THE HOUSE

Perched on a hill overlooking San Francisco, the house was magnificent, built in 1923 by a wealthy man for the woman he adored. For her and for this house, he would spare no expense and overlook no detail, from the endless marble floors to the glittering chandeliers. Almost a century later, with the once-grand house now in disrepair, a young woman walks through its empty rooms. Sarah Anderson, a perfectly sensible estate lawyer, is about to do something utterly out of character. An elderly client has died and left her two gifts. One is a general inheritance. The other a priceless message: to use his money for something wonderful, something daring. And in this old house, surrounded by crumbling grandeur, Sarah knows just what it is.

THE HOUSE

Danielle Steel

WINDSOR
PARAGON

First published 2006
by
Transworld Publishers
This Large Print edition published 2006
by
BBC Audiobooks Ltd by arrangement with
Transworld Publishers Ltd

Hardcover ISBN 10: 1 4056 1490 0
           ISBN 13: 978 1 405 61490 0
Softcover ISBN 10: 1 4056 1491 9
           ISBN 13: 978 1 405 61491 7

British Library Cataloguing in Publication Data available

Printed and bound in Great Britain by
Antony Rowe Ltd., Chippenham, Wiltshire

To my beloved babies,
Beatie, Trevor, Todd, Nick, Sam, Victoria,
  Vanessa, Maxx, and Zara,
May your lives and homes be blessed,
May your history be something you cherish,
and may all those who come into your lives
  treat you with tenderness, kindness, love
  and respect.
May you always be loved and blessed

I love you.
Mom/d.s.

CHAPTER 1

Sarah Anderson left her office at nine-thirty on a Tuesday morning in June for her ten o'clock appointment with Stanley Perlman. She hurried out of the building at One Market Plaza, stepped off the curb, and hailed a cab. It occurred to her, as it always did, that one of these days when she met with him, it would really be for the last time. He always said it was. She had begun to expect him to live forever, despite his protests, and in spite of the realities of time. Her law firm had handled his affairs for more than half a century. She had been his estate and tax attorney for the past three years. At thirty-eight, Sarah had been a partner of the firm for the past two years, and had inherited Stanley as a client when his previous attorney died.

Stanley had outlived them all. He was ninety-eight years old. It was hard to believe sometimes. His mind was as sharp as it had ever been, he read voraciously, and he was well aware of every nuance and change in the current tax laws. He was a challenging and entertaining client. Stanley Perlman had been a genius in business all his life. The only thing that had changed over the years was that his body had betrayed him, but never once his mind. He was bedridden now, and had been for nearly seven years. Five nurses attended to him, three regularly in eight-hour shifts, two as relief. He was comfortable, most of the time, and hadn't left his house in years. Sarah had always liked and admired him, although others thought he was irascible and cantankerous. She thought he was a

1

remarkable man. She gave the cabdriver Stanley's Scott Street address. They made their way through the downtown traffic in San Francisco's financial district, and headed west uptown, toward Pacific Heights, where he had lived in the same house for seventy-six years.

The sun was shining brightly as they climbed Nob Hill up California Street, and she knew it might be otherwise when they got uptown. The fog often sat heavily on the residential part of the city, even when it was warm and sunny downtown. Tourists were happily hanging off the cable car, smiling as they looked around. Sarah was bringing Stanley some papers to sign, nothing extra-ordinary. He was always making minor additions and adjustments to his will. He had been prepared to die for all the years she had known him, and long before. But in spite of that, whenever he seemed to take a turn for the worse, or suffered from a brief illness, he always rallied and hung on, much to his chagrin. He had told her only that morning, when she called to confirm her appointment with him, that he had been feeling poorly for the last few weeks, and it wouldn't be long.

'Stop threatening me, Stanley,' she had said, putting the last of the papers for him in her briefcase. 'You're going to outlive us all.'

She was sad for him at times, although there was nothing depressing about him, and he rarely felt sorry for himself. He still barked orders at his nurses, read *The New York Times* and *The Wall Street Journal* daily, as well as the local papers, loved pastrami sandwiches and hamburgers, and spoke with fascinating accuracy and historical

2

detail about his years growing up on the Lower East Side of New York. He had come to San Francisco at sixteen, in 1924. He had been remarkably clever at finding jobs, making deals, working for the right people, seizing opportunities, and saving money. He had bought property, always in unusual circumstances, sometimes preying on others' misfortunes, he readily admitted, and making trades, and using whatever credit was available to him. He had managed to make money while others were losing it during the Depression. He was the epitome of a self-made man.

He liked to say that he had bought the house he lived in for 'pennies' in 1930. And considerably later, he had been among the first to build shopping malls in Southern California. Most of his early money had been made in real estate development, trading one building for another, sometimes buying land no one else wanted, and biding his time to either sell it later or build office buildings or shopping centers on it. He had had the same intuitive knack later on, for investing in oil wells. The fortune he had amassed was literally staggering by now. Stanley had been a genius in business, but had done little else in his life. He had no children, had never married, had no contact with anyone but attorneys and nurses. There was no one who cared about Stanley Perlman, except his young attorney, Sarah Anderson, and no one who would miss him when he died, except the nurses he employed. The nineteen heirs listed in the will that Sarah was once again updating for him (this time to include a series of oil wells he had just purchased in Orange County, after selling off several others, once again at the right time) were

3

great-nieces and -nephews he had never met or corresponded with, and two elderly cousins who were nearly as old as he was, and whom he said he hadn't seen since the late forties but felt some vague attachment to. In truth, he was attached to no one, and made no bones about it. He had had one mission throughout his lifetime, and one only, and that had been making money. He had achieved his goal. He said he had been in love with two women in his younger days, but had never offered to marry either and had lost contact with both of them when they gave up on him and married other men, more than sixty years ago.

The only thing he said he regretted was not having children. He thought of Sarah as the grandchild he had never had, but might have, if he had taken the time to get married. She was the kind of granddaughter he would have liked to have. She was smart, funny, interesting, quick, beautiful, and good at what she did. Sometimes, when she brought papers to him, he loved to sit and look at her and talk to her for hours. He even held her hand, something he never did with his nurses. They got on his nerves and annoyed him, patronized him, and fussed over him in ways he hated. Sarah never did. She sat there looking young and beautiful, while speaking to him of the things that interested him. She always knew her stuff about new tax laws. He loved the fact that she came up with new ideas about how to save him money. He had been wary of her at first, because of her youth, and then progressively came to trust her, in the course of her visits to his small musty room in the attic of the house on Scott Street. She came up the back stairs, carrying her briefcase,

4

entered his room discreetly, sat on a chair next to his bed, and they talked until she could see he was exhausted. Each time she came to see him, she feared it would be the last time. And then he would call her with some new idea, some new plan that had occurred to him, something he wanted to buy, sell, acquire, or dispose of. And whatever he touched always increased his fortune. Even at ninety-eight, Stanley Perlman had a Midas touch when it came to money. And best of all, despite the vast difference in their ages, over the years she'd worked with him, Sarah and Stanley had become friends.

Sarah glanced out the window of the cab as they passed Grace Cathedral, at the top of Nob Hill, and sat back against the seat, thinking about him. She wondered if he really was sick, and if it might be the last time. He had had pneumonia twice the previous spring and each time, miraculously, survived it. Maybe now he wouldn't. His nurses were diligent in their care of him, but sooner or later, at his age, something was going to get him. It was inevitable, although Sarah dreaded it. She knew she'd miss him terribly when he was gone.

Her long dark hair was pulled neatly back, her eyes were big and almost cornflower blue. He had commented on them the first time he saw her, and asked if she wore colored contact lenses. She had laughed at the question and assured him she didn't. Her usually creamy skin was tan this time, after several weekends in Lake Tahoe. She liked to hike and swim, and ride a mountain bike. Weekends away were always a relief after the long hours she spent in her office. Her partnership in the law firm had been well earned. She had graduated from Stanford law school, magna cum laude, and was a native San Franciscan. She had lived here all her life, except for the four years she spent as an undergraduate at Harvard. Her credentials and hard work had impressed Stanley and her partners. Stanley had grilled her extensively when they met, and had commented that she looked more like a model. She was tall, thin, athletic-looking, and had long legs that he always silently admired. She was wearing a neat navy blue suit, which was the kind of thing she always wore when she visited him. The only jewelry she wore was a pair of small diamond earrings that had been a Christmas gift from Stanley. He had ordered them by phone for her himself from Neiman Marcus. He was not usually generous, he preferred to give his nurses money on holidays, but he had a soft spot for Sarah, just as she had for him. She had given him several cashmere throws to keep him warm. His house always seemed cold and damp. He scolded the nurses soundly whenever they put the heat on. Stanley preferred to use a blanket than be what he thought of as careless with his money.

Sarah had always been intrigued by the fact that he had never occupied the main part of the house, only the old servants' rooms in the attic. He said he had bought the place as an investment, had always meant to sell it, and never had. He had kept the house more out of laziness than any deep affection for it. It was a large, beautiful, once-luxurious home that had been built in the twenties. Stanley had told her that the family that had built it had fallen on hard times after the Crash of '29, and he had bought it in 1930. He had moved into one of the old maids' rooms then, with an old brass bed, a chest of drawers the original owners had abandoned there, and a chair whose springs had died so long ago that sitting on it was like resting on concrete. The brass bed had been replaced by a hospital bed a decade before. There was an old photograph of the fire after the earthquake on the wall, and not a single photograph of a person anywhere in his room. There had been no people in his life, only investments, and attorneys. There was nothing personal anywhere in the house. The furniture had all been sold separately at auction by the original owners, also for nearly nothing. And Stanley had never bothered to furnish it when he moved in. He had told her that the house had been stripped bare before he got it. The rooms were large and once elegant, there were curtains hanging in shreds at some of the windows. Others were boarded up, so the curious couldn't look in. And although she'd never seen it, Sarah had been told there was a ballroom. She had never walked around the house, but came in straight from the service door, up the back stairs, to his attic bedroom. Her only purpose in coming here was to see Stanley. She had no reason to tour the house, except that she knew that one day, more than likely, after he was gone, she would have to sell it. All of his heirs were in Florida, New York, or the Midwest, and none of them would have an interest in owning an enormous white elephant of a house in California. No matter how beautiful it had once been, none of them would have any use for it, just as Stanley hadn't. It was hard to believe he had lived in it for seventy-six years and neither furnished it nor moved from the attic. But that

7

was Stanley. Eccentric perhaps, unassuming, unpretentious, and a devoted and respected client. Sarah Anderson was his only friend. The rest of the world had forgotten he existed. And whatever friends he had once had, he had long since out-lived them.

The cab stopped at the address on Scott Street that Sarah had given the driver. She paid the fare, picked up her briefcase, got out of the cab, and rang the back doorbell. As she had expected, it was noticeably colder and foggy out here, and she shivered in her light jacket. She was wearing a thin white sweater under the dark blue suit, and looked businesslike, as she always did, when the nurse opened the door and smiled when she saw her. It took them forever to come downstairs from the attic. There were four floors and a basement, Sarah knew, and the elderly nurses who tended to him moved slowly. The one who opened the door to Sarah was relatively new, but she had seen Sarah before.

'Mr. Perlman is expecting you,' she said politely, as she stood aside to let Sarah in, and closed the door behind her.

They only used the service door, as it was more convenient to the back staircase which led up to the attic. The front door hadn't been touched for years, and was kept locked and bolted. The lights in the main part of the house were never turned on. The only lights that had shone in the house for years were those in the attic. They cooked in a small kitchen on the same floor that had once served as a pantry. The main kitchen, a piece of history now, was in the basement. It had old-fashioned iceboxes and a meat locker. In the old

8

days the iceman had come, and brought in huge chunks of ice. The stove was a relic from the twenties, and Stanley hadn't worked it since at least the forties. It was a kitchen that had been meant to be run by a flock of cooks and servants, overseen by a housekeeper and butler. It had nothing to do with Stanley's way of life. For years, he had come home with sandwiches and take-out food from diners and simple restaurants. He never cooked for himself, and went out every morning for breakfast in previous years before he was bedridden. The house was a place where he slept in the spartan brass bed, showered and shaved in the morning, and then went downtown to the office he had, to make more money. He rarely came home before ten o'clock at night. Sometimes as late as midnight. He had no reason to rush home.

Sarah followed the nurse up the stairs at a solemn pace, carrying her briefcase. The staircase was always dark, lit by a minimal supply of bare bulbs. This had been the staircase the servants had used in the house's long-gone days of grandeur. The steps were made of steel, covered by a narrow strip of ancient threadbare carpet. The doors to each floor remained closed, and Sarah saw daylight only when she reached the attic. His room was at the end of a long hall, most of it taken up by the hospital bed. To accommodate it, his single narrow dresser had been moved into the hall. Only the ancient broken chair and a small bed table stood near the bed. As she walked into the room, he opened his eyes and saw her. He was slow to react this time, which worried her, and then little by little a smile lit his eyes and took a moment to reach his mouth. He looked worn and tired, and she was suddenly afraid that maybe this time he was right. He looked all of his ninety-eight years now, and never had before.

'Hello, Sarah,' he said quietly, taking in the freshness of her youth and beauty. To him, thirty-eight was like the first blush of her childhood. He laughed whenever Sarah told him she felt old. 'Still working too hard?' he asked, as she approached the bed, and stood near him. Seeing her always restored him. She was like air and light to him, or spring rain on a bed of flowers.

'Of course.' She smiled at him, as he reached up a hand for hers and held it. He loved the feel of her skin, her touch, her warmth.

'Don't I always tell you not to do that? You work too hard. You'll end up like me one day. Alone, with a bunch of pesky nurses around you, living in an attic.' He had told her several times that she needed to get married and have babies. He had scolded her soundly when she said that she wanted to do neither. The only sorrow of his life was not having children. He often told her not to make the same mistakes he had. Stock certificates, bonds, shopping centers, and oil wells were no substitute for children. He had learned that lesson too late. The only joy and comfort he had in his life now was Sarah. He loved adding codicils to his will, and did it often. It gave him an excuse to see her.

'How are you feeling?' she asked, looking like a concerned relative and not an attorney. She worried about him and often found excuses to send him books or articles, mostly about new tax laws or other topics she thought might be of interest to him. He always sent her handwritten notes afterward, thanking her, and making comments. He was as sharp as ever.

'I'm tired,' Stanley said honestly, keeping a grip on her hand with his frail fingers. 'I can't expect to feel better than that at my age. My body's been gone for years. All that's left is my brain.' Which was as clear as it had ever been. But she saw that his eyes looked dull this time. Usually, there was still a spark in them, but like a lamp beginning to dim, she could see that something had changed. She always wished that there were some way to get him out in the air, but other than occasional trips by ambulance to the hospital, he hadn't left the house in years. The attic of the house on Scott Street had become the womb where he was condemned to finish his days. 'Sit down,' he said to her finally. 'You look good, Sarah. You always do.' She looked so fresh and alive to him, so beautiful, as she stood there looking tall and young and slim. 'I'm glad you came.' He said it a little more fervently than usual, which made her heart ache for him.

'Me too. I've been busy. I've been meaning to come for a couple of weeks,' she said apologetically.

'You look like you've been away somewhere. Where did you get the tan?' He thought she looked prettier than ever.

'Just Tahoe for the weekends. It's nice up there.' She smiled as she sat down on the uncomfortable chair and set down her briefcase.

'I never went away on weekends, or for vacations for that matter. I think I took two vacations in my whole life. Once to Wyoming, on a ranch, the other time to Mexico. I hated both. I felt

11

like I was wasting time, sitting around worrying about what was happening in my office and what I was missing.' She could just imagine him fidgeting as he waited for news from his office, and probably went home sooner than planned. She had done her share of that herself, when she had too much work to do, or brought files with her from the office. She hated leaving anything unfinished. He wasn't entirely wrong about her. In her own way, she was as compulsive about work as he was. The apartment where she lived looked scarcely better than his attic room, just bigger. She was nearly as uninterested in her surroundings as he was. She was just younger and less extreme. The demons that drove them both were very much the same, as he had surmised long since.

They chatted for a few minutes, and she handed him the papers she had brought him. He looked them over, but they were already familiar to him. She had sent several drafts over by messenger, for his approval. He had no fax machine or computer. Stanley liked to see original documents, and had no patience with modern inventions. He had never owned a cell phone and didn't need one.

There was a small sitting room next to him set up for his nurses. They never ventured far from him, and were either in their tiny sitting room, his room in the uncomfortable chair, watching him, or in the kitchen, preparing his simple meals. Farther down the hall, on the top floor, there were several more small maids' rooms, where the nurses could sleep, if they chose, when they went off duty, or rest, when there was another nurse around. None of them lived in, they just worked there in shifts. The only full-time resident of the house was

Stanley. His existence and shrunken world were a tiny microcosm on the top floor of the once-grand house that was crumbling and falling into disrepair as silently and steadily as he was.

'I like the changes that you made,' he complimented her. 'They make more sense than the draft you sent me last week. This is cleaner, it leaves less room to maneuver.'

He always worried about what his heirs would do with his various holdings. Since he had never met most of them, and those he had were now so ancient, it was hard to know how they would treat his estate. He had to assume they'd sell everything, which in some cases would be foolish. But the pie had to be cut nineteen ways. It was a very big pie, and each of them would get an impressive slice, far more than they knew. But he felt strongly about leaving what he had to relatives and not to charity. He had given his share to philanthropic organizations over the years, but he was a firm believer that blood was thicker than water. And since he had no direct heirs, he was leaving it all to his cousins, and great-nieces and -nephews, whoever they were. He had researched their whereabouts carefully, but had met only a few. He hoped that what he left them would make a difference in quality of life to some of them, when they received this unexpected windfall. It was beginning to look like it would be coming to them soon. Sooner than Sarah wanted to think about as she looked at him.

'I'm glad you like it,' Sarah said, looking pleased, trying not to notice or acknowledge the lackluster look in his eyes, which made her want to cry. The last bout of pneumonia had left him drained and looking his age. 'Is there anything you want me to add to it?' she asked, and he shook his head in answer. She was sitting in the broken chair, quietly watching him.

'What are you going to do this summer, Sarah?' he asked, changing the subject.

'A few more weekends in Tahoe. I don't have anything special planned.' She thought he was afraid that she'd be away, and wanted to reassure him.

'Then plan something. You can't be a slave forever, Sarah. You'll wind up an old maid.' She laughed. She had admitted to him before that she dated someone, but had always said it wasn't serious or permanent, and it still wasn't. It had been a casual relationship for four years, which he had also told her was foolish. He had told her that you don't do 'casual' for four years. Her mother told her the same thing. But it was all she wanted. She told herself and everyone else that she was too involved in her work at the law firm to want more than casual for the moment. Her work was her first priority, and always had been. Just like him.

'There are no "old maids" anymore, Stanley. There are independent women, who have careers and different priorities and needs than women had years ago,' she said, convincing no one but herself. Stanley didn't buy it. He knew her better, and was wiser about life than she.

'That's hogwash and you know it,' he said sternly. 'People haven't changed in two thousand years. The smart ones still settle down, get married, and have kids. Or they wind up like me.' He had wound up a very, very rich man, which didn't seem like such a bad thing to her. She was

14

sorry that he had no children, and had no relatives nearby, but living as long as he had, most people wound up alone. He had outlived everyone he had ever known. He might even have lost all his children by then, if he'd had any, and would have only had grandchildren or great-grandchildren to comfort him. In the end, she told herself, no matter who we think we have, we leave this world alone. Just as Stanley would. It was just more obvious, in his case. But she knew, from the life her mother had shared with her father, that you can be just as alone, even if you have a spouse and children. She was in no hurry to saddle herself with either. The married people she knew didn't look all that happy to her, and if she ever married and it didn't work out, she didn't need an ex-husband to hate and torment her. She knew too many of those, too. She was much happier like this, working, on her own, with a part-time boyfriend who met her needs for the moment. The thought of marrying him never crossed her mind, or his. They had both agreed from the beginning that a simple relationship was all they wanted from each other. Simple, and easy. Especially since they were both busy with jobs they loved.

Sarah could see then that Stanley was truly exhausted, and she decided to cut the visit short this time. He had signed the papers, which was all she needed. He looked like he was about ready to fall asleep.

'I'll come back and see you soon, Stanley. Let me know if you need anything. I'll come over whenever you like,' she said gently, patting the frail hand again after she stood up and took the papers from him. She slipped them into her briefcase as

15

he watched her with a wistful smile. He loved watching her, just the easy grace of her movements as she chatted with him, or did ordinary things.

'I might not be here,' he said simply, without self-pity. It was a simple statement of fact that they both knew was possible but that she didn't like to hear.

'Don't be silly,' she chided him. 'You'll be here. I'm counting on you to outlive me.'

'I'd better not,' he said sternly. 'And next time I see you, I want to hear all about some vacation you took. Take a cruise. Go lie on a beach somewhere. Pick up a guy, get drunk, go dancing, cut loose. Mark my words, Sarah, you'll be sorry one day if you don't do it.' She laughed at his suggestions, visualizing herself picking up strangers on a beach. 'I mean it!'

'I know you do. I think you're trying to get me arrested and disbarred.' She smiled broadly at him, and kissed his cheek. It was an uncharacteristically unprofessional gesture, but he was dear to her, and she to him.

'Screw getting disbarred. It might do you good. Get a life, Sarah. Stop working so hard.' He always said the same things to her, and she took them with a grain of salt. She enjoyed what she did. Her work was like a drug she was addicted to. She had no desire to give up the addiction, and maybe not for years, although she knew his warnings were heartfelt and well intended.

'I'll try,' she lied, smiling at him. He really was like a grandfather to her.

'Try harder.' He scowled at her, and then smiled at the kiss on his cheek. He loved the feel of her velvet skin on his face, the softness of her breath so

16

close to him. It made him feel young again, although he knew that in his youth he would have been too foolish and intent on his work to pay any attention to her, no matter how beautiful she was. The two women he had lost, due to his own stupidity at the time, he realized now, had been just as beautiful and sensual as she. He hadn't acknowledged that to himself until recently. 'Take care of yourself,' he said as she stood in the doorway, holding her briefcase and turned back to look at him.

'You too. Behave yourself. Don't chase your nurses around the room, they might quit.' He chuckled at the suggestion.

'Have you looked at them?' He laughed out loud this time, and so did she. 'I'm not getting out of bed for that,' he said, grinning, 'not with these old knees. I may be stuck in bed, my dear, but I'm not blind, you know. Send me some new ones, and I might give them a run for their money.'

'I'll bet you would,' she said, and with a wave at him, finally forced herself to leave. He was still smiling as she left, and told the nurse she could find her way downstairs on her own.

She clattered down the steel stairs again, her steps resonating on the iron staircase, as the sound reverberated in the narrow hall. The threadbare carpet did little to muffle the din. And it was a relief when she stepped out of the service door into the noon sunshine that had finally come uptown. She walked slowly down to Union Street, thinking of him, and found a cab there. She gave the driver the address of her office building, and thought of Stanley all the way downtown. She was afraid he wouldn't last much longer. He seemed to be finally sliding slowly downhill. Her visit had perked him up, but even Sarah knew it wouldn't be much longer. It was almost too much to hope that he would reach his ninety-ninth birthday in October. And why? He had so little to live for, and he was so alone. His life was so confined by the tiny room he lived in, and the four walls of the cell where he was trapped for the remainder of his days. He had lived a good life, or at least a productive one, and the lives of his nineteen heirs would be forever changed when he died. It depressed Sarah to think about it. She knew she would miss Stanley when he was gone. She tried not to think about the many warnings he gave her about her own life. She had years to think about babies and marriage. For now, she had a career that meant the world to her, and a desk full of work waiting for her at the office, although she appreciated his concern. She had exactly the life she wanted.

It was shortly after noon as she hurried back to her office. She had a partners' meeting at one o'clock, meetings scheduled with three clients that afternoon, and fifty pages of new tax laws to read that night, all or some of which would be pertinent to her clients. She had a stack of messages waiting on her desk, and she managed to return all but two of them before the meeting with her partners. She would return the other two, and whatever new ones she had, between client meetings later that afternoon. She had no time for lunch . . . any more than she did for babies or marriage. Stanley had made his choices and mistakes in life. She had a right to make her own.

CHAPTER 2

Sarah continued to send books and relevant articles to Stanley, as she always did, through July and August. He had a brief bout of flu in September, which didn't require a hospital stay this time. And he was in remarkably good spirits when she visited him on his ninety-ninth birthday in October. There was a sense of victory to it. It was a remarkable achievement to reach ninety-nine years of age. She brought him a cheesecake and put a candle in it. She knew it was his favorite, and reminded him of his childhood in New York. For once, he didn't scold her about how hard she was working. They talked at length about a new tax law that was being proposed, which could prove advantageous to his estate. He had the same concerns about it she did, and they both enjoyed batting theories back and forth with each other, about how current tax laws might be affected. He was as clear and sharp as ever and didn't seem quite as frail as he had on her previous visit. He had a new nurse who was making a real effort to make him eat, and Sarah thought he had even gained a little weight. She kissed him on the cheek, as she always did, when she left, and told him that they'd be celebrating his hundredth birthday the following October.

'Christ, I hope not,' he said, laughing at her. 'Whoever thought I'd make it this far,' he said as they celebrated together.

She left him a stack of new books, some music to listen to, and a pair of black satin pajamas that seemed to amuse him. She'd never seen him in better spirits, which made the call she got two weeks later, on the first of November, more shocking somehow. It shouldn't have been. She had always known it would come. But it caught her off guard anyway. After more than three years of doing legal work for him, and enjoying their resulting friendship, she really had begun to expect him to live forever. The nurse told her that Stanley had died peacefully in his sleep the night before, listening to the music she had given him and wearing the black satin pajamas. He had eaten a good dinner, drifted off to sleep and out of this world, without a gasp or a whimper, or a final word to anyone. The nurse had found him when she went to check on him an hour later. She said the look on his face was completely peaceful.

Tears sprang to Sarah's eyes as she heard it. She'd had a hard morning at the office, after a heated debate with two of her partners over something they'd done that she didn't agree with, and she felt they'd ganged up on her. And the night before, she'd had a fight with the man she dated, which wasn't all that unusual, but upset her anyway. In the past year, they had begun to disagree more. They both had busy days, and stressful lives. They confined their time together to weekends. But sometimes she and Phil got on each other's nerves over minor irritations. Hearing about Stanley dying in the night was the topper. She felt suddenly bereft, reminded of when her father had died when she was sixteen, twenty-two years before.

In an odd way, Stanley was the only father figure she'd had since then, even though he was a client.

He was always telling her not to work too hard, and to learn from his mistakes. No other man she knew had ever said that to her, and she knew how much she was going to miss him. But this was what they had prepared for, why she had come into his life, to plan his estate, and how it would be dispersed to his heirs. It was time for her to do her job. All the groundwork had been laid over the past three years. Sarah was organized and ready. Everything was in order.

'Will you make the arrangements?' the nurse asked her. She had already notified the other nurses, and Sarah said she'd call the funeral parlor. He had long since selected the one he wanted, although he had been emphatic that there be no funeral. He wanted to be cremated and buried, without fuss or fanfare. There would be no mourners. All his friends and business associates were long dead, and his family didn't know him. There was only Sarah to make the arrangements.

She made the appropriate phone calls after speaking to the nurse. She was surprised to see that her hand shook as she made the calls. He was to be cremated the next morning, and buried at Cypress Lawn, in a spot he had purchased in the mausoleum a dozen years before. They asked if there would be a service, and she said no. The funeral home picked him up within the hour, and she felt somber all day, particularly as she dictated the letter to his unsuspecting heirs. She offered a reading of the will in her offices in San Francisco, which Stanley had requested, should they wish to come out, at which time they might like to inspect the house they had inherited, and decide how they wished to dispose of it. There was always the remote possibility that one of them would want to keep it, and buy out the others' shares, although she and Stanley had always considered that unlikely. None of them lived in San Francisco, and wouldn't want a house there. There were a multitude of details to attend to. And she had been advised by the cemetery that Stanley would be interred at nine o'clock the next morning.

She knew it would be several days, or longer, before she began hearing from his heirs. For those who didn't wish to come out, or couldn't, she would send them copies of the will, as soon as it had been read. And his estate had to be put into probate. It would take some time to release the assets. She set all the wheels in motion that day.

By late afternoon, the head nurse had come to the office to bring all the nurses' keys to her. The cleaning woman who had come in for years, just to clean the attic rooms, was going to continue working. There was a service that came in once a month to clean the rest of the house, but nothing was changed for them. It was startling how little had to be done at this point. And Stanley had so few personal effects and so little furniture, that when they cleaned out the house for a real estate broker, Goodwill could take it all away. There was nothing the heirs would want. He was a simple man with few needs and no luxuries, and he had been bedridden for years. Even the watch he wore was of no consequence. He had bought a gold watch once, and had long since given it away. All he had were properties and shopping malls, oil wells, investments, stocks, bonds, and the house on Scott Street. Stanley Perlman had had an enormous fortune, and few things. And thanks to

Sarah, his estate was totally in order at the time of his death, and long before.

Sarah stayed at the office until nearly nine o'clock that night, poring over files, answering e-mails, and filing things that had sat on her desk for days. She realized finally that she was avoiding going home, almost as though the emptiness of Scott Street now might have been transmitted to her own home. She hated the feeling that Stanley was gone. She called her mother, and she was out. She called Phil, glanced at her watch, and realized he was at the gym. They rarely, if ever, saw each other during the week. He went to the gym every night after work. He was a labor attorney in a rival firm, specialized in discrimination cases, and his hours were as long as hers. He also had dinner with his children twice a week, since he didn't like seeing them on weekends. He liked keeping his weekends free for adult pursuits, mostly with her. She tried his cell phone, but it was on voice mail when he was at the gym. She didn't leave a message because she didn't know what to say to him. She knew how stupid he'd make her feel. She could just imagine the conversation. 'My ninety-nine-year-old client died last night and I'm really sad about it.' Phil would laugh at her. 'Ninety-nine? Are you kidding? . . . Sounds like he was way overdue, if you ask me.' She had mentioned Stanley once or twice to Phil, but they rarely talked about their work. Phil liked to leave his at the office. She brought hers home with her, in many ways. She brought files home to work on, and worried about her clients, their tax problems and plans. Phil left his clients at the office, and their worries on his desk. Sarah carried them around

23

with her. And her sadness over Stanley weighed heavily on her.

There was no one to say anything to, no one to tell. No one to share the overwhelming feeling of emptiness with her. What she felt was impossible to explain. She felt bereft, just as she had when her father died, only this was worse. There was none of the shock she'd had then, and none of the relief. There was no real loss when her father died, except the loss of an idea. The idea of the father he'd never been. He had been the phantom father her mother had created for her. The fantasy her mother had propagated for him. At the time her father died, although they lived in the same house, Sarah hadn't really talked to him in years. She couldn't. He was always too drunk to talk or think, or go anywhere with her. He just came home from work and drank himself into a stupor, and eventually didn't even bother to go to work. He just sat in the room he and her mother shared, drinking, while her mother attempted to cover for him, and worked to support all three of them, selling real estate, and coming home during the day to check on him. He died at forty-six, of liver disease, and had been a total stranger to her. Stanley had been her friend. And in some strange way this was worse. With Stanley gone, there was actually someone to miss.

She sat in her office and cried, finally, as she thought about it, and then she picked up her briefcase and left. She took a cab home and let herself into her apartment in Pacific Heights, a dozen blocks from Stanley's house on Scott Street, and walked straight to her desk. She checked her messages. Her mother had left her one earlier. At

24

sixty-one, she was still working, but had shifted from real estate to interior design. She was always busy, with friends, at book clubs, with clients, or at the twelve-step groups she still attended after all these years. She had been going to Al-Anon for nearly thirty years, even all these years after her alcoholic husband died. Sarah said she was addicted to twelve-step groups. Her mother was always busy and spinning her wheels, but she seemed happy doing it. She had called Sarah to check in, and said she was on her way out for the evening. As she listened to the message, Sarah sat down on the couch, staring straight ahead. She hadn't eaten dinner and didn't care. There was two-day-old pizza in the fridge, and she knew she could have made a salad if she wanted one, but she didn't. She didn't want anything tonight except the comfort of her bed. She needed time to grieve, before doing everything she had to do for Stanley. She knew the next day she'd be fine, or thought she would, but right now she needed to let go.

She stretched out on the couch and hit the remote for the TV. All she needed was sound, voices, something to fill the silence and the void she felt welling up in her. Her apartment was as empty as she was tonight. The apartment itself was in as much disarray as she felt. She never noticed it and didn't now. Her mother nagged her constantly about it, and Sarah always fobbed her off, and said she liked it that way. She liked to say her apartment looked studious and intelligent. She didn't want fluffy curtains, or a bedspread with ruffles. She didn't need cute little cushions on the couch, or plates that matched. She had a battered old brown couch she had had since college, a coffee table she'd bought at Goodwill in law school. Her desk was an old door she'd found somewhere and put on two sawhorses. She had rolling file cabinets stashed underneath it. Her bookcases took up one wall, full of law books that were crammed into the shelves, with the overflow stacked up in piles on the floor. There were two very handsome brown leather chairs that had been a gift from her mother, along with a big mirror that hung over the couch. There were two dead plants, and a fake silk ficus tree her mother had found somewhere, a tired-looking beanbag seat Sarah had brought back from Harvard, and a small battered dining table with four unmatched chairs. She had venetian blinds instead of curtains, but they worked fine for her.

Her bedroom looked no better. She made the bed on the weekends before Phil came over, if he did. Half the dresser drawers no longer closed. There was an old rocking chair in the corner, with a handmade quilt thrown over it that she'd found in an antique store. She had a full-length mirror with a small crack in it. Another dead plant sat on the windowsill, and the bedside table had another stack of law books on it, her favorite bedtime reading. And in the corner, a teddy bear she had salvaged from her childhood. It wasn't likely to be a spread in *House & Garden* or *Architectural Digest*, but it worked for her. It was livable, serviceable, she had enough plates to eat dinner on, enough glasses to have a dozen friends in for drinks, when she felt like it and had time, which wasn't often, enough towels for her and Phil, and enough pots and pans to make a decent meal, which she did about twice a year. The rest of the time she brought home takeout, ate a sandwich at the office, or made salad. She just didn't need more than she had, no matter how much it upset her mother, who kept her own apartment looking as though it were going to be photographed any minute. As she put it, it was her own calling card for her interior design business.

Sarah's apartment looked no different than any of hers had since she had been in college and law school. It was functional, if not beautiful, and it served her needs. She had a stereo system she liked, and Phil had bought her the TV, since she didn't have one, and he liked watching it when he was at her place, mostly for sports. And she had to admit, now and then she enjoyed it, like tonight. She liked hearing the droning of the voices on some innocuous sitcom, and then her cell phone rang. She debated answering it, and then realized it might be Phil, returning her call. She picked it up, glanced at the caller ID, and saw that it was. She saw his number with a mixture of dread and relief. She knew if he said the wrong thing, it would upset her, but she had to take the chance. She needed some form of human contact tonight, to make up for Stanley's absence from now on. She turned down the volume on the TV with the remote in one hand, flipped open her cell phone with the other, and put it to her ear.

'Hi,' she said, feeling her mind go blank.

'What's up? I missed a call, and saw that it was you. I'm just leaving the gym.' He was one of those people who insisted he needed to go to the gym every night to ward off stress, except when he saw his kids. He stayed at the gym for two or three hours after work, which made dinner with him during the week impossible, since he never left his office till at least eight. One of the things that appealed to her about him was that he had a sexy voice. It sounded good to her tonight, whatever the words. She missed him and would have loved him to come over. She wasn't sure what he'd say if she asked. Their long-standing agreement, mostly unspoken, though occasionally put into words, was that they saw each other only on weekends, and alternated between her place and his, depending on whose was the bigger mess. Usually it was his. So they stayed at hers, although he complained that her bed was too soft and hurt his back. He put up with it to be with her. It was only for two days a week, if that.

'I had kind of a shit day,' she said in a monotone, trying not to feel all she did, and have it make sense to him. 'My favorite client died.'

'That old guy who was about two hundred years old?' he asked, sounding as though he were struggling with something, like getting into his car, or picking up a heavy bag.

'He was ninety-nine. Yeah, him.' They spoke with a shorthand they had developed over four years. Like their relationship, there wasn't a lot of romance to it, but it seemed to work for them. Their alliance wasn't a perfect match by any means, but she accepted it. Even if not totally satisfying, it was familiar and easy. They both lived in the here and now, and never worried about the future. 'I'm really sad. I haven't felt this bad over something like this in years.'

'I always tell you not to get too involved with your clients. It just doesn't work. They're not our friends. You know what I mean?'

28

'Well, in this case I did. He didn't have anyone but me, and a bunch of relatives he'd never even met. He didn't have kids, and he was really a nice man.' Her voice was soft and sad.

'I'm sure he was. But ninety-nine years is a hell of a good run. You can't exactly say you're surprised.' She could hear by then that he was in the car, on his way home. He lived six blocks from her, which was convenient a lot of the time, particularly if they switched locations from her place to his, halfway through the weekend, or had forgotten something they meant to bring.

'I'm not surprised. I'm just sad. I know it sounds dumb, but I am. It reminds me of when my father died.' She felt vulnerable admitting it to him, but after four years, they had no secrets from each other, and she could say whatever she wanted to, or needed to at the time. Sometimes he got it, and sometimes he didn't. So far, he didn't tonight.

'Don't even go there, babe. This guy wasn't your father. He was a client. I had kind of a shit day myself. I was in deposition all day, and my client in this case is a total asshole. I wanted to strangle the son of a bitch halfway through the deposition. I figured opposing counsel would do it for me, but he didn't. I wish to hell he had. We'll never win the case.' Phil hated losing cases, just like he hated losing at sports. It put him in a bad mood sometimes for weeks, or days at least.

He played softball in the summer on Monday nights. And rugby in winter. He had played ice hockey at Dartmouth, and had lost his front teeth, which had been beautifully replaced. He was a very handsome man. At forty-two, he still looked thirty, and was in fantastic shape. Sarah had been bowled

29

over by his looks the first time they met and, much as she hated to admit it, ever since. There was some sort of powerful chemistry between them, which defied reason or words. He was the sexiest man she'd ever met. It wasn't enough to justify the four years they had spent in a weekends-only relationship, but it was definitely part of it. Sometimes he drove her nuts with his inflexible opinions, and frequently disappointed her. He wasn't deeply sensitive, or overly attentive, but he definitely turned her on.

'I'm sorry you had such a lousy day,' she said, feeling as though his didn't even begin to compare to hers, although admittedly depositions could be a bitch, and so could bad clients, particularly in his line of work. Labor law was incredibly stressful. He handled a lot of discrimination and sexual harassment cases, mostly for men. He seemed to have better rapport with male clients, maybe because he was such a jock. And his firm had a lot of female partners, who worked better with their female clients. 'Do you want to come over on your way home? I could use a hug.' It was a request she almost never made of him, except when it was direly needed. And it was tonight. She felt terrible about Stanley, no matter what his age when he died. He was still her friend, and not just her client, whatever Phil said and even if he was right about it being unprofessional. Phil never got emotionally involved with his clients, or anyone else, except her to some degree, and his three kids. They were all in their teens, and he had been divorced for twelve years. He hated his ex-wife with a passion. She had left him for another man, as it happened, a running back for the 49ers, which had nearly driven Phil insane at the time. He had lost to an even bigger jock, which was the ultimate insult to him.

'I'd love to, babe,' Phil said, in response to her request. 'I really would. But I'm wiped out. I just played squash for two hours.' She knew he must have won, or he would have been in a rotten mood, which he didn't seem to be, just tired. 'I've got to be back in the office at eight in the morning, to get ready for another deposition. I'm in depos all this week. If I come over, one thing will lead to another, and I won't get to bed till late. I need my sleep, or I'll be a mess at the depos.'

'You can sleep here if you want'—she would have liked that—'or just a drive-by hug. I'm sorry to be a pain. I'd just love to see you for a minute.' She hated herself for it, but she knew she was whining, and felt unbearably needy. He hated that. He always said his ex-wife had been a whiner, and made fun of her for it. He didn't like it in Sarah, either. He thought needy women were a drag, and he liked Sarah because she wasn't. Her feelings and request tonight were out of character for her. She knew the rules of their relationship. 'Don't ask. Don't whine. No bitching. Let's have a good time when we see each other.' And most of the time, they did. However time-limited it was, it had worked for both of them for four years.

'Let's see how it goes tomorrow. I just can't tonight.' Phil stuck to his guns, as he always did. He had firm boundaries. 'I'll see you Friday.' In other words, no. She got the message, and knew that pushing, or out-and-out begging, would only make him mad.

'Okay. I just thought I'd ask.' She tried to hide the disappointment in her voice, but there were tears in her eyes. Not only had Stanley died, but she had run right into Phil's worst feature. He was a narcissist, not a nurturer. It was not a news flash to her. She had made her peace with it over the past four years. You could only get so much from him, and usually not by asking. Asking him for anything made him feel cornered, or controlled. As he said himself at every opportunity, he only did what he wanted. And tonight he didn't want to drop by to hug her. He had made that clear. She always got more from him if she wasn't needy. And tonight she was. Shit luck for her.

'You can always ask, babe. If I can, I can. If I can't, I can't.'

No, if you won't, you won't, not can't, Sarah thought.

It was a debate she had had with him for years, and was not about to tackle with him tonight. It was why the relationship worked for her sometimes and at other times it didn't. She always felt that Phil should make adjustments for special circumstances, like Stanley's death for instance. Phil was rarely if ever swayed from his path, and only when it suited him, not others. He didn't like being asked for special favors, and she knew it. But they liked each other, and were familiar with each other's quirks and styles. Sometimes it was easy, sometimes it was hard. He said he never wanted to get married again, and had always been straightforward with her about it. She had told him just as honestly that marriage wasn't a priority for her, or even of interest to her, and Phil liked that about her a lot. She didn't think she wanted kids. She had told him that right in the beginning. She said she wasn't about to give anyone a childhood as

32

lousy as hers, with an alcoholic father, although Phil wasn't an alcoholic. He liked a drink now and then, but was never excessive. And he already had kids, and didn't want more. So it had been a good fit in the beginning. In fact for the first three years, it had suited them both to perfection. The shoe had only begun to pinch slightly for the last year, when Sarah mentioned that she'd like to see more of him, like maybe one weekday evening. Phil was outraged the first time she said it, and felt her request was intrusive. He said he needed weekday evenings to himself, except those he spent with his kids. After three years Sarah felt it was time to take a small step forward into more time together. Phil was adamant about it, Sarah had gotten nowhere on the subject for the past year, and they argued about it often now. It was a sore subject for her.

He didn't want to spend more time with her, and said the beauty of their relationship had always been mutual freedom, weekdays to themselves, companionship on weekends to the degree they wanted, and not having to make a serious commitment, since neither of them wanted to get married. All he wanted was what they had. A great time in the sack on weekends, a body to cuddle up with two nights a week. He wasn't willing to give her more than that, and probably never would. They had been stuck on the same argument for the past year, and gotten nowhere with it, which had begun to seriously annoy her. How hard was it to see her one extra night a week for dinner? Phil acted like he'd rather have root canal than do it, which Sarah said was insulting. It was slowly becoming a bitter battle whenever the subject came up.

But by now, she had four years invested in the relationship, and she didn't have the time or energy to go out and audition anyone else. She knew what she had with Phil and was afraid she might find someone worse, or no one at all. She was nearly forty years old, and the men she knew liked younger women. She wasn't twenty-two or -four or -five years old anymore. Her body was pretty damn good, but it didn't look the way it had when she was in college. She worked a fifty- or sixty-hour week at least, in a high-stress job, so when was she going to be dating to find someone else who might want more than just weekends? It was easier to stay with Phil, and live with his gaps and lapses. He was the devil she knew, and for now that was good enough. Maybe not great. But the sex was better than she'd ever had. It was the wrong reason to stay in a relationship, she knew, but it had kept her involved with him for four years.

'I hope you feel better,' he said, as he pulled into his garage six blocks away. She could hear the garage door close, and he had probably driven by her house, while telling her he couldn't stop by to give her a hug. She tried to ignore the knot in her stomach that his doing that had caused. Was it so unreasonable to ask him for a hug? Midweek it was, from his perspective. He didn't want to fill her emotional cup, or even deal with it, on weekdays. He had his own problems, and better things to do with his time.

'I'm sure I'll feel better tomorrow,' Sarah said numbly. It didn't matter if she did or not, she felt lousy then, and as usual he had stuck to his narcissistic guns. Phil was smart, charming when he wanted to be, sexy, and good-looking, but he was all about himself, and no one else. He had never claimed otherwise, but after four years she expected him to mellow a little and be more flexible. He wasn't. Phil took care of his own needs first. She knew that about him, and didn't always like it.

At first he had told her how devoted he was to his kids, that he coached Little League and went to all their games. She had realized eventually that he was just a sports fanatic, and gave up coaching because it ate up too much of his time. And he didn't see his kids on weekends, because he wanted the time to himself. He saw them for dinner twice a week, but never let them spend the night, because they drove him insane. They were thirteen, fifteen, and eighteen. He had one in college now, the other two were still at home with their mother, but as far as he was concerned, they were his ex-wife's problem. The two younger kids were girls, and he figured dealing with them was ample punishment for his ex-wife having left him for someone else.

More than once, Sarah had felt he was transferring his anger at his ex-wife onto her, for crimes Sarah had never committed. But someone had to be punished, not only for his ex-wife's sins, but worse yet, for those of his mother, who had had the audacity to die and thus abandon him when he was three. He had a lot of scores to settle, and what he couldn't accuse Sarah of, he blamed on his ex-wife or kids. Phil had 'issues' up the gazoo. But then there were all the rest of the things that she liked about him, well enough to stick around. She had considered it a stopgap relationship at first and it was hard to believe that it had lasted for four years. Much as she hated to admit it to herself, or to her mother, God forbid, Phil defined dead-end relationship. Once in a while, Sarah hoped that eventually there would be more substance to it, not marriage, but just more time. By now, she expected him to be closer to her, but he wasn't. He kept distance between them by only seeing her twice a week and maintaining separate lives.

'I'll call you tomorrow, on my way home from the gym. And I'll see you Friday night . . . I love you, babe. Gotta go in now. It's freezing in the garage.' She wanted to say 'good,' but she didn't. He made her so mad sometimes, and hurt her feelings when he disappointed her, which he often did, and she disappointed herself by putting up with it.

'I love you, too,' she said, wondering what that meant to him. What does love mean to a man whose mother died and abandoned him, whose ex-wife left him for another man, and whose kids wanted more from him than he had to give? *I love you.* What did that mean exactly? I love you, but don't ask me to give up the gym, or see you on a weekday night . . . or come by for a hug on a night we're not supposed to see each other, just because you're sad. There was a limited amount to what he had to give. He just didn't have it in his emotional piggy bank, no matter how hard she shook.

She lay and stared mindlessly at the TV for another hour, trying not to think of anything, and then she fell asleep on the couch. It was six in the morning when she woke up, and thought about Stanley again, and then knew what she wanted to do. She wasn't going to let them put him away in the mausoleum with no one to be there for him. Maybe it was unprofessional, as Phil said, but she wanted to be there for her friend.

She stood in the shower for nearly an hour after that, crying for Stanley, her father, and Phil.

CHAPTER 3

Sarah drove to the cemetery in Colma, past the long line of car dealerships, and reached Cypress Lawn just before nine. She let the secretary in the office know why she had come, and she was waiting in the mausoleum for the cemetery people to arrive with Stanley's ashes at nine o'clock. They placed the urn inside a small vault, and it took another half hour to seal it up with the small marble slab, while Sarah watched. It unnerved her to see that the slab was blank, and they assured her that the one with his name and dates on it would replace it in a month.

Forty minutes later it was over, and she stood outside in the sunlight, looking dazed, wearing a black dress and coat. She felt momentarily disoriented, looked up at the sky and said, 'Good-bye, Stanley.' And then she got in her car, and drove to the office.

Maybe Phil was right, and she was being unprofessional. But whatever this was, it felt awful. She had work to do for him now, the work they had completed so carefully in the three years they had worked together, meticulously preparing his estate, and discussing tax laws. She had to wait to hear from his heirs. She had no idea how long it would take, or if she would have to proactively pursue some of them. Sooner or later, she knew she'd round them up. She had a lot of good news for them, from a great-uncle they didn't even know.

She tried not to think of Phil, or even of Stanley, on the drive back. She went over a mental list of things she had to do today. Stanley had been buried, as simply and unpretentiously as he had wanted. She had put the wheels in motion to probate the estate. She had to call a realtor to discuss putting the house on the market, and have it appraised. Neither she nor Stanley had had a precise idea of what it was worth. It hadn't been appraised in a long time, and the real estate market had gone up drastically since the last time it was. But the house also hadn't been touched, remodeled, or even freshened up in more than sixty years. There was a huge amount of work to do. Someone was going to have to restore the house from basement to attic. More than likely it would cost a fortune. She was going to have to ask the heirs, when they surfaced, how much work they wanted to do, if any, before they put it on the market. Maybe they would just want to sell it as it was, and let the new owners worry about it. It was their decision. But she wanted to at least get a current appraisal for the heirs before they turned up for the reading of the will.

She called a realtor as soon as she got to her office. They made an appointment to meet at the house the following week. It was going to be the first time Sarah got a full tour of the house herself. She had the keys now, but she didn't want to go there on her own. She knew it would make her too sad. It felt intrusive to her somehow and would be easier to do with the realtor, keeping things professional, as Phil had said. She was doing her job for a client, not just a friend. She had watched his interment as his friend.

She had just hung up after talking to the realtor, when her secretary buzzed her and told her that her mother was on the line. Sarah hesitated for a moment, took a breath, and answered the call. She loved her mother, but not the way she never failed to invade her space.

'Hi, Mom,' she said, sounding bright and breezy. She didn't like telling her mother her woes. It always led to things she didn't want to discuss with her. Audrey was never afraid to push her way past whatever boundaries Sarah had. Audrey's many years in twelve-step groups, and therapy, had failed to teach her that. 'I got your message last night, but you said you were going out, so I didn't call,' Sarah explained.

'You sound awful. What's wrong?' So much for bright and breezy.

'I'm just tired. I have a lot going on at the office. One of my clients died yesterday, and I'm trying to organize everything for the estate. It's a big job.'

'That's too bad.' Audrey sounded briefly sympathetic, which was at least nice of her. Sarah didn't mind the sympathy, she just didn't want everything else that usually went with it. Her mother's questions, and even her gestures of kindness, were always invasive and excessive. 'Is something else wrong?'

'No. I'm fine.' Sarah could feel her voice get small, and hated herself for it. Up, up, up, she told herself, or Mom will nail you. Audrey always knew when Sarah was upset, no matter what she did to hide it, and then the interrogation, and eventually accusations would begin. And worse yet, the advice. It was never what Sarah wanted to hear. 'How are you? Where did you go last night?' Sarah tried to distract her mother. Sometimes that worked.

'I went to a new book club with Mary Ann.' Mary Ann was one of her mother's many women friends. She had spent the twenty-two years of her widowhood hanging out with other women, playing bridge, taking classes, going to women's groups, even taking trips with them. She had dated a few men over the years, who always turned out to be alcoholic, problematic, or secretly married. She seemed to draw dysfunctional men to her like a magnet. And after she disposed of them, she then went back to hanging out with other women. She was in one of her celibate phases again, after a brief romance with an owner of a car dealership, who had turned out to be yet another alcoholic, or so she said. It was hard for Sarah to believe there were that many on the planet. But if there was one in the area, Audrey was sure to find him.

'That sounds like fun,' Sarah said, referring to the book club. She couldn't think of anything worse than attending a book club with a flock of women. Just thinking about things like that kept her seeing Phil on weekends. She didn't want to end up like her mother. And despite years of her mother's entreaties, she had never gone to Adult Children of Alcoholics, a twelve-step group her mother was absolutely certain was right for Sarah. Sarah had seen a therapist briefly between college and law school, and felt she had dealt with at least some of her 'issues,' as much about her mother as about her father. She had never dated an alcoholic. The men she chose were emotionally unavailable, her specialty, because in a way, despite his physical presence in the house, she had never really known her father, thanks to his drinking. He had been shut off from all of them.

'I wanted to let you know that we're having Thanksgiving at Mimi's.' Mimi was Audrey's mother, and Sarah's grandmother. She was eighty-two years old, had been widowed for ten years, after a long and happy marriage, and had a far more normal dating life than her daughter's or even Sarah's. There seemed to be a limitless supply of nice, normal, happy widowers at her age. She was out nearly every night, and very rarely with other women, unlike her daughter. She was having a lot more fun than either of them.

'That's fine,' Sarah said, making a note of it on her calendar. 'Do you want me to bring anything?'

'You can help cook the turkey.'

'Is anyone else coming?' Sometimes her mother brought one of her friends who had nowhere else to go. And her grandmother sometimes invited friends, or even her current boyfriend, which always irritated Audrey. Sarah suspected she was jealous, but never said it.

'I'm not sure. You know your grandmother. She said something about inviting one of the men she's going out with, because his children live in Bermuda.' Mimi had a vast supply of men and friends, and had never been to a book club in her life. She had far more entertaining fish to fry.

'I just wondered,' Sarah said vaguely.

41

'You're not bringing Phil, are you?' Audrey asked pointedly. The way she said it spoke volumes. She had pegged him correctly as a problem, right from the beginning. Audrey was the expert in screwed-up men. She said it as though asking if Sarah was bringing a test tube of leprosy to their dinner. She asked the same question every year, which never failed to annoy Sarah. Audrey knew the answer without asking. Sarah never brought Phil to Thanksgiving. He spent holidays with his children and never invited Sarah to join them. In four years, she had never spent a holiday with him.

'Of course not. He'll be with his children, and then they're going skiing in Tahoe.' They did the same thing every year, as Audrey knew only too well. This year was no different. Nothing in the relationship had changed in four years.

'I assume he's not inviting you, as usual,' her mother said in an acid tone. She had hated Phil the first time she laid eyes on him, and things had worsened since then. The only things she had not accused him of were being gay or alcoholic, neither of which he was. 'I think it's disgraceful that he doesn't invite you. That ought to tell you what the relationship means to him. You're thirty-eight years old, Sarah. If you ever want to have children, you'd better find a new guy and get married. Phil is never going to change. He has too many issues.' Her mother was right, of course, and Sarah knew he had an aversion to any form of therapeutic help.

'I'm not worried about that this morning, Mom. I have other things to take care of, here at the office. He needs to be with his children. It's nice for him to be alone with them.' She would never

42

have admitted it to her mother, but it had bothered her too in the last year or two. She had met his children several times, but he never invited her on weekends away with them, or vacations. He told her exactly what she had just said to her mother. He said he needed time alone with his children. It was sacred. Like going to the gym five nights a week, which precluded their seeing each other anytime except on weekends. After four years, she would have liked being invited on his vacations, but it was not part of the deal she had with him. She was strictly his weekend girlfriend. It was hard for her to admit, even to herself, that she had put up with it for that long. Four years had just slipped by, and nothing ever changed. Even without marriage as their ultimate goal, a little mellowing of his rigid rules, over four years, would have been nice for her.

'I think you're kidding yourself about him, Sarah. He's a deadbeat.'

'No, he isn't. He's a very successful attorney,' Sarah said, feeling twelve years old while talking to her mother. Audrey always made her feel defensive, and backed her into corners.

'I'm not talking about his career. I'm talking about your relationship with him, or lack of one. Just where do you think this is going, after four years?' She had never expected it to go anywhere except to maybe seeing him one or two more days a week. But being put on the spot by her mother always made her uncomfortable, and feel as though she were doing something wrong.

'It's right where we want it for now, Mom. Why don't you just relax and back off about it? I don't have time for more than that right now. I'm busy with my own career.'

'I had a career *and* a child at your age,' Audrey said smugly, while Sarah resisted the urge to remind her that her husband had been a real deadbeat, in every possible way. He had been a zero as a husband *and* a father, and couldn't even hold down a job. But Sarah said nothing, as usual. She didn't want a battle with her mother, least of all today.

'I don't want a child right now, Mom.' Or maybe ever. Nor a husband, if there was even a remote chance he'd turn out like her father. 'I'm happy the way I am.'

'When are you going to get a new apartment? For God's sake, Sarah, the place you're living in is a dump. You need to get a decent place, and throw out all that crap you've been dragging around since college. You need a real apartment, like a grown-up.'

'I *am* a grown-up. And I *like* my apartment.' Sarah was talking through clenched teeth. She had buried her friend and favorite client that morning, Phil had disappointed her the night before, and the last thing she needed was her mother dragging her through barbed wire over her apartment and her boyfriend. 'I've got to get to work now. I'll see you on Thanksgiving.'

'You can't run away from reality forever, Sarah. You need to face your issues. If you don't, you'll waste years with Phil, or men just like him.' What she said was truer than Sarah wanted it to be. She needed to ask more of Phil, but she wasn't sure it would make a difference. And if she did, and he walked out on her, then she would have no one to spend weekends with. The loneliness of that

44

possibility didn't appeal to her, and she didn't want to replace him with book clubs, like her mother. It was a problem Sarah hadn't solved yet, and wasn't ready to face at the moment. And being badgered by her mother was definitely not what she wanted. It just made it all seem worse.

'Thanks for your concern, Mom. This isn't the time to talk about it. I have a lot on my plate at the office.' To her own ears, she sounded just like Phil. Avoidance. One of his best games. And denial. She had played that one for years herself.

She was unnerved after she hung up the phone. It was hard putting her mother's pointed questions and criticisms out of her head. Her mother always wanted to strip away her defenses, and leave her standing there naked, while she looked over every pore. Her scrutiny was intolerable, and her judgments about everything in Sarah's life just made her feel worse. She was dreading Thanksgiving. She wished she could go to Tahoe with Phil. At least her grandmother would keep things lively. She always did. And more than likely, Mimi would invite one of her boyfriends. They were always very nice men. Mimi had a knack for meeting them, wherever she went.

Sarah heard from her grandmother shortly thereafter, reiterating the Thanksgiving invitation Sarah had already had via her mother. In contrast, the conversation with Mimi was lively, loving, and brief. Her grandmother was a gem. After that, Sarah tied up the last loose ends on Stanley's estate, made a list of questions to ask the realtor, and made sure the letters had gone out to notify the heirs. Then she turned to her work for other clients. It turned into another thirteen-hour day before she even realized it. It was nearly ten o'clock when she got home, and midnight when she heard from Phil. He sounded tired too and said he was going to bed. He said he hadn't gotten home from the gym till eleven-thirty. It was strange knowing he was a few blocks away, yet acted as though he lived in another city five days a week. It was hard not to feel as close to him as she wanted, particularly when other things were rocky in her life. It was impossible to understand sometimes why seeing her once in a while during the week would have been such a travesty to him. To Sarah, after four years, it didn't seem a lot to ask.

They spoke on the phone for five minutes, talked about what they would do that weekend, and ten minutes after Sarah talked to him, she fell into a troubled sleep, alone in the bed she hadn't made all week.

She had nightmares about her mother that night, and woke up twice during the night, crying. She told herself she was just upset about Stanley, when she woke up the next morning, with a stomachache and a headache. It was nothing a cup of coffee, two aspirins, and a hard day at the office wouldn't fix. They always did.

CHAPTER 4

By the time Friday night rolled around, Sarah felt as though she had been run over by a tank. One of Stanley's heirs had contacted her, but she had heard nothing so far from the others. She had an appointment at the house for the following

46

Monday, with the realtor she'd called. She was curious now to see the rest of the house. It had been an enigma to her for years. She had never even glimpsed the other floors, and couldn't wait to see it all on Monday.

In the call with her grandmother, just after the one from her mother earlier in the week, Mimi told her to bring whoever she wanted to Thanksgiving. Mimi had always welcomed Sarah's friends. She didn't mention Phil specifically, but Sarah knew the open invitation included him as well. Unlike Audrey, she never pried, criticized, or asked questions that might make Sarah uncomfortable. Sarah's relationship with her grandmother had always been easy, accepting, and warm. She was an incredibly nice person, and Sarah had never met anyone who didn't love her, man, woman, or child. It was hard to believe that this gentle, happy human being had spawned a child who was as abrasive as Audrey. But Audrey's life and marriage had not turned out as well as her mother's, and the mistakes she had made had cost her. Mimi's long, happy marital history had been a lot smoother, and the man she'd married and stayed with for more than fifty years had been a gem. Unlike Sarah's father, who had turned out to be a total lemon. Audrey had been sour, critical, and suspicious ever since. Sarah hated that about her, although she didn't entirely blame her. Sarah's father and his rampant alcoholism, and failure to be there for anyone, even himself, had damaged her as well.

By the time Sarah got home on Friday night, she was physically exhausted and emotionally drained. Seeing Stanley's ashes sealed away in the

47

mausoleum had been a huge emotional blow to her. It was so final, and so sad. A long life, but in many ways an empty one. He had left a fortune behind him, but very little else. And she couldn't help but remember now all his warnings about how she led her life as well. There was more to life than just work, and she was suddenly more acutely aware of it than ever before. His words over the last three years had not been lost on her. They had begun to color how she viewed everything that week, even Phil's weekday unavailability to her. She was suddenly really tired of it, and having trouble buying the excuses he had given her for four years. Even if it wasn't right for him, and didn't fit into his program, she needed and wanted more. His refusal to drop by to see her, and comfort her, the night Stanley died, had left a sour taste in her mouth. Even if they never planned to marry, four years together should have counted for something. An ability and desire to meet each other's needs and be there for each other in hard times, if nothing else. And Phil steadfastly refused to offer her that. And if that was the case, what was the point? Was it only sex? She wanted more than that. Stanley was right. There should be more to life than working sixty hours a week and ships passing in the night.

Phil usually showed up at her place, by tacit agreement, every Friday around eight o'clock, after the gym. Sometimes nine. He insisted that he needed at least two hours, sometimes three, at the gym, to unwind, and get over the stress of his daily work life. It also kept his body looking fantastic, which he was well aware of and wasn't lost on her, either. Sometimes it annoyed her. He was in much

48

better shape than she was. She stayed at her desk twelve hours a day, and exercised only on weekends. She looked great, but she wasn't as toned as he was with twenty hours spent at the gym every week. She didn't care as much about it, and she didn't have the time. He made time for himself, hours of it, every day. Something about it had always bothered her, but she had tried to be magnanimous about it. It was getting to be harder and harder, considering how little time she got to spend with him, especially during the week. She was never his first priority, which really bugged her. She wanted to be, but knew she wasn't. She had always thought she would become more important to him in time, but in recent months, hope of that had begun to wane. He was holding firm. Nothing between them ever grew or changed. He diligently maintained the status quo. They seemed to be frozen in time, and she felt like nothing more than a four-year two-night stand. She wasn't sure why, but just in the few days since Stanley's death, she was more acutely aware than ever before that maybe that just wasn't enough. She needed more. Not marriage perhaps, but kindness, emotional support, and love. After Stanley's death, she felt more vulnerable somehow.

Not getting what she needed made her feel resentful toward Phil now. She deserved more than just two casual nights a week. But she also knew that if she wanted to continue the relationship with him, she had to accept the terms that they had agreed to in the beginning. He wasn't going to budge. And letting go of Phil had always scared her. She'd thought of it before, but was afraid to wind up alone, like her mother. The specter of

Audrey's life terrified her. Sarah preferred to hang on to Phil than wind up at bridge games and book clubs, like her mother. In the past four years she hadn't met any other man who appealed to her as much. But the relationship she had with Phil was settling for a two-day-a-week physical relationship born of habit, and not a matter of the heart, not in the real sense. Being with him, she was giving up a lot. The hope of something better, and the love of a man who might be kinder or love her more. It seemed like more of a dilemma to her now than it had in a long time. Stanley's death had shaken her up a lot.

Phil turned up earlier than usual that night. He let himself in with the keys she'd given him, walked in, and sprawled out on the couch. He grabbed the remote and turned on the TV. Sarah found him there when she got out of the shower. Phil glanced over his shoulder at her, lay his head back on the arm of the sofa, and groaned audibly.

'Oh God, I had such a shit week.' Lately, she had begun noticing that he always told her about his week first. Questions about hers came after if at all. It was amazing how many things about him had begun to annoy her lately. And yet she still hung on. She watched her own feelings about him now, and her reactions to him, with dispassionate fascination, as though she were another person, a deus ex machina hanging somewhere off the ceiling, observing what was happening in the room, and commenting silently on it to herself.

'Yeah, me too.' She bent over him to kiss him, wrapped in a towel, still dripping, with her long hair still wet from the shower. 'How were your depos?'

'Endless, boring, and stupid. What do we have for dinner? I'm starving.'

'Nothing yet. I didn't know if you'd want to go out or stay in.' They often stayed home on Friday nights, because they were both exhausted from their long days at work, particularly Sarah. But Phil worked hard too, and his area of law was admittedly more stressful than hers and he was frequently involved in litigation, which he enjoyed, but was far more anxiety causing than her endless hours of trying to ferret out new tax laws to assist her clients, or protect them from others that could hurt them. Her work was painstaking and filled with minute details that were tedious at times. His was more flamboyant.

She and Phil rarely, if ever, made set plans for Friday nights, or even Saturdays. They just played it by ear when they got together.

'I don't mind going out, if you want to,' she suggested, thinking it might cheer her up. She was still depressed about Stanley's passing. It had cast a pall over everything she did all week. And in spite of her unspoken complaints and questions, or even doubts about him, she was happy to see Phil on Friday night. She always was. He was familiar, and seeing him on the weekend was an easy way to unwind, and sometimes they had a lot of fun. He looked so beautiful and healthy and alive, lying on her couch, watching TV. He was nearly six foot four, his hair was sandy blond, and instead of blue like hers, his eyes were green. He was a beautiful example of the male species, with broad shoulders, a small waist, and legs that seemed endless. He looked even better naked, though she wasn't feeling overly sexual this week. Depression, like

51

hers over Stanley, always dampened her libido. She was more interested in cuddling with Phil this week, which wasn't a problem. They rarely made love on Friday nights, they were both too tired usually. But they made up for it on Saturday mornings, or nights, and then again sometime on Sunday, before he went back to his own apartment, to get organized for the week. She had tried for years now to get him to stay over on Sunday nights, but he said he liked leaving for work from his place on Monday morning. He always felt disorganized at her house, without all his things there. And he didn't like her staying over at his place on a work night. He said that before he went back into the ring on Monday morning, he needed a night of undisturbed sleep, and she was too distracting. He meant it as a compliment, but it disappointed her anyway.

She was always looking for ways to increase their time together, while he found better ones to keep it in check. So far, he was winning. Or lately, maybe losing, in more important ways. His stubbornness about limiting their time together was beginning to turn her off, and made her feel unimportant to him. Although Sarah hated to admit it, maybe her mother was right. Maybe she needed more in her life than Phil would ever give her. Not marriage, since that wasn't on Sarah's agenda either, but at least some weekday nights and occasional vacations. She was beginning to feel as though she was re-evaluating her life, and what she wanted from it, in the few days since Stanley had died. She realized she didn't want to end her life alone, with only money and professional achievements, as Stanley had. There had to be something more. And Phil didn't seem to be it, nor want to be. She was suddenly questioning everything now, in ways she never had before. Maybe Stanley had been right, with all his nagging and advice about her working too hard and not having a life.

'Do you mind if we just order takeout tonight?' Phil asked her, stretching happily. 'I'm so comfortable here on the couch, I'm not sure I can move.' He was blissfully unaware of the deep concerns that had troubled her all week. She looked normal to him.

'Sure, that's fine.' She had a stack of menus from places they frequently ordered from: Indian, Chinese, Thai, Japanese, Italian. The possibilities were endless. Most of the time she lived on take-out food. She didn't have the time or patience to cook, and had fairly limited skills, which she willingly admitted. 'What speaks to you tonight?' she asked, deciding she was actually happy to see him. She liked having him there. Whatever his flaws or limitations, alone was worse for her. His physical presence next to her seemed to dispel some of the doubts she'd had about him that week. She liked being with him, which was why she wanted to see more of him.

'I don't know . . . Thai? . . . Sushi? . . . I'm sick of pizza. I've been eating it in the office all week . . . How about Mexican? Two beef burritos and some guacamole would hit the spot. Okay with you?' Phil suggested. He loved hot spicy food.

'Sounds great,' she said, smiling. It sounded good to her, too. She liked their lazy Friday nights, sitting on the floor and eating, watching TV, and unwinding after a long week. They almost always met and ate at her place, and sometimes slept at his. He preferred his own bed, but was willing to sleep in hers on weekends. The advantage of sleeping at her place, for him, was that he could leave whenever he wanted, the next day, to do his own thing.

She ordered the Mexican dinner he'd asked for, with chicken and cheese enchiladas for herself, a double order of guacamole, and tucked herself onto the couch next to him after she'd made the call, while they waited for the food to arrive. He put an arm around her and pulled her close, while they both stared mindlessly at the TV. They were watching a special on diseases in Africa, which didn't really interest either of them, but it was something to look at while their exhausted minds defrosted after their frantic week. Like racehorses that needed to cool off after a long race. They both worked hard.

'What do you want to do tomorrow?' she asked him. 'Are the kids in any games this weekend?'

'Nope. I have no fatherly duties. I've been dispensed with.' His son had left for UCLA in August, for his first year in college, and both his girls were busy with their friends every weekend. With his son gone now, he had far fewer sports events to attend for his children. His daughters were more interested in boys than sports, which made life easier for him. His older daughter was a powerhouse in tennis, and he enjoyed playing with her. But at fifteen, the last people she wanted to spend time with on weekends were her parents, so he was off the hook. And the youngest one had never been athletic. Sports seemed to be the only way Phil interacted with his children. 'Anything you want to do?' he asked Sarah casually.

'I don't know. Maybe a movie. There's a great photography show at the MOMA, we can take a look if you want.' She'd been wanting to see it for weeks, but they hadn't gotten to it yet. She was hoping to see it before it closed.

'I have a lot of errands to do tomorrow,' he suddenly remembered. 'I need new tires, I have to get my car washed, pick up my dry cleaning, do my laundry, the usual garbage.' She knew what that meant. He would leave her early the next morning, after they woke up, and return in time for dinner. It was a game he had played often, first he told her he had nothing to do, then stayed busy from morning to night, doing things he said she didn't need to bother doing with him. He preferred doing his chores on his own. He said it was quicker, and why waste her time, too. She would have preferred doing them with him. It made her feel more connected to him, which was what he avoided at all cost. Too much connection was uncomfortable for him.

'Why don't we spend the day together? You can do your laundry here on Sunday,' Sarah suggested. She had machines in her building, though not in her apartment. They were no better or worse than the ones in his building, and they could watch a movie on TV together, or a video, while he did it. She didn't even mind doing his laundry for him. Sometimes she liked doing little domestic things like that for him.

'Don't be silly, I'll do it at my place. I can even go out and buy more underwear.' He did that often when he was too lazy to do his laundry, or too busy. It was a trick most bachelors did. He also bought shirts when he didn't have time to pick up his dry cleaning. As a result, he had mountains of underwear, and a closet full of shirts. It worked for him. 'I'll get the tires in the morning. I want to do it in Oakland. Why don't you go to the museum while I get all my stuff done? Photography really isn't my thing.' Neither was spending Saturdays with her in the daytime. He preferred his independence and doing his own thing, and then coming back to her in the evening.

'I'd rather be with you,' she said firmly, feeling pathetic as the doorbell rang. It was their dinner. She didn't want to argue with him about his errands, or what they'd both be doing the next day.

The food was good, and he stretched out on the couch again, after they ate. She put away the leftovers, in case they wanted to eat them later in the weekend. Sarah sat down on the floor next to Phil, and he leaned over and kissed her. She smiled at him. This was the nice part about their weekends, not the errands she didn't get to do with him, but the affection he shared with her when he was with her. Despite the distance he kept between them much of the time, he was a surprisingly warm person. He was an interesting dichotomy, both independent and sometimes cozy.

'Have I told you today that I love you?' he asked, pulling her closer to him.

'Not lately.' She smiled up at him. She missed him during the week, so damned much. Things just got good between them on the weekends, and then on Sunday he was gone for five days. It made the contrast of his absence more acute. 'I love you, too,' she said, returning the kiss, and then stroking his silky blond hair, as she nestled against him.

They sat there, watching the eleven o'clock news together. Friday evenings always went by quickly. By the time they had dinner, unwound for a few hours, chatted about their weeks, or just sat quietly together, the evening was over. Half of their weekend was already gone before she had a chance to catch her breath, relax, and enjoy it. She could never believe how fast it went.

They woke up relatively early on Saturday morning. It was a cold, gray November day. A drizzle of rain was misting up her windows as they got out of bed, he went to shower, and she went to cook breakfast for them. Sarah was always the breakfast chef. Phil said he loved her breakfasts. She made great French toast, waffles, and scrambled eggs. She had more trouble with over easy and omelettes, but had made fantastic eggs Benedict once. This time she made scrambled eggs, heaps of bacon, fried crisp and lean, and English muffins, with a big glass of orange juice for him, and a latte she made with expertise from her own espresso machine. He had given it to her for Christmas their first year. It hadn't been a romantic gift, but it had served them well for the past four years. She only used it when he was there. The rest of the time, when she was running to work, she stopped at Starbucks and bought herself a cappuccino, which she took to work with her. But on weekends they luxuriated in the sumptuous breakfasts she prepared.

'This is fantastic,' he said happily as he ate the eggs and gobbled the bacon. She reached outside her door for the newspaper and then handed it to him.

It was the perfect lazy Saturday morning, and

she would have loved to go back to bed with him and make love. They hadn't made love since the week before. Sometimes they missed a week, when one of or both of them were too tired, or sick. Most of the time she loved the regularity and dependability of their love life. They knew each other well, and had had a great time in bed with each other for the past four years. It would have been hard to give that up. There were lots of things about him she didn't want to lose: his companionship, his intelligence, the fact that he was a lawyer too and was usually interested in what she was doing, at least to some degree, although admittedly, tax law wasn't as exciting as what he did.

They had a good time together when they saw each other, liked the same movies, and enjoyed the same food. She liked his kids, though she saw little of them, maybe a few times a year. And whenever they went out with her friends or his, they seemed to like the same people, and had the same comments to make about them afterward. There was a lot that worked about the relationship, which was why it was so frustrating that he didn't want more than they had. Lately, she had thought that she might like living with him one day, but there was no chance of that. He had told her right from the beginning that he was interested neither in cohabitation nor in marriage, only dating. And this was dating. It was more than enough for him, and had been for her for four years.

Lately she felt a little too old for this kind of arrangement of nearly total noncommitment. They were sexually exclusive, and had a standing weekend date. Beyond that, they shared nothing.

And sometimes she felt she had been dating for too long. At thirty-eight, she had dated too many people for too many years, as a teenager, a student, a law student, a young lawyer, and now a partner of the firm. She had moved up the ranks in business and life, but she still had the same kind of relationship she had had when she was a kid at Harvard. There was nothing she could do about it, given Phil's stubbornness on the subject and the firm boundaries he set. He had always been completely clear about the limits on the relationship he wanted. But doing the same old thing year after year made her feel like she was trapped in the twilight zone sometimes. Nothing ever moved backward or forward. Nothing ever changed. It just hung in space, eternally, while only she got older. It seemed weird to her. But not to him. In Phil's mind, he was still a kid, and he liked it that way. She didn't want babies and marriage, but she definitely wanted more than this, only because she liked him, and loved him in some ways, although she knew he was selfish at times, self-centered, could be arrogant and even pompous, and had different priorities than she did. But no one was perfect. To Sarah, the people she cared about always came first. To Phil, he did. He always reminded her that in the safety video on the airplane, they told you to put on your own oxygen mask first and help others later. But tend to yourself first. Always. He considered that a lesson in life, and justification for the way he treated people. The way he put it made it hard to argue with him, so she didn't. They were just different. She wondered sometimes if it was the basic difference between women and men, and not anything particularly deficient about him. It was hard to say. But there was no hiding from the fact that Phil was selfish, always put himself first, and did what was best for him. It gave her no wiggle room at all to ask for more.

After breakfast, he went off to do his errands, while Sarah made her bed. He had said something about staying there that night, so she changed the sheets, and put fresh towels up in the bathroom. She did the breakfast dishes, then went out to pick up her own dry cleaning. She never had time to do that either during the week. Single working people never did. Her only day to do errands was Saturday, which was why Phil was doing his. She would just have liked to do them together. He laughed at her when she said that, made light of it, and then reminded her that that was what married people did, single people didn't. And they weren't married. They were single, he always said loud and clear. They did laundry separately, errands separately, had separate lives, apartments, and beds. They came together a couple of days a week to have fun, not to join their two lives into one. He said it to her often. She understood the difference. She just didn't like it. He did. A lot.

Sarah came back to the apartment to put her dry cleaning away, and after that she went to the photography exhibit at the museum, and found it beautiful and interesting. She would have liked to share it with Phil, but she knew he wasn't crazy about museums. She went for a walk on the Marina Green after that, to get some exercise and air, and she was back at her apartment at six o'clock, after stopping at Safeway to buy some groceries. She had decided to cook Phil dinner, and maybe after that they could rent a video or go to a movie. They didn't have much of a social life these days. Most of her friends were married and had children, and Phil found them incredibly boring. He liked her friends, but no longer liked their lifestyles. The people they had met together in the beginning of their relationship were now all married. And he said he found it depressing to try and have an intelligent conversation, while listening to their toddler and brand-new baby screaming either for their dinner or from earaches. He said he had done all that years before. His own friends now were mostly men his age or younger who had never been married, or who had been divorced for years, liked it that way, and were bitter about their ex-wives, or their kids who had supposedly been corrupted by their despicable ex-wives, and the men hated the spousal support they were paying, which they always insisted was too much. They were unanimous in the belief that they had gotten screwed, and were emphatic about not letting it happen again. He found her friends too domestic these days, although he had liked them in the beginning, and she found his superficial and bitter, which limited their social life a lot. She noticed that most of the men Phil's age were now dating seriously younger women. When they went to dinner with them, she found herself trying to have conversations with young women who were barely more than half her age, and she had nothing in common with them. So lately she and Phil had been keeping to themselves, and for the moment that worked well, although it isolated them. They saw fewer and fewer friends now.

He saw his own friends during the week, either

at the gym, or before or after for a drink, which was another reason he had no time to see Sarah during the week, and objected to her trying to take his weekday independence from him. He was very open with her about the fact that he needed to see his friends, whether she liked them or not, or approved of who they dated. So weekday nights were his.

Phil didn't call her on her cell phone all day Saturday, and she assumed he was busy, so she didn't call him, either. She knew he'd turn up at her apartment when he was finished doing what he had to do. He finally walked in at seven-thirty, in blue jeans and a black turtleneck that made him look sexier than ever. She almost had dinner ready for him, and handed him a glass of wine the minute he walked in. He smiled, kissed her, and thanked her.

'My, how you spoil me . . . it smells delicious . . . What's for dinner?'

'Baked potatoes, Caesar salad, steak, and cheesecake.' His favorites, but it sounded good to her, too. And she had bought a nice bottle of French Bordeaux. She liked it better than Napa Valley.

'Sounds fantastic!' He took a sip of the wine and made a yummy sound, and ten minutes later they sat down to dinner at her battered dining table. He never objected to the grim furnishings of her apartment, and seemed not to see them whenever he hung out there. He complimented her lavishly on the dinner. She had made the steak exactly the way he liked it, just rare enough but not too rare. He heaped sour cream and chives that she had chopped into his baked potato. Sometimes she really enjoyed being domestic, and even the Caesar salad was delicious. 'Wow! What a meal!' He loved it, and she was pleased. He was always generous with kind words and praise, and she loved that about him. Her mother had been critical of her all her life, and her father had been too out of it to know she existed. It meant a lot to her to have someone acknowledge the nice things she did. Most of the time, Phil did.

'So what did you do today?' she asked happily, as she served him a slice of the cheesecake. She preferred chocolate herself but always bought cheesecake for him. She knew he loved it. 'Did you get the tires and all the other stuff done?' She assumed he had, since they had been apart for nine hours. He should have been able to get everything done by the time he got back to her apartment just in time for dinner.

'You won't believe it, you'll never believe how lazy I was. I got back to my place, got all organized, and wound up watching some stupid old gladiator movie on TV. It wasn't *Spartacus,* but a poor man's version of it. I sat there for three hours, and by then I was really lazy. I took a nap. I called a couple of people. I went to pick up my dry cleaning, and ran into Dave Mackerson, I hadn't seen him in years, so I went out to lunch with him, then I went to his place and played video games. He just moved into a fantastic house in the marina, with a view of the whole bay. We polished off a bottle of wine, and by the time we did, I came back here. I'll pick up the tires next week. It was just one of those days when I didn't accomplish a damned thing, but it felt good. It was great to see Dave again. I didn't realize he got divorced last year. He has a mighty cute girlfriend.' He laughed easily then, as Sarah tried not to stare at him. 'She's about the same age as his oldest kid. In fact, I think she's a year younger. He gave Charlene the house in Tiburon, but I like his new place a lot better. More style, more modern, and Charlene was always a bitch.' Sarah sat listening to Phil, feeling breathless. She said nothing. She had left him alone all day, so he could do his errands, and because she didn't want to crowd him, while he had watched TV at his place, had lunch with a friend, and played video games all afternoon. He could have spent the afternoon with her, if he wanted to do that. But the painful reality was that he didn't want to. He would rather have spent the afternoon with his buddy, talking about what a bitch his ex-wife was, and admiring his twelve-year-old girlfriend. Sarah nearly cried as she listened, but did everything in her power not to. It was always so hurtful and disappointing when he did things like that. And Phil had absolutely no idea that she was upset, or why she would be. That was the core of the problem. Everything he had done that day seemed fine to him, including leaving Sarah out of his life, in spite of the fact that this was the weekend. But in his mind, it was his life. Not 'their' life: only his. She had accepted it for four years, but now it infuriated her. His priorities were so insulting and hurt her feelings. And saying it to him, as she had tried to on occasion, made her sound like a bitch to him, or so he said. More than anything, he hated complaints, and wanted total freedom about how he spent his time.

'Did you meet her?' Sarah asked, staring into her plate. She knew that if she looked at Phil, she

64

would say something she shouldn't and might regret later, like start a fight with him, which would go on all night. She was really angry, more than hurt this time. She felt as though he had stolen the day from her.

'Charlene? Of course. I went to college with her. Don't you remember? I went out with her my freshman year, which is how Dave met her. She got knocked up, and he married her. Glad it was him and not me. Christ, I can't believe they were married for twenty-three years. Poor bastard. She really took him to the cleaners. They always do,' Phil said, polishing off his cheesecake with a satisfied look, as he complimented Sarah again on the dinner. She seemed quiet to him, but he assumed she was probably just full, or tired from the cooking. To Sarah, everything he had just said sounded so disrespectful, about Charlene, their marriage, about women in general. As though all women were lying in wait for men, plotting to marry them, and then divorce them and screw them out of everything they had. Some did that, she knew. Most didn't.

'I didn't mean Charlene,' Sarah said quietly. 'I meant the girlfriend. The one younger than his oldest kid.' In Dave's case, Sarah knew that meant she was twenty-two. She could do the math. She just couldn't stomach what that looked like, or said about Phil's old college roommate. What was wrong with all these guys, that they were out there, lusting after girls who were barely more than children? Didn't any of them want a grown-up woman with a brain? Or some experience or maturity? Sitting there, at the table with Phil, she felt like a relic. At thirty-eight, those girls could almost be her children. It was a frightening thought. 'Did you meet the girlfriend?' Sarah repeated the question, and Phil looked at her strangely, wondering if she was jealous. As far as he was concerned, that would have been stupid, but you never knew with women. They got upset about the damnedest things. He was almost positive that Sarah wasn't old enough to be sensitive about her age, or anyone else's. In fact, she was, and even more sensitive about how he had spent his day, without including her. She had spent her whole day alone, while he hung out in his apartment, and then played video games with his friend. The reality of that hurt like hell.

'Yeah, of course I did. She was hanging around. She played pool with us for a few minutes. She's a cute girl, not much upstairs, but she looks like a *Playboy* bunny. You know Dave.' He said it almost admiringly. The girl was obviously considered a trophy of sorts, even to Phil. 'She got kicked out of her apartment by her roommates, and I think she's living with him.'

'How lucky for him . . . or maybe for her,' Sarah said in an acid tone, and felt like a bitch as she said it.

'Are you pissed off about something?' It was written all over her face. Helen Keller would have sensed it. And Phil was watching her closely. He was beginning to get it.

'Yes, actually, I am,' Sarah said honestly. 'I know you need space to do your own stuff. So I didn't call you all day. I figured you'd call me when you were through. Instead, you were at your place, watching TV, and then hanging out with Dave, and his dumbass bimbo, playing video games and shooting pool, instead of spending it with me. I see little enough of you as it is.' She hated the tone of her own voice, but couldn't help it. She was livid.

'What's the big deal? Sometimes I need some time to chill. We weren't having an orgy, for chrissake. The girl's a kid. That may be Dave's cup of tea, but it's not mine. I love you,' he said, leaning over to kiss her, but this time she didn't respond and turned her face away, and Phil was starting to look annoyed. 'For chrissake, Sarah! What are you? Jealous? I came home to you, didn't I? We just had a nice dinner. Don't screw it up.'

'With what? My feelings? I'm disappointed. I would have liked to spend that time with you.' She sounded sad and tense, as much as angry.

'I just ran into him. It happened. It's not a big deal.' He sounded defensive and resentful.

'Maybe not to you. But it is to me. We could have done something together. I missed you all afternoon. I wait all week for these weekends.'

'Then enjoy them. Don't bitch about them. Fine, next time I run into an old friend on a Saturday afternoon, I'll call you. But I don't think you'd have enjoyed hanging out with her, while I talked to him.'

'You've got that right. It's all about the priorities thing again. You're my priority. I just don't feel like yours.' She had been feeling that way for months, now more than ever. It felt like he had just demonstrated, yet again, how inconsequential she was to him.

'You're my priority, too. He invited me to dinner, and I told him I couldn't. You can't keep me on a leash, for chrissake. I need time for myself, to unwind and have some fun. I work my ass off all week.'

'So do I. I still want to be with you. I'm sorry you don't think it's as much fun to spend time with me.' She hated the timber of her own voice, but there was no hiding her anger or resentment.

'I didn't say that. I need both in my life. Time with my guy friends, and time with you.' She knew it was an argument that would go nowhere. He didn't get it, and maybe never would. He didn't want to get it. She had fallen in love with the Ray Charles of relationships. The music was wonderful, and romantic at times, he just couldn't see a thing. Not about her point of view, at least. In order to end the argument before it got out of hand, she stood up and put the dishes in the sink. He helped her for a minute, and then went and sat down on the couch and turned on the TV. He was tired of defending himself, and didn't want to argue with her, either. He didn't see her crying, with her back to him, as she scrubbed the pans in the sink. It had been a shit week. First Stanley, and now this. It really did feel like a big deal to her. Maybe more so because her mother was always nagging her about Phil. And he never failed to prove her right. Now she had Stanley's words in her head, as well as her mother's and her own. There had to be more to life than this.

By the time she came and sat next to him on the couch, half an hour later, she looked calmer again. She said nothing more about Dave, or his new *Playboy* bunny friend. She knew there was no point, but she was depressed about it anyway. Given Phil's attitude and defenses, she felt powerless to change it. Feeling helpless always

68

depressed her.

'Are you tired?' Phil asked her gently. He thought it was stupid that she'd gotten upset, but he wanted to make it up to her. She wasn't tired, and shook her head. 'Come on, babe, let's go to bed. We've both had a long day, and a long week.' She knew he wasn't inviting her to sleep, and for once she felt ambivalent about it. It wasn't the first time she had felt that way, but it seemed worse to her tonight.

He surfed the channels for a while instead, and found a movie they both liked. They watched it until midnight, and then they both took showers, and went to bed. Predictably, the inevitable happened. As always, it was exceptionally good, which made it harder to stay mad at him. Sometimes she hated to respond to him, when she didn't like what was happening in the relationship, but she was only human. And the sex between them was very, very good. Almost too good. At times she thought it blinded her to all else. She fell asleep in his arms, relaxed and physically sated. She was still upset about how he had spent his Saturday, but hurt feelings were the nature of her relationship with him, and so was great sex. Sometimes she was afraid it was an addiction. But before she could make her mind up about it, or mull it over further, she fell asleep.

CHAPTER 5

Phil and Sarah woke up late on Sunday morning. The sun was out and streaming across her bedroom. He got up and showered before she was fully awake, as she lay on her side of the bed, thinking of him, and everything that had happened the day before. The day without him, his spending it with his friend without calling her, the way he talked about Dave's ex-wife and his girlfriend, and the exceptionally good sex she and Phil had had. All put together, it made for a puzzle where none of the pieces fit smoothly. She felt as though she were trying to fit pieces together that showed trees, sky, half a cat, and part of a barn door. All together they didn't make a picture. She knew what the images were, but none of them was complete, and she didn't feel whole, either. She reminded herself that she didn't need a man to be complete. But so much of the relationship she had with Phil was constantly half-assed. Maybe that was all she needed to know, and eventually act on. There never seemed to be a real connection between them. For the very simple reason that Phil didn't want to be truly connected, to anyone.

'What are you looking so gloomy about?' he asked when he got out of the shower. He was standing stark naked before her, and his flawless body was enough to knock any woman senseless.

'I was just thinking,' she said, lying back against the pillows. She wasn't aware of it, but she looked beautiful herself. Her body was long and lean and lithe, her long dark hair fanned out against her pillow, her eyes the color of bright blue sky. Phil was well aware of how beautiful she was. Sarah had never traded on her looks or even thought about them.

'What were you thinking about?' he asked, sitting down on the edge of the bed, as he

70

towel-dried his hair. He looked like a naked Viking sitting there.

'That I hate Sundays, because the weekend is over, and in a few hours you'll be gone.'

'Look, silly, enjoy me while I'm here. You can get depressed after I leave, although I don't know why you would. I'll be back again next week. I have been for four years.' That was the problem, for her. Though obviously not for him. What they had was a severe conflict of interests. As attorneys, that should have been clear to both of them, but it wasn't to him. Sometimes denial was a great thing. 'Why don't we go out to brunch somewhere?' She nodded. She liked going out with him, and also being at home with him. And then, as she looked at him, she had an idea.

'I'm getting an appraisal on Stanley Perlman's house tomorrow. I've got the keys. I'm meeting the realtor there before I go to the office. Do you want to go over there today, after brunch? I'm dying to have a look around. It might be fun. It's an amazing place.'

'I'm sure it is,' he said, looking uncomfortable, as he stood up, with the full beauty of his body facing her. 'But I'm not that into old houses. And I think I'd feel like a cat burglar sneaking around.'

'We wouldn't be sneaking. I'm the attorney of record for the estate, I can go in anytime I want. I'd love to look at it with you.'

'Maybe another time, babe. I'm starving, and after that I really need to get home. I have a full week of depos ahead of me again this week. I brought two file boxes of shit home. I've got to get back to my place after brunch.' In spite of her best efforts not to, Sarah looked crestfallen over what

71

he had just said. He always did that to her. She expected to spend the day with him, or hoped to, and he found some reason why he couldn't.

He rarely stayed till lunchtime on Sunday, and today would be no different, which made his spending Saturday with Dave that much worse, which was why she had been so upset. But this time she said nothing. She got up without a word or comment. She was tired of being the beggar in the relationship. If he didn't want to spend the day with her, she would find something to do by herself. She could always call a friend. She hadn't been hanging out with her old friends recently, because especially on weekends, they were busy with their husbands and kids. She liked her time alone with Phil on Saturdays, and on Sundays she had no desire to be a fifth wheel with other people. She spent her Sundays in museums or antique shops, walking on the beach at Fort Mason, or doing work herself. Sundays had always been hard for her. They had always seemed like the loneliest day of the week. They were worse now. They always seemed acutely bittersweet after Phil left. The silence in her apartment after his departure depressed her no end. She could already tell that today would be no different.

She tried to figure out what to do with herself, as she got dressed. She tried to at least feign good spirits, as they walked out of her apartment on the way to brunch. He was wearing a brown leather bomber jacket, jeans, and an immaculate, perfectly pressed blue shirt. He kept just enough of his things at her place so that he could spend the weekend with her, and be decently dressed. It had taken him nearly three years to do that. And

72

maybe in another three, she thought gloomily, he might even stay till Sunday night. Or maybe that would take five, she thought sarcastically as she followed him down the stairs. He was whistling, and in a great mood.

In spite of herself, Sarah had a good time with him at brunch. He told her funny stories, and a couple of really outrageous jokes. He did an imitation of someone in his office, and even though it was stupid and meant nothing, he made her laugh. She was sorry that he wouldn't go with her to see Stanley's house. She didn't want to go there alone, so she decided to wait until she met with the realtor on Monday morning.

Phil was in good spirits, and ate an enormous brunch. Sarah had cappuccino and toast. She could never eat when he was about to leave. Even though it was a weekly occurrence, it never failed to make her sad. She felt rejected somehow. This had been an okay weekend, but for her the day before had been a bust. The lovemaking the night before had been fabulous. But Sunday mornings were always too short. This one was going to be no different. Just another lonely, depressing day after he left. It was the price she was paying for not being married or having kids, or being in a more committed relationship. Other people always seemed to have someone to spend Sundays with. She didn't, when Phil left after breakfast. And she would have cut off her arms and her head before she called her mother. As far as Sarah was concerned, that was no solution. She preferred to be alone. She just wished she could have spent the day with Phil.

She had gotten good at concealing all she felt when he left on Sunday mornings. She managed to look cheerful, and even amused sometimes, when he kissed her lightly on the mouth, dropped her off at her place, and drove home. This time she told him to leave her at the restaurant. She said she wanted to walk down Union Street and check out the shops. What she didn't want was to go home to her empty apartment. She waved gamely, as she always did, when he drove away, back to his own life. End of weekend.

She walked down to the marina eventually, sat on a bench, and watched people flying kites. In the late afternoon, she walked all the way back up the hills to Pacific Heights, and her apartment. She didn't bother to make the bed when she got back. She didn't eat dinner that night, and then finally, she made herself a salad, and took some files out of her briefcase. They were Stanley Perlman's files, and the one thing she was excited about was seeing his house. She had a million fantasies about it. She wished she knew its history. She was going to ask the realtor to research it for her before they put it on the market. But first she wanted to see the house. She had a feeling it was going to be remarkable. She thought of it again as she lay in bed that night.

She was almost asleep when her phone rang. It was Phil. He said he had been working on preparing his depos all night, and he sounded tired.

'I miss you,' he said in a loving voice. It was the voice that always made her heart do flip-flops, even now. It was the voice of the man who had made passionate and highly skilled love to her the night before. She lay in bed and closed her eyes.

'I miss you, too,' she said softly.

'You sound sleepy.' He sounded nice.

'I am.'

'Were you thinking about me as you drifted off to sleep?' He sounded sexier than ever, and this time she laughed.

'No,' she said, turning over on her side, and looking at the side of the bed where he had slept the night before. It seemed so empty now. His pillow was somewhere on the floor. 'I was thinking about Stanley Perlman's house. I can't wait to see it tomorrow.'

'You're obsessed with the place,' he said, sounding disappointed. He liked it when she was thinking about him. As Sarah often said to him, everything was always about him. Sometimes he even agreed.

'Am I?' she said, teasing him. 'I thought I was obsessed with you.'

'You'd better be,' he said, sounding pleased with himself. 'I was just thinking about last night. It gets better and better with us, doesn't it?' She smiled.

'Yeah, it does,' she conceded to him, but she wasn't entirely sure that was a good thing. More often than not, the good sex they shared clouded her vision, and she didn't want it to. It was hard to weed out the wheat from the chaff in their relationship. Their sex life was definitely wheat. But there was a lot of chaff as well, on a variety of subjects.

'Well, I've got to be up early tomorrow. I just wanted to kiss you good night before I went to bed, and tell you that I miss you.' She wanted to remind him that there was an easy solution to it if he missed her, but didn't say a word.

'Thank you.' She was touched. It was a sweet

75

thing for him to do. He was sweet, even though he disappointed her at times. Maybe all men did, and it was just the nature of relationships, she told herself. She was never sure. This was the longest relationship she had ever had. She had always been too busy before that with school and work to commit herself fully to a man.

'I love you, babe . . .' he said in the husky voice that turned her guts to mush.

'I love you too, Phil . . . I'll miss you tonight.'

'Yeah, me too. I'll call you tomorrow.' The sad thing was that whenever they got closer to each other on weekends, he somehow managed to dispel it during the week, and put distance between them again. He was never willing or able to maintain whatever intimacy they established. He seemed to feel safer keeping her at arm's length. But they certainly hadn't been at arm's length the night before.

She lay in bed thinking about him after they hung up. He had gotten his wish. She was thinking about him, and not Stanley's house. As she lay there, her eyes drifted closed, and the next thing she knew, the alarm had gone off and the sun was streaming in her windows. It was Monday morning, and she had to get up.

An hour later, she was dressed, rushing out the door, and on her way to Starbucks. She needed a cup of coffee before meeting the realtor at Stanley's house. She felt as though she were about to go on a treasure hunt. She drank her coffee and read the paper in her car, while waiting for the realtor in Stanley's driveway. She was so intent on the newspaper that she didn't notice the woman approach until she tapped on Sarah's car window.

Sarah quickly pressed the button, and the window sped down. The woman standing there facing her was somewhere in her fifties, and her appearance was between businesslike and frumpy. Sarah had dealt with her on estates before, and had liked her. Her name was Marjorie Merriweather, and Sarah looked at her with a warm smile.

'Thanks for meeting me this morning,' Sarah said as she got out of her car. It was a small dark blue convertible BMW she had bought the year before. She usually left it in her garage and took a cab to work. She didn't need a car downtown, it just cost a fortune to leave it sitting all day in the garage. But this morning, it had been easier to drive.

'I'm delighted to. I've always wanted to get in and see this house. It's a treat for me,' Marjorie said with a broad smile. 'This house has a lot of history to it.' Sarah was pleased to hear it, she had always suspected it had, but Stanley insisted he knew nothing about it.

'I think we should do some research before we put the house on the market. It will give the place some more cachet, and it may make up for turn-of-the-century electricity and plumbing,' Sarah said with a laugh.

'Do you know when the interior was last remodeled?' Marjorie asked her with a businesslike air, as Sarah took the keys out of her handbag.

'Well, let's see,' Sarah said cautiously, as they walked up the white marble steps to the front door. It was glass with an exquisite bronze grille over it, which was itself a work of art. Sarah had never come through the front door, but she didn't want to bring the realtor in through the kitchen. She wasn't sure Stanley had ever used the front door during his entire tenancy of the house. 'Mr. Perlman bought the house in 1930. He never mentioned a remodel to me, and he always intended to sell it. He bought it as an investment, and then somehow never divested himself of it. More by accident, I think, than by design. He just got comfortable and stayed here.' She thought of his tiny little room in the attic as she spoke, the maid's room, where he had spent seventy-six years of his life. But she didn't tell the realtor that. She would probably notice it herself when they toured the house. 'My guess is that it hasn't been remodeled to any significant degree since they built the house. I think Mr. Perlman said that was in 1923. He never told me the name of the family that built it.'

'They were a very well-known family that made their money in banking during the Gold Rush. They came over from France with a number of other bankers from Paris and Lyon. I believe they remained in banking for several generations here in the States until the family died out. The man who built this house was Alexandre de Beaumont, with the French spelling. He built the house in 1923 for his beautiful young wife, Lilli, when they married. She was a famous beauty at the time. It was a very sad story. Alexandre de Beaumont lost his entire fortune in the Crash of '29. I believe she left him after that, roughly around 1930.' The realtor knew a lot more about the house than Sarah did, or Stanley ever had. Although he had lived there for three-quarters of a century, he had

had little or no emotional attachment to the house. It had remained for him, until the end, merely an investment, and the place where he slept. He had never decorated it, or moved to the main portion of the house. He was happy living in the maid's room in the attic.

'I think that's when Mr. Perlman bought the house, in 1930. He never said a word to me about the de Beaumonts.'

'I think Mr. de Beaumont died sometime after his wife left him, and as far as I know, she vanished. Or maybe that's just the romantic version of the story. I want to research it some more for the brochure.'

They both fell silent as Sarah struggled with the keys, and slowly the heavy bronze and glass door creaked open. Sarah had told the nurse to remove the chain closing it before she left, so that she could bring the realtor in through the front door. The door opened and revealed a yawning darkness. Sarah walked in first, and looked around for a switch to turn on the lights. As she stepped inside, the realtor followed. They both had an odd, eerie sense as they entered the house, part trespassers, and part curious children. The realtor opened the door wider behind them, so the sunlight could enter the house and light their path, and then they both saw the light switch. The house was eighty-three years old, and neither of them had any idea if the switch would still work. There were two buttons in the marble entranceway where they stood. Sarah pushed each button in turn, and nothing happened. In the dim light, they could see that the windows in the entrance hall were boarded up. Beyond them they could see nothing.

'I should have brought a flashlight,' Sarah said, sounding annoyed. This was not going to be as easy as she had hoped. As she said it, Marjorie reached into her bag, and handed one to Sarah. She had brought another for herself.

'Old houses are my hobby.' They both turned their flashlights on, and peered around. There were heavy boards on the windows, a white marble floor beneath their feet that seemed to stretch for miles, and overhead an enormous chandelier that was electrified, but the connections to the switch must have decayed over the years, along with everything else.

The hallway itself had beautiful molded panels and was very large, the ceiling high. And then on either side, they saw small receiving rooms that must have been rooms where people waited when they came to visit. There was no furniture anywhere to be seen. The floors of the two receiving rooms were beautiful old parquet, and the walls were carved antique boiseries that looked as though they had come from France. The two smaller rooms were exquisite. And in each there was a spectacular chandelier. The house had been stripped before Stanley bought it, but he had mentioned to Sarah once that the previous owners had left all the original sconces and chandeliers. They both saw then, too, that there were also antique marble fireplaces in each of the rooms. Both receiving rooms were identical in size. Both would have made exquisite studies or offices, depending on what the house became in its next life. Perhaps a fabulously elegant small hotel, or a consulate, or a home for someone incredibly wealthy. The interior had the feel of a small château, and the exterior had always suggested that to Sarah as well. It was the only house even remotely like it in the city, or perhaps even in the state. It was the kind of house, or small château, one expected to see in France. And according to Marjorie, the architect had been French.

As they proceeded farther into the enormous white marble hallway, they could see a large staircase in the center of it. Its steps were white marble, and there were bronze handrails on either side. It swept grandly toward the upper floors, and it was easy to envision men in top hats and tailcoats and women in evening gowns walking up and down those stairs. Overhead was a chandelier of incredibly vast scale. They both stepped gingerly away from it, each of them with the same thought at the same time. There was no way of knowing how secure anything was, after all those years. Sarah was suddenly terrified that it might come crashing down. And as they stepped away from it, they saw an immense drawing room beyond, with curtains covering the windows. Marjorie and Sarah both walked toward them, to see if they were boarded up. The heavy curtains shredded in their hands as they pushed them aside. The windows were actually French doors into the garden. There was a whole wall of them, and here they were only boarded with semicircles of wood at the top. The rest of the windows were filthy but uncovered, they saw, as soon as the curtains were pushed aside. Sunlight entered the room for the first time since Stanley Perlman had bought the house, and as they looked around the room they were standing in, Sarah's eyes grew wide and she gasped. There was a gigantic fireplace on one side, with a marble mantel, boiseries, and mirrored panels. It almost looked like a ballroom, but not quite. The parqueted floors looked several hundred years old. They too had obviously been removed from a château in France.

'My word,' Marjorie said in a hushed whisper. 'I've never seen anything like it. Houses like this just don't exist anymore, and never did out here.' It reminded her of the 'cottages' in Newport that had been built by the Vanderbilts and Astors. Nothing on the West Coast had ever compared to this. It looked like a miniature of Versailles, which was precisely what Alexandre de Beaumont had promised his wife. The house had been a wedding gift to her.

'Is this the ballroom?' Sarah asked, looking impressed beyond words. She knew there was one but had never even remotely imagined anything as beautiful as this.

'I don't think so,' Marjorie said, loving every minute of their tour. This was so much better than anything she had hoped. 'Ballrooms were usually built on the second floor. I think this might be the main drawing room, or one of them.' They found another like it, though slightly smaller, on the other side of the house, with a small rotunda adjoining the two. The rotunda had inlaid marble floors, and a fountain in the center that looked as though it had worked at one time. If one closed one's eyes, one could imagine grand balls here, and the kind of parties of a bygone era that one only read about in books.

There were also several smaller rooms, which Marjorie explained were fainting rooms, where in earlier days in Europe, ladies could rest and loosen their corsets. There was also a large series of pantries and service rooms, where food had obviously been sent up from the kitchen, but not prepared. In a modern world, one could turn the pantries into kitchens, since no one today would want their kitchen in the basement. People no longer had dozens of servants to run food and trays up and down the stairs. There was a row of dumbwaiters, and when Sarah opened one of them to inspect it, one of the ropes broke in her hands. There was no sign of rodents or damage in the house. Things had not been chewed, nothing was damp or mildewed. Stanley's monthly cleaning crew had kept it clean, but there were obvious signs nonetheless of the ravages of time. They also found six bathrooms on the main floor, four of them in marble, for guests, and two simpler tiled ones, obviously for servants. The backstairs area for the huge staff of domestics they must have had was vast.

By then, they were ready to move upstairs. Sarah knew there was an elevator in the house, but Stanley had never used it. It had long since been sealed off, as even he acknowledged that it would be far too dangerous for current use. Until his legs had finally failed him completely, he had valiantly marched up and down the back stairs. And once he could no longer walk, he never came downstairs.

Marjorie and Sarah made their way cautiously toward the grand staircase that ran up the center of the house, admiring every inch and detail around them as they went, floors, marquetry, boiseries, moldings, windows, and chandeliers. The ceiling over the grand staircase was three stories high. It ran up the main body of the house. Above it was the attic where Stanley had lived, and below it the basement. But the staircase itself, in all its grandeur and elegance, took up a vast amount of space in the central part of the house.

The carpeting on it was faded and threadbare but looked as though it was Persian, and the fittings holding the carpet in place were exquisite antique bronze, with small cast antique lion's heads at the end of each rod. Every detail of the house was exquisite.

On the second floor, they found two more splendid living rooms, a day parlor facing the garden, a card room, a conservatory, where the grand piano had once been, and finally the ballroom they had both heard about. It was in fact an exact replica of the Hall of Mirrors in Versailles, and utterly beyond belief. As Sarah pulled the curtains back yet again, as she had in almost every room, she nearly cried. She had never seen anything so beautiful in her life. She couldn't even imagine now why Stanley had never used the house. It was much too beautiful to stand empty all these years, unloved. But grandeur on that scale, and elegance of the kind they were seeing, had clearly not been his thing. Only money was, which suddenly struck her as sad. She finally understood now what he had been saying to her. Stanley Perlman had not wasted his life, but in so many important ways, it had passed him by. He hadn't wanted the same thing to happen to her, and now she could see why. This house was the symbol of everything he had owned but never really had. He had never loved it or enjoyed it, or allowed himself to expand into a bigger life. The maid's room where he had spent three-quarters of a century was the symbol of his life, and everything he'd never had, neither companionship, nor beauty, nor love. Thinking about it made Sarah sad. She understood it better now.

As they reached the third floor, they were faced with enormous double doors at the head of the grand staircase. Sarah thought they were locked at first. She and Marjorie pulled and tugged and nearly gave up, when they suddenly sprang open, and revealed a suite of rooms so beautiful and welcoming, they had obviously been the master suite. Here the walls were painted a faded, barely discernible pale powder pink. The bedroom was a confection worthy of Marie Antoinette. It looked down onto the garden. There was a sitting room, a series of dressing rooms, and two extraordinary marble bathrooms, each one larger than Sarah's apartment, that had obviously been built for Lilli and Alexandre. The fixtures were exquisite, the floor in hers pink marble, and in his beige marble, of a quality worthy of the Uffizi in Florence.

There were once again two small sitting rooms on the same floor, flanking the entrance to the master suite, and on the opposite side of the house what must have been the nursery for their two children, obviously one for a girl and the other a boy. There were beautiful painted tiles in their dressing rooms and bathrooms, with flowers and sailboats on them. Each child had had a large bedroom, with big, sunny windows. There was an enormous playroom for both of them, and several smaller rooms that must have been for the governesses and maids who tended to their every need. And as she looked around with tender amazement, something occurred to Sarah. She turned and asked Marjorie a question.

'When Lilli vanished, did she take her children with her? If she did, no wonder it broke Alexandre's heart.' The poor man must have lost not only his beautiful young wife but the boy and girl who had lived here, and on top of it, his money. It would have been enough to destroy anyone, particularly a man, to lose so much and have to give all this up.

'I don't think she took the children with her,' Marjorie said pensively, wondering the same thing herself. 'The story I read about them, and the house, didn't say much about it. It said that she 'vanished.' I didn't get the impression they vanished with her.'

'What do you suppose happened to them, and to him?'

'God knows. Apparently, he died relatively young, of grief, they implied. It said nothing about his family. And I think the family died out. There is no prominent family in San Francisco by that name anymore. Maybe they went back to their roots in France.'

'Or maybe they all died,' Sarah said, sounding sad.

After they left the nursery, Sarah led Marjorie to the back stairs and the attic floor she was so familiar with from her many visits to Stanley. She stood in the hallway with her eyes cast down, while Marjorie inspected the rooms without her. She didn't want to see the room where Stanley had lived. Sarah knew it would make her too sad. All that had mattered to her, of him, was in her heart and her head. She didn't need to see his room, or the bed where he had died, and never wanted to again. What she had loved of him, she had taken with her. The rest was unimportant. She was reminded of the Saint-Exupéry book *The Little Prince,* which she had always loved. Her favorite quote from it was 'What is essential in life is invisible to the eyes, and only seen by the heart.' She felt that way about Stanley. He was forever in her heart. He had been a great gift in her life during the three years of their friendship. She would never forget him.

Marjorie followed her back down the stairs to the third floor again, and reported that there were twenty small servants' rooms on the attic floor. She said that if several of the walls between them were knocked down, a new owner could get several good-size bedrooms out of them, and there were six working bathrooms, although the ceilings were much lower than on the three main floors below.

'Do you mind if I walk back through the house again and make some notes and sketches?' Marjorie asked politely. They were both in awe of what they'd seen. It was totally overwhelming. Neither of them had ever before seen such beauty, and exquisite detail and workmanship except in museums. The master craftsmen who had built the house had all come from Europe. Marjorie had read that in the story. 'I'll send someone in to do official plans, and photographs of course, if you let us sell it for you. But I'd like to have a few quick sketches to remind myself of the shape of the rooms, and number of windows.'

'Go right ahead.' Sarah had set aside the entire morning to spend with her. They'd been there for two hours by then, but she didn't have any appointments in the office until three-thirty. And she was impressed by how serious and respectful Marjorie was. Sarah knew she had chosen the right woman to sell Stanley's house.

Marjorie took out a small sketch pad in the master suite, and worked quickly, walking off distances and making notes to herself, as Sarah looked at the bathrooms again, and wandered through the dressing rooms, opening a multitude of closets. She didn't think she'd find anything there, but it was fun to imagine the gowns that had hung in them when Lilli was in residence. She must have had a mountain of jewels, incredible furs, and even a tiara. Those had all been sold off, undoubtedly, nearly a century before. Thinking about it, and the grief that had come to them, financially and otherwise, made Sarah sad. In all her years of visiting Stanley there, she had never thought about the previous owners much before. Stanley never said anything about them, and seemed to have no interest in them himself. He had never even mentioned them to her by name. Suddenly the name de Beaumont seemed all-important to her. With the little Marjorie had shared with her, her imagination was full of the people they must have been, even their children. And the name did ring a bell even for her. She must have heard about them at some point. They had been an important family in the city's history at one time. She knew she had heard the name before, although she no longer remembered where, or in what context. Maybe during some field trip she had participated in as a child at school, visiting a museum.

As she opened the last closet, which had a musty smell to it but still the rich smell of cedar, she realized it had been one of the closets where Lilli kept her furs, probably ermines and sables. As Sarah glanced into the darker recesses of the closet, as though expecting to find one there, something on the floor of the closet caught her eye. She used the flashlight Marjorie had given her and saw that it was a photograph. She got down on all fours and reached for it. It was covered with dust and very brittle. It was a photograph of an exquisite young woman coming down the grand staircase in an evening gown. Looking at her, Sarah thought she was the loveliest creature she had ever seen. She was tall and statuesque, with the lithe body of a young goddess. Her hair was arranged in some sort of fashionable hairdo of the times, with a bun at the back, and waves framing her face. And just as Sarah would have expected her to, she was wearing an enormous diamond necklace and a tiara. She almost looked as though she were dancing down the stairs, pointing one foot in a silver sandal. She looked as though she were laughing, and she had the most piercing, mesmerizing, enormous eyes Sarah had ever seen. The photograph was haunting. She knew instantly it was Lilli.

'Find something?' Marjorie asked as she hurried past with her tape measure and notebook. She didn't want to take up too much of Sarah's time, and was trying to do everything she needed to quickly. She stopped to glance at the photograph only for an instant. 'Who is it? Does it say on the back?'

Sarah hadn't even thought to look, and turned it over. There, in long-faded but still legible ink and lacy ancient handwriting, was written, 'My darling

Alexandre, I will love you forever, your Lilli.' Tears sprang to Sarah's eyes as she read it. She felt the words go straight to her heart, almost as though she'd known her, and could feel her husband's sorrow when she left. The essence of their story tore at Sarah's heart.

'Keep it,' Marjorie said as she moved on, back to the master bedroom. 'The heirs will never miss it. You were obviously meant to find it.' Sarah didn't argue with her, and looked at it repeatedly, fascinated by it, as she waited for Marjorie to finish. Sarah didn't want to put it in her purse, for fear that she would hurt it. Knowing what had happened to them, at a later date, the photograph and the inscription behind it were even more meaningful and poignant. Had Lilli forgotten the photograph in the closet when she vanished? Had Alexandre ever seen it? Had someone dropped it when they stripped the house, and he sold it to Stanley? The oddest thing about it was that Sarah had the overwhelming feeling that she had seen the photograph somewhere before, but she couldn't remember where she'd seen it. Maybe in a book or a magazine. Or maybe she had imagined it. But it was hauntingly familiar. She had not only seen the woman in the photograph, but she knew she had seen the actual photograph somewhere. She wished she could remember but didn't.

The two women made their way from floor to floor, as Marjorie made notes and sketches. An hour later they were back at the front door, with faint light streaming in from the large salon on the main floor toward the hallway. There was no longer a gloomy feeling or an aura of mystery to it. It was just an extremely beautiful house that had

90

been long unloved and abandoned. For the right person, with enough money to bring it back to life, and a sensible use for it, it would be an extraordinary project to give this house back its life, and restore it to its rightful place as an important piece of history for the city.

They stepped outside into the November sunshine. Sarah locked the door carefully. They had made a quick tour of the basement and seen the ancient kitchen there, which was a relic from another century, the enormous servants' dining room, the butler and housekeeper's apartments, and twenty more maids' rooms, as well as the boiler, the wine cellars, the meat locker, the ice room, and a room for arranging flowers, with all the florist's tools still in it.

'Wow!' Marjorie said to Sarah as they stood looking at each other on the front steps. 'I don't even know what to tell you about what I think of it. I've never seen anything like it, except in Europe, or Newport. Even the Vanderbilts' house isn't as beautiful as this. I hope we find the right buyer. It should be brought back to life and treated as a restoration project. I almost wish someone would turn it into a museum, but it would be even more wonderful if someone actually lived in it who loved it.' She had been shocked to discover that Stanley had lived upstairs all his life, in the attic, and realized that he must have been extremely eccentric. Sarah had just said quietly that he was unpretentious and very simple. Marjorie ventured no further comment, as she could see that the young attorney had been very fond of her ancient client, and spoke of him with awe.

'Do you want to talk about it now?' Sarah asked.

It was noon, and she didn't want to go back to the office yet. She wanted to absorb what she'd seen of the house.

'I'd love to. I need to think about it though. Do you want to get a cup of coffee?' Sarah nodded, and Marjorie followed her in her own car to Starbucks. They took a quiet corner table, bought cappuccinos, and Marjorie glanced at her notes. Not only was the house itself remarkable, but it was on a huge lot, in a prime location, with an extraordinary garden, although nothing had been planted there in years. But there again, in the hands of the right person, both the house and garden could be a dream.

'What do you think the house is worth? Unofficially, obviously. I won't hold you to it.' She knew Marjorie had to make calculations and take official measurements. This had just been a reconnaissance mission, for them both. But they both felt as though they had found one of the greatest treasure troves ever seen.

'Lord, Sarah, I don't know,' the older woman said honestly. 'Any house you look at, big or small, is only worth what someone is willing to pay for it. It's an imperfect science at best. And the bigger the house and the more unusual, the harder to predict.' She smiled then, and took a sip of her cappuccino. She needed it. It had been an incredible morning, for them both. Sarah was dying to tell Phil. 'There sure are no comparables on this,' Marjorie continued with a grin. 'How do you assess a house like that? There's absolutely nothing like it, except maybe the Frick in New York. But this isn't New York, it's San Francisco. Most people will be scared to death of a house this size. It will cost a fortune to restore and furnish it, and it would take an army of people to run it. No one lives like that anymore. The neighborhood isn't zoned for a hotel, or a bed-and-breakfast. No one will buy it as a school. Consulates are closing their residences, and renting apartments for their staff. This is going to take a very special buyer. Whatever price we put on it will be an arbitrary number. Sellers and brokers always talk about offshore buyers, an important Arab, or maybe Hong Kong Chinese, maybe a Russian. The reality is that someone local will probably buy it. Maybe someone from the high-tech world in Silicon Valley, but they have to want a house like this and understand what they're getting . . . I don't know . . . Five million? Ten? Twenty? But if no one wants to deal with something like this, the heirs may be lucky to get three, or even two. It could sit here, unsold, for years. It's impossible to predict. How anxious are they to sell it? They may want to price it for a quick low-ball sale, and get rid of it as is. I just hope the right person buys it. I fell in love with it,' she said honestly as Sarah nodded. So had she.

'Me too.' She had left the photograph of Lilli sitting on the front seat of her car, terrified to hurt it. Something about the young woman in the photograph seemed magical to her. 'I'd hate to see the heirs just dump it for very little money. The house deserves to be treated with more respect than that. But I haven't met with any of them yet. I've only heard from one of them, and he lives in St. Louis, Missouri. He's the head of a bank there, he's not going to want a house here.' From what Sarah knew, none of them would. They all lived somewhere else, and since they didn't know

Stanley, there was no sentiment involved in it for them. Even he hadn't been sentimental about the house. Far from it. For them, as for him, it would be about the money. And surely none of them would want to restore a house in San Francisco. It made no sense for them. She was sure they would want to sell the house quickly, and as it was.

'We could try to put a coat of paint on it, and clean it up a bit,' Marjorie suggested. 'We probably should. Polish the chandeliers, get the boards off the windows that have been boarded up, throw away the tattered curtains. Wax the floors, oil the paneling. But that won't bring the electricity back to life, or the plumbing. Someone will have to build a new kitchen, probably in those main-floor pantries. It'll need a new elevator. There's some real work to do, and that costs money. I don't know how much they'll want to invest in selling it. Maybe nothing. I hope the termite reports are good.'

'He replaced the roof last year, so at least that's done,' Sarah explained, and Marjorie nodded, pleased.

'I didn't see any evidence of leaks, which is surprising,' Marjorie said matter-of-factly.

'Can you give me a number of estimates? A price for selling it as is, another to clean it up slightly. Maybe a price someone could get if it's restored.'

'I'll do what I can,' Marjorie promised her. 'But I have to be honest with you. We're in uncharted waters. It could sell for twenty million, or as low as two. It all depends on who we get, and how fast the heirs want to sell it. If they want to dump it, they'll be lucky to get two. It could even sell for less. Most buyers will be scared to death of a house like this, and the problems they'll find once they start the project. The exterior looks good to me, which is good news, although some of the windows need replacing. Dry rot, that's pretty common, even in a new house. I had to replace ten windows in my own house last year.' The stone exterior appeared to be solid and in good condition. The garages in the basement were accessible, though the driveway had been built for the narrow cars in the twenties and would have to be widened. There was no question in either of their minds, there was a lot of work to do. 'I'll try to get you some answers, and some ballpark figures by the end of the week. There's an architect I'd like to call, to get his impression of what's involved here. He and his partner specialize in restoration. He does good work, although I'm sure he's never tackled anything like this, either. Although I know he's done some work on the Legion of Honor Museum, which is comparable at least. And he studied in Europe. His partner is a woman, and she's very good, too. I think you'll like them. Could we take them through the house if they're not too busy?'

'Anytime you like. I have the keys. I'll make myself available to you. I really appreciate your help with this, Marjorie.' They both felt as though they had been in a time warp all morning, and had just been dropped back into their own century. It had been an unforgettable experience.

The two women left each other outside Starbucks, and Sarah headed back to her office. It was nearly one o'clock by then. She called Phil on her car phone as she wended her way downtown, still feeling dazed, and glancing at the photograph of Lilli on the seat next to her. She reached Phil on

95

his cell phone. He was on a lunch break from the deposition and in a rotten mood. Things weren't going well for his client. They had come up with some surprise evidence against him that he hadn't told Phil about previously. He had lost two earlier sexual harassment suits in Texas, before moving to San Francisco. That made Phil's client look like hell.

'I'm sorry,' Sarah said sympathetically. He sounded stressed out of his mind, and ready to kill his client. It was another one of those weeks. 'I've had the most incredible morning,' she said, still excited about it, and on a high from all they'd seen. Whatever the heirs decided to do with the house, Sarah was grateful to have seen it first.

'Yeah? Doing what? Inventing new tax laws?' He sounded sarcastic and dismissive. She hated it when he was like this.

'No. I went through Stanley Perlman's house with the realtor. It's the most beautiful place I've ever seen. Like a museum, only better.'

'Great. Tell me about it later,' he said, sounding harassed and anxious. 'I'll call you tonight after the gym.' He clicked off before she could say good-bye, or tell him anything about the house, or the photograph of Lilli, or the history she'd learned about the house from Marjorie. It wasn't Phil's kind of thing anyway. He was interested in sports and business. Historical houses had never been of interest to him.

Sarah parked her car in the garage at work, and gingerly put the photograph of Lilli in her purse, careful not to damage it, or ruffle the edges. Ten minutes later she was sitting at her desk, took it out, and stared at it again. She knew that somewhere in her lifetime she had seen this photograph, and she hoped that wherever Lilli had gone when she disappeared, she had found what she was looking for, or escaped what she'd been fleeing from, and that whatever had happened to her, life had been kind to her children. Sarah propped the photograph up on her desk, debating about whether to show it to the heirs. The face that looked across her desk at her was unforgettable, full of youth and beauty. Lilli's face, like Stanley's warnings to her over the years, reminded Sarah that life was brief and precious, and love and joy were fleeting.

CHAPTER 6

By Thursday, Sarah had heard from all of Stanley's heirs save two. They were the two elderly cousins in New York, who were in nursing homes. She finally decided to call them herself. One was the subject of a conservatorship and had severe Alzheimer's. Sarah was referred to the man's daughter. She explained to her about the reading of Stanley's will, and the bequest he had made to her father. Sarah explained to her that the money would presumably be held in trust, depending on the probate laws in New York, and would pass on to her and whatever siblings she had, whenever her father died. The woman cried, she was so grateful. She said they were having trouble paying for the nursing home. Her father was ninety-two years old, and unlikely to last much longer. The money Stanley had left had come in the nick of time for all of them. She said she had never even heard of Stanley, or a cousin of her father's in California. Sarah promised to send her a copy of the portions of the will that applied to her, after the official reading, assuming there would be one. The man she had spoken to the previous week, who had called her from St. Louis, had assured her that he would come to San Francisco, although he too had never heard of Stanley. He sounded vaguely embarrassed about it, and given his position as a bank president, Sarah had the feeling he didn't need the money.

The second heir who hadn't responded to her said he was ninety-five years old, and hadn't answered her because he thought it was some sort of joke someone had played on him. He remembered Stanley well and said they had hated each other as children. And then he laughed loudly. He sounded like a character, and said he was stunned that Stanley even had any money. He said the last time he had seen or heard from him, he was a crazy kid, heading for California. He told Sarah he had assumed he had died by then. She promised to send him a copy of the will, too. She knew she would have to be contacting him again to ask how he wished to dispose of the house.

By late Thursday afternoon, the reading of the will had been set for the following Monday morning, in her office. Twelve of the heirs were coming. Money had a way of making people willing to travel, even for a great-uncle no one knew or remembered. He had clearly been the black sheep of his family, whose fleece had become white as snow, as a result of the fortune he had left them. She was unable to tell any of them how large an amount it was, but she assured them it was a sizable sum. They would have to wait to hear the rest on Monday morning.

Her last call of the day was from Marjorie, the realtor, who asked if Sarah would mind meeting the two restoration architects with her at the house the following day. She said it was the only day and time they could make it. They were leaving for Venice that weekend, to attend a conference of restoration architects. For Sarah, the timing was perfect. It would give her more information to share with the heirs at the reading of the will on Monday. She promised to meet Marjorie and the architects on Friday afternoon at three o'clock. She was going to make it her last meeting of the day. She would go home after that, to start her weekend. It would give her time to unwind and relax, before Phil showed up several hours later, after the gym. She had hardly spoken to him all week. They had both been busy. And he had been in a rotten mood every time she spoke to him. Opposing counsel had made mincemeat of him and his client in the depositions. She hoped Phil's mood would improve dramatically by Friday night, or it was going to be a very unpleasant weekend. She knew what he was like when he was losing, at anything. It wasn't pretty. And she at least wanted to spend a decent weekend with him. For the moment, she wasn't optimistic.

Marjorie and the two architects were waiting for her at the house when Sarah showed up promptly at three o'clock on Friday. Marjorie said they had been early, and not to worry about it. She introduced Sarah to both of the people with her. The man was tall, pleasant-looking, and had hair as dark as Sarah's, with gray at the temples. He had eyes that were a warm brown, and he smiled during the introduction. He had a firm handshake, and an easy manner. He was wearing khaki slacks, a shirt and tie, and a blazer. And he looked as though he was somewhere in his early forties. There was nothing exciting about him. He wasn't excessively handsome, and he looked competent, interested, and easy going. She liked his smile, which seemed to light up his face and improve his looks. He had a nice personality, one could tell instantly, and she could see why Marjorie liked working with him. Even after the exchange of a few words, one had the sense that he had a sense of humor, and didn't take himself too seriously. His name was Jeff Parker.

His partner, on the other hand, was exactly the opposite of everything he was. Where he was noticeably tall, at least as tall as Phil, if not taller, Sarah noticed, she was tiny. His hair was dark and subdued, hers was bright red, her eyes were green, and she had creamy skin with a smattering of freckles. He was smiling as Sarah approached. She was frowning. She looked irritable, difficult, and angry. He was pleasant, she wasn't. She was wearing a bright green cashmere jacket, blue jeans, and high heels. He seemed modest in his appearance, she was showy, and chic in an offhanded sexy way. He looked classically American with his blazer and khaki pants, and Sarah realized the moment the woman spoke to her that she was French, and looked it. She had style and a certain panache about the way she'd put herself together. She also seemed to exude a kind of testiness, and looked as though she were annoyed to be there. Her name was Marie-Louise Fournier, and although her accent was noticeable, her English was impeccably fluent. She made Sarah feel instantly uncomfortable, and seemed to be in a hurry. Jeff was relaxed, interested in the house, and looked as though he had all day to be there. Marie-Louise looked at her watch several times as Sarah unlocked the house, and said something to Jeff in French. Whatever he said back to her in English in an undertone seemed to reassure her, but she still looked almost angry to be there.

Sarah wondered if it was because she knew they were unlikely to be asked to do the work. They were there only for a consultation. Marjorie had warned them that the house was more than likely going to be sold in its existing condition. Which meant to Marie-Louise that they were wasting their time at the meeting. Jeff wanted to come anyway. Everything Marjorie had told them about the house fascinated him. He loved old houses like this with a passion. Marie-Louise didn't like wasting time. To her, time was money. Jeff explained to Sarah that they had been partners, privately and professionally, for fourteen years. They had met at the Beaux-Arts in Paris while he was studying there, and had been together ever since. He explained with a smile that Marie-Louise was an unwilling hostage in San Francisco, and went back to France for three months every year. He said somewhat humorously that she hated living in the States, but stayed there for him. Her eyes flashed as he said it, but she didn't comment. She looked about Sarah's age, and had an incredible figure. Everything about her seemed

101

prickly and unfriendly in the extreme. But even she looked mollified as Sarah led them into the house, and she and Marjorie gave them the tour of all they'd seen and discovered earlier that week. Jeff stood at the foot of the grand staircase in awe, staring up at the three-story-high vaulted ceiling and the incredible chandelier. Even Marie-Louise looked daunted by it, and said something about it to her partner in hushed tones.

They walked around for two hours, examining everything diligently, while Jeff made copious notes on a yellow pad, and Marie-Louise made terse comments. Sarah hated to admit it to herself, but she didn't like her. The female partner of the team looked like a huge pain in the neck to her. And even without subtitles, she sounded like a bitch. Marjorie didn't like her much either, she admitted to Sarah sotto voce when they reached the master suite, but she said they both did great work, and were an excellent team. Marie-Louise was just very difficult, and didn't seem like a happy person. Sarah could see she wasn't. But Jeff more than made up for it, with his warm, easy manner, and extensive explanations. He said the boiseries were exceptionally valuable, were probably early eighteenth century, and had been removed from a château somewhere in France, which caused a comment from Marie-Louise, this time in English.

'It's amazing how Americans stripped our country bare of treasures that should never have been let out of the country. They would never get away with it today.' She looked at Sarah as though she had been personally responsible for this travesty on French culture. All Sarah could do was nod and appear to agree with her. There was nothing else to say. The same was true of the floors, which were clearly far older than the house on Scott Street and had presumably been removed from a château in France and sent to the States. Jeff said he hoped that the heirs didn't try to strip the house of the parquet floors and boiseries in order to sell them separately, probably at Christie's or Sotheby's. He said they would go for a fortune, but he hoped they would stay here, which was Sarah's hope as well. It would have seemed a crime to her to cannibalize the house now, after it had survived intact for so long.

They sat down on the steps of the grand staircase at the end of their tour, and he gave Sarah an informal assessment. In his opinion, bringing the house up to modern code, electrically and otherwise, with copper plumbing, would cost a new owner close to a million dollars. If they cut corners but stayed within code, they might be able to do it for half as much, but it would be a major challenge. He wasn't overly worried by the dry rot on the windows and French doors, he said that was to be expected. He was surprised it wasn't far worse. He didn't know what was under the floors or behind the walls of course, but he and Marie-Louise had restored houses older than this in Europe. It was a lot of work, but certainly not impossible. And he added that he loved this kind of challenge. Marie-Louise didn't comment, or say a word.

Jeff said that putting in a kitchen wasn't a monumental task, and he agreed with Sarah and Marjorie about the location of a new kitchen on the main floor. He thought the entire basement should be stripped and turned into storage space.

The elevator could be given modern workings, while preserving its original look. And the rest he thought should remain as it was. Craftsmen should be brought in to restore the wood, treat it, and oil it. The boiseries had to be handled with great care and precision. Everything else needed paint or varnish or polishing. The chandeliers were perfect and could be made to work again. There were a lot of details that could be played with and highlighted. Hidden lighting could be installed. It all depended on how much work and money a new owner wanted to put into it. The exterior was in good shape, and the house was well built. It needed a modern heating system. There was a vast range of things a new owner could do, depending on how much they wanted to spend, and how intent they were on showing off. He personally loved the bathrooms as they were. He thought they were beautiful, and integral to the house, as he put it. They could be redone with modern plumbing, without interfering with their current look.

'Essentially, you could spend as much money here as you want. A million dollars would work wonders here, and get everything where you'd want it to be. If someone wanted to be careful about it, you could probably do it for half of that, if the new owner was a nut like me and liked doing a lot of the work himself. If they wanted to drop two million here, they could, or even three, but it's not necessary. It's a rough guess, and I could work up some figures for you, to show a serious prospective buyer. For a million dollars, they could restore the house to everything it once was. And they could probably do it for half of that,' he reiterated, 'if they knocked themselves out, keeping the costs

104

down. It would take longer that way, but a project like this shouldn't be rushed anyway. It has to be done right, with great care, otherwise important details of the house will get damaged or broken, and no one would want that. I would recommend a small crew working here for six months to a year, loving owners who know what they're doing and want this as a project, and an honest architect who won't soak them. If they go to the wrong ones, it could cost them five million dollars, but that shouldn't happen. Marie-Louise and I restored two châteaux in France last year. We did both for under three hundred thousand in costs, and both houses were larger and older than this. It's easier to find the craftsmen there, but we have good resources in the Bay Area.' As he said it, he handed Sarah their card. 'You can give a prospective buyer our names. We'd be happy to meet with them for a consultation, whether they want to hire us for the job or not. I love houses like this. I'd love to see someone really care enough to restore it and do it right. I'd be happy to do whatever I can to help. And Marie-Louise is a genius with the details. She's a perfectionist. Together we get the job done.' Marie-Louise smiled at him finally, as he said it. Sarah realized then that she was probably nicer than she looked. They were an interesting pair. Marie-Louise looked intelligent and capable, she just wasn't very warm. She seemed prickly and very French. Jeff was warm, easy, and friendly, and Sarah felt comfortable with him already. Working with Marie-Louise would be a challenge.

'Marjorie told me that you and your wife are leaving for Venice tomorrow,' Sarah said as they walked slowly through the main floor on the way out. They had been there for more than two hours. It was after five o'clock.

'We are.' He smiled pleasantly at Sarah. He liked her devotion to the project, and her obvious deep respect for her late client's house.

Sarah wanted to get as much information as she could for his heirs, and be realistic about it, although she doubted they'd want to do the work. They would get a much better price for the house ultimately if they made some modern improvements, but she also knew that they probably wouldn't want to be bothered. All she could do was offer them the information. What they did about it was up to them. She had no decisions to make here. Her orders were to come from them.

'We'll be in Italy for two weeks,' Jeff explained to her. 'You can call our European cell phone if you need to. I'll give you our number. We'll be at the conference in Venice for a week, then a few days in Portofino to relax. And we'll spend the last few days with Marie-Louise's family in Paris. And by the way,' he said casually, 'we're not married. We're partners in every sense of the word.' He smiled at Marie-Louise as he said it, and she looked suddenly mischievous and very sexy. 'But my associate here doesn't believe in marriage. She thinks it's a Puritan institution, and corrupts a good relationship. She must be right, because we've been together for a long time.' They exchanged a smile.

'Much longer than I expected,' Marie-Louise said succinctly. 'I thought it was a summer romance, and then he dragged me here, against my will. I'm a prisoner in this city,' she said, rolling her eyes, and he laughed at her. He had heard it all for years. He didn't seem bothered by it. They seemed to like working together, although Sarah thought he had a much easier manner with clients than she did. She was incredibly abrasive, to the point of being rude.

'She's been trying to talk me into moving to Paris since she got here. But I grew up here and I like it. Paris is too much of a big city for me, and so is New York. I'm a California boy, and Marie-Louise will never admit it, but she likes it here a lot of the time. Especially in winter, when it's so cold and gray in Paris.'

'Don't be so sure!' She was quick to respond. 'One of these days I'm going to surprise you, and move back to Paris.' It sounded more like a threat than a warning to Sarah. But Jeff let the sharpness of her words roll off his back.

'We have a great house in Potrero Hill, which I restored myself, before it was fashionable to be there. Ours was the only decent house on the block for years. Now it's gotten very "in," and there are a lot of beautiful houses around us. I did all the work myself, with my own hands. I love that house,' he said proudly.

'It's not as nice as the one in Paris,' Marie-Louise said primly. 'Our house there is in the Seventh. I did that one myself. I stay there every summer, while Jeff insists on freezing in the fog here. I hate the summers in San Francisco.' They were admittedly cold and foggy. She definitely had not made a commitment to life in San Francisco, and made it sound as though she was still planning to go back. Jeff didn't look worried. He probably knew they were empty threats. Although Sarah thought it was interesting that after fourteen years together, they still weren't married. Marie-Louise looked extremely independent. But in his own way, so was Jeff. She complained a lot, but never pulled him off his path.

Sarah thanked them both for their consultation and his honest assessment of what a restoration could cost her clients. There was a broad range, depending on what a new owner would want, how far they'd want to take it, and how much work they were willing to do themselves. All she could do was relay the information to the heirs.

She wished them both a good trip to Venice, Portofino, and Paris, and a few minutes later Marie-Louise and Jeff drove off in an ancient Peugeot that Marie-Louise said she had brought from France. She said as they got into it that she didn't trust American cars. 'Or anything else!' Jeff added, and they all laughed.

'She's a piece of work, isn't she?' Sarah commented to Marjorie, as they walked back to their cars.

'She's hard to work with, but she's good at what she does. She has great taste and a lot of style. She treats him like dirt, and he seems to love it. That's always the way, isn't it? The bitches always get the great guys.' Sarah laughed at the comment. She hated to admit it, but it seemed to be true a lot of the time. 'He's a hunk, isn't he?' Marjorie said admiringly, and Sarah smiled.

'I don't know if I'd call him that.' Phil was a hunk, in her eyes. Jeff wasn't. But he seemed like a nice man. 'But he's a very nice guy, and he seems to know his stuff.' He obviously had a passion for old houses, and loved his work.

'They both do. They complement each other. Sweet and sour. It seems to work. At home and in the office. Although I think they've had their ups and downs. Every now and then she gets fed up, and goes back to France. She left him for a year once, while he was working on a big project I referred to him. But she always comes back, and he takes her back when she does. I guess he's crazy about her, and she knows she's got a good thing. He's solid as a rock. It's too bad they never got married. He'd be great with kids, though she doesn't look like the motherly type to me.'

'Maybe they will someday,' Sarah said, thinking of Phil. Their weekend was due to begin in a few hours. This part of the week was her reward for all the hard work she did at her law firm.

'Who knows what makes people's relationships work,' Marjorie said philosophically, and then wished Sarah luck with Stanley's heirs on Monday.

'I'll let you know what they decide, after the meeting.' They were obviously going to sell the house—the only question was in what condition, restored or not, and to what extent. Sarah would have loved to oversee the project, but she knew there was almost no chance of that. They weren't likely to want to spend a million dollars to restore Stanley's house, or even half that, and then wait six months or a year to sell it. She was sure that on Monday she'd be telling Marjorie to put it on the market as is.

Sarah said good-bye to her, and drove home, to get ready for Phil. She changed her sheets and made the bed, and then collapsed onto the couch with a stack of work she had brought home from the office. It was seven o'clock when her phone rang. It was Phil, calling from the gym. He sounded awful.

'Is something wrong?' she asked. He sounded sick.

'Yeah. We settled the case today. I can't tell you how pissed off I am. We got buried by opposing counsel. My fucking client got caught with his pants down a few times too often. There was no other choice.'

'I'm sorry, sweetheart.' She knew how he hated to give up. It must have been a really rotten case for him to do that. Usually, he battled to the bitter end. 'What time are you coming over?' She was looking forward to seeing him. It had been an interesting week for her, particularly dealing with Stanley's house. She still hadn't had time to tell him much about it. He'd been too absorbed in his depositions. They had hardly spoken to each other all week. And whenever they did, he was too busy to talk.

'I'm not coming over tonight,' he said bluntly, and Sarah was shocked. He very rarely canceled a weekend night completely, except if he was sick.

'You're not?' She had been excited about seeing him, as she always was.

'I'm not. I'm in a shit mood, and I don't want to see anyone. I'll feel better tomorrow.' She was instantly disappointed when he said it, and wished he'd make the effort to come over anyway. It might cheer him up.

'Why don't you just come here after the gym and chill out? We can order takeout, and I'll give you a massage.' She sounded hopeful, and tried to be convincing.

110

'No, thanks. I'll call you tomorrow. I'm going to stay here for a few hours. I may play some squash, and get my aggression out. I'd be lousy company tonight.'

He sounded like it, but she was upset not to see him anyway. She had seen him in black moods before, and he wasn't fun to be around. But it would have been nicer having him there, even in a rotten mood, than not seeing him at all. Relationships weren't just about seeing each other on good days. She expected to share bad days with him, too. But he was adamant about staying at his own place that night. She tried to talk him into it, but he cut her off. 'Just forget it, Sarah. I'll call you in the morning. Have a good night.' He had hardly ever done that in four years. But when Phil was upset, the whole world stopped, and he wanted to get off.

There was nothing she could do about it. She sat on the couch for a long time, staring into space. She thought of the architect she'd met that day, and his difficult French partner. She remembered Marjorie saying that Marie-Louise had left Jeff several times and gone back to Paris, but she always came back. So did Phil. She knew she'd see him in the morning, or sometime on Saturday, whenever he felt up to calling her. But it was small consolation on a lonely Friday night. He didn't even call her when he got home. She stayed up till midnight, working, hoping she'd hear from him. She didn't. Whenever Phil was upset about something, there was no room for anyone else in his life. The world revolved around Phil. At least he thought it did. And for the moment, he was right.

111

CHAPTER 7

Sarah didn't hear from Phil until four o'clock on Saturday. He called her on her cell phone while she did errands, and said he was still in a bad mood, but promised to take her out to dinner to make up for it. He showed up at six in a sports coat and sweater, and had made reservations at a new restaurant she'd been hearing about for weeks. It turned out to be a really lovely evening, and made up for the time together they'd missed. He even stayed later than usual on Sunday, and it was early evening when he finally left her house. He always made it up to her when he let her down in some way, which made it hard to stay angry at him. It was why she had never walked away, so far. He reeled her in, and out.

She had told him about her visit to Stanley's house, over dinner at the new restaurant, but it was obvious he wasn't interested in it. He said it sounded like an old dump to him. He couldn't imagine anyone wanting to do all that work. He changed the subject before she could tell him about the meeting with the architects. It just wasn't his thing. He was more interested in talking about a new case he was handling. It was another sexual harassment case, but this one was a lot cleaner than the one he'd had to settle that week. It was actually fascinating legally, and Sarah discussed it with him at great length on Sunday afternoon. They watched a video at her apartment, and made love before he left. The weekend had been short but sweet. Phil had an incredible knack for salvaging things, calming her down, and keeping her in it, just as he had for four years. It was an art.

She was in good spirits when she went to work on Monday, and excited about meeting Stanley's heirs. Five had been unable to leave their jobs and lives in other cities. Twelve were coming, and the two cousins in New York were too old and ill. She had asked her secretary to set up the conference room for them, with coffee and Danish pastries. She knew that what was coming to them was going to be a big surprise for them. A few of them were already waiting in the hallway when she reached her office. She set down her briefcase and went out to meet them. The first one she saw was the bank president from St. Louis. He was a distinguished-looking man in his early sixties. He had already told her he was widowed, and had four grown children, and she had gathered in the conversation that one of them had special needs. Perhaps, although he had money, the bequest from Stanley would be of some use to him.

It was nearly ten o'clock when the last of the heirs finally drifted in. There were eight men and four women. Several of them knew each other, far better than they knew Stanley, who had only been a name to some of them. Others had never even heard of him and knew nothing of his existence. Two of the women and three of the men were siblings. They lived all over the country, from Florida to New York to Chicago to St. Louis to Texas. The man from Texas was wearing a cowboy hat and boots that looked well broken in. He was the foreman of a ranch he had worked on for thirty years, lived in a trailer, and had six kids. His wife had died the previous spring. The cousins were

113

enjoying talking to each other, as Sarah made her way through the group. She was going to offer to show them Stanley's house that afternoon. If nothing else, she thought they should see it before they decided what to do with it, or how they wanted to dispose of it. She had explored the options for them, and had them carefully outlined on a single sheet, with the appraisal from Marjorie, which was more of a guesstimate, since nothing even remotely comparable to it had been sold for years, or existed anymore, and the condition it was in affected the price they could ask for it. There was no accurate way to assess what it would bring. Sarah wanted to attend to the reading of the will first.

The bank president from St. Louis, Tom Harrison, sat next to her at the conference table. She almost felt as though he should be calling the meeting to order. He was wearing a dark blue suit, white shirt, conservative navy tie, and had impeccably cut white hair. And as Sarah looked at him, she couldn't help thinking of her mother. He was the perfect age, and a cut above anyone her mother had gone out with in years. They would make a handsome couple, Sarah thought with a smile, as she looked around the table at the heirs. All four women were seated next to each other to her right, Tom Harrison was on her left, and the rest of them fanned around the table. The cowboy, Jake Waterman, had taken the foot of the table. He was having a feast on the Danish, and was on his third cup of coffee.

They all looked attentive, as Sarah called the meeting to order. She had the documents in a file in front of her, along with a sealed letter Stanley had given to one of her partners six months before, and had written himself. Sarah had no previous knowledge of it, and when she gave it to her that morning, Sarah's partner said Stanley had instructed her not to open it until the reading of the will. Stanley had told Sarah's associate that it was an additional message to his heirs, but in no way altered or jeopardized what he and Sarah had set up before. He had known to add a line ratifying and confirming his previous will, and assured Sarah's partner it was in order. Out of respect for Stanley, Sarah had left the letter sealed that morning, per his request, and planned to read it after the will.

The heirs were looking at her with open expectation. She was glad that they had been respectful enough to come in person, and didn't just tell her to send the money. She had the feeling that Stanley would have enjoyed meeting all or most of them. She knew two of the women were secretaries and had never been married. The other two were divorced and had grown children. Most of them had children; some were younger than others. Only Tom looked as though he didn't need the money. The others had made an effort to leave their jobs, and pay their way to come to San Francisco. For the most part, they looked as though the windfall they were about to receive would leave their lives forever changed. Sarah knew better than anyone that the size of that windfall was going to amaze them. It was exciting for her to share this moment with them. She only wished that Stanley could be there, and hoped he was in spirit. She looked around the faces of the people seated at the conference table. There was dead silence as they waited for her to speak.

'I want to thank you all for coming. I know it took some real effort for some of you to be here. I know it would have meant a lot to Stanley that you came here today. I'm sad for all of you that you didn't know him. He was a remarkable man, and a wonderful person. In the years we worked together, I came to admire and respect him a great deal. I am honored to be meeting you, and to have worked on his estate.' She took a sip of water then, and cleared her throat. She opened the file in front of her and took out the will.

She sped through most of the boilerplate, explaining to them what it meant as she went along. Most of it related to taxes, and how they had protected his estate. He had set aside more than enough money to pay the taxes when it went through probate. The shares he had left for them, of his holdings, would be unaffected by the taxes the estate owed the federal government and the state. They looked reassured. Tom Harrison understood better than the rest of them what she was reading to them. And then she reached the list of bequests, which were in nineteen equal shares.

She listed their names alphabetically, including those who were not present. She had a copy of the will for each of them, so they could study it later, or have it examined by their own attorneys. Everything was in order. Sarah had been meticulous in her work.

She read off the list of assets to them, with current up-to-the-minute assessments of their worth, wherever possible. Some assets were more nebulous, in the case of properties he had held on to for years, like shopping malls in the South and

Midwest, but in those instances, she had listed comparable recent values, to give them an idea of what they were worth. Some of it they were going to be able to keep individually, and in other cases they would have to make decisions about holding on to them as a group, selling the assets, or buying each other out. She explained each case separately, and said she would be happy to advise them, or discuss it with them at any time, or their attorneys, and make recommendations based on her experience with his portfolio and assets. Some of it still sounded like gibberish to them.

There were stocks, bonds, real estate developments, shopping malls, office buildings, apartment complexes, and the oil wells that had become his greatest asset in recent years, and still the most valuable for the future, in her opinion, particularly in the current international political climate. There was a fair amount of liquidity in his estate at the time of his death. And then there was the house, which she said she would explain to them in further detail after the reading of the will, and she had several options for them to consider in relation to its disposal. They continued to stare at her silently, trying to wrap their minds around the concepts she was exposing them to, and the list of assets that reached from one end of the country to the other. It was a lot to absorb at one time, and none of them was exactly sure what it meant. It was almost a foreign language to them, except to Tom, who was staring at her intently, unable to believe what he was hearing. Although he didn't know the details, he could figure out the implication of what she was saying, and was keeping track of it in his head.

'We will get you completely accurate appraisals of each asset in the days to come. But based on what we already have, and some fairly close assessments, your great-uncle's estate is currently valued, after taxes, which have been handled separately, at just over four hundred million dollars. In our estimation, that will give each of you a bequest of approximately twenty million dollars, give or take. Which, after taxes for you, should come to roughly ten million dollars each. There may be some float in that, by several hundred thousand dollars, depending on current market values. But I think that it's safe to assume that your after-tax inheritance will come to roughly ten million dollars each.' She sat back and took a breath as they stared at her in total silence, and then suddenly there was pandemonium in the room, as they talked with animation and astonishment. Two of the women were crying, and the cowboy let out a whoop that broke the ice, and made them all laugh. They felt exactly as he did. It was impossible to believe. Many of them had lived on small salaries all their lives, or even hand to mouth, just as Stanley had in the beginning.

'How on earth did he ever make all that money?' one of the great-nephews asked. He was a policeman in New Jersey, and had just retired. He was trying to start a small security business, and like Stanley had never married.

'He was a brilliant man,' Sarah said quietly, with a smile.

It was a remarkable thing to participate in a moment and event that changed so many lives. Tom Harrison was smiling. Some of them looked embarrassed, especially those who'd never heard his name. This was like winning the lottery, only better in some ways, because someone they didn't even know had remembered them, and meant for them to have it. Although he had no family of his own, those he was related to meant everything to Stanley. Even if he'd never met them. In his mind, they were the children he had never had. It was his one moment, after death, to be their loving father, and benefactor. Sarah was honored to be part of it, and only wished he could have seen it.

The cowboy was wiping his eyes, then blew his nose and said he was going to buy the ranch, or start his own. His kids were in state schools, and he said he was going to send them all to Harvard, except the one he said was in jail. He told the assembled group he was going to go home now, kick his son's ass, and get him a decent lawyer. He had been caught stealing horses, and had been on drugs all his life. Now maybe he had a chance. They all did. Stanley had given them that. It was his posthumous gift to all of them, even those who hadn't shown up. He cared about them all equally. Sarah was nearly in tears herself. It might have been unprofessional of her, but it was an unforgettable experience, sharing this with them. It was her brightest and most meaningful single event in the twelve years she'd been a lawyer. Thanks to Stanley.

'You all have a lot to think about,' Sarah explained to them, and brought them back to order. 'There are assets you will own individually. Others you now hold jointly. I've listed them all separately, and I'd like to have a conversation with you today about what you want to do about them. It will be simpler for you if you sell the joint holdings, where reasonable to do so, and divide up the profits, depending on what our financial advisers recommend to you. In some cases, this may not be the right time to sell them. But if that's what you decide, we'll wait for the right time to sell, and advise you.' She knew better than any of them that it was going to take months, and in some cases years, to unravel. But she also explained to them that the individual portion of their bequests was in the vicinity of seven or eight million dollars each. The rest would come to them later after the joint assets were disposed of. Stanley had tried to keep it as clean as possible for them, without hindering his investments. He didn't want to cause a battle among nineteen of his relatives, whether he knew them or not. And he had done a brilliant job, with Sarah's help, of dividing up his estate, so it could be easily disposed of.

'There is also the matter of the house that your great-uncle lived in. I went through it with a realtor last week, to try and get a realistic appraisal. It's a remarkable place, and I think you should see it. It was built in the twenties, and unfortunately, it hasn't been remodeled, renovated, or modernized since. It's almost like a museum. Your great-uncle lived in a small portion of the house, the attic actually. He never occupied the main portion of the house. It has remained untouched since 1930, when he bought it. I had renovation architects, who specialize in this kind of project, look at it on Friday, to give me an assessment of what it would cost to bring it up to current code and get it in shape. There's a broad range of possibilities of what that work would entail. You could spend as little as five hundred thousand dollars to clean it up, make it livable, and bring it up to code, or ten times that if you really want to do it up and make a showplace of it. The same is true of selling the house. The realtor said we could get anywhere from a million to twenty million for it, depending on who buys it, and current real estate market values. In the current condition it's in, you won't get much for it, because it would be an enormous project for someone to undertake, and not many people want to live in a house that large anymore. It's roughly thirty thousand square feet. No one wants to employ staff to run a house that size these days, or can even find them. My recommendation to you would be to sell it. Maybe clean it up, take the boards off the windows, polish up the floors, and maybe put a coat of paint on the walls, but put it on the market essentially as is, without undertaking the more costly work of electricity and plumbing and renovation according to current code. That could cost a fortune. Unless of course one of you would like to buy the others out, and move to San Francisco and live there. I thought we could go to see it this afternoon. It might help you make the decision. It's a beautiful old home, and if nothing else, it's worth a visit.'

Before she had finished, they were all shaking their heads. None of them had plans to move to San Francisco, and they agreed, talking about it, that a renovation project of that magnitude was the last thing they wanted. Voices all around the table were saying 'Sell it . . . get rid of it . . . unload it . . . put it on the market . . .' Even the coat of paint and minor clean-up she had suggested to them was of no interest. It made her sad to hear it. It was like throwing away a once-great beauty. Her

121

time had passed, and no one wanted anything to do with her. The other heirs had to be consulted, of course, but since they hadn't even come to San Francisco for the meeting, it was unlikely they would feel any different.

'Would you like to see it this afternoon?' Only Tom Harrison said he had time to, although he too felt they should sell it. He said he could stop by on the way to the airport. The others all had flights back to their own cities early that afternoon, and they unanimously told Sarah to put the house on the market, and sell it as it was. Their bequests from Stanley were so large, and so exciting to them, that the sale of the house and what they got seemed to make little difference to them. Even if they got two million for it, it would only give them an additional hundred thousand dollars each. And after taxes, even less. To them now, it was a pittance. An hour before it would have been a windfall. Now it meant nothing to them. It was amazing how life could change in a single unexpected moment. She smiled as she looked around the table. They all looked like decent people, and she had the feeling Stanley would have liked them. Those who had come looked like wholesome, nice individuals, whom he would have enjoyed being related to. And they were certainly ecstatic over having been related to him.

She brought them to order once again, though with increasing difficulty. They were all anxious to leave the conference room, and contact spouses, siblings, and children. This was major news for all of them, and they wanted to share it. She assured them that the money would begin to come in within the next six months, sooner if they could get

122

it through probate. The estate was extremely clean.

'I have one last matter of business. Apparently Stanley, your great-uncle, asked me to read you a letter. I just learned today that he gave it to one of my partners six months ago, and I'm told it contains a codicil to his will, which I have not yet seen. My associate gave it to me this morning. I'm told Stanley wanted it read, after the reading of the will, which we've done now. I received it sealed myself, and have no idea what it contains. I've been assured that nothing in its contents alters the will in any way. With your permission, I'll read it now. I can make copies of it for you after I do. It's been sealed, per his instructions, since my colleague received it.' Sarah could only assume it was some sort of thoughtful message, or minor addition, to the heirs he knew he would never meet. It was the sweet and gruffly sentimental side of Stanley that Sarah had known and loved. She slit it open with a letter opener she had brought to the meeting for that purpose. They attempted to listen politely, although there was an almost palpable electricity and excitement in the room, from all that they had heard before. They could hardly sit still, and who could blame them? She was excited for them, too. It had been a thrill for her just announcing the gift to them. She was only the messenger, but even that had been a joy for her. She would like to have had some small sentimental token from him for herself, but there were none to have. All he had were books, and the clothes they had given to Goodwill. He didn't own a single item or memento worth having. All he had had was his vast fortune, and his house. He literally had no other worldly possessions at all. Just money. And nineteen strangers to leave it to. It was a big statement about his life, and who he had been. But he had been important to her, as much as he now was to them. In his final years, Sarah was, in fact, the only person he had loved. And she had loved him.

Sarah cleared her throat again, and began reading the letter. She was surprised to notice that she held it in trembling hands. There was something deeply moving about seeing his tremulous handwriting stretched out across the pages, and as he had promised her, there was a line at the bottom, ratifying his current will and witnessed by two of his nurses. Everything was in order. But she knew these were the last words from her friend Stanley that she would ever read, even if official, and not directed at her. It was like his last whisper from the grave, a final farewell to all of them. She would never see that handwriting, or hear his voice again. The thought of that brought tears to her eyes, as she fought to keep her voice steady. In some ways, he had meant more to her, as a friend and client, than he had to any of them.

'To my dear relatives, and to my friend and attorney, Sarah Anderson, who is the best attorney in the business, and a wonderful young woman,' she began, as the tears clouded her eyes, and she took a deeper breath, then went on. 'I wish I had known you. I wish I had had children of my own, and grown old knowing them, and their children, and you. I spent my life, all of it, making the money that I have left you. Use it well, do things that are important to you. Let it make a difference in your life. Don't let it *be* your life, as it was for me. It's only money. Enjoy it. Make your lives better because of it. Share it with your children. If you don't have children, have some, soon. They will be the best gift you ever had. This is my gift to you. Maybe it's time for you to enjoy new lives, or new opportunities, new worlds you wanted to discover, and can now, before it's too late. The gift I want to leave with you is one of options and opportunity, of a better life for you, and those who are important to you, not just money. In the end, the money means nothing. Except for the joy it gives you, what you do with it, and the lives you touch, the difference you make to the people you love. For most of my life, I loved no one. I just worked hard and made money. The only person I loved in the last years of my life was Sarah. I wish she had been my daughter, or my granddaughter. She is everything I would want a child of mine to be.

'Don't feel sorry for me. I had a good life. I was happy. I did what I wanted to do. It was exciting to build a fortune, to create something out of nothing. I came to California at sixteen with a hundred dollars in my pocket. It grew a lot in all these years, didn't it? Which shows what you can do with a hundred dollars. So don't waste this money. Do something important with it. Something that matters to you. Give yourselves better lives, give up jobs you hate, or that stifle you. Let yourselves grow and feel free with the gift I am leaving you. My wish for you is happiness, whatever that means to you. For me, happiness was building a fortune. In retrospect, I wish I had taken the time to build a family, too, but I didn't. You are my family, even though you don't know me, and I don't know you. I didn't leave my money to the SPCA, because I never liked dogs and cats much. I didn't leave it to charity, because they get enough

125

of other people's money. I left it to you. Use it. Have fun with it. Don't waste it, or hoard it. Be better and happier and freer now because you have it. Let it help you make your dreams come true. That is my gift to you. Follow your dreams.

'I also want to acknowledge my dear, beloved Sarah, my young friend and attorney. She has been like a granddaughter to me, the only family I ever had, since my parents died when I was a boy. I am very proud of her, although she works too hard. Don't you, Sarah! I hope you will learn a lesson from me. We talked a lot about it. I want you to go out and have a life now. You've earned it. You've already worked harder than some people do in their whole life, except maybe me. But I don't want you to be like me. I want you to be better. I want you to be you, the best you that you can be. I haven't said this to anyone in fifty years, but I want you to know that I love you, like a daughter, or a grandchild. You are the family I never had. And I am grateful for every moment you spent with me, always working too hard, helping me to save my money from taxes, so I could give it to my relatives. Thanks to you, they have more money and I hope they will have better lives now because of your work and mine.

'I want to make a gift to you. And I want my relatives to know why I did that. Because I love you, and you deserve it. No one deserves it more than you. No one deserves a good life more than you, even a great life. I want you to have that, and if my relatives give you a hard time about it, I'm going to come back from the grave and kick their asses. I want you to enjoy the gift I am leaving you, and do something wonderful with it. Don't just

126

invest it. Use it for a better life. Being of sound mind, and completely deteriorating body, dammit, I hereby bequeath to you, Sarah Marie Anderson, the sum of seven hundred and fifty thousand dollars. I thought a million would make you nervous, and might piss them off, and half a million didn't seem like enough to me, so I compromised. Above all, darling Sarah, have a wonderful happy life, and know that I will be watching over you, with love and thanks, always. And to all of you, you have my best wishes and my love, along with the money I have left you. Be well, go well, and may your days be happy and worthwhile, and filled with people you love.

'I am, on this date, Stanley Jacob Perlman.' He had signed it in his all-too-familiar handwriting, which Sarah had seen on so many documents before this. It was his last good-bye to her and to all of them. There were tears rolling down her cheeks, as she set the letter down, and looked at the others. She spoke to them in a hoarse voice, filled with emotion. She had never, ever expected to receive anything from him, and wasn't even sure she should now. But she was also aware that his doing the codicil via one of her partners, and not with her, made it legal. He had done everything by the book.

'I had no idea what was in this letter. Do any of you object to it?' She was willing to give up the bequest. They were his relatives, she was only his attorney, although she had genuinely loved him, which they hadn't.

'Of course not,' the women said in unison.

'Hell, no,' Jake, the cowboy, added. 'You heard what he said, he said if we did, he'd come back and kick our asses. I don't need no ghost giving me a hard time. Ten million after-tax dollars will do just fine for me and my kids. I may even buy myself a sexy young wife.' The others laughed at what he said, and there were nodding heads of assent around the room. Tom Harrison spoke up, as he patted her hand. One of the women handed her a tissue to blow her nose. Sarah was so moved, she was almost sobbing. The best part was that he had said he loved her. Although he was almost a hundred years old in the years she knew him, he had been the father she'd never had, the man she had respected most in her life, in fact the only one. Good men had not been abundant in her life.

'It sounds like you deserve the bequest a lot more than we do, Sarah. You obviously brought him a lot of comfort and joy, and saved us a lot of money,' Tom Harrison said as everybody nodded and smiled. 'I'm sorry for your loss,' Tom added, which only made her cry harder.

'I really miss him,' she said, and they could see she did. Several of them almost wished they could put their arms around her, but didn't. She was the attorney, and they didn't know her, although all their emotions were running high. Stanley had affected them all profoundly, and shaken their respective worlds to the core.

'You made his last days a lot happier, from everything he said in that letter,' one of the women said kindly.

'Hell, yes, and you're almost a millionaire now,' Jake added, and Sarah laughed.

'I have no idea what I'll do with the money.' She made a good salary as a partner, shared in the firm's profits, and had never had big financial needs. There was really nothing she wanted. She was going to make some good, solid investments, in spite of Stanley's entreaties to do otherwise. She was hardly about to quit her job and start buying mink coats and taking cruises, although he might have liked that. But it wasn't Sarah's style to indulge herself, even now that she could. She saved a lot of what she made.

'Neither do we,' several voices said around the room. 'We'll all have to figure out what to do with the money. It's obvious he wanted all of us to have a good life,' a man next to Jake said solemnly. He was seated between the cowboy from Texas and the policeman from New Jersey. She hadn't put faces to all the names yet. 'And you, too, Sarah,' he added. 'You heard what he said. Use it. Don't hoard it. Follow your dreams.' She had no idea what her dreams were. She had never taken the time to ask herself that question.

'I'm more of a hoarder than a spender,' Sarah admitted, and then she stood up, smiling at all of them. There were handshakes around the room, and hugs. Several people hugged her. Everyone looked as though they were in shock by the time they left. It had been an overwhelming morning. The receptionist called cabs for all of them, to get to the airport. Sarah's secretary handed each of them a manila envelope, with a copy of the will and whatever additional documents there were, about their investments. Their last word on the house was to sell it as it was. They instructed Sarah to put it on the market immediately, and get whatever she could for it. Tom Harrison had agreed to see it with her only to be polite, but she could tell, he wasn't interested in it, either. No one was. It was a white elephant in another city, which none of them wanted or needed. And they hardly even needed the money. The house on Scott Street meant nothing to them. It only meant something to her because it was beautiful, and because her beloved friend Stanley, now her benefactor to an incredible degree, had lived in the attic. But even she, with her newfound fortune, had no use for the house, although she had no voice in how it was disposed of. The decision to sell it had been theirs.

She left Tom Harrison in the conference room, and called Marjorie from her office. She told her their decision, and asked if she would mind meeting her at the house in half an hour, to show it to one of the heirs. But she said it was purely a visit of formality. They had each signed a release, instructing her to sell the house, in the condition it was presently in, at a price Sarah and Marjorie agreed on. They had left it all up to her.

'Are we going to get to doll it up a little?' Marjorie asked hopefully.

'I'm afraid not. They said to get a janitorial service in, get rid of the debris, like boards on the windows and curtains, and sell it the way we found it.' Sarah was still trying to wrap her mind around the bequest Stanley had given her, and recover from the loving words in his letter that had gone straight to her heart. For once, she sounded less businesslike, somewhat shaken, and distracted. With his loving words to her in the letter, and the astounding gift, she missed him more than ever.

'It's going to hurt our price, if we do that,' Marjorie said sadly. 'I hate to sell a house like that as a fire sale. It deserves better than that. It'll be a real steal for someone to get that at a bargain-

130

basement price.'

'I know. I hate to do it, too. But they don't want the headache. It doesn't mean anything to them, and after you divide it nineteen ways, in relation to everything else, the money doesn't mean much, either.'

'That's really too bad. I'll meet you there in half an hour. I have a showing at two, fairly close by. It shouldn't take us long, particularly if it's just a token visit, with no real interest behind it.'

'See you there,' Sarah promised, and went back to find Tom Harrison in the conference room. He was on his cell phone, talking to his office, and got off quickly.

'This has been quite a morning,' he said, still trying to catch his breath. Like the others, he was in shock. He had assumed it was a modest estate, and had come out of respect for a relative who had left him a bequest. It seemed like the least he could do.

'Yes, for me, too,' Sarah admitted, still dazed by Stanley's letter and what it meant for her. Seven hundred and fifty thousand dollars. It was beyond amazing. It was breathtaking. Stunning. With what she had saved herself over the years of her partnership in the law firm, she now had well over a million dollars, and felt like a rich woman. Although she was determined not to let it change her attitudes or her life, despite Stanley's warnings. 'Would you like a sandwich or something to eat before we see the house?' she asked Tom Harrison politely.

'I don't think I could eat it. I need a little time to absorb what just happened. But I have to admit, I'm curious to see the house.' The others weren't.

She drove him there herself. Marjorie was waiting for them. And Tom Harrison was as impressed with the house as they all had been. Once he saw it, though, he was glad they had collectively decided to sell it. It was a remarkable and venerable piece of history, but utterly unlivable, in his opinion, in today's world.

'No one lives like this anymore. I have a four-thousand-square-foot house just outside St. Louis, and I can't even find anyone to clean it. A house like this would be a total nightmare, and if you can't sell it as a hotel in this neighborhood, we're probably going to be stuck sitting on it for a long time.' The zoning in the area would not have allowed a hotel to operate there.

'That could happen,' Marjorie admitted. Although she knew the real estate market was full of surprises. Sometimes a house she thought she could never sell went five minutes after she put it on the market, and the ones she swore would be gone instantly and sell for their full asking price, didn't. There was no predicting taste or sometimes even value in the real estate market. It was all very personal and quixotic.

Marjorie regretfully suggested putting it on the market for two million dollars, given its condition. Sarah knew they didn't care if it sold for less, they just wanted to get rid of it, and Tom agreed. 'We'll put it on the market for two, and see what happens,' Marjorie told them. 'We can always entertain offers. I'll get a service in to clean it up, and then have a broker's open house. I'm not sure I can get it done by Thanksgiving,' which was the following week. 'But I promise to have it on the market the week after. I'll have a broker's open

132

house the Tuesday after Thanksgiving. It can go on the market officially the day after. Someone will probably buy it, and hope to win a battle with the city to change the zoning. It would make a gorgeous little hotel, if the neighbors will put up with it, though I doubt it.' They both knew a battle like that could go on for years, and the person who undertook it wasn't likely to win. San Franciscans put up a lot of resistance over commercial enterprises in their residential neighborhoods, and who could blame them.

Tom asked to see the part of the house where Stanley had lived, and with a heavy heart, Sarah walked him up the back stairs to show him. It was the first time she had ever seen it without Stanley. The hospital bed was still there, but he wasn't. It looked like an empty shell now. She turned away with tears in her eyes and walked back into the hall, as Tom Harrison patted her shoulder. He was a nice man, and seemed as though he would have been a nice father to his children. She had discovered, as they waited for the meeting to start, that his special needs daughter was blind and brain-damaged, from lack of oxygen when she was born prematurely. She was thirty years old now, still lived in his home, and was cared for by nurses. It had been particularly hard for him to manage her after his wife died. She had devoted almost all her time to her. But he didn't want the girl in an institution. Like many things in life, it was a major challenge. He looked like he was equal to it.

'I can't believe Stanley lived in a maid's room in the attic all his life,' Tom said, shaking his head sadly as they walked back down the stairs. 'What an amazing man he must have been.' And more

133

than a little eccentric.

'He was,' Sarah said softly, thinking once again of the incredible bequest he had left her. She still hadn't absorbed it, nor had the others with theirs. Tom still looked shell-shocked over his inheritance. Ten million dollars.

'I'm glad he remembered you in his will,' Tom said generously, as they reached the main hall again. The cab she had called to take him to the airport was waiting outside. 'Call if you ever come to St. Louis. I have a son about your age. He just got divorced, and has three adorable children.' She laughed at the suggestion, and then suddenly he looked embarrassed. 'I assume, from what Stanley said in his letter, that you're not married.'

'No, I'm not.'

'Good. Then come to St. Louis. Fred needs to meet a nice woman.'

'Send him to San Francisco. And call me too if you ever come out on business,' Sarah said warmly.

'I'll do that, Sarah,' he said, sounding fatherly as he gave her a hug. They had become friends in a single morning, and felt nearly related. They were, through Stanley. They were bonded through his generosity and benevolence, which had blessed them all. 'Take care of yourself,' Tom said kindly.

'You too,' she said, as she walked him to the cab, and then smiled at him in the pale November sunshine. 'I'd love to introduce you to my mother,' she said mischievously, and he laughed at her.

She was teasing, though it wasn't a bad idea. Although she thought her mother would give any man a pain in the neck. And Tom looked far too normal for her. There was nothing dysfunctional about him. She'd have no reason to go to a twelve-step group if she got involved with him, and then what would Audrey do? Without an alcoholic in her life, she'd be bored. 'Fine. I'll bring Fred out here, and we'll have dinner with your mother.'

Sarah waved at Tom as the cab drove away, and then went back in the house to wrap up the details with Marjorie. Sarah was glad she'd gone to Stanley's room with Tom. It broke the spell for her. There was nothing to hide from or mourn for there. It was just an empty room now, the shell in which he had lived, and which he had shed. Stanley was gone, and would live forever in her heart. It was hard to realize that suddenly her circumstances had changed, dramatically in fact. She had far less to adjust to than the others did, but it had been a huge windfall for her. She decided not to tell anyone for the moment, not even her mother or Phil. She needed to get used to the idea herself.

She and Marjorie discussed plans about the janitorial service, and the broker's open house. She signed a release confirming the asking price, on behalf of the heirs. They had signed a power of attorney at her office, allowing her to sell the house and negotiate for them. An identical document had been sent by fax to those who weren't present, for them to sign as well. She and Marjorie agreed that it was unlikely to move quickly, and unless a prospective buyer had real imagination, or a love of history, it was not going to be an easy sell. A house this size, in the condition it was in, was going to scare most people to death.

'Have a nice Thanksgiving,' Marjorie said to her, 'if I don't see you before that. I'll let you know how the broker's open goes.'

'Thanks. Have a nice holiday.' Sarah smiled at her, as she got into her car. Thanksgiving was the following week, still ten days away. Phil would be away with his kids, as usual. It was always a quiet weekend for her. She had the coming weekend with him to look forward to before that.

He called her on her cell phone as she was on the way back to her office, and asked how the meeting with Stanley's heirs had gone.

'Were they blown away?' he asked with interest. She was surprised he had remembered and even called to inquire. Often he forgot what she was working on, but this time he had kept track.

'They sure were.' She had never told him how much money was involved, but he had figured out himself that it was a lot.

'Lucky bastards. That's one way to make a fortune.' She didn't tell him she just had, too. She wanted to keep it to herself. But she smiled at his comment, and wondered what he would say if she told him she was a lucky bastard, too. Shit, not just lucky, she had suddenly become a rich girl. She felt like an heiress as she drove downtown. And then he startled her, as he sometimes did.

'I have bad news for you, babe,' he said, as she felt the usual drag of an anchor on her heart. Bad news, with him, usually meant less time he could spend with her. And she was right. 'I have to go to New York this week, on Thursday. I'll be there till next Tuesday or Wednesday, taking depositions for a new client. I'm not going to see you till after the Thanksgiving weekend. I'll have to pick up my kids the night I get home. We're heading straight up to Tahoe. You know how that goes.'

'Yes, I do,' she said, trying to be a good sport about it. Hell, she had just inherited nearly a million dollars. How bad could life be? She was just disappointed not to see him. It would be nearly three weeks before she saw him again, since the previous weekend. It was a long time for them. 'That's too bad.'

'You'll be with your mom and grandmother on Thanksgiving anyway.' He said it as though trying to convince her that she would be too busy to see him, which wasn't the case. She would be at her grandmother's house for a few hours, as she always was, and then she would have three lonely days over the weekend without him. And of course he wouldn't compensate for it by seeing more of her the following week. She'd have to wait a whole week, till the next weekend, to see him. God forbid he should miss the gym one night, or an opportunity to play squash with his friends.

'I have an idea,' she said, trying to sound ebullient about it, as though it were a novel idea she had never suggested to him before. In fact, she had every year, and never with good results. 'Why don't I come up to Tahoe on Friday for the weekend? The kids are old enough not to be shocked by my being there. It might be fun. I can always get my own room at the hotel, so we don't upset the kids,' she said, sounding jollier than she felt, and trying to be convincing. His voice was firm when he answered.

'You know that won't work, babe. I need time alone with my kids. Besides, my love life is none of their business. You know I like to keep those things separate. Besides, their mother doesn't need a firsthand report on my life. I'll see you when I get back.' So much for that. She never got anywhere with that suggestion, but each year she tried. He kept a firm division between church and state. Between her and his children. He had put her in a pigeonhole years ago, and kept her there. 'Weekend piece of ass.' It wasn't a reality she liked. She had inherited nearly a million dollars that day, which opened a thousand new doors for her, except the one she wanted so much with him. No matter how rich she had suddenly become, nothing had changed in her love life. Phil was as unattainable as ever, except on his terms. He was emotionally and physically unavailable to her, except when he chose to be otherwise. And on holidays, he didn't. As far as he was concerned, holidays belonged to him and his kids, and he expected her to fend for herself. That was their deal. The terms had been set by him right from the beginning and never changed.

'I'm sorry we're going to miss this weekend,' he said, sounding apologetic but busy.

'So am I,' she said sadly. 'I understand. I'll see you in about three weeks.' As always, she had done the math quickly. She could always figure out in the flicker of an eye how long it had been since she'd last seen him, and before she'd be seeing him again. This time it would be two weeks and five days. It felt like an eternity to her. It wouldn't have been as bad if they could see each other over the Thanksgiving weekend. No such luck.

'I'll call you later. I've got someone waiting outside my office,' Phil said in haste.

'Sure. No problem.' She hung up and drove the rest of the way to her office. She tried to convince herself not to let it spoil her day. Wonderful things had already happened. Stanley had left her a fortune. So what if Phil was going to New York, and she couldn't spend Thanksgiving weekend with him, or even if she didn't see him for nearly three weeks? What the hell was wrong with her priorities? she asked herself. She had inherited three-quarters of a million dollars, and she was worried about not seeing her boyfriend? But it wasn't her priorities she was concerned about. The real question was, what the hell was wrong with his?

CHAPTER 8

Thanksgiving had always been important to Sarah and her family. It was a special time they shared not only with each other but with special friends. Sarah's grandmother had made a point of inviting what she called 'lost souls' every year, people she liked and who had nowhere else to go. Inviting friends, even a few of them, gave the day a festive atmosphere, and made the three women feel less alone. And the people they invited to join them were always deeply grateful to be included. In recent years, the festivities had always been enlivened even more by the inclusion of one of her grandmother's current suitors. Over the past ten years, there had been a lot of them.

Mimi, as everyone called her, was an irresistible human being, small, pretty, 'cute,' funny, warm, and sweet. She was everyone's ideal grandmother, and nearly every man's ideal woman. At eighty-two, she was lively, happy, had a great attitude about life, and never dwelled on anything unpleasant. Her outlook was always positive, and she was interested and open to new people. She exuded happiness and sunshine. As a result, people wanted to be with her. Sarah smiled to herself, thinking about her, on the way to her grandmother's house, on Thanksgiving afternoon.

She had heard from Phil the night before, when he breezed through town on the way to pick up his kids. He had gotten back from New York late the night before but hadn't had time to see her. She wasn't even angry at him now, or sad, only numb. She had wished him a happy Thanksgiving when he called the night before, and got off the phone. Talking to him had depressed her. It just reminded her of everything they didn't share and never would.

When Sarah got to her grandmother's house, Mimi's two women friends were already there, both women older than she, and both widowed. They looked like little old ladies, but Mimi didn't. Mimi had snow-white hair, big blue eyes, and perfect skin. She hardly had any wrinkles, and still had a trim figure. She watched an exercise program on television every day, and did everything they showed her how to do. She walked at least an hour a day. She still played tennis once in a while, and loved to go dancing with her friends.

She was wearing a pretty silk dress in a deep turquoise, and high-heeled black suede shoes, with beautiful turquoise earrings and a matching ring. They hadn't had a huge fortune when Sarah's grandfather was alive, but they were comfortable, and she had always been well dressed and stylish.

140

They had made a handsome couple for more than fifty years. She rarely, if ever, spoke of her childhood. She liked to say that she'd been born on her wedding day to Leland. Her life had begun then. Sarah knew that Mimi had grown up in San Francisco, but she knew little more than that. She didn't even know where her grandmother had gone to school, or what her maiden name had been. They were things Mimi simply didn't talk about. She never dwelled on the past, she lived in the present and the future, which made her so appealing to everyone who knew her. There was nothing depressing about her. She was a happy woman through and through.

Her current favorite beau was in the living room when Sarah walked in. He was a few years older than her grandmother, had been a stockbroker, and played eighteen holes of golf every day. He had children he got along well with and enjoyed, and he liked to dance as much as Mimi. He was standing at the bar in her small, neatly arranged living room, and offered to make Sarah a drink.

'No, thanks, George.' She smiled at him. 'I'd better report for duty in the kitchen.' She knew her mother would be holding court there, watching over the turkey and complaining about its size, as she did every year. It was either too big or too small, too old or too young, and once it was cooked it would be too moist or too dry, and not nearly as good as the one they had last year. Mimi, on the other hand, always said it was perfect, which was the basic difference between the two women. Mimi was always satisfied with whatever life doled out to her, and enjoyed herself. Her daughter was always disgruntled with her lot, and perennially angry, upset, or worried. The two women were peering into the oven as Sarah walked into the kitchen. Sarah was wearing a new brown velvet suit she had bought herself as a gift, to celebrate her windfall from Stanley. She had bought brown suede shoes to go with it and looked very stylish. Mimi complimented her on it the minute Sarah walked into the kitchen. She was very proud of her only granddaughter, and bragged about her to everyone she knew. Audrey did too, although she never admitted it to Sarah.

'Are we having hot dogs tonight?' Sarah asked, as she set down her new brown suede bag on a chair in the kitchen. Her mother turned to look at her and raised an eyebrow.

'Hardly,' she said in answer to Sarah's question. 'Are you going somewhere? A party after dinner?'

'Nope. I'm coming here. Coming to Mimi's is the best party in town.'

'You never say that when you come to my house,' Audrey said, looking hurt. She was wearing a good-looking black suit, with a string of pearls and a gold pin on the lapel. She looked chic, but severe. Since her husband's death twenty-two years before, she rarely wore color, although she was an attractive woman. She had Sarah's and her mother's blue eyes, dyed her hair blond, and wore it in a bun or French twist. She looked like an older but almost equally pretty Grace Kelly. She also had lovely skin, few wrinkles, and a good figure. She was as tall as Sarah, unlike Mimi, who was tiny. Audrey's father had been tall.

'Yes, I do say I love coming to your house, Mom.' Sarah kissed them both, and her mother went back to checking the turkey with a disgruntled expression, predictably muttering about its size.

Mimi went back to the living room to her two friends and George. It was interesting that Mimi had invited three people, but neither Audrey nor Sarah had anyone to bring. Audrey had invited her friend Mary Ann, but her book club buddy had gotten sick at the last minute. They had met years before at Al-Anon, when both their husbands were drinking. Sarah liked Mary Ann but always found her a little depressing. She was never a truly happy addition to the group, and seemed to drag her mother down, which wasn't hard to do. More often than not, Audrey's view of life was pessimistic, unlike her mother's.

'The turkey is too small this year,' Audrey said, as Sarah laughed, checking in the pots that were on the stove. There were mashed potatoes, peas, carrots, sweet potatoes, and gravy. And sitting on the kitchen table were rolls, cranberry sauce, and salad. Their standard Thanksgiving meal. There were three pies cooling on the counter, mince, pumpkin, and apple.

'You always say that, Mom.'

'No, I don't.' Audrey bridled, covering her suit with an apron. 'Where'd you get the new suit?'

'At Neiman's. I bought it this week. For Thanksgiving.'

'I like it,' Audrey said as Sarah smiled at her.

'Thanks, Mom.' She walked over to her and gave her a hug. And then Audrey unnerved her again with her next question.

'Where's Phil?'

'In Tahoe. Remember? Just like he does every year.' She turned away to check the mashed

143

potatoes then, so her mother wouldn't see the disappointment in her eyes. Some days it was harder than others to hide. Holidays were always tough without him.

'I don't know why you put up with it. I assume he's not inviting you up this weekend,' Audrey said grimly. She hated Phil, and always had.

'Nope. He's not. I'm fine. I have a lot of work to do for a new client next week. Things always get crazy before the holidays. I wouldn't have had time to see him anyway.' It was a lie, and they both knew it, but this time Audrey let her save face. She was busy with the turkey, which she was afraid would be too dry.

Half an hour later they were seated at Mimi's dining table, in the small, elegant dining room Audrey had decorated for her. The vegetables were all on the table in serving bowls, and George had carved the turkey. Everything looked perfect. Mimi said grace, as she always did, and after that the table was alive with chatter. Mimi's two women friends were going on a cruise to Mexico, George had sold his city house and was moving into an apartment, Audrey was talking about a house she was doing for a client in Hillsborough, and Mimi was planning a Christmas party. Sarah smiled as she listened to all of them. She could hardly get a word in edgewise. It was nice to see them all happy. Their enthusiasm was contagious.

'What have you been up to, Sarah?' Mimi asked her halfway through the meal. 'You've been very quiet.' Her grandmother always loved hearing what she was doing.

'I've been settling a large estate. There are nineteen heirs from all over the States. They all got quite a windfall from their great-uncle. It's been keeping me busy. I'm selling a house for them, it's a beautiful old place. It's going to go for next to nothing. The house is enormous, which is hard to sell these days.'

'You couldn't talk me into a big house again for anything in this world,' Mimi said emphatically, as Audrey looked at Sarah pointedly.

'You should do something about your apartment.' Her mantra. 'At least buy a pair of flats. It would be a good investment.'

'I don't want the headache of a tenant. It's an invitation to a lawsuit,' Sarah said practically, although with the money Stanley had left her, she had been thinking of just that this week. But she didn't want to give her mother the satisfaction of admitting it to her. She had almost decided to buy a condo. She liked the idea of that better than a pair of flats.

The conversation drifted along on a variety of subjects. The pumpkin, mince, and apple pies came and went, with whipped cream and ice cream, and Sarah helped her mother clear the table and do the dishes. They had just finished cleaning up the kitchen when Sarah wandered into her grandmother's bedroom, to use her bathroom. One of the other ladies was in the second bathroom, so Sarah had decided to use Mimi's. She walked past the dresser where her grandmother kept so many framed photographs that most of them were concealed by the others. Sarah stopped to look at a photograph of herself when she was five or six, at the beach with her mother. There was another of Audrey on her wedding day. And one at the back, of Mimi on her wedding day during the war, in a white satin gown with a tiny waist and enormous shoulders. She managed to look both demure and stylish, and then another photograph caught her eye, of another young woman in an evening gown. The photograph had been hidden by the one of Mimi and her husband. Sarah stopped and stared at the photograph as she held it, and her grandmother walked into the room. Sarah turned to look at her, still holding the photograph with a dazed expression. This was where she'd seen it. It was the same photograph she had found in the closet of the master suite in the house she was selling for Stanley's estate, on Scott Street. She knew who it was, but she had to ask. She wanted to know. Suddenly she had to have confirmation.

'Who is this?' Sarah asked her as their eyes met. Mimi looked serious for a moment as she took it from her and looked at it with a wistful air.

'You've seen this before.' It was the only photograph Mimi had of her. All the others had vanished when she did. This one had been her father's. She had found it in his papers after he died. 'It's my mother. It's the only photograph I have of her. She died when I was six.'

'Did she die, Mimi?' Sarah asked gently. She knew the truth now, as she realized clearly for the first time that her grandmother had never spoken to her of her own mother. And Sarah's mother had told her that her own grandmother had died when Mimi was six, so Audrey had never met her.

'What makes you ask something like that?' Mimi asked sadly, her eyes locked onto Sarah's.

'I saw that same photograph this week in a house we're selling for a client on Scott Street.

146

We're selling it for his heirs actually. That's the house I mentioned at dinner. Twenty-forty Scott Street.'

'I remember the address,' Mimi said, as she put the photograph back on the dresser and turned to smile at Sarah. 'I lived there till I was seven. My mother left when I was six, and my brother was five. It was 1930, the year after the crash. We moved a few months later to an apartment on Lake Street. I lived there until I married your grandfather. My father died that year. He never really recovered after the crash, and my mother left him.' It was an amazing story, the same one she had heard from Marjorie Merriweather about the family that had built the house on Scott Street. But more startling was the news that Mimi's mother had not died, but left. It was the first time Mimi had said it. Sarah wondered if her own mother knew the truth and never told her. Or if Mimi had lied to her, too.

'I never realized until I thought about it recently that I never knew your maiden name. You don't talk about your childhood,' Sarah said gently, grateful for her grandmother's candor now. Mimi looked uncharacteristically unhappy as she answered.

'It was de Beaumont. My childhood wasn't a happy time for me,' she said honestly, for the first time. 'My mother disappeared, my father lost all his money. The governess I loved was sent away. It was all about loss, and losing people I had loved.' Sarah knew her brother had died during the war, which was how she had met the man she married. Sarah's grandfather had been Mimi's brother's best friend, and he had come to see them and bring

147

them some of her brother's belongings. He and Mimi had fallen in love, and got married shortly after. That much Sarah knew, but she had never heard the earlier part of the story.

'What happened after she disappeared?' Sarah asked, touched that her grandmother was finally telling her what had happened. She didn't want to be invasive, but suddenly it had all become terribly important. The house that Stanley had lived in for seventy-six years, and that she was selling now for his estate, had been built by her great-grandfather for her great-grandmother. She had been in it dozens of times over the years to visit Stanley, and she had never suspected that it had a deep connection to her. And now, suddenly, she was fascinated by it and wanted to know all.

'I don't know much about what happened. No one ever spoke about her when I was a child, and I wasn't allowed to ask. It always upset my father. I don't think he ever recovered, from any of it. Divorce was a shocking thing in those days. I learned later that she left my father for another man, and went to live in France with him. He was a French marquis, and very dashing, I was told. They met at a diplomatic party and fell in love. Several years after my father died, I learned that she had died of pneumonia or tuberculosis during the war. I never saw her again after she left us, and my father would never speak of her to me. As a child I never knew why she disappeared, or what happened.'

And yet, with all that tragedy in her life, Mimi was one of the happiest people Sarah had ever known. Mimi had lost her entire family—mother, brother, father—at a remarkably young age, and

148

the whole way of life she'd known as a young child. And yet she was cheerful, unassuming, and content, and brought joy to everyone. Sarah understood now why she had always said that she had been born on the day she got married. It had been a whole new life for her. Not as luxurious as the one she'd lived as a child, but it had been solid and stable and secure, with a man who loved her, and their child.

'I don't think my father ever really got over it,' Mimi went on. 'I don't know if it was losing my mother, or the money, probably both. It must have been devastating for him, and totally humiliating, to have his wife leave him for another man, and worse yet, a year after the crash. They would have had to give up the house anyway, and I think they were selling things already then. After that, my father worked in a bank, and became a recluse for the rest of his life. I don't remember him ever going out socially, until he died fifteen years later. He died right after I got married. He built that house for my mother. I remember the house as though it was yesterday, or at least I think I do. I remember their parties in the ballroom.' There was a dreamy look in her eyes as she said it, and it was even more remarkable for Sarah, knowing she had been in that same ballroom, and her grandmother's childhood nursery, only the week before.

'Would you like to see the house again, Mimi?' Sarah asked softly. She could easily take her to visit it before they sold it. It wasn't going on the market until the following week, after the broker's open house on Tuesday after Thanksgiving. 'I have the keys. I could take you there this weekend.'

149

Mimi hesitated and then shook her head with a nostalgic expression.

'It sounds silly, but I think it might upset me. I don't like doing things that make me sad.' Sarah nodded. She had to respect that. She was so touched by the history her grandmother had finally shared with her, after all these years. 'I went to see the château where she had lived with the marquis she married, when I was in Europe with your grandfather, after your mother was born. But it was all boarded up and deserted. I knew she had died by then, but I just wanted to see where she had lived after she left us. The locals said her husband, the marquis, had died during the war as well. In the Resistance. They had no children. I wondered if I might find someone who knew her, some small piece of information or history about her. But no one knew anything, and neither your grandfather nor I spoke French. They just said the marquis had died, and she did, too. My father died around the same time she did, oddly. He always acted as though she had died, from the moment she left. And that is what I always told people when I was growing up. It was simpler. I told your mother that too.' Mimi looked apologetic for the lie, and Sarah's heart went out to her as she listened. What a tragedy it had been for Mimi. Sarah was grateful that Mimi had decided to finally tell her the truth. It felt like a gift.

'How awful for you,' Sarah said sadly. She put her arms around Mimi and gave her a hug. She couldn't even imagine what those years had been like for her. Losing her mother, her father's years of depression, and then to lose her only brother in the war. He had been killed at Iwo Jima, which she had always said had been the fatal blow for her father. He died less than a year later. Mimi had lost the last of her family, nearly at one gulp. And now, almost mysteriously, the house her great-grandfather had built had drifted into Sarah's life, bringing all its history and secrets with it.

'What's going on here?' Audrey asked sharply, as she walked into her mother's bedroom and saw Sarah give Mimi a hug. Audrey was always slightly jealous of the warm, easy relationship her mother and her daughter shared. Her relationship with Sarah was much more tense.

'We're just talking,' Mimi said, turning to smile at her daughter.

'About what?'

'My parents, actually,' Mimi said simply, as Audrey stared.

'You never talk about that, Mother. What brought that up?' Audrey had stopped questioning her mother about her childhood years before.

'I'm selling her parents' house for an estate,' Sarah explained. 'It's a beautiful old house, although not in very good shape. It hasn't been touched since it was built.' Mimi drifted out of the room then, to look for George. They'd said enough.

'You didn't upset her, did you?' Audrey asked her daughter conspiratorially. 'You know she doesn't like to talk about that stuff.' Audrey had heard rumors that her grandmother had abandoned her mother as a child, but Mimi never confirmed it and she knew very little else. As a result of handling Stanley's estate, Sarah now knew far more.

'I may have,' Sarah said honestly. 'I tried not to.

151

I found a photograph of her mother in the house this week. I didn't know who it was, but I realized I'd seen it somewhere before. I just saw it on her dresser.' She pulled the photograph of Lilli out and showed her mother. She didn't want to share her grandmother's confidences until Mimi said she could, or chose to do so herself.

'How strange.' Audrey looked pensive and then put it back. 'I hope Mimi's not too upset.'

But when they walked back into the living room, Mimi seemed to have regained her composure, and was having an animated conversation with George. He was teasing the three ladies surrounding him, listening raptly, but his gaze was firmly attached to Mimi. He clearly had a soft spot for her. And she appeared to enjoy him as well.

Sarah finally left an hour later. Audrey stayed for a few more minutes, and then said she was meeting a friend. She didn't invite Sarah to join her, but Sarah wouldn't have anyway. She had a lot to think about, and wanted to be alone in her apartment to digest what her grandmother had shared. When she walked in, and saw the dirty dishes on the kitchen counter, the unmade bed, the laundry on her bathroom floor, she realized what her mother meant about her apartment. The place really was a shambles. It was dirty, dark, depressing. There were no curtains, the venetian blinds were broken. There were old wine stains on the carpet, and the couch she'd dragged through her life since college should have been thrown out years before.

'Shit,' Sarah said, as she sat down on the couch and looked around. She thought of Phil with his children in Tahoe, and felt lonely. Everything in her life suddenly seemed depressing. Her apartment was ugly, she had a weekend relationship with an inattentive boyfriend who didn't even bother to spend holidays with her after four years. All she really had in her life was work. She could hear the echo of Stanley's warnings, and could suddenly envision herself in an apartment like this one, or worse, ten or twenty years from now, with a boyfriend even worse than Phil, or none at all. She had stayed in the relationship with him because she didn't want to rock the boat, or lose the little she had. But what did she have? A solid career as a tax attorney, a partnership in a law firm, a mother who picked on her frequently, an adorable grandmother who adored her, and Phil, who used every excuse he could dream up not to spend time or holidays with her. It felt as though her personal life couldn't get much worse. In fact, she barely had one.

Maybe a nicer apartment would be a start, she thought, as she sat there on her ancient couch. And then what? What would she do after that? Who would she spend her time with, particularly if she decided what she had with Phil wasn't enough, and broke it off? It was terrifying thinking of all of it. And suddenly she wanted to clean house and get rid of everything, and maybe Phil with it. She looked at the two dead plants in her living room, and wondered why she hadn't noticed them in almost two years. Was this all she thought she deserved? A bunch of cast-off furniture she'd had since her days at Harvard, dead plants, and a man who didn't love her, no matter what he said. If he did, why wasn't she in Tahoe with him? She thought of how brave her grandmother must have been, how hard it was to lose her mother, brother, father, and still soldier on like a ray of sunshine, bringing joy to everyone in her life. She thought of Stanley then, in his attic room in the Scott Street house, and she suddenly made a decision. She was going to call Marjorie Merriweather in the morning and find a new apartment. She had the money, and it wouldn't solve everything, but it was a start. She had to do something different. If she didn't, she would be trapped here forever, alone on holidays, with dead plants and an unmade bed.

Phil didn't bother to call her that night, to wish her a happy Thanksgiving. She didn't even matter that much to him. And he never liked her to call him when he was with his kids. He considered it an intrusion and said as much if she called. She knew that when he did call, he'd have some complicated though plausible excuse why he hadn't. And swallowing whatever he said to her would only make it that much worse. It was time to pick up her skirts and do something about her life. She decided to tackle the apartment first. Thanks to Stanley, that was the easy part. But maybe once she dealt with that, the rest would be easier for her. She lay on the couch in the dark, thinking about it. She deserved so much better than this. And if Mimi could turn her history into a happy life, Sarah knew she could do it, too, whatever it took.

CHAPTER 9

Sarah called Marjorie on the Friday after Thanksgiving at nine in the morning. She wasn't in her office, but Sarah got her on her cell. Marjorie thought she was calling about the house on Scott Street. The janitorial service had been there, the boards and curtains had been put in a dumpster, and the place was immaculate after a full-time cleaning crew had scrubbed, polished, and shined it all week. The broker's open house was Tuesday. All the brokers were aware of it, and so far the response had been good. Marjorie said she was expecting a full house, with nearly every broker in town.

'I wasn't actually calling about that,' Sarah explained, after Marjorie had given her the full report on Scott Street, and added that the brokers even liked the price they'd put on it. Given the condition the house was in, balanced by the enormous amount of square footage, and incomparable antique details, they thought the price was fair. 'I was actually calling about a new apartment. For me. I think I'd like to find a condo, something really nice, in Pacific Heights. My mother has been bugging me about it for years. Do you suppose we could find something?' Sarah asked hopefully.

'Of course.' Marjorie sounded delighted. 'You're looking at about half a million dollars in Pacific Heights, if that feels right to you. Flats would be more expensive, and would run closer to a million, if they're in decent shape. A house would be closer to two. Unless we start looking in other areas, but then you're going to get into houses that may need a lot of work. Tear-downs these days cost close to a million dollars, even in neighborhoods where you won't want to live. Real estate's not cheap in San Francisco, Sarah.'

'Wow, at those prices, maybe we should be asking more for Scott Street.' But they both knew that was a special house, and there was a ton of work to do there.

'We'll find you something pretty, don't worry,' Marjorie reassured her. 'I have a few things on my books right now. I'll check on their status, and make sure they're not in escrow. When do you want to look?'

'Do you have any time today? My office is closed till Monday, and I'm pretty much at loose ends.'

'I'll call you back in an hour,' Marjorie promised. Sarah did her laundry while she waited, and threw out the dead plants. She couldn't believe how long they'd been there and that she'd never noticed them before. It was a hell of a statement about her, she reproached herself. When Marjorie called back, she said she had four condos to show her. Two were lovely, one was so-so, and one was kind of interesting, though maybe too small for her, but worth a look. The last one was on Russian Hill, which wasn't Sarah's first-choice neighborhood, but she was willing. The other three were in Pacific Heights a few blocks from her. Sarah agreed to meet her at noon. She was suddenly excited about it, although she knew it would probably take time to find the right thing. Maybe her mother could help her with the decorating. The domestic arts were not Sarah's strong suit.

She had already calculated that if she put ten percent down on a condo she purchased, she would still have plenty of Stanley's money to invest. Ten percent of half a million, if she spent

156

that much, was only fifty thousand. That would leave her with seven hundred thousand to invest. If she went totally crazy and bought a house for two million dollars, she'd have to put up two hundred thousand. She'd still have half a million of Stanley's money left. And she made enough money at the law firm to pay a mortgage. She didn't want a house. She didn't need that much space. An apartment seemed like a much better solution to her.

She ran down the steps of her building at eleven-thirty, stopped at Starbucks, and met Marjorie promptly at noon at the first address. They started on Russian Hill, and Sarah didn't like it. Marjorie was right. It was a converted garage that had been made into a house, and it just didn't work for her. Neither did the ones in Pacific Heights, all three of which were apartments, but none of them seemed warm and welcoming to her. They were cold and small and cramped. For half a million dollars she wanted to buy something that had soul and that she loved. She was disappointed, but Marjorie told her not to be discouraged. There were going to be lots more on the market before the end of the year. And after Christmas, there would be even more. People didn't want to be bothered selling their houses over the holidays, she explained to Sarah. This was a whole new world for her. She was discovering the horizons Stanley had alluded to in his letter. She was doing just what he had urged her and the others to do. He had opened an important door for her.

She and Marjorie talked about a house again, as they walked back to their cars at the last address. Sarah still thought it would be too much for her. It

157

might turn out to be depressing to have too much space and no one to share it with. Marjorie smiled at what she said.

'You're not going to be alone forever, Sarah. You're still very young.' Compared to the real estate broker, she was. She looked like a child to Marjorie, but Sarah shook her head.

'I'm thirty-eight. That's not so young. I want something I'll be comfortable in by myself.' Those were, after all, the realities of her life.

'We'll work on it,' Marjorie promised her. 'And we'll find exactly the right thing. Houses and apartments are like romance. When you see the right one, you know it, and everything else falls into place. You don't have to beg, plead, push, or force it to work.' Sarah nodded, thinking of Phil. She had done a lot of begging, pleading, and pushing in the last four years, and it was starting to hurt. She hadn't heard from him in two days. He obviously wasn't pushing himself, or even thinking of her.

He finally called her late that night, after she went to a movie by herself. The movie was lousy and the popcorn was stale. When the phone rang, she was lying on her bed, still dressed, feeling sorry for herself.

'Hi, babe, how are you? I tried to get you earlier, but your cell phone was off. Where were you?'

'I was at a movie. It sucked. It was one of those stupid foreign films where nothing happens, and people snore in the audience so loud you can't hear the movie.' He laughed at her description, and sounded like he was in a great mood. He said he was having fun with his kids. 'Thanks for the call on Thanksgiving,' she said acidly. If she was

158

miserable, she thought he should be, too. It was irritating to hear him so happy, especially when she wasn't included.

'I'm sorry, babe. I meant to call. It got late. I was at some disco up here with the kids till two in the morning. I forgot my cell phone in the room, and by the time we got back it was too late to call you. How was Thanksgiving?'

'Fine. My grandmother and I talked about some interesting stuff, about her childhood. That's rare for her. It was nice.'

'What did you do today?' He sounded as though he were calling one of his children, not a woman he was in love with. And the reference to the disco he'd been to on Thanksgiving night wasn't wasted on her either. She didn't feel like part of his life, not an important part in any case. It sounded almost like a duty call, and she was too depressed to enjoy it. It just depressed her more, for everything it wasn't, and probably never would be. She was just a woman he spent weekends with. She wanted more than that. He didn't. It was the same deal it always was with him.

'I looked at apartments. Condos actually,' she said in a dead voice.

'What brought that on?' He sounded startled. It was unlike her to think about where she lived. And condos were expensive. She was obviously doing better than he thought. He was momentarily impressed.

'Actually, my couch and my dead plants brought it on,' she said, and then laughed at herself.

'You can get a new couch and throw the plants out instead of buying a condo. That's a pretty radical solution for a couple of dead plants.'

159

'I thought it might be fun to look,' she said honestly.

'Was it?'

'Actually, no. It depressed the hell out of me. But I decided I really want to move. The broker says we'll probably find something after Christmas.'

'Christ, leave you alone for a couple of days, and you get into all kinds of mischief.' He was teasing her, and she didn't bother correcting him. It hadn't been 'a couple of days.' She hadn't seen him in two days shy of two weeks, between the holiday and his trip to Tahoe with his kids, where she couldn't be included, his week in New York before that for depositions, and their insane policy of only seeing each other on weekends. And it would be yet another week before she saw him again. Hell, why not make it a month? she wanted to say, but didn't. It was almost as though he were trying to prove something, except he wasn't. He was just being Phil. 'Well, don't move before I get back. I've got to go check on the kids. They're downstairs in the hot tub with a bunch of college boys.' And who was he in the hot tub with? She couldn't help but wonder. It didn't matter really. All that mattered was that he was not in the hot tub with her, or anywhere else for that matter. They were living in separate worlds, and she was tired of it. It was too lonely here without him, particularly over a holiday weekend.

She slept fitfully that night and woke up at six o'clock the next morning, forgot that it was Saturday, and started to get ready to go to work. And then she remembered what day it was, and went back to bed. She had two more days of the

160

weekend to get through before she could escape into her work at the office. She had finished all the files she'd brought home with her. She had checked the newspaper for condos, had seen all the movies she wanted to. She called her grandmother, who was busy all weekend, and she didn't want to see her mother. Calling her married friends would just depress her. They were busy with husbands and kids she didn't have. What had happened to her life? Had all she accomplished for the past ten years been work, lose track of friends, and find a weekend boyfriend? She had no idea what to do with herself with spare time on her hands. She needed a project. She decided to go to a museum, and drove by the house on Scott Street on her way. She hadn't done it on purpose, she had just turned, and there it was as she drove past it. It was even more meaningful to her now that she knew it had been built by her great-grandfather, and her grandmother had been a child there. She couldn't help wondering who would buy it, and hoped they'd love it, as the house deserved.

She found herself thinking of the two architects Marjorie had introduced her to, and wondered if they were having fun in Venice and Paris. She started to think about taking a trip. Maybe she should go to Europe herself. She hadn't been in years. She didn't like traveling by herself. She wondered if maybe for something like that, Phil would join her. She was suddenly trying to fill in the gaps in her life, to make it all make sense, and give her life some meaning and movement. Somewhere, sometime, somehow, she felt as though the engine of her life had died. She was trying to jump-start it and had no idea how.

161

She wandered around the museum aimlessly, looked at paintings she didn't care about, and then drove slowly home, still pondering a trip to Europe, and without thinking, she found herself driving past Stanley's house again. She stopped the car, got out, and stood staring up at it. The idea that had just come to her was the craziest she'd ever had. It wasn't just crazy. It was more than that. It made no sense whatsoever. Phil was right for once. Instead of buying a new couch and throwing out her plants, she was thinking of buying a condo. She could claim that was an investment at least. But this, this was a money pit. It would not only eat up the money Stanley had so unexpectedly left her, it would eat up everything else she had saved. But if what Marjorie said was true, an ordinary little Pacific Heights house would cost her just as much, and this was a piece of history, her own history. Her great-grandfather had built it, her grandmother had been born there. A man she had loved and respected had lived tucked away in the attic. And if what she needed was a project, this was the project to end all projects.

'No!' she said to herself out loud, as she reached into her bag, found the keys, walked up the front steps, looked at the heavy bronze and glass door, and unlocked it. It was as though something more powerful than she was forcing her to move forward and step inside. She felt suddenly as though she had been picked up by a riptide in a rushing river with no free will of her own. She walked slowly into the main hallway.

As Marjorie had promised, it was immaculate. The floors gleamed, the chandeliers sparkled in the afternoon light, and the white marble staircase shone. The ugly old carpet had vanished, although the bronze rods were still there. The banisters had been polished to perfection. The house was clean, but all its problems were still there, the ancient electrical wires, the plumbing that hadn't been replaced in years. The kitchen that had to be moved to another floor, the furnace that had to be replaced with a more modern system. The elevator was roughly eighty years old. There was almost nothing in the house, except the floors and boiseries, that didn't require some kind of attention. Jeff Parker had said it could be done for half a million dollars by someone who did some of the work themselves and kept a careful eye on the budget. But she knew nothing about how to restore a house. She lived in a two-room apartment, and she couldn't even take care of that. What was she thinking? She stood there wondering if she had gone totally insane. Maybe loneliness had done that to her, or arguing with Phil about how much time he would spend with her, or too much work, or losing Stanley, or inheriting too much money. But all she could think of now was if she paid them two million for the house and put two hundred thousand down for the mortgage, she would have five hundred and fifty thousand of Stanley's dollars left to restore the house.

'Oh my God,' she said out loud, as she put her hands over her mouth and stood there. 'I must be crazy.' But the oddest thing was she didn't feel it. She felt totally sane, completely clear, and suddenly she was laughing and looking up at the gigantic chandelier. 'Oh my God!' she said louder still . . . 'Stanley, I'm going to do it!!!' She danced around the hallway then, like a child, ran back to the front door, exited, locked it, and dashed back to her car. She called Marjorie from her cell phone, sitting in her car.

'Don't be discouraged, Sarah. We'll find you something,' Marjorie reassured her instantly, anticipating what she was going to say.

'I think we just did,' Sarah said in barely more than a whisper. She was shaking. She had never been so terrified or so excited in her entire life. Passing the bar had been nothing compared to this.

'Did you see something today? If you give me the address, I can check the listing. It may be one of ours.'

'It is,' Sarah said with a crazed giggle. She felt giddy.

'Where is it?' Marjorie thought she sounded strange, and wondered if she'd been drinking. It wouldn't have surprised her. Sarah had looked depressed to her the day before.

'Cancel the broker's open.'

'What?'

'Cancel the broker's open house.'

'Is something wrong? Why?'

'I think I just went insane. I'm going to buy it. I want to make the heirs an offer.' She had already figured out the exact amount, and they had already told her they would accept the first offer they got, no matter what it was. She could have offered less but she didn't think it was right to do that. 'I want to offer them one point nine million. That gives each of the heirs a hundred thousand dollars.'

'Are you serious?' Marjorie asked, sounding dumbstruck. She had never expected Sarah to do anything remotely like it. She had said only hours before that she wanted an apartment, not a house.

164

And what on earth was she going to do with a thirty-thousand-square-foot house that needed two years and close to a million dollars' worth of work? 'Are you sure?' Marjorie sounded stunned.

'I am. I just found out yesterday that my great-grandfather built it. My great-grandmother was the Lilli who ran away.'

'Good Lord, you never mentioned anything about the connection.'

'I didn't know it. I knew I'd seen that photograph somewhere before. I saw it yesterday on top of my grandmother's chest of drawers in her bedroom. Lilli was her mother. She never saw her again after she left.'

'What an amazing story. If you're serious about this, Sarah, I'll draw up the papers, and we'll make an offer on Monday.'

'Do it. It sounds crazy, but I know it's right. I think it was fate that this house came into my life. And Stanley left me the money to buy it. He didn't know he was doing that, but he left me a bequest that will allow me to buy and restore the house. If I do it the way Jeff Parker suggested, doing a lot of the work myself, and watching every penny.' She knew she sounded like a madwoman as she raced through all of it. But suddenly it was as though new vistas had opened up and everything she saw on the horizon was beautiful and alive. More than ever before in her life. Overnight, Stanley's house had become her dream. 'I'm sorry to sound so crazed, Marjorie. I'm just so excited. I've never done anything like this in my life.'

'What? Buy a ninety-year-old thirty-thousand-square-foot house in need of total overhaul and restoration? No kidding? I thought you did this

165

every day.' They were both laughing as she said it. 'Well, I'm glad we didn't make any offers on the piddly stuff I showed you yesterday.'

'Me too,' Sarah said happily. 'This is it for me.'

'Okay, kiddo. I'll bring you the offer to look over tomorrow. Will you be home?'

'I will. I'm going to be throwing all my belongings into the garbage.'

'I wouldn't want you to be hasty or anything.' Marjorie smiled, shaking her head. 'You can sign the papers tomorrow, if they look okay to you.'

'I guess I could call them with the offer myself on Monday. Or maybe fax it to them.' She couldn't see it being a problem, from everything they'd said at the meeting the week before, but who knew? Sarah didn't want to count on it until they agreed. 'I'd better call the bank, too.' There was a possibility they would advance her the money until Stanley's bequest came through. She had excellent credit, and a long-standing relationship with her bank.

'Remember what I said to you?' Marjorie reminded her with a knowing tone in her voice. 'Houses are like romance, Sarah. When you find the right one, you know it. You don't have to beg, plead, fight, or push. It just happens. And everything falls into place. I guess this is the one for you.'

'I honestly believe it is.' It felt meant to be.

'You know what, Sarah?' Marjorie said, happy for her. She was a nice woman, and she deserved this, if it was what she wanted. 'I think this is the one for you, too. It just feels good.'

'Thank you,' Sarah said, feeling calmer than she had in several minutes. This was the most exciting

166

thing she had ever done in her life. And the scariest too.

Marjorie promised to come by with the offering papers the following morning. Sarah started her car and drove home. She had never felt calmer, more certain about anything, or happier, ever. She parked her car, walked up the front steps of her apartment building, and went inside with a broad smile. Twenty-forty Scott Street was beckoning to her on the horizon. She could hardly wait!

CHAPTER 10

Marjorie came by with the papers on Sunday morning. They looked fine to Sarah, who signed them and handed them back to her. Marjorie gave Sarah a copy so she could send the offer by fax to Stanley's heirs from her office. It was all a little incestuous, since she was the attorney for the estate. But everything was above-board.

'You should call Jeff and Marie-Louise when they get back from Europe,' Marjorie reminded her. Sarah had already thought of it herself. She had said nothing to Phil when he called the night before. He had been shocked on Friday when she said she'd been looking at condos. He would think she'd lost her mind entirely if she told him that the next day she'd made an offer on a thirty-thousand-square-foot house.

She went out for breakfast by herself, read *The New York Times,* did the crossword puzzle, and went back to her apartment. When she got in, she looked for their card and decided to leave a message for Jeff Parker and Marie-Louise Fournier. She knew they were probably still in Europe, but when they got back, they could call her. She wanted to go through the house with them again, this time with a fine-tooth comb. Once the offer was accepted, if it was, she needed to start making lists of everything she'd have to do. The electrical and plumbing work would have to be handled by a contractor, but she was going to try and do a lot of the more menial manual work herself. She was going to need their help, and lots of advice. She hoped they wouldn't charge her a fortune for their services, but she had no other choice. She was flying blind.

She called their office number and waited for their machine to come on. Jeff had given her both their European and American cell phone numbers, but there was nothing they could do for her at this distance. It could wait until the offer was accepted, and they came back to San Francisco, so she could meet them again at the house. Sarah heard the machine come on, and then over it a male human voice. They both tried to talk over the machine, and then he told her to wait while he turned the machine off. He came back on the line a moment later, and Sarah tried again. She hadn't recognized the voice that answered.

'Hi, my name is Sarah Anderson, and I'm trying to leave a message for Jeff Parker and Marie-Louise Fournier for when they get back from Europe. Could you ask either of them to call me at my office, please?' She hoped it would be Jeff, and not his disagreeable French partner, but she was prepared to deal with whichever of them had the time to help her.

'Hi, Sarah. This is Jeff.' As he had before, he sounded easy-going and warm.

'What are you doing here? I thought you were in Italy, or Paris.' She had lost track of their trip and where they were supposed to be at what time.

'I was. Marie-Louise is still there. I came back early. I had some work to do for a client. We were running behind.'

She took a breath and jumped right in. 'I'm going to make an offer on the house.'

He sounded confused for a moment. 'What house?'

'Twenty-forty Scott Street,' she said proudly, and this time at his end, he was stunned. Sarah could hear it if not see it.

'*That* house? Wow! There's a surprise, and a brave thing to do.' The way he said it was a little daunting. As though he thought she was crazy.

'Do you think I'm nuts to do it?'

'No, I don't,' he said thoughtfully. 'Not if you love the house.'

'I do,' she said, more calmly. 'My great-grandfather built it.'

'Now *that* really is cool. I love things like that, that come full circle. It seems like the right order of things somehow. I hope you're ready to take on a big job,' he said, with a smile in his voice, and she laughed.

'I am. I hope you are, too. I need your help, and a lot of guidance and direction. I'm going to follow plan A.'

'Which one was that?'

'The one where you spend half a million to restore the house, do a lot of the work yourself, and watch every penny.'

'Oh, that one. I would do exactly the same thing in your shoes, particularly if my family owned the house originally.'

'The difference is that you're an architect. I'm an attorney. I know tax laws and property trusts inside out. I don't know beans about restoring a house, or even hammering a nail.'

'You'll learn. Most people who work on their houses have no idea what they're doing. You'll figure it out as you go, and if you make mistakes, you'll fix 'em.' He was very encouraging, and as friendly as he'd been before. Sarah was relieved that Marie-Louise wasn't there. She wouldn't have been nearly as pleasant as he.

'I'd like you to see the house again when you have time, if you're not too busy. You can charge me for it, of course. But I really need your advice about what to do first. Electrical, plumbing, wiring. I need some direction to get me started, and I'm going to need a lot of advice along the way.'

'That's what we're here for. What does your week look like? When do you want me to drop by? I don't think Marie-Louise will be back for a few more weeks. I know her when she gets together with her family in Paris. She delays her return day by day. I just factor in about three extra weeks. We can wait till she comes back, if you like, or I can start working with you myself.'

'To be honest, I'd rather not wait.'

'Okay by me,' he said easily. 'Tell me about your week.'

'The usual insanity.' She was thinking about the meetings with clients that she remembered, and work she was still doing on the probate of Stanley's estate. She had to go to court on Tuesday morning for a probate hearing. It was going to be a pretty crazy week.

'Me too,' he said, glancing at his book. 'I have an idea. Are you busy this afternoon?'

'No, but you are,' Sarah said, feeling guilty. 'I assume you're not sitting there reading a book or watching TV.'

'No, but I got a lot done yesterday and this morning. I can take a few hours off now, if you want me to meet you at the house. Besides, now you're a client. This *is* work.'

'I'd love it.' She had nothing to do all afternoon. The house was already filling her days.

'Perfect. I'll meet you there in half an hour. Actually, do you want to grab a sandwich before we go? We can talk about your plans over lunch.'

'That works for me,' she said happily. She hadn't been this excited since she got into Harvard.

'I'll pick you up in ten minutes. Where do you live?' She gave him the address, and he rang her bell fifteen minutes later. She ran down the stairs to meet him, and climbed into the Jeep he had driven to pick her up.

'What happened to the Peugeot?' Sarah asked with interest.

'I'm not allowed to drive it.' He smiled at her, and they stopped at a deli on Fillmore Street for sandwiches and lemonade. Less than an hour after he picked her up, they were at the house Sarah hoped would be hers. With any luck, it would be. She warned him that it was not yet a done deal, and he smiled at her, unconcerned. 'It will be. I feel it in my bones.'

'Me too,' she giggled, as she let them both into the house.

He took his work very seriously. He had brought two cameras, an industrial tape measure, a sketch pad, and a series of tools and implements to measure things, and check others out. He explained to her that the floors and boiseries would have to be protected while there was work being done in the house. He recommended two plumbing contractors for her to choose between, and three electricians whom he told her wouldn't charge a fortune. The arrangement Jeff suggested he make with her was an hourly fee, based on work he actually did, not a percentage of costs, to run the project. He said an hourly would be cheaper for her. He was being extremely reasonable, got under things, climbed over things, rattled things, knocked on walls, and checked wood, tile, and plaster.

'The house is amazingly sound, considering its age,' he said, after they'd spent an hour there. There was no question that the plumbing and electrical were a disaster, although he liked the fact that there were no visible leaks anywhere in the house, which he said was unheard of.

'Stanley took pretty good care of it on the outside. He didn't want to live in the main part of the house, but he didn't want it to fall apart, either. He just put on a new roof.'

'He was smart. Water damage screws up everything, and sometimes leaks are hard to follow.' They were there till nearly six o'clock, and by the time they left, they were both using powerful flashlights. Sarah felt completely at home there. She'd had a fun afternoon going over everything with Jeff. And this was only the beginning. He had already filled one notebook

172

with notes and sketches. 'And there will be no charge for today,' he said as she locked the front door and he helped her into the Jeep.

'Are you kidding? We've been here for five hours.'

'It's Sunday. I had nothing better to do, and I enjoyed it. Today was a gift. I had so much fun, you should charge me. Your hourly rate is probably higher than mine,' he teased her. They seemed to be fairly comparable, given the prices he had quoted to her over the phone.

'I think it's a wash in that case.'

'Good. Do you have time for dinner, or are you busy? We could start going over my notes. I want to do some renderings for you tomorrow morning.' They were off and running.

'You're not sick of me yet?' She felt like a bit of a mooch, taking advantage of him, since she was planning to do some of the work herself. But he knew that, and didn't seem to mind. It had originally been his suggestion.

'I'd better not be sick of you, or the house. Or you of me. You're going to see a lot of me for the next six months, or longer, depending on how long it takes for us to finish. Sushi?' he asked as they drove off.

'Perfect.'

He took her to a sushi restaurant just off Union, and they continued talking about the house with energy and enthusiasm. He was going to be fun to work with. He obviously loved his profession, and the house she was buying was rapidly becoming his passion. It was like the projects he had done in Europe.

He dropped her back at her place just after

eight-thirty, and promised to call her in the morning. The phone was ringing when she walked into her apartment.

'Where were you?' It was Phil. He sounded anxious.

'Just out eating sushi,' she said calmly.

'All day? I've been calling you since two o'clock. I brought the kids back early. You've been out all day. I've been leaving messages on your cell phone.' She hadn't checked her messages since noon. She'd been too busy on Scott Street.

'I'm sorry. I didn't think you'd call me,' she said sincerely.

'I was going to take you to dinner.' He sounded piqued, and she teased him.

'On a Sunday? Now, there's a new twist.'

'I had pizza. I gave up on you at seven. Do you want me to come over?'

'Now?' She sounded surprised, and was filthy dirty. They'd been crawling around the house all day, even in the basement. The janitorial service had done a good job, but they'd gotten dusty anyway. There was still dirt in some of the remoter nooks and crannies.

'Are you busy?' Phil asked.

'No. I just look a mess. You can come over if you want. I'll hop in the shower.' He had the keys, and had for two years. She had nothing to hide from him. In spite of the inadequacy of their arrangement, from her perspective, she had always been faithful to him, and he to her. She couldn't help wondering why he was coming over. She was drying her hair, after the shower, when he walked into the apartment, frowning.

'What's with you?' he asked, looking worried.

'You're out every time I call you. You went out for sushi. You never go to dinner alone. You went to a movie alone on Friday. And you've been looking at condos.' She smiled mysteriously as he said it. She was thinking about the house on Scott Street. 'And you look weird.'

'Gee, thanks,' she said, laughing at him. What did he expect? He left for a weekend with his kids, and didn't invite her. Maybe he thought she'd sit locked in the apartment all weekend waiting to see him the following weekend. Not this time, although it had happened before. 'I was just keeping busy. And I decided not to buy a condo.'

'Well, at least that's normal. I was beginning to think you were seeing another guy or something.' She smiled at him and put her arms around him.

'Not for the moment,' she said honestly, 'but one of these days, I will, if we don't start seeing more of each other.'

'For chrissake, Sarah, don't start that again.' He seemed nervous.

'I'm not. You asked me.'

'I just thought you were acting strange.' Stranger than he could ever dream of. And if she got the house, it was going to get a lot stranger. Now she could hardly wait to tell him. But she wanted to talk to her bank, and wait to hear from all the heirs first.

He lay down on the couch and turned on the TV, and then he pulled her down next to him. Within moments he got amorous, and half an hour later, they moved to her bedroom. The bed was unmade and the sheets hadn't been changed, but he didn't seem to mind it. In fact, he never noticed. He spent the night with her, nestled next to her,

175

holding her, even on a Sunday night. And he made love to her again the next morning. It was funny, Sarah thought to herself as she drove downtown, how people sensed when things were different. And her life was about to get even more so. If she got the house, her life would change radically.

CHAPTER 11

Sarah drafted a letter to all nineteen heirs of Stanley's estate on Monday. She faxed it to those who had fax machines, FedExed it to the others, and added the official offer form that Marjorie had prepared as the realtor. Everything was official, and had been sent out into the ether by ten A.M.

At eleven, Tom Harrison called her from St. Louis. He was laughing when she took the call in her office. 'I was wondering if you were going to do that, Sarah. Your eyes lit up when you walked into that house. Good for you. I think that's exactly what Stanley meant when he told us all to look for new horizons. I have to say, I'd pay you twice that much not to get saddled with a white elephant like that. But if you love it, do it. You have my full approval. I accept your offer.'

'Thanks, Tom.' She was thrilled as she listened.

She heard from four more of them that day. And nine on Tuesday. That left five she hadn't heard from. Two of them gave her their approval on Wednesday. And by then she had heard from her bank. There was no problem getting a mortgage, or even giving her a line of credit to cover the down payment until her bequest came through from Stanley. Marjorie had suggested she get a termite report, just to be on the safe side, and that was fine. There were a few surprisingly minor problems, which were to be expected in an old house. Nothing that couldn't be fixed. Stanley had had a seismic report done, just to make sure the house wouldn't fall on him in an earthquake. So the only problems were the obvious ones she knew about.

The last three approvals came in on Thursday, and as soon as they did, Sarah called the bank, Marjorie, and Jeff Parker. They were the only ones who knew of her insanity. Jeff gave out a whoop of glee when she told him. He had called her on Tuesday to check, but then she still had five approvals missing. All the heirs were delighted to get the house sold and out of the estate, and they were happy with the price. It was a complication and headache none of them had wanted. They had agreed to a three-day escrow, which was almost unheard of. It meant that technically the house would be hers on Sunday.

'We have to do something to celebrate,' Jeff said, when he heard the news. 'How about another sushi dinner?' It was easy and quick, and they agreed to meet at a different restaurant on Fillmore, after they both finished work. They agreed on seven-thirty, and she had to admit, it was nice having something to do, and someone to meet with during the week. It was more fun than eating a sandwich at her desk while she worked, or going home to stare at the TV and skip dinner completely.

She and Jeff talked incessantly about the house for two hours, over dinner. He'd had a million ideas since the last time they spoke on Tuesday. He wanted to see if he could help her do something more elegant with the back staircase, and he had designed an entire kitchen for her on the main floor. It was only a rough sketch, of course, but she loved it. He was suggesting a gym in the basement, where the old kitchen had been, and had even included a sauna and steam room.

'Won't that cost a fortune?' she asked, looking worried, although Phil would love it. She hadn't told him about the house yet, but was going to that weekend.

'It doesn't have to. We can use prefab units. We can even put in a hot tub.' She laughed at the suggestion.

'Now we're really getting fancy.' She especially loved his design for the kitchen, it was functional and pretty. There was even room for a large, comfortable dining table in front of the windows facing the garden. He was putting a lot of time and thought into her project. Occasionally, it made her wonder what his bill would look like. But he was obviously as passionate about the house on Scott Street as she was. It was just his cup of tea.

'God, I love this house, Jeff. Don't you?' She beamed at him.

'I do.' He smiled happily at her, looking relaxed after they finished dinner. They were both drinking green tea. 'I haven't enjoyed anything this much in years. I can hardly wait to sink my teeth into it and start.' She told him she had called the electrical and plumbing contractors that week. She had appointments with all of them the following week so they could make bids. They had all told her they couldn't start the actual work until after

Christmas. Like Jeff, she could hardly wait to start. 'Just wait till we have the place ripped apart, get everything cleaned up, and then put it all back together.'

'You make it sound scary,' she said, smiling at him. But he was so calm and reassuring, if anyone could make it happen, he could.

'It is scary at times, but when you get it all done, it's the most incredible feeling.'

Sarah was hoping that the house would look respectable again by the summer. Or at worst, by the following Christmas. Jeff didn't think it would take a full year. He paid the check, and then looked at her with a quizzical expression. He had a boyish face, but a wise man's eyes. He seemed both old and young at the same time, and was only six years older than she was. He was forty-four years old. And he had mentioned in passing that Marie-Louise was forty-two, although Sarah thought she looked much younger. There was something about her spicy, somewhat racy look that made her seem even younger than Sarah, who had an entirely different, more businesslike look, at least on days she went to the office. As she sat at dinner with Jeff, Sarah was wearing a simple navy blue pantsuit. On Sunday she'd been wearing jeans, Nikes, and a red sweater. He liked that look. When his mother had met Marie-Louise, she had said she looked like a hooker, although there were times when he had to admit that he liked that look, too. Sarah looked more American, more natural and wholesome, like a Ralph Lauren model, or the Harvard student she had once been.

'Tell me something,' Jeff said, with his more boyish look. 'If we're going to be spending all this

179

time together, working on the house, am I allowed to ask personal questions?' He had been curious about her since they met, and even more so once she told him she was buying the house. That was a hell of a brave thing for her to do, and he admired her for it.

'Sure,' she said with a look of innocence and openness that he loved about her. Sarah always looked as though she had no secrets. Marie-Louise looked as though she had many, some of them decidedly unpleasant. She was not an easy person. 'Shoot.'

'Who's moving into that house with you?' He looked embarrassed after he said it, but Sarah didn't.

'No one. Why?'

'Are you kidding? *Why?* You're moving into a five-story, thirty-thousand-square-foot house, and you're asking me why I was wondering who was moving in with you? Shit, Sarah, you could invite in a whole village.' They both laughed as the waiter poured them each more tea. 'I just wondered.'

'Nope. Just me.'

'Is that how you want it?' He sounded as though he were volunteering, but they both knew he wasn't. He had lived with Marie-Louise for the past fourteen years, and even if she seemed difficult to Sarah, apparently she suited him.

'Now, that's a more complicated question,' she said honestly, looking at him over her cup of tea. 'That depends on what you mean. Am I looking for a husband? No, I don't think so. I've never been convinced that marriage is the answer for me. It seems like a lot more trouble than it's worth. But I guess that depends on who you marry. Do I want

180

kids? I don't think so. At least I never have. Having children sounds too scary to me. Would I like to live with someone? Probably, or at least have someone who wants to be around pretty full-time, even if he has his own life. I think that's probably what I'd want. I like the idea of sharing my life with someone on a daily basis. That seems to be pretty hard to find. I may have missed the boat on that one.' He laughed at her answer, although he had listened seriously up until the end.

'At your age? Your boat hasn't even come into port yet. These days all the women I know wait until they're forty, or your age at least, to settle down.'

'You didn't. You must have settled down with Marie-Louise when you were thirty.'

'That's different. Maybe I was stupid. None of my friends got married till their thirties. Marie-Louise and I had a very passionate relationship with each other when we were students. It still is a lot of the time, but we've had our ups and downs. I guess most people do. Sometimes I think it makes it harder that we work together. But I like being with someone every day. She says I'm too insecure, needy, and possessive.' Sarah smiled at the description.

'You look fine to me.'

'That's because you don't live with me. She may be right. I tell her she's too cold-blooded and independent, and too goddamned French for her own good. She hates it here, which is hard, too. She goes home every chance she gets, and then stays there for six weeks instead of two.'

'That must be rough for your business,' Sarah said sympathetically. She wouldn't have liked that,

181

either.

'Our clients don't seem to mind it. She works from over there, and stays in touch with all of them by e-mail. Basically, she just hates living in the States, which is rough on me. A lot of the French are like that. Like their best wines, they don't travel all that well.' She smiled again at what he said about her. It wasn't mean, but more than likely true. She hadn't seemed happy or pleasant when Sarah met her. That would be hard to live with. 'So what about you? There's no everyday person in your life now?' She didn't feel he was putting the make on her in Marie-Louise's absence, just trying to be friends. She suspected he was lonely, and so was she.

'No,' Sarah said honestly. 'There's someone I see on weekends. We have very different needs. He's divorced, and has been for twelve years. Three teenage kids, whom he sees for dinner once or twice a week. He goes away on holidays with them. He doesn't see more of them than that, and he never sees them on weekends, they're too busy, and I don't think he'd want to. He hates his ex-wife with a passion, and his mother, and sometimes all that anger spills over onto me. He's an attorney, too, and he's very busy. But mostly he likes to do his own thing, during the week anyway, and sometimes on weekends. He doesn't have much tolerance for closeness, or someone in his space all the time. We spend Friday and Saturday nights together. It's strictly a weekends-only deal. He goes to the gym every night during the week, and he flat out refuses to see me, except on weekends. Holidays are not included.'

'Does that work for you?' Jeff asked her with

interest. It didn't sound good to him. It was probably an arrangement Marie-Louise would have liked, if she could get away with it, but with him, she couldn't. He would never have tolerated what Sarah had just described to him, and he was surprised to hear that she did. She looked like a woman who wanted more than that, and needed it. But maybe he was wrong, and she didn't.

'Honestly?' she answered him. 'No, it doesn't work for me. Weekends-only is the pits. I hate it. It was fine at first, but it got to me after the first couple of years. I've been upset and complaining about it for the last year, but he doesn't want to hear about it. That's the deal that's on the table. Take it or leave it. He's a tough negotiator, and a very good attorney.'

'Why do you put up with it, if you don't like it?' Jeff was ever more curious about her.

'What else is there?' she asked sadly. 'I'm not that young anymore. There aren't a lot of decent guys out there at our age. Most of them are commitment phobic. They've had a bad marriage and don't want another one, or even a full-time commitment. The ones who've never been married are usually dysfunctional, and can't tolerate any relationship at all. The good ones are married by now and having children. Besides, I'm busy. I work too hard. When am I supposed to go out and meet someone? And where? I don't go to bars. I almost never go to parties anymore. I don't drink enough to enjoy them. The guys I work with are all married. And I don't do married men. So that leaves what I've got. I keep thinking that eventually he'll want to spend more time with me. But he doesn't. At least not so far. And maybe never. This works for him, better than it does for me. He's a nice guy, though he's selfish sometimes. And most of the time I enjoy him, when I don't upset myself worrying about how little I see him.' And she didn't want to add to Jeff that the sex was great, even after four years.

'He'll never spend more time with you,' Jeff said clinically. They were becoming friends as they put their emotional cards on the table, and they liked each other. 'Why should he? He's got what he wants. A weekend woman who's there for him, and doesn't give him a lot of grief, because you probably don't want to rock the boat too badly. He's got comfort when he wants it, two days a week, and freedom the rest of the time. Hell, for him, it's the perfect arrangement. For a guy who's already been married and has kids, and doesn't want more than he's got with you now, he has it made in the shade with you.' She smiled at the expression, and she didn't disagree with him.

'I just haven't had the guts to walk away till now. My mother says the same thing you do. She calls him a deadbeat. But I know what weekends all alone look like, and to be honest with you, Jeff, I hate them. I always did. I'm just not ready to face that again. Not yet.'

'You'll never find a better one, unless you're willing to go through it.'

'You're right, but it's goddamn hard to do,' she said honestly.

'Tell me about it. That's why Marie-Louise and I keep winding up together. That, and a house we bought together, and a business, and an apartment we share in Paris, that I pay for and she uses. But every time we break up, we both look around and

184

it scares the shit out of us, so we wind up back together. After fourteen years, at least we know what we're getting. She's not psycho, I'm not dysfunctional. We're not ripping each other off, or cheating on each other. At least I hope not,' he said with a rueful grin, since she was six thousand miles away in Paris. 'But one of these days I suspect she'll go back to Paris and stay there, and we'll have to pull apart our business, which wouldn't be a great thing for either of us. We make pretty decent money working together. She's a good woman. We're just very different. Maybe that's a good thing. But she always says she doesn't want to grow old here. And I can't see myself moving to Paris. For one thing, I still don't speak decent French. I get by, but it would be hard to work there. And if we're not married, I can't get work papers. Marie-Louise says she'll never get married, and in her case, she means it. And she sure as hell doesn't want children.' Neither did Sarah. She and Marie-Louise had that in common, although everything else about them was different.

'God, things are so complicated these days, aren't they? Everyone has such screwed-up ideas about relationships and how they want to live. Everyone has 'issues.' Nothing is easy. People don't just say 'I do' and walk off into the sunset together and make it work. We construct these crazy arrangements that sort of work and sort of don't, and maybe could work, but then again they couldn't. I wonder if it was always like that. I just don't think so,' Sarah said, looking thoughtful as she mused about it.

'We're probably all like that because none of us saw happy marriages at home when we were

185

growing up. Our parents' generation stayed together and hated each other. Ours either doesn't get married at all, or gets divorced at the drop of a hat. Nobody tries to work it out. If it's not comfortable, and they get a wedgie and their shorts bunch up, they dump it,' he said, and Sarah laughed at how he described it. But she didn't disagree with him.

'Maybe you're right,' Sarah said, looking pensive. It was an interesting theory.

'What about your parents? Were they happy?' he asked, watching her. He liked her. He could sense that she was a truly decent person, with integrity and good values. But so was Marie-Louise, she just had very sharp edges. And she'd had a tough childhood, which impacted her still, whether she admitted it or not.

'Of course not.' Sarah laughed at the question he'd asked her. 'My father was a raging alcoholic, and my mother covered for him. She supported all of us, while he lay around in the bedroom too drunk to move and she made excuses for him. I hated him for doing that. And then he died when I was sixteen. I can't even say I missed him. It was almost as though he'd never been there. In fact, it was easier once he wasn't.' And for much of her early life, she wished he hadn't been. And then felt guilty about it after he died.

'Did she remarry?' he asked with interest. 'She must have been young when she was widowed, if you were only sixteen.'

'She was a year older than I am now, come to think of it. She sold real estate, and then became an interior decorator and made pretty decent money. She paid my way through Harvard, and

186

then Stanford law school. But she never remarried. She's had a bunch of very temporary boyfriends. They're always alcoholic or dysfunctional, or she thinks they are. Mostly she hangs out with her girlfriends now, and goes to book clubs.'

'That's sad,' Jeff said sympathetically.

'Yeah, it is, although she claims she's happy. I don't believe her. I wouldn't be. That's why I hang on to my weekend guy. I don't want to wind up twenty years from now doing book clubs like my mom.'

'You will anyway,' Jeff said bluntly. 'He's taking up real estate in your life. You really think he'll stick around for twenty years?'

'Probably not,' she said honestly, 'but he's here now. That's the problem. I guess one of these days it'll fall apart, but I'm in no hurry to push it. I hate those lonely weekends.'

'I know. I get it. So do I. I don't mean to sound smug about it. I don't have the answers either.'

They left the restaurant after that. And they had come in separate cars, so they hugged each other and she drove home. The phone was ringing off the hook when she got in. She glanced at her watch and was surprised to see that it was eleven. She had turned her cell phone off during dinner.

'Where the fuck were you?' Phil was livid.

'Jesus. Relax. I went out to dinner. It was no big deal. I had sushi.'

'Again? With who?' He nearly came through the phone at her, and she couldn't help wondering if he was jealous, or just being an asshole. Maybe he'd been out himself and had been drinking.

'What difference does it make?' she asked, sounding annoyed. 'You're not here during the week anyway. I went out with someone I'm working on a project with. It was strictly business.' That was true.

'What is this? Revenge? Because I need to go to the gym after work and get some exercise? Punishment? Christ, that's childish.'

'I'm not the one screaming,' she pointed out. 'You are. What's the big deal here?'

'For four years you come home every night and lie on your ass in front of the TV, and suddenly you're out for sushi every night. What are you doing? Fucking a goddamned Japanese?'

'Watch your mouth, Phil. And your manners. I go out for sushi with you, too. This was business. Since when do we tell each other that we can't go out for business dinners during the week?' She felt faintly guilty, because she had enjoyed herself, and after the first hour or two, it had felt more like friendship. But it was true. It had been business, too. 'If you're so hot to keep track of me during the week, why don't you try cutting your gym time short and hanging out here? You're welcome to do that anytime. I'd much rather go out for sushi with you.'

'Fuck you!' he said, and hung up on her. There had been no other possible response because she was right and he knew it. He couldn't have it both ways, total freedom during the week, yet be assured that she would be chained to a wall, waiting to see him on weekends. Maybe he'd like to give her a chastity belt, too. He was just damned lucky, Sarah told herself, that Jeff Parker was living with someone. Because she thought he was a hell of a nice guy. And all the assessments he'd made about Phil and the level of commitment he had to

188

her were true. The relationship she and Phil had now was anything but ideal.

Phil called her back later to apologize, but she let the machine answer it. She'd had a nice time that night, and she didn't want to spoil it now by talking to Phil. What he had said really upset her. He was accusing her of cheating, something she never, ever did. Never had, and never would. She just wasn't that kind of person.

Phil called her back again while she was rushing to dress for work the next morning. It was Friday. He sounded nervous again. 'Are we still on for tonight?'

'Why? Do you have other plans?' Sarah asked him coldly, but she was afraid to push it.

'No. I was afraid you did.' He didn't sound warm and cozy, either. It was going to be a great weekend.

'I was planning to see you, since we haven't seen each other in three weeks,' she said somewhat acidly.

'Let's not get into that now. I had to be in New York for a week, to take depositions. And I was with my kids last week. You know that.'

'Point taken, counselor. Now what?'

'I'll come by tonight after the gym.'

'See ya,' she said, and hung up. They were off on a bad foot. They were both clearly harboring resentments. She over the three weeks she hadn't seen hide nor hair of him, although he could have dropped by during the week. And he because he didn't like her being out for dinner and turning off her cell phone. And this was the weekend she was planning to tell him about the house on Scott Street and maybe even show it to him. Even Phil's temper tantrum hadn't put a damper on it for her.

She called Jeff on her way to work and thanked him for a delightful evening.

'I hope I wasn't too outspoken,' he said apologetically. 'I have a way of doing that when I drink too much tea.' She laughed, and so did he. And he told her he had had some more ideas for her kitchen, and maybe even her gym. 'Do you have time to get together this weekend? Or will you be busy with him?'

'His name is Phil. He always leaves by noon on Sundays. We could get together in the afternoon.'

'Great. Call me when he leaves.' She didn't tell him that Phil had had a jealous fit over him the night before. And she loved the thought that the house was going to keep her busy now. It would make things less depressing when Phil left on Sundays, and every night during the week. With a house that size to remodel, she was going to have a lot to do. It would take up all her spare time.

She stopped and bought groceries on the way home that night, and was thinking of cooking dinner, since they hadn't seen each other for so long. She was surprised to see Phil walk in just after seven.

'Didn't you go to the gym?' He never got to her place before eight.

'I thought you might like to go out to dinner tonight,' he said, looking slightly mollified. He rarely apologized verbally, but always tried to make it up to her in other ways, if he had offended her in some way.

'That would be nice,' she said pleasantly, and got up to give him a kiss. She was surprised by the strength with which he hugged her, and the fervor of his kiss. Maybe he really had been jealous. She almost thought that was sweet. She'd have to go out for sushi and turn her cell phone off more often, if it had this effect on him.

'I missed you,' he said lovingly, and she smiled at him. The relationship they had was so weird. Most of the time he didn't want to see her, and then when she fended for herself, he was jealous, had a tantrum, and said he missed her. It seemed as though one of them always had to be uncomfortable. One end of the seesaw had to be up and the other down. They could never be on an even keel at the same time. It somehow seemed a shame.

He took her out to dinner that night, at a restaurant she liked, and he seemed to be making an effort. And as soon as they got back to the apartment, he insisted he was tired and wanted her to come to bed with him. She knew what he had in mind, and she had no objections. It had been three weeks since the last time they made love. And she could tell when they did that night that he had been hungry for her. She had missed him, too, but not as much since she was distracted by the house. She hadn't said anything to him about it at dinner. She wanted to wait until after breakfast on Saturday morning. She somehow thought he'd be in a better mood. And she didn't know exactly why, but she had the feeling he'd disapprove. Phil hated change, and there was no denying it was an outlandishly big house.

She made him scrambled eggs and bacon in the morning, with blueberry muffins she had bought the night before. She even made him a mimosa, with champagne and orange juice, and brought him the paper while he was still in bed.

'Uh-oh,' he said with a sly smile, as she handed him a cappuccino with little flecks of chocolate on it. 'What are you buttering me up for?'

'What makes you think I am?' she said with a mischievous smile.

'The breakfast was too good. The cappuccino was perfect. You never bring me the paper in bed. And the champagne and orange juice was outrageous.' And then he looked at her with worried eyes. 'You're either going to dump me, or you've been screwing around.'

'Neither,' she said with a victorious look, as she sat down on the end of the bed. She couldn't contain her excitement any longer. She was dying to share it with him, and know what he thought. She was hoping to take him over to see it that afternoon. 'I have something to tell you.' She smiled at him.

'No kidding,' he said, looking anxious. 'I could figure that much out. What did you do?'

'I'm moving,' she said simply, and he suddenly looked panicked.

'Away from San Francisco?'

She laughed and was pleased. He actually looked frightened. That was a good sign.

'No. Just a few blocks away.' He looked relieved.

'You bought a condo?' He seemed surprised. 'You told me you decided not to.'

'I did. I didn't buy a condo. I bought a house.'

'A house? Just for you?'

'Just for me. And you on weekends, if you like.'

'So where is it?' He looked skeptical. She could see that he thought it was a bad idea. He had already done the house thing, in his marriage. He

192

didn't want anything more than the small apartment he had. All he had at his was one big bedroom, and a tiny back room with a triple bunk for his kids. They hardly ever stayed there, and it was easy to see why. They had to be contortionists to fit in. When he wanted to spend time with them, he took them away. The rest of the time they stayed at his old house with his ex-wife. He was perfectly satisfied just seeing them for dinner once or twice a week.

'It's on Scott Street, not far from here. We can go over and see it this afternoon, if you want to.'

'When do you close escrow?' He took a sip of the cappuccino as he listened.

'Tomorrow.'

'Are you kidding? When did you make the deal?'

'Thursday. They accepted my offer. I bought it as is. It needs a lot of work,' she said honestly.

'Jesus, Sarah. That's a headache you don't need. What do you know about fixing up a house?'

'Nothing. I'm going to learn, and I want to do a lot of it myself.'

He rolled his eyes. 'You're dreaming. What were you smoking when you decided to do this?'

'Nothing. I admit, it's a little crazy. But it's good crazy. This is my dream.'

'Since when? You didn't even start looking till last week.'

'It was my great-grandparents' house. My grandmother was born there.'

'That's no reason to buy it.' He thought he had never heard anything so stupid in his life, and he didn't know the whole story yet. She was getting there slowly. And he was more skeptical by the minute. 'How old is it?'

'My great-grandfather built it in 1923.'

'When was it last remodeled?' he asked, interrogating the witness.

'Never,' Sarah said with a sheepish grin. 'Everything's original. It's never been touched. I told you it needs a lot of work. I figure it might take me a year. I'm not going to move right away.'

'I hope not. It sounds like you bought yourself a giant headache. It's going to cost you a fortune.' She didn't tell him she had one now, thanks to Stanley Perlman. Phil never asked her about money, nor she him. It was something they each kept to themselves. 'How big is it?'

She smiled at Phil. That was the clincher. She almost laughed when she said it. 'Thirty thousand square feet.'

'Are you nuts?' He shoved the breakfast tray aside and jumped out of bed. 'Have you gone insane? Thirty *thousand* square feet? What was it? A hotel? It sounds like the fucking Fairmont, for chrissake.'

'It's even prettier,' she said proudly. 'I want you to come and see it.'

'Does your mother know you did this?' As though that mattered to either of them. He had never even mentioned her before. He disliked Audrey as much as she did him.

'Not yet. I'll tell them at Christmas dinner. I want to surprise my grandmother. She hasn't seen the house since she was seven.'

'I don't know what's gotten into you,' he said, glaring at her. 'You're behaving like a lunatic. You've been acting weird for weeks. You don't just go out and buy a house like that, unless you bought it as an investment, and you're going to sell it for a profit, after you redo it, but even that doesn't make sense. You don't have time to take on a project like that. You work as hard as I do. You're a lawyer, for chrissake, not a contractor or a decorator. What are you thinking?'

'I have more spare time than you do,' she said demurely. She was tired of his being insulting about it, and about her. She wasn't asking him to pay for it. He acted as though she was, which was hardly the case.

'Really? How do you figure you have more spare time? Last I heard, you were working fourteen-hour days.'

'I don't go to the gym. That gives me free evenings five days a week. And I can work on it on weekends.'

'And what am I supposed to do?' he asked, looking outraged. 'Twiddle my thumbs while you wash windows and sand floors?'

'You could help. You're never here in the daytime on weekends anyway, Phil. You always end up doing your own thing.'

'That's bullshit and you know it. I just can't believe you would do something this stupid. And you're going to live in a house that size?'

'It's gorgeous. Wait till you see it.' She was offended by everything he'd said, and hurt by the way he said it. If he had bothered to look, he'd have seen it in her eyes. He didn't. He was too busy putting her down. 'It even has a ballroom,' she said quietly.

'Great. You can rent it out to Arthur Murray, and maybe pay for the repairs. Sarah, I think you're nuts,' he said, and sat down on the bed again.

195

'Apparently. Thanks for being so supportive.'

'At this point in our lives, everything is about simplifying things. Going smaller. Having less. Being less involved. Who needs a headache like that? You have no idea what you're getting into.'

'Yes, I do. I spent four hours with the architect on Thursday night.'

'So that's where you were.' He sounded smug, and relieved. He had actually been worried about it for two days. It was why he had taken her out to dinner the night before. 'You've already hired an architect? You didn't waste any time, did you? And thanks for asking for my advice.'

'I'm glad I didn't, if this is what you would have said.'

'You must have money to burn. I had no idea your firm was doing that well.' She didn't comment on that. How she had gotten the money was none of his business. She had no intention of explaining it to him.

'Let me tell you something, Phil,' she said, with an edge in her voice. 'You may be "simplifying," as you put it, and "going small." I'm not. You've been married, you have kids, you've had a big house. You've had all that. I haven't. I haven't done any of it. I've been living in this crappy apartment since I passed the bar, with the same shit furniture I had when I left Harvard. I don't even have a goddamned plant. And maybe I want big, and beautiful, and something exciting to do. I'm not going to sit here for the rest of my life with a bunch of dead plants, waiting for you to show up on weekends.'

'What are you saying?' His voice got louder, and so did hers.

'I'm saying that this is exciting for me. I can't wait to do it. I love it. And if you can't get behind it, or be supportive of me, or even polite, for chrissake, then to hell with you. I'm not asking you to pay for it, or even help me. All you have to do is smile and nod and encourage me a little. Is that so fucking hard for you to do?' He didn't answer her for a long moment, and then got up and stormed into the bathroom and slammed the door. She had hated everything about his reaction, and she had no idea why he was doing that to her. Maybe he was jealous, or threatened, or hated change. Whatever it was, it wasn't nice, or even pretty to watch.

When he came out of the bathroom, with his hair wet, wrapped in a towel, she was wearing a sweatshirt and jeans. She looked at him sadly. There was nothing gracious or kind about anything he'd said. He'd been just plain mean.

'I'm sorry I wasn't happy for you about your house,' he said grimly. 'I just think it's a really bad idea. I'm worried for you.'

'Don't be. If it's too much for me to handle, I'll sell it. But I'd at least like to try. Do you want to see it?'

'Not really,' he said honestly, as she looked at him. It was all about control. He liked the status quo, and didn't want anything to change. Ever. He wanted her here in this apartment, which he was familiar with, at home on weekday nights, so he knew where she was. He wanted her sad, lonely, and bored, while she waited for him to show up two nights a week, just as she had said to him. She had never seen it as clearly. He didn't want her to have any excitement in her life, even if she paid for

197

it herself. That wasn't the point. He wanted his independence and freedom, but he couldn't deal with hers. 'I'll just get mad if I see it,' he said honestly. 'I've never heard such a stupid thing in my life. I'm playing tennis today anyway.' He glanced at his watch. 'I'm late, thanks to you.'

She didn't say a word. She went into the bathroom and closed the door. She sat down on the toilet and burst into tears. And when she came out twenty minutes later, he was gone. He had left her a note, saying he'd be back at six. 'Thanks for a great Saturday,' she said, as she read the note. Things were just getting worse. It was as though he wanted to see how far he could push her. But she wasn't ready to let go yet. She thought of what Jeff Parker had said, as she put the dishes in the sink but didn't wash them. And she didn't make the bed. She didn't care anymore. What was the point? He really was an asshole. Nothing he had said that morning showed any respect for her. Or even kindness. Saying he loved her meant nothing if this was how he behaved. She remembered Jeff asking her the other night what it would take for her to let go, and she had told him she wasn't sure. Whatever it was, Phil was getting close. He was crossing boundaries he never had before.

She drove to the house that afternoon, let herself in, and looked around. She started to wonder if Phil was right. If this was just too insane. It was the first sign of buyer's remorse she'd had, but as she walked through the master suite, she thought of the beautiful young woman who had lived there, and then run off to France and abandoned her husband and children. And the old man she had loved who had lived in the attic, and never had a life. She wanted to make this a happy house now. The house deserved it, and so did she.

She went back to her apartment just before six, and thought about what to say to Phil. She had thought all day about telling him it was over. She didn't want to, but she was beginning to feel she had no other choice. She deserved a lot better than he was giving. But when she got in, she saw that the apartment was clean, the dishes were done, she could smell food cooking, and there were two dozen roses in a vase on her ugly table. Phil walked out of the bedroom and looked at her.

'I thought you were playing tennis,' she said bleakly. She'd been depressed all day, over him, not the house.

'I canceled. I came back to apologize for being an asshole and raining on your parade, but you were gone. I called your cell phone, but it was turned off.' She had turned it off because she didn't want to talk to him. 'I'm sorry, Sarah. What you do about the house is none of my business. I just don't want you to get in over your head. But it's up to you.'

'Thank you,' she said sadly, and saw that he had made the bed, too. She'd never seen him do any of that before. And she had no idea now if what she was seeing was manipulation or real. But one thing was clear. He didn't want to lose her, either. He wasn't willing to do it right, and he wasn't willing to let go. He was no different than she was, except that she wanted a real relationship with him, one that actually moved forward and grew, and he didn't want that. He wanted it just as it was, frozen in time, and stagnant. It didn't work for her, but it was hard to say any of that to him with the effort he had just made.

'I started dinner,' he said, as he came to put his arms around her. 'I love you, Sarah.'

'I love you too, Phil,' she said, and turned her head away, so he wouldn't see her tears.

CHAPTER 12

Phil took Sarah to brunch the next day at Rose's Café on Steiner. They sat outside under the heaters in the winter sunshine. He read the paper and she said nothing. They ate in silence. They hadn't made love the night before. They had watched a movie on TV and gone to bed early. It had been an exhausting day, and she felt drained.

She didn't invite him to see the house again. She didn't want to hear what he had to say about it. It was too painful, and spoiled her fun. She didn't object this time when he said he had work to do after brunch. It depressed her even more to realize that she was relieved when he left. Their relationship was on its last legs, and she knew it, even if he didn't, or wouldn't admit it. There was very little good stuff left, just a lot of resentment and bad feelings, on both sides. That much was clear from the force of his tirade about the house the day before. It wasn't about the house, she realized, it was about them. He was tired of her pulling on him, begging for more, and she was tired of asking. It was a stalemate. And for some reason, her buying the house on Scott Street threatened him. Just as his distance and absences threatened her.

She called Jeff at noon, as she had promised she would. He was in his office, waiting for her call.

'I'll meet you at the house in half an hour,' she said quietly, and he could hear in her voice that the weekend hadn't gone well. She didn't sound like a woman who'd been comforted and loved. She sounded lonely and sad and out of sorts.

She was touched when he arrived at the house with a picnic basket. He had brought pâté, cheese, sourdough bread, fresh fruit, and a bottle of red wine.

'I thought we could have a picnic.' He smiled at her. He didn't ask how the weekend had been. He could see it. They went outside with the basket and sat on a stone wall in the garden. The flowers were long gone, there was nothing out there but weeds. But she looked better after lunch. And then he showed her his new ideas for the kitchen. His whole vision came to life as he described it.

'I love it,' she said, her eyes bright with excitement. She looked like a different person than the one who had arrived an hour before. She had felt dead all weekend. Now, looking at the house with Jeff, she felt alive again. She wasn't sure if it was him or the house, or the combination. But in any case, it was a lot better than the abuse she had taken from Phil the day before. It was becoming abusive. A power war no one would win.

They walked through the upper floors again, and he brushed against her, as they tried to figure out what to do with the closets in the dressing room. She said she didn't have that many clothes.

'Maybe you should buy some,' he teased her. Marie-Louise was using nearly all of their closets. She always came back with trunkloads of new things from Paris, and dozens of pairs of new shoes. They had nowhere to put them.

'I'm sorry I was such a downer when I got here,' she apologized, as they walked through what had been her grandmother's room as a child. 'I had a shit weekend.'

'I figured. Did he show up?'

'Yeah. He always does on weekends. He had a fit about the house. He thinks I'm nuts.'

'You are.' Jeff smiled at her gently. There was so much he liked about her. 'But nice nuts. There's nothing wrong with having a dream, Sarah. We all need that. It's not a sin.'

'No.' She smiled wistfully at him. He felt like her friend now, although she hardly knew him. But she felt as though she had known him for years, and so did he with her. 'But you have to admit, it's a pretty big dream.'

'There's nothing wrong with that. Big people have big dreams. Small people have none at all.' He already hated Phil from the look on her face. He could see she'd been hurt. Just from the little she'd said on Thursday night, he thought Phil was a jerk. She didn't like Marie-Louise, either. But she didn't say that to Jeff.

'It's not going well,' she admitted as they walked back downstairs.

They hadn't done as much work today, but they were both relaxing and getting to know the house. They had explored every nook and cranny. He liked being able to do that with her. Marie-Louise had called that morning, and he had said he was having lunch with a client, but he didn't say who. He had never done that before, and he wasn't sure why he had now. Except that Marie-Louise hadn't

202

liked Sarah either when they met. She had made unpleasant comments about her when they drove away, and again in Venice. She was too American for Marie-Louise's taste. And she had hated the house. Jeff wasn't going to ask her to work on it with him. It wouldn't be fair to Sarah to have an architect who disliked the house. Marie-Louise thought it was an impossible job, and thought the place should be torn down, which was a travesty to him.

'I could see it wasn't going well when you arrived,' Jeff said as they put the leftover food back in his basket. He had bought it at the flea market in Paris, and it was very old.

'I don't know why I stay with him. He was such a jerk about the house yesterday, that I was thinking about ending it last night. And then I got home, and he was cooking dinner, cleaned the house, gave me two dozen roses, and apologized. He's never done any of that before. It's hard to end it when he does things like that.'

'Maybe he sensed you were fed up. Some people have remarkable survival instincts in relationships. Maybe that was more about him than about you. He probably isn't ready to give you up, either. Sounds like a panic move to me.' She smiled at the male assessment.

'Damned if I know. I'd rather he had been nice about the house than buy me roses. He said a lot of really ugly stuff. I feel like such a wimp for staying in it.'

'You'll give it up when you're ready, if it's the right thing to do. You'll know,' he said wisely.

'What makes you so smart about these things?' she asked him, and he smiled.

203

'I'm older than you are, and I've been there before. But I'm no smarter or braver than you are. Marie-Louise called this morning.' He didn't tell Sarah about his lie about her, only about the rest. 'All she did was bitch about coming back, and tell me how much she hates it here. I get tired of hearing it, too. If she hates it so much here, maybe she should just stay there. She will one of these days anyway. I know it.' It was the second time he had said it and he sounded depressed. She was always threatening never to come back.

'Then why do you stay in it?' Sarah wanted to know. Maybe it would teach her something about herself.

'It's hard to give up fourteen years, and admit you might have been wrong. And I'm never sure if I am.'

'It's hard enough to give up four,' she admitted.

'Try adding ten onto that. It only gets worse, the longer you hang in.'

'I thought it was supposed to get better if you stuck it out.'

'That only works if it's the right person.'

'How the hell do you ever know, Jeff?'

'I don't know. My life would be a lot simpler if I did. I ask myself a lot of questions, too. Maybe it's never an easy fit between two people. That's what I tell myself.'

'So do I. I make a lot of excuses for his shit behavior.'

'Don't. At least see it for what it is.' She nodded, thinking about what he'd said, and she was looking out at the garden from the living room, when she felt Jeff standing close to her, and she turned to face him. He was taller than she was, and her face

204

was turned up to him as their eyes met and held. His lips found hers effortlessly, their arms were wrapped around each other, and the kiss seemed to last forever. She had forgotten what that could feel like, and so had he. This wasn't difficult. It was easy. But it was also new, and forbidden fruit. They were both committed to other people, however difficult it was with them.

'I think that was a mistake,' she said softly afterward. She felt guilty, but not very. She liked Jeff a lot. He was a hell of a lot nicer than Phil.

'I was afraid of that,' Jeff said in answer. 'But I'm not so sure it was a mistake. It didn't feel like one. What do you think?'

'I don't know.' She looked confused.

'Maybe we should try again just to be sure.' As he said it, he kissed her again, and this time she pressed her body against his. He felt powerful, and she felt safe and warm in his arms. 'Mistake or not?' he whispered, and this time she laughed.

'We're going to get ourselves in a hell of a mess with Phil and Marie-Louise,' she said, as he hugged her. It felt so damned good.

'Maybe it's all they deserve. It's not right to be hard on people the way they've been on us.' Jeff was tired of his problems, too.

'If that's true, then maybe we're supposed to have the guts to walk away from them,' she said sensibly. It would have been the honorable thing to do.

'Oh that,' Jeff said, smiling at her. It had turned into an exceptionally lovely afternoon, particularly in the last few minutes. 'I have. Many times. So has she. We always wind up in the same place, starting over again.'

'Why?'

'Habit. Fear. Laziness. Familiarity. Ease.'

'Love?' she asked honestly. She asked herself the same question about Phil. Did she love him or not? She was no longer sure.

'Maybe. After fourteen years, sometimes it's hard to know. I think it's mostly habit with us. And work, too. It would be a mess to try and divide up the business. It's not like we sell shoes. Most of our clients buy us as a team. And with work, we're good. I like working with her.'

'That's not a good reason to stay together,' Sarah commented. 'Privately anyway. Could you work together if you broke up?' She was checking it out, and so was he.

'Probably not. She'd go back to Paris anyway. Her brother is an architect, too. She always tells me she'll go to work with him. They have an important firm there.'

'Nice for her.'

'I'm not afraid to work on my own. I just don't like the mess of getting there.' Sarah nodded. She understood. But she also didn't want to be 'the other woman' in his life. That would be an even bigger mess than the ones they had now. 'Sometimes one has to let life unfold,' he said philosophically. 'It's all about the right thing at the right time. I think when it's right, you know. I've always had a tremendous attraction to the wrong thing,' he admitted, looking sheepish. 'I liked dangerous women when I was young. Or women who were hard to get along with. Marie-Louise is a bit of both.'

'I'm not,' Sarah added cautiously, and he smiled.

'I know. I love that about you. I must finally be

206

growing up.'

'And you're not mean.' She thought about it. 'Although you are unavailable. That's my specialty. You're living with another woman. I don't think this is a good idea for either of us right now. Dangerous for you. Unavailable for me. That's a no-no.' They both knew she was right, but it was very tempting, and the kisses had been sweet. But if it was right, it would wait.

'Let's see what happens,' Jeff said sensibly. They were going to be spending a lot of time together working on her house. It was going to be better for both of them if things developed over time.

'When is she coming back?' Sarah asked as they walked out the front door onto Scott Street.

'She says in a week. Probably more like two or three, or four.'

'Will she be back for Christmas?'

'I hadn't thought of that,' he said pensively as he walked her to her car. 'I'm not sure. Maybe not. You never know with her. One day she just turns up, when she runs out of excuses to stay there.'

'She sounds like Phil. If she doesn't come back by then, would you like to have Christmas with my family? It's just my grandmother, my mother, and me, and probably my grandmother's boyfriend. They're very cute together.'

He laughed. 'I could probably do that even if she's back. She hates holidays and refuses to celebrate them. I like Christmas a lot.'

'Me too. But I'd rather not do that if she's back. I'd feel rude not inviting her, and I don't want to. If that's okay with you.'

He kissed her gently on the lips as she got into her car. 'Anything you do is okay with me, Sarah.'

There was so much he liked about her. She was a woman of substance, principle, integrity, and brains, with an enormous heart. There was no better combination in his book. She had it all.

She thanked him for the lunch he'd brought, and drove away with a wave. And as she drove back to her apartment, she wondered what to do about Phil. She didn't want any decision she made to be about Jeff. It wasn't about Jeff. It was about Phil. And Jeff had Marie-Louise. She wasn't going to let herself forget that. She wasn't going to do the unavailable thing again, even in a different format this time. Jeff was a truly lovely man. But unavailable was off-limits for her. She wasn't going to allow herself to do that again. Whatever she did this time, it had to be right. Phil wasn't, from all she could see. And she didn't know yet if Jeff was.

CHAPTER 13

Just as they always did, Phil and Sarah celebrated Christmas with each other the night before he left for Aspen with his kids. He always left on the first Saturday of their school vacation, and stayed until just after the New Year. It left her alone for the holidays, which was hard for her, but it was the same old story. He wanted to spend the time alone with his kids. And Sarah had to fend for herself for Christmas and New Year's, which was hard. She knew she would hear a lot about it from her mother, as she always did. This was in fact the fifth Christmas she had spent without him, as their relationship had just entered its fifth year.

He took her to Gary Danko for dinner on their last night together. The food was exquisite, the wines he chose were expensive and superb. Afterward they went back to her place, exchanged gifts, and made love. He gave her a new espresso machine, because hers was getting tired, and a pretty silver bracelet from Tiffany, which she loved. It was a simple bangle that she could wear to the office, or anytime. It wasn't showy. She gave him a new briefcase he needed desperately and a great-looking blue cashmere sweater from Armani. And as always, when he left in the morning, she hated to see him go. He lingered more than usual. It was going to be two weeks before she saw him again. Two very significant weeks over the holidays. Holidays that she would once again spend alone.

'Good-bye . . . I love you . . .' she said again as he kissed her one last time before he left. She was going to miss him terribly, as she always did, and she didn't argue with him about going this time. There was no point. The only thing different about the holidays this year was that she was going to be busy with her house.

Sarah had been spending a lot of time there on weekends, sanding, cleaning, measuring, making lists. She had bought herself an impressive-looking tool kit, and was going to try and build a bookcase herself, in her bedroom. Jeff had said he'd show her how.

Marie-Louise had finally come back to the city the week before. She sounded more French than ever, whenever Sarah talked to her, but she was not involved in the project. She had come back to handle her own, as most of her clients were clamoring for her return. Sarah talked to Jeff now almost every day. They had agreed, before Marie-Louise got back, not to pursue a romance with each other, but to keep their dealings and friendship entirely centered on her house. If anything else developed later, if their current relationships failed, that would be a bonus, but Sarah had made it clear to him that it was too uncomfortable for her to harbor romantic feelings for him, while he was living with and totally enmeshed with Marie-Louise, whether he was happy with her or not. Jeff agreed.

They had lunch with each other the day after Phil left. It was a Sunday, and Marie-Louise was stuck at her desk, trying to catch up. Sarah was touched and startled when, after omelettes at Rose's Café, Jeff slipped a little package toward her across the table. She unwrapped it carefully, and her breath caught when she saw the beautiful little antique pin he had given her. It was a small gold house with tiny diamonds in the windows, and was the perfect gift. He had been both generous and thoughtful.

'It's not as big as your house,' he said sheepishly, 'but I thought it was pretty.'

'I love it!' she said, looking touched. She could wear it on the jackets of all the suits she wore to the office, to remind her of him and her house. She was learning so much from him, about how to restore her house. He also gave her a book, explaining about carpentry and house repairs, which would be very useful. He had given her the perfect gifts, carefully chosen.

She in turn had given him a set of beautiful old leatherbound books on architecture, which were

210

first editions. She had found them in a musty old bookstore downtown. They had cost her a fortune, and he loved them. They were a handsome addition to the library he added to whenever possible, and cherished.

'What are you doing over the holidays?' he asked her over coffee at the end of the meal. He was looking tired and more than a little stressed. He had a lot of projects to finish, and now that Marie-Louise was back, his life was busier and less peaceful. She always occupied his space like a tornado. Over the years, he had found most of the things they said about redheads to be true. She was fiery, dynamic, and had a fearsome temper. But she was passionate as well, about everything, both good and bad.

'I'll be working on my house,' Sarah said easily. She was looking forward to it. With Phil gone, she could work through the weekends, and even late into the nights. She was hoping it would help the holidays speed by. 'I'm having Christmas Eve dinner with my grandmother and mom, and whoever they invite. The rest of the time, I'll work on the house. Our office is closed between Christmas and New Year's.'

'So is mine. Maybe I'll come over and help you. Marie-Louise hates holidays so much, she's always particularly irritable at this time of year. She not only hates celebrating them herself, she takes it personally when anyone else does, especially me.' He laughed as he said it, and Sarah smiled. Nothing was ever easy, for anyone, no matter how it looked from the outside. 'She's thinking of going skiing over New Year's. I don't ski, so I'll probably stay here and get some work done. I used to go

211

with her, and sit around the lodge bored all day, and she was too tired to go anywhere at night. She almost made the Olympics as a kid, so she's a hotshot skier. She tried to teach me a long time ago, but I'm hopeless. It's one sport I'm really not good at and don't like. I hate the cold.' He smiled. 'And falling on my ass, which I did a lot of, while she laughed at me. Now she goes up to Squaw alone. We both prefer it.'

'Come over anytime you want,' Sarah said warmly. She knew that their time together at the house would be more circumspect now. He had never kissed her again since the day of their picnic there. They had both agreed that that wasn't a good idea, and would just get them into trouble, and someone would get hurt. Sarah didn't want it to be her, nor did he. He had conceded that she was right, although it was hard not to reach out and take her in his arms when they were alone together. For her sake, as much as his own, he resisted the impulse now. Instead they worked together for hours, side by side, without ever touching. Admittedly, sometimes it was hard. But he respected her judgment and her wishes. And he had no real desire to complicate his situation with Marie-Louise.

'What do you two do on Christmas Day, since she doesn't celebrate holidays?' Sarah was always curious what their life was like. They seemed so different from each other.

Jeff smiled before he answered. 'Usually, we fight. I bitch about how her attitude screws up the holidays for me. She tells me I'm insincere, crass, and commercial, that I'm a victim of institutions that sold me a bill of goods when I was a child, and too weak and stupid to know better now and resist it. You know, ordinary stuff like that.' Sarah laughed. 'She had a Dickensian childhood, mostly spent with relatives who hated her or abused her and each other. She doesn't have much respect for family ties, tradition, or religious-based events. She still spends a lot of time with her family, but they all hate each other.'

'How sad for her.'

'Yes, I suppose so. She covers up the sadness with rage. It works for her.' He smiled as he said it. He accepted her as she was, although it didn't make her easy to live with.

They walked slowly down Union Street together, to where they had left their cars. The stores were decorated for the holidays, and there were lights twinkling on the trees, even in the daylight. It all looked very festive.

'I'll call you when our offices are closed,' he promised. 'I'll come over and help whenever you want.'

'Marie-Louise won't mind?' Sarah asked cautiously. She was afraid to step on the woman's toes. From all Sarah knew of her, she thought she was a viper. But still, she respected Jeff's bond to her, as he did, despite his grousing about her at times.

'She won't even notice,' he assured her. And he wasn't planning to tell her, although he didn't say that to Sarah. He knew how honorable she was. He felt that how he dealt with Marie-Louise was up to him. He knew her better, and what their boundaries were. And like Sarah, he was determined now not to let his attraction to her get out of hand. They had agreed to just be friends.

213

They thanked each other for the gifts, and Sarah went back to her apartment. A little while later, she went back to the house on Scott Street, with her new book from Jeff under her arm. She stayed there working until long after midnight that night. And on Christmas Eve, she wore the pretty gold pin he had given her, of a house. Her mother commented on it almost the moment Sarah sat down. She had forgotten Phil's silver bracelet on her dresser. She hadn't heard from him then in three days. He was always that way in Aspen. He was having too much fun to call.

'I like that,' her mother commented about the pin. 'Where'd you get it?'

'A present from a friend,' Sarah told her cryptically. She was planning to tell them about the house that night. She could hardly wait.

'Phil?' Her mother looked surprised. 'I didn't think he had taste like that.'

'He doesn't,' Sarah said, and turned to speak to George, her grandmother's boyfriend. He had just bought a house in Palm Springs and was excited about it. He had invited them all to come down and visit. Mimi had already been to see the house and loved it. He was teaching her to play golf.

Christmas Eve dinner was easy and warm. Audrey made roast beef and Yorkshire pudding, which she was masterful at. Mimi had done the vegetables and baked two pies, which got rave reviews. Sarah had brought wine, which everyone complimented her on. And George had given Mimi a beautiful little sapphire bracelet that made her eyes light up when she showed it off, and everyone oohed and aahed, which pleased George no end.

Sarah waited until the excitement had died down, after they finished eating. Audrey was serving coffee, as Sarah looked around the table.

'You look like the cat that swallowed the canary,' her mother said, praying that she wasn't about to announce her engagement to Phil. If so, Audrey assumed that he would at least have shown up for that. And there was no ring on her finger, thank God. So Audrey felt reassured it wasn't that.

'Not exactly a canary,' Sarah said, unable to conceal her excitement. 'I finally took Mom's advice,' she said to the assembled company, as Audrey rolled her eyes and sat down.

'That would be a first,' Audrey interrupted, and Sarah smiled benevolently at her. All was forgiven.

'Actually, I did, Mom. I bought a house.' She breathed the words like a woman announcing she was having a baby, excited, ecstatic, and proud.

'You did?' Audrey looked delighted. 'When did you do that? You didn't tell me!'

'I am now. I bought it a few weeks ago. It's all been very unexpected and unplanned. I started looking for condos, and a rare opportunity landed in my lap. It's kind of a dream come true, a dream I didn't even know I had until it happened and I fell in love with it.'

'How wonderful, sweetheart!' Mimi was quick to share her excitement, as was George, who was thrilled with his own new house. As always, Audrey looked slightly more suspicious.

'It's not in some awful neighborhood, is it? And you're going to change the world by moving there?' She knew her daughter was capable of it. Sarah shook her head.

'No, I think you'll approve. It's only a few blocks

from where I am now, in Pacific Heights. It's extremely respectable, and totally safe.'

'So what's the catch? I hear one coming.' Audrey was relentless. Sarah wished she would find a boyfriend who would distract her. But if so, they'd have to sedate her, to keep her mouth shut. She scared them all away, or dumped them. Her edges were too sharp, especially for Sarah, who was often cut to the quick by the razor blades on her mother's tongue.

'No catch, Mom. It needs work. A lot of it, but I'm excited about doing it, and I got it at a great price.'

'Oh God, it's a dump. I know it.'

Sarah shook her head and persisted. 'No, it's gorgeous. It'll take me six months or a year to get it in shape, and then you'll be bowled over by it.' She looked at her grandmother as she said it. Mimi was nodding, entirely willing to believe her. She always was, unlike Audrey, who challenged her at every turn.

'Who's going to help you?' Audrey asked practically.

'I hired an architect, and I'm going to do a lot of the work myself.'

'I guess it's safe to assume we won't be seeing Phil wielding a hammer on weekends. Your law firm must be doing well if you're hiring an architect.' Audrey pursed her lips, and Sarah nodded. The bequest from Stanley was none of their business, either. 'When do you take possession?'

'I already own it,' Sarah said with a proud smile.

'That was fast,' Audrey said suspiciously.

'Very,' Sarah admitted. 'It was love at first sight,

once I decided. I've known the house for a long time, and it just came on the market. I never thought I'd own it, or anything like it.'

'How big is it?' Audrey asked matter-of-factly, and Sarah laughed out loud at the question.

'Thirty thousand square feet,' she said proudly, as though she had said 'one' or 'two.' The assembled company stared at her in disbelief.

'Are you joking?' Audrey asked, wide-eyed.

'No, I'm not. That's why I got it for such a great price. No one wants a house that size anymore.' And then she turned to her grandmother and spoke softly. 'Mimi, you know the house. You were born there. It's your parents' house at Twenty-forty Scott Street. That's a big part of why I bought it. It means a lot to me, and I hope it will to you, too, when you see it.'

'Oh, my dear . . .' Mimi said, as tears sprang to her eyes. She didn't even know if she wanted to see the house again. In fact, she was almost sure she didn't. She had such poignant memories there, of her father before depression crushed his spirit, and the last times she saw her mother before she disappeared. 'Are you sure? . . . I mean . . . it's such a big house for you to manage on your own. No one lives that way anymore . . . My parents had nearly thirty employees there, or maybe more.' She looked worried, and almost frightened, as though a ghost from her past had reached out and touched her. The ghost of her mother. Lilli.

'Well, I won't have thirty employees, I can promise you that,' Sarah said, still smiling, despite her mother's scowling at her, and her grandmother's look of panic. Even George looked a little stunned. His new house in Palm Springs was

217

five thousand square feet, which he was afraid might be too much for him. Thirty thousand defied the imagination. 'I might have a cleaning person come in once a week. The rest of the staff is me. But it's so beautiful, and when I'm finished restoring it to what it once was, or as close as I can get to it, I think you'll all love it. I already do.'

Audrey was shaking her head, as though she was convinced now, indisputably, that her daughter was crazy. 'Who's owned it for all these years?' she asked, vaguely curious.

'My late client, Stanley Perlman,' Sarah said simply.

'Did he leave it to you?' her mother asked bluntly. She would have asked if Sarah had been sleeping with him, except she remembered Sarah telling her he was about a hundred years old.

'No, he didn't.' The rest was between her and Stanley and nineteen other heirs. 'The heirs put it on the market at a remarkably low price, and I bought it. It cost me less than a small house in Pacific Heights would have, and I love it a whole lot more. Besides, it means a lot to me to have it back in our family, and I hope it does to you, too,' she said to both her grandmother and her mother. Both women remained silent. 'I was hoping you'd both come and see it tomorrow. It would mean a lot to me.' For a long moment, neither answered, as disappointment fluttered over Sarah's heart like a moth.

As always, her mother spoke first. 'I can't believe you bought a house that size. Do you have any idea what it's going to take to restore it and bring it up to code, let alone decorate and furnish it?' Her words never failed to sound like

218

accusations to her daughter's ears.

'I do. Even if it takes years, it's important to me. And if it's too much for me at any point, I can sell it.'

'And lose your shirt in the process,' Audrey said with a sigh, as Sarah's grandmother reached over and took her grandchild's hand in hers. She still had lovely, delicate hands, even at her age, and beautiful, long thin fingers.

'I think you did a wonderful thing, Sarah. I think we're all just a little surprised. I'd like very much to see it. I never thought I'd see that house again. I never thought I wanted to, but now that it's yours, I do . . .' It was exactly the right thing to say. Mimi always came through, unlike Audrey.

'Could we go tomorrow, Mimi?' It would be Christmas Day. Sarah felt as she had as a child, showing her grandmother some project she had made, or a new puppy. She wanted Mimi to be proud of her, and her mother. It had always been harder to win praise from her mother.

'We'll go first thing in the morning,' Mimi said firmly, struggling to overcome her own emotions and fears. It was not an easy thing for her to go back there, but for Sarah, she would have braved every demon in hell, even her own private hell and painful memories. And George said he would go with her. That left Audrey.

'Fine. But don't expect me to tell you that you did the right thing. I don't think you did.'

'I wouldn't expect anything less of you, Mom.' Sarah looked pleased. She left a little while later, and drove home. She drove past Scott Street and smiled at the house. She had put a wreath on the door the day before. She couldn't wait to move in.

Phil called her at midnight, to wish her a merry Christmas. He said his children were having a great time, and so was he. He told Sarah he missed her, and she said the same to him, and felt sad after they hung up. She couldn't help wondering if she would ever have a man to spend holidays with. Maybe one day. Maybe even Phil.

The next morning she thought about calling Jeff to wish him a merry Christmas, but she was afraid Marie-Louise would answer. In the end, she didn't call. She went straight to the house on Scott Street, puttered around, and waited for her family to show up at eleven, as promised. They arrived only a few minutes late. Her mother had picked Mimi and George up, and pretended not to know they had spent the night together. They were inseparable these days. George definitely had the inside track now over Mimi's other suitors, Sarah teased her and said it was the golf lessons. Audrey said it was the house in Palm Springs. Whatever it was, it seemed to be working, and Sarah was happy for them. At least one woman in the family had a decent relationship. And it might as well be Mimi, she was so cute, and deserved to spend the remainder of her life happily. Sarah thought George was perfect for her.

Mimi was the first to come through the front door, looking around as though afraid to see ghosts. She walked slowly into the main hallway, with the others behind her, and went straight to the bottom of the grand staircase and looked up, as though she still saw familiar people there. As she turned to Sarah, there were tears rolling slowly down her cheeks.

'It looks exactly the way I remember it,' she said

220

softly. 'I always remember my mother coming down those stairs in beautiful evening gowns, with all her jewels and furs, and my father waiting at the bottom of the staircase in his tailcoat and top hat, smiling as he looked up at her. She was so wonderful to look at.' Sarah could easily imagine it, just from the single photograph she'd seen of her. There was something magical about Lilli, almost mesmerizing. She looked like a movie star or a fairy princess, or a young queen. Seeing her grandmother in the house now brought it all to life for Sarah in ways that nothing else ever could.

They wandered around the main floor for nearly an hour, as Sarah explained her plans for the house, and the location and design of the new kitchen. Audrey was very quiet as she examined the paneling and moldings and boiseries. She commented on the exquisite parquet floors that had come from Europe. And George was in awe of the chandeliers. Who wouldn't be?

'My father brought them over from Austria for my mother,' Mimi explained as they stood beneath them. They still couldn't be lit, but Jeff had already had someone come in to make sure they were firmly attached and wouldn't fall on anyone. So it was safe now to stand underneath them. 'My governess told me about them once,' Mimi said thoughtfully. 'I think two of them are Russian, the others are from Vienna, and the one in my mother's bedroom was from Paris. My father pillaged châteaux all over Europe when he built the place.' It was easy to see. The results were exquisite.

They spent another half hour on the second floor, looking at the sitting rooms, and standing in the ballroom, with its gilt and mirrors, paneling and inlaid floors. It was a work of art in itself. And then they went upstairs. Mimi went straight to her bedroom and her brother's. She felt as though she had last seen them yesterday. She couldn't even speak, standing there, as George put a gentle arm around her shoulders. Standing in these rooms again was a deeply emotional journey for her. Sarah almost felt guilty putting her through it, but at the same time, she hoped it might heal old wounds.

Mimi explained to them all about her mother's bedroom and dressing rooms, the furniture that had been there, the pink satin curtains and priceless Aubusson carpet. It had fetched a fortune at auction even in 1930, she had read later. She told them about her mother's gowns in the various closets, the outfits she had worn, the breathtaking hats that had been made for her in Paris. It was a legend like no other, and a history lesson listening to her. Audrey had been remarkably quiet the entire time they were there. In all her sixty-one years, she had never heard her mother speak to that extent, or any, about her childhood, and was amazed to realize how much she remembered. She had always thought that she was able to recall nothing. All she had known herself growing up as a child was that her mother's family had lost everything in the Crash of '29, that her father had died shortly after, and had left nothing. Audrey knew nothing about the people who had populated her mother's life as a child, the details of the disappearance of her maternal grandmother, or even of the existence of this house. Mimi had never spoken of any of it, and now the memories and stories tumbled out, like jewels from deep coffers, unlocked and spilling everywhere at last. It was a rich history they shared.

They examined the attic and basement for good measure, though there wasn't much to see there. Mimi remembered the elevator and how much she loved riding in it with her father, and the favorite downstairs maid she had sneaked up to see in the attic, whenever she could escape her governess.

It was nearly two o'clock by the time they finished their tour. Mimi looked exhausted, and even the others looked drained. It had been more than just a house tour, or a history lesson, it had been a trip into the past to visit people long forgotten, and revisited now because Sarah had pursued her dream, and included them.

'Well, what do you think?' Sarah asked, as they stood in the front hall, about to leave.

'Thank you,' Mimi said, and hugged her. 'God bless you,' she said, as tears sprang to her eyes again. 'I hope you will be happy here, Sarah. They were, for a time. I hope you always will. You deserve to be. You're doing a wonderful thing bringing this place back to life. I'd like to do whatever I can to help you,' she said, and meant it. George reached over and hugged Sarah, too.

'Thank you, Mimi,' Sarah said, hugging her back, and then she looked at her mother, her eyes full of the trepidation she always felt when she looked for her mother's approval. It was not easy to achieve, and had never been.

Audrey nodded, and seemed to hesitate, and then spoke with an audible frog in her throat and a misty expression. 'I was going to tell you that you were crazy. I thought you were . . . but now I

223

understand. You're right. This is important, for all of us . . . and it's a beautiful old house . . . I'll help you decorate it, if you like, when you're ready.' She smiled lovingly at her daughter. 'It's going to take a hell of a lot of fabric to do this place . . . the curtains alone are going to break the bank . . . I'd like to help . . . I have some ideas for all those sitting rooms, too. You know, you could rent it out for weddings, once it's finished. It might give you a nice little income. People are always looking for elegant locations for weddings. This would be perfect, and you could charge a fortune.'

'That's a great idea, Mom,' Sarah said, with tears in her own eyes. Her mother had never offered to help her before, just told her what to do. In an odd way, the house was bringing them all closer. It hadn't been her original intention, but it was an unexpected bonus she was enjoying, too. 'I never thought of it.' Sarah thought it was actually a good idea.

The three women stood smiling at each other before they left the house, as though they shared a very special secret. The descendants of Lilli de Beaumont had come home at last, under the roof Alexandre had built for her. It had been a house filled with love once, and in Sarah's hands all three of them knew it would be again.

CHAPTER 14

Sarah spent every waking moment of her Christmas break from the office working on the house. Audrey got into the habit of dropping by.

She had gone to the library to research the history of the house, and found some interesting bits and pieces she shared with Sarah, and she had some surprisingly good suggestions about construction and future decoration. For the first time in years, Sarah was enjoying her mother's company. Mimi dropped by several times, too. She brought Sarah sandwiches to keep her fed while she hammered, sanded, and sawed. The bookcase she was building was taking shape, and she was oiling the paneling and boiseries diligently. They were beginning to almost glow.

Jeff spent several evenings there with her when Marie-Louise went skiing. They were working hard one night in separate rooms. He didn't charge her for the time he spent there, only his designs and drawings and liaison to contractors during that time. He said it relaxed him working on the house. He came to check on her progress, trying a new wax on one of the paneled rooms. She looked exhausted, her hands were a mess, her hair was piled high on her head, and she wore overalls and workboots. She stopped working for a few minutes, as he handed her a beer.

'I feel like my arms are going to fall off,' she said, as she sat down on the floor to take a break, and he looked down at her with a grin. They had shared a pizza earlier.

'Do you know what day this is?' he asked, setting down a small sander as he sipped the beer he had opened for himself.

'I have no idea.' She lost all sense of time when she was working. They had set up temporary lights, which shone on the areas they worked on. The rest of the room was bathed in shadows. It had a gentle feeling, but wasn't spooky. She never felt ill at ease here, even late at night, when she worked alone. But it was nice having him there.

He had just checked the date on his watch, and smiled when he saw it. 'It's New Year's Eve.'

'It is?' She looked amazed. 'That means I have to go back to the office in two days. It's been great having every day free to work here. I'm going to hate going back to just being here on weekends. Maybe I can do some things here at night after work.' The faster she worked, and the more days she spent doing it, the faster they would be finished.

She couldn't wait to move in. She hoped it was far enough along to do that by spring. And then she remembered what he'd said. 'What time is it?'

'Eleven fifty-three. Seven minutes to the New Year.' She held up her beer in his direction, as she sat on the floor and he stood near her, and toasted him. It was a nice way for her to see in the new year, and for him, too. Easy and comfortable, with a good friend, which was what they had become. 'I hope it's a good one for both of us.'

'Me too. Next year at this time, I'll be living here, and I can give a New Year's Eve party in my ballroom.' It didn't seem a likely scenario to her, but it was fun to imagine.

'I hope you invite me,' he said, smiling at her, teasing her a little, and she gave it right back to him.

'Yeah, sure. You and Marie-Louise. I'll send you an invitation.'

'Please do,' he said with a gracious bow. Marie-Louise was skiing in Squaw Valley. She didn't care about New Year's Eve, and neither did he. Phil was still in Aspen with his children. He had called her the day before, but didn't mention New Year's Eve, nor did she. He was due back in the coming week, when the kids had to be back at school. 'Eleven fifty-eight,' Jeff announced, checking his watch again, as Sarah stood up with her beer. She set down the bottle in her tool chest, and wiped her hands on her overalls. She was filthy from head to toe, and even had streaks of dust and wax on her face. She caught a glimpse of herself in a mirror set into a panel and laughed.

'Nice outfit for New Year's Eve, huh?' He laughed too, and she was happy they were there together. It might have been too quiet otherwise. She was far less lonely working here than she had ever been in her apartment.

'Eleven fifty-nine.' He kept his eyes on his watch this time and took a step toward her. She didn't move away or step back. 'Happy New Year, Sarah,' he said softly. She nodded, as though giving him permission. Just this once. For New Year's Eve.

'Happy New Year, Jeff,' she said softly as he put his arms around her and kissed her. They hadn't done that for a while, and had meant not to. They stayed in each other's arms for a long time, and then slowly came apart, and stood there looking at each other. 'Thanks for being here.'

'I wouldn't want to be anywhere else.' Slowly, they went back to the projects they'd been doing, without commenting on the kiss or whether it should have happened. They left together at three o'clock in the morning.

When she got home, there was a message from Phil on her machine. He had called at midnight, her time, to wish her a happy New Year. He hadn't called on her cell phone. She had had it on at the house, just in case. He called her back in the morning and woke her at eight o'clock.

'Where were you last night?' he asked with interest. He was calling from his cell phone, riding up on the chair lift, and the connection was poor. He kept breaking up.

'Working at the house. I came home at three, and found your message. Thanks for calling.' She stretched and yawned.

'You and that crazy house. I miss you,' he said, and then momentarily broke up, and then came back on the line.

'Me too.' She did. But she had kissed Jeff last night at midnight, and it had been nice.

'I'll see you when I get back,' he said, and then they lost the connection as he reached the top of the mountain. Sarah got up then, and was back at the house by ten.

Jeff joined her there at noon. He didn't tell her that he had had a fight on the phone with Marie-Louise that morning. She hadn't called him at midnight the night before, but she had wanted to know where he'd been. He told her the truth, and said it was innocent. She didn't believe in his innocence, regarding his devotion to Sarah and her house. He reminded Marie-Louise that he had nothing better to do than work on the house on New Year's Eve. She had told him to go fuck himself, and hung up. She was due back that night. He spent the rest of the day with Sarah, and left her at six. Neither of them made any reference to their midnight kiss of the night before, but it was on her mind. She had sternly reminded herself again that morning not to be pulled in by his

228

unavailability. But he was so sexy and attractive. She loved his brain, his heart, his looks. And maybe the fact that he lived with someone else. Sarah was always hard on herself.

In spite of her concerns about him, they had a good time that day working on the house together, as always. The sections of paneling she had waxed look gorgeous. She was determined to do it throughout the house.

'I guess I won't have nails again for another year.' She laughed as she looked at her hands. 'I'm going to have to think of an excuse for clients. They're going to think I moonlight digging ditches with my bare hands.' She could never get her hands clean now, but she didn't mind. It was worth it.

She stayed that night till nine, and then went home to collapse in front of the TV. The holidays had been perfect this year. Or almost. They would have been nicer with Phil, or maybe not. They had been nice with Jeff, working on the house. It had been lucky for both of them that Marie-Louise was out of town, too.

Sarah went back to work the next morning, and Phil got back into town the day after. He called her as soon as he got to his apartment, but didn't offer to stop by and see her. And she didn't ask. She knew better. He would just tell her that he was too busy, had a mountain of work waiting on his desk, and had to go to the gym. She was tired of being disappointed. It was simpler to wait until the weekend. He said he'd see her on Friday, and no matter how many times he did this to her, it was still an odd feeling to know that he was back in town, in his apartment only a few blocks away, and she couldn't see him. It gnawed at her for days.

She was trying to get to the house every night now to work on the paneling she was waxing, and on Thursday night, she did some work on the bookcase she was building. She made a mess of it a few times, and had to pull the nails out and start again. It was frustrating and she felt awkward, and finally she decided to give it up around eleven. She was driving home, when she realized she was within a block of Phil's apartment. She was seeing him the next day, but suddenly it seemed like a fun idea to drop by his place and give him a kiss on her way home, or slip into his bed, and wait for him to come home from the gym. She didn't do that sort of thing often, but once in a while she had. And she had his keys with her. He had finally given them to her the year before, a year after she had given him hers. He was always slower to reciprocate. And he knew she didn't abuse the privilege. Except for something like this, to surprise him, she would never have gone there when he wasn't there. She had a strong respect for his privacy, as he did hers. They rarely dropped in on each other and always called first. It just seemed nicer and more respectful. Their mutual respect was one of the reasons why the relationship had lasted for four years.

She parked down the street from his apartment, still wearing her workboots and overalls. The overalls were covered with the wax she used on the panels, and her hair was piled on top of her head to keep it out of her way when she worked.

As she walked toward the building, she could see that the lights were out in his apartment. And she suddenly loved the idea of slipping into his bed and waiting for him. She giggled to herself as she used his keys to get through the outer door, and then into his apartment on the second floor. The apartment was dark when she walked in. She didn't bother to turn on the lights, because she didn't want to tip him off that she was there, if he was just walking down the street himself, on his way home from the gym, and happened to look up at his windows.

She walked straight down the hall in the dark to his bedroom, opened the door, and walked in. In the dim light, she could see that the bed was unmade and quickly started to take off her overalls and T-shirt. As she took her shirt off, she suddenly heard a moaning sound and jumped about a foot. It sounded like someone was injured, and she turned in the direction of the sound in terror. Suddenly from under the comforter, two human forms sat up, and a male voice said 'Shit!' He snapped on the light, and saw Sarah in her bra and underpants and workboots, and she saw him in all his hunky nakedness with an equally naked blonde woman beside him. Sarah stared at them in blind confusion just long enough to register that the girl looked about eighteen years old, and she was gorgeous.

'Oh my God,' she said, staring at him, holding her discarded T-shirt and overalls in her trembling hands. For a moment she thought she would faint.

'What the *fuck* are *you* doing here?' he asked with a startled look and vicious tone of voice. Afterward she realized it could have been worse, although not much. He could have been plunging into the spectacular blonde when she walked in, instead of whatever they were doing concealed under the covers. Fortunately, it had been a cold

231

night, and his apartment was always freezing, so they had stayed under the duvet.

'I came to surprise you,' Sarah said in a trembling voice, choking back tears of grief, rage, and humiliation.

'You sure as hell did,' he said, running a hand through his hair as he sat up. The girl lay flat on the bed after turning on the light, not sure what to do. She knew Phil wasn't married. And he hadn't said he had a girlfriend. The woman standing at the foot of the bed in her underwear looked a mess. 'What do you think this is?' He didn't know what else to say, and the nubile blonde said nothing, staring at the ceiling, waiting for it all to go away.

'It looks like cheating to me,' Sarah said, staring him right in the eye. 'I guess that's what all the weekends-only bullshit was about all along. What a fucking crock of shit,' she said, not sure herself if she was referring to his dating policy with her, or to him. She pulled on her T-shirt with shaking hands, and managed to get it on inside out. She wanted to run out the door but didn't want to walk back into the street in her bra and underpants. Then she climbed back into the overalls and only bothered to hook one side. They were drooping badly.

'Look, go home. I'll call you. This isn't what it looks like.' He glanced from Sarah to the blonde and back. But he couldn't get out of bed, for obvious reasons. He was naked, and probably still had a hard-on.

'Are you joking?' Sarah asked, shaking from head to foot. 'This *isn't* what it looks like? How dumb do you think I am? Was she in Aspen with you? Have you been pulling this shit for four years?'

'No . . . I . . . look . . . Sarah . . .'

The girl sat up in bed then and looked at Phil with a blank expression. 'Do you want me to go?'

Sarah answered for him. 'Don't bother.' And with that, she hurried down the hall, slammed out the front door, threw his keys on the floor as she left, and ran down the stairs, out of the building, and back to her car. She was shaking so hard she could hardly drive. She had wasted four years of her life. But at least she knew now. No more manipulation and lies. No more disappointment. No more agonizing self-examinations about why she put up with his bullshit. It was finally over. She told herself she was glad, but tears were pouring down her cheeks as she walked into her apartment. It had been a hell of a shock. The phone was ringing as she unlocked the door. She didn't answer. There was nothing left to say. She heard him leave a message on her answering machine. She knew the voice. The voice of conciliation. She walked over to her machine and erased it without listening to him. She didn't want to hear it.

She lay in bed awake for hours that night, replaying the ugly scene in her head, that fucking unbelievable moment when he had sat up in bed and she realized there was a woman with him. It was like watching the collapse of a building imploding on itself, or a bomb going off. Their very own twin towers. The whole fantasy world she had shared with him for four years, however inadequate it was, had come falling down around them. And there was no putting it back together. She didn't want to. And even in her shaken state, she knew it was a mercy. She probably would have

233

accepted weekends-only for many more years.

The phone continued to ring all night, and finally she unplugged it, and turned off her cell phone. It was gratifying to know he cared that much. He just didn't want to look bad. Or maybe the weekends had been comfortable after all, and he didn't want to lose her. She no longer cared. Cheating was one thing she wasn't going to put up with. She had put up with far too much already. But this was finally, and irreversibly, the last straw.

She tried to tell herself in the morning that she felt better. In truth, she knew she didn't. But she felt certain she would eventually. He had finally given her no choice whatsoever. She dressed for work, and got to her office on time. Her mother called her ten minutes after nine and sounded worried.

'Are you all right?'

'I'm fine, Mom.' The woman had goddam radar.

'I tried to call you last night. The phone company said your phone was out of order.'

'I was working on a brief, so I unplugged it. Honestly, I'm fine.'

'Good. I was just checking. I have a dentist appointment. I'll call you later.'

After she hung up, Sarah called Phil's apartment, knowing he would have left for work by then, and left a message. She asked him to messenger her keys back. 'Don't drop them off, don't bring them. Don't mail them. Messenger them. Thank you.' It was all she said. He called her six times that day at her office. She didn't take the calls, and then finally, on the seventh call, she did. She told herself she didn't need to hide from him. She had done nothing wrong. He had.

All she said was hello when her secretary put the call through. He sounded panicked, which surprised her. He was such a cocky son of a bitch, she figured he'd try to bullshit his way through it, but he didn't. 'Look, Sarah . . . I'm sorry . . . it's the first time in four years . . . these things happen . . . I don't know . . . maybe it was the last gasp of my freedom . . . we need to talk . . . maybe we should see each other a couple of times during the week . . . maybe you're right . . . I'll come over tonight and we'll talk about it . . . Babe, I'm sorry . . . you know I love you . . .' She finally cut in.

'Do you?' she said coldly. 'Funny way to show it. Love by proxy. I suppose she was standing in for me.'

'Come on, babe . . . please . . . I'm human . . . so are you . . . it could happen to you one day . . . I'd forgive you . . .'

'No, it couldn't happen to me, actually. Because I'm incredibly stupid. I believed the garbage you told me. I let you leave me at home for weekends and holidays with your kids. I've spent every goddamned Christmas and New Year's alone for four years, while you tell me how busy you are during the week and that you're going to the gym, when you're really fucking someone else. The difference between us, Phil, is that I'm honest, I have integrity. You don't. That's what it boils down to. It's over. I'm not going to see you again. Send me back my keys.'

'Don't be stupid, Sarah.' He started to sound testy. It didn't take him long to get there. 'We have four years invested in this.'

'You should have thought of that last night before you got into bed with her, not after,' Sarah said coldly. She was shaking again, and she had feelings for him, but there was no turning back. She didn't want to. Now, finally, at long long last, she wanted out.

'Is it *my* goddamned fault that you barged into my apartment and walked in on me? You should have called.'

'*You* shouldn't have been fucking another woman, whether I "barged" in or not. I'm glad I did. I should have done it a lot sooner. I could have saved myself a lot of grief and four wasted years. Good-bye, Phil.'

'You'll regret this,' he warned her. 'You're thirty-eight years old, and you'll wind up alone. For chrissake, Sarah, don't be stupid.' He was almost threatening her, but she wouldn't have taken him back now if he was the last man on the planet.

'I was alone when I was with you, Phil,' Sarah said quietly. 'Now I'll only be by myself. Thanks for everything,' she said, and without hearing what he had to say in answer, she hung up. He didn't call her back. He tried a few more times that night, after she plugged her phone in again, and this time she had unplugged her message machine, she didn't want to hear his voice ever again. It really was over. She shed a few tears over him that night, and tried to get the awful scene of the night before out of her head. Her keys came back to her by messenger the next morning. He sent them to the apartment. It was Saturday morning. He had included a note saying that he was there for her, anytime she wanted to call him, and he hoped she would. She threw the note away after glancing at it, and packed up the things he had left there. There weren't many, toiletries, some jeans, underwear, shirts, a pair of Nikes, flip-flops, and loafers. A leather jacket he left there for weekends. She realized as she packed his things that he had been more fantasy in her life than real. He was the embodiment of hope, and the culmination of her own neurosis, her terror of being alone, and abandoned by a man, as she had been by her father. So she put up with the crumbs he gave her, and never demanded more. She asked for it, but was willing to tolerate it when he gave her less than she deserved. And on top of it, he was cheating on her. He had done her a huge favor the night he went to bed with the young blonde. She was actually surprised to discover that she didn't feel as bad as she had feared she would after the breakup. By late that afternoon, she was at the house, hammering away on the bookcase. She thought the hammering would do her good, and it did. She didn't even hear the doorbell ring at first, and when she did finally, she was afraid that it was Phil. She peered downstairs cautiously, from a second-floor window, and saw that it was Jeff. She ran down the grand staircase to the front door to let him in.

'Hi,' he said easily. 'I saw your car in the driveway and thought I'd stop in for a minute.' He noticed that she looked distracted and observed her more closely. 'Are you okay?'

'I'm fine,' she reassured him, but didn't look it. Something was off, but he couldn't quite put his finger on what it was. He could see it in her eyes.

'Tough week at the office?'

'Yeah. More or less.' He followed her back upstairs and checked her work on the bookcase. It was surprisingly good for an amateur. She was diligent in her work. Her eyes met his then, and he smiled at her.

'What's up, Sarah? You don't have to tell me if you don't want to, but something's wrong.' She nodded, but didn't cry.

'I broke up with Phil two days ago. Long overdue.' She set down the hammer for a minute and brushed her hair out of her eyes.

'What happened? Big fight when he got back from Aspen?'

'Not really,' she said quietly. 'I walked in on him with another woman. That was a novel experience. Something new and different.' She said it in a monotone, and considering that, Jeff thought she looked pretty good.

'Wow!' he whistled. 'That must have been unpleasant.'

'It was. I looked like an idiot. She looked like a whore. And he looked like a total asshole. Maybe he's been doing that all along. I threw his keys on the floor and walked out. I sent back his stuff this morning. He's been calling like crazy.'

'You really think it's over, or do you think you'll take him back?' Marie-Louise had cheated on him years before, and he had relented when she came back and begged him to forgive her. Afterward he was sorry he had. She had done it again. But never after. That time he had put his foot down. They'd been through a lot in fourteen years.

'No, I won't take him back,' Sarah said sadly. She was sadder about the fool she'd been for so long than about losing him. 'I'm finished. I should have been a long time ago. He's a jerk. And a liar and a cheat. All those nice things.'

'He won't let you go that easily,' Jeff predicted.

'Maybe not. But I have. I could never forgive him. It was a disgusting scene. I was about to climb into his bed to surprise him, when I discovered someone else already had. I've never felt so stupid in my life, or been so shocked. I thought I'd have a heart attack when I left. Anyway, it's over, and here I am, back at work on the house. Brave new world. I can hardly wait to move in,' she said, changing the subject, and he nodded. He got the drift. He was curious to see if she would stay away from Phil. She sounded very firm about it now. But it had only been two days since the unhappy event. It sounded awful to him, as it had been.

'When do you think you'll be able to move in?'

'I don't know. What do you think?' The electrical work was starting the following week, the plumbing the week after. There would be crews all over the house for months. They weren't starting on the kitchen till February or March, when the other work was done or at least well under way.

'Maybe April,' he said thoughtfully. 'It depends how steadily they stay on it. If they stick with it, you may be able to camp out here in March, if you can stand the dust and the noise.'

'I'd love it.' She smiled at him. 'I'm dying to get out of my apartment.' She had outgrown it, especially now that Phil was gone. She wanted to move on. Desperately. It was time.

Jeff hung around for a while and kept her company while she worked. He didn't have time to work on the house himself today, he had things to do. But he felt badly leaving her there alone, particularly after what had just happened. Finally, two hours later, he told her he'd try to come back the next day, and left her hammering on the

239

bookcase. She stayed there till nearly midnight, and then went home to her empty apartment. Her message machine was still off, and so was her cell phone. There was no one she wanted to hear from, no reason to take calls. And as she slipped into her unmade bed that night, she thought of Phil and the woman she'd caught him making love to. She wondered if he was with her, or someone else. She wondered, too, how many women he had cheated on her with, over the years, while he told her he couldn't see her during the week, and only on weekends. It was depressing to realize what a fool she'd been. There was nothing she could do about it now, except make sure he stayed gone forever. She never wanted to lay eyes on him again.

CHAPTER 15

By the end of January, Sarah was feeling better. She was busy at the office, and working at the house every weekend. Jeff was right. Phil hadn't given up easily. He had called her many times, written to her, sent her roses, and even dropped by unannounced at the house on Scott Street. She had seen him from an upstairs window, and hadn't let him in. She responded to none of his calls or messages, didn't thank him for the roses, and threw away his letters. She had meant what she said. There was nothing to discuss. She was finished. She assumed now that he had probably cheated on her for years. The way he had arranged their lives, he had had every opportunity. And now she knew she couldn't trust him. That was enough for her. She was done. It took him nearly a month to stop calling. And when he did, she knew he had moved on. He had admitted to her once that he had cheated on his wife at the end, but he had blamed it on her, and said that she had driven him to it. Maybe now, Sarah thought, he was blaming it on her.

Stanley's estate was nearly settled. They had already disbursed a considerable amount of the assets to the heirs. She had received her bequest as well, from the liquid portion of his estate. She was doling it out carefully to the contractors Jeff was hiring for her. One of them had put a lien on her house, which he insisted was standard procedure, and she had forced him to remove it. So far the restoration was within her budget, and Jeff was supervising all the subcontractors for her. She was doing a huge amount of work herself, and loving every minute of it. It was incredibly gratifying doing manual work, after all her more cerebral stresses in the office. And she was surprised to find she didn't miss Phil as much as she had feared. Working at the house on weekends helped a lot.

Sarah was pleased to hear from Tom Harrison the last week of January. He said he was coming to San Francisco on business the following week, and invited her to dinner. She offered to show him her progress on the house, and he said he'd be delighted. She made a date to pick him up at his hotel the night he arrived.

The day he came it was pouring rain, which was typical weather at that time of year. But he said it was better than snow in St. Louis. She took him to the house on Scott Street, on the way to dinner, and he was vastly impressed by what she'd accomplished in a short time. She was no longer as aware of her progress herself, since she was there almost every day.

'I'm amazed at what you've done here, Sarah,' he said with a broad smile. 'To be honest, I thought you were crazy to buy it. But now I can see why you did. It's going to be a beautiful place when you're finished.' Although enormous, certainly, for her. But she couldn't resist salvaging a piece of history, her own particularly, and a gem like this.

'It was built by my great-grandfather,' she explained to him, and told him the story of Lilli over dinner. She had taken him to a new restaurant that had delicious French and Asian food. They had a lovely time, which didn't surprise her. She had liked him from the first moment they met. He was in town for two days of meetings, and then she remembered her earlier idea. 'Are you free for lunch tomorrow?' she asked cautiously. She didn't want him to think that she was putting the make on him, and he smiled when she asked.

'I could be. What did you have in mind?' Everything about him was wholesome, intelligent, and kind. He treated her like a daughter, not a woman he was pursuing, which was comfortable for Sarah.

'I know this probably sounds silly. But I'd like you to meet my mother. I mentioned it when we met, but it wasn't the right time. She's a pain in the neck as a mother, but she's actually a nice woman. I just had the feeling that you might like her, and she might like you.'

'My, my,' he said, laughing at her, but he didn't seem offended. 'You sound just like one of my daughters. She keeps fixing me up with the

242

mothers of all her friends. I have to admit, there have been some real lulus, but I guess at my age, you have to be a good sport about it when you find yourself alone.'

She knew he was sixty-three years old, and her mother was sixty-one, and still a good-looking woman. Sarah was happy to hear that he was dating the mothers and not the daughters. Most men his age were more interested in the daughters, or worse yet, girls who were young enough to be their granddaughters. At times, even at thirty-eight she felt over the hill. And there were fewer and fewer takers for women her mother's age. She knew a lot of Audrey's friends had tried computer dating services, sometimes with good results. But otherwise the men in Audrey's age group, for the most part, were dating women Sarah's age. She thought Tom Harrison would be perfect, as long as Audrey didn't get pushy or aggressive and scare him away.

They made a date for lunch the next day at the Ritz-Carlton, and she called her mother as soon as she got home.

'Sarah, I can't.' Audrey sounded embarrassed. She had been amazingly nice to Sarah for the past month, ever since she'd come to see the house on Christmas. It had somehow given them a common interest and a new bond. 'I don't even know the man. He's probably interested in dating you, and he's just being polite.'

'No, he isn't,' Sarah insisted. 'I swear, he's normal. He's just a nice, decent, attractive, intelligent, well-dressed widower from the Midwest. People are probably a lot more respectable there than they are here. He treats me

243

like a kid.'

'You are a kid.' Her mother laughed at her, sounding uncharacteristically girlish. If nothing else, she was flattered. She hadn't had a date in months. And the last blind date she'd had had been a total dud. He was seventy-five years old, had false teeth that kept slipping, he was deaf as a stone, rabidly right wing, refused to leave a tip at dinner, and hated everything she believed in. She wanted to kill the friend who had set her up and had been upset that Audrey didn't think he was 'sweet.' He wasn't sweet. He was a curmudgeon. And there was no reason to think Tom Harrison would be any better, except that Sarah insisted that he was. Finally, Audrey relented when Sarah reminded her that it was not espionage, open-heart surgery, or marriage, it was only lunch. 'All right, all right, what'll I wear? Serious or sexy?'

'Conservative, but not depressing. Don't wear your black suit.' Sarah didn't want to tell her it made her look too old. 'Wear something happy that makes you feel good.'

'Leopard? I have a terrific new leopard-print suede jacket. I saw it in a magazine with gold shoes.'

'*No!*' Sarah nearly screamed at her. 'You'll look like a hooker . . . sorry, Mom.' Sarah backed off as she could hear her mother stiffen.

'I have *never* looked like a hooker in my *life!*'

'I know you haven't. I'm sorry,' Sarah said more gently. 'That just sounded a little racy for a banker from St. Louis.'

'He may be from St. Louis, but I'm not,' Audrey said haughtily, and then relaxed a little. 'Don't worry about it. I'll figure it out.'

'I know you'll look gorgeous, and you'll knock his socks off.'

'Hardly,' her mother said demurely.

Sarah was more nervous than either of them when she met them both in the lobby of the Ritz-Carlton at noon. She was late, they had both been on time, and were already chatting happily by the time Sarah got there. Tom had figured out who Audrey was. And Sarah was proud of her when she saw her. She looked just right. She was wearing a red wool dress that set off her figure, without looking vulgar. It had a high neck and long sleeves, and she was wearing high heels and pearls, her hair done in a neat French twist. She was wearing a beautifully cut black wool coat over it that she had had for years, but looked well on her. And he was wearing a dark blue pin-striped suit, white shirt, and a good-looking blue tie. They looked wonderful together, Sarah thought, and the conversation flowed like water. She could hardly get a word in edgewise, as they talked about their children, travels, late spouses, interest in gardens, the symphony, ballet, movies, and museums. They seemed to agree on nearly everything. Sarah almost wanted to clap her hands in glee, as she sat quietly eating a club sandwich, and they made their way through soup and crab salad. He talked about how much he liked San Francisco, while Audrey said she had never been to St. Louis, but had always loved Chicago. They talked about so much for so long that Sarah finally had to leave them to go back to the office. She was already late for a meeting, and they were still talking a mile a minute when she left. Bingo! she said to herself, beaming proudly as she left the hotel. Success!

She called her mother late that afternoon when she got out of the meeting, and Audrey confirmed that Sarah was right, he was a lovely man.

'A little geographically undesirable maybe,' Sarah confessed. St. Louis was not exactly around the corner, or easy for a dating situation. But they had each made a new friend. 'He has a special needs daughter, by the way, Mom. I think she's blind and brain damaged, and she lives with him.' She had forgotten to mention it to her before lunch, but thought she should at least now.

'I know. Debbie,' her mother said, as though she knew everything about him, and he was her friend, not Sarah's. 'We talked about her after you left. Such a tragedy for him. She was premature and got damaged at the delivery. Something like that would never happen today. He said he has wonderful people taking care of her. It must be very hard for him now that he's alone.' Sarah was utterly amazed.

'I'm glad you liked him, Mom,' Sarah said, feeling as though she had won the lottery herself. They had been cute to watch over lunch.

'He's a very handsome man, and so nice,' Audrey went on about him.

'I'm sure you'll hear from him the next time he comes to town. He looked like he was enjoying you, too.' Audrey could be charming when she wanted to be, especially with men. It was only with her daughter that she was so unrelenting at times and could be so tough. Sarah still remembered how good she had been to her father, no matter how drunk he was. And she was absolutely certain that Tom Harrison was not a drunk.

'We're having dinner tonight,' Audrey

246

confessed.

'You are?' Sarah sounded stunned.

'He had other plans with his business associates, but he canceled them. It's a shame he's leaving tomorrow,' she said, sounding wistful.

'It sounds like he'll be back.'

'Maybe so,' Audrey said, sounding unconvinced, but she was enjoying it for now. And so was her daughter. It was perfect. She wished she could do as well matchmaking for herself. But she didn't want to date right now anyway. She wanted some time off after Phil, he had just been too disappointing and too hurtful. And she was busy with her house. For now at least, Sarah didn't want a man. And Audrey hadn't had a real one in a long time.

'Have fun tonight. You looked beautiful at lunch.'

'Thank you, sweetheart,' Audrey said, sounding softer than she had in a long time. 'Mimi can't have all the fun!' she said, and they both laughed. Her grandmother was very busy these days with George, and all her other suitors seemed to have been discarded. She had explained to Sarah after Christmas that she and George were 'going steady.' Sarah had almost asked her if she'd been 'pinned' or had his high school ring. It was nice to see them happy. There was a sweet innocence about them.

Sarah didn't hear from her mother until several days after her dinner date. By then, Tom had left town. He had left Sarah a message thanking her for the introduction to her very charming mother, and he promised to get in touch again when he came back to San Francisco. Sarah had no idea when that might be, and when she stopped by her mother's house on Saturday to drop off Audrey's dry cleaning, which she had promised to pick up for her, she noticed a vase full of long-stemmed red roses.

'Let me guess,' Sarah said, looking puzzled. 'Mmm . . . who could those be from?'

'An admirer,' Audrey said, looking girlish again as she took her dry cleaning from Sarah. 'All right, all right. They're from Tom.'

'Very impressive, Mom.' She could see at a glance that there were two dozen of them. 'Have you heard from him since he left?'

'We're e-mailing,' Audrey said demurely.

'You are?' Sarah looked amazed again. 'I didn't even know you had a computer.'

'I bought a laptop the day after he left,' she admitted, and then blushed. 'It's fun.'

'Maybe I should open a dating service,' Sarah commented, amazed at all that had happened in just a few days.

'You could use your services yourself.' Sarah had told her that she and Phil had broken up. She hadn't explained it, she just said that they had run out of gas, and for once Audrey just let it go at that.

'I'm too busy right now with the house,' Sarah said. She was wearing overalls again and on her way there.

'Don't use that as an excuse, the way you do your work.'

'I'm not,' she said, looking stubborn.

'Tom said he would love to introduce you to his son. He's a year older than you are, and recently divorced.'

'I know, and he lives in St. Louis. That's not going to do me much good, Mom.' Or maybe Audrey, either, but it had boosted her spirits and her self-esteem to meet Tom.

'What about the architect you hired to work on the house? Is he single, and decent-looking?'

'He's fine, and so is the woman he's lived with for fourteen years. They own the business together, and a house in Potrero Hill.'

'I guess that won't work. Well, someone will turn up when you least expect it.'

'Yeah, like the Hillside Strangler or Charles Manson. I can hardly wait,' Sarah said cynically. She was feeling bitter about men these days. Phil had left a bad taste in her mouth, after his final escapade.

'Don't be so negative,' her mother scolded her. 'You sound depressed.'

'No'—Sarah shook her head—'just tired. I had a lot of work at the office this week.'

'When don't you?' her mother said, walking her to the door, and then they both heard the bell on her laptop ring and say 'You've got mail!' Sarah raised an eyebrow and smiled at her mother.

'Cupid calls!'

They kissed each other, and Sarah left. She was glad her mother's introduction to Tom had gone so well. Nothing much could come of it, with him in St. Louis, but it was nice for both of them. She had a feeling he was lonely, and Audrey was as well. Everybody needed roses from time to time. And e-mail from a friend.

CHAPTER 16

By the end of February, Sarah had copper pipes throughout the house, and parts of the house had new wiring as well. They were doing it floor by floor. In March they started laying the groundwork for the kitchen. It was exciting watching things come in. She had picked her appliances from books in Jeff's office, he was buying them for her wholesale. The house wasn't ready for her to move in yet, but it was going well. They told her the rest of the electrical work would be complete by April.

'Why don't you go on a vacation?' Jeff suggested one night when they were laying down templates in the kitchen, to make sure all her appliances would fit. She was putting in a big butcher-block island in the center, and he was afraid it would be too crowded, but Sarah insisted it would work. As it turned out, she was right.

'Are you trying to get rid of me?' She laughed at him. 'Am I driving you crazy?' No, he told her, but Marie-Louise was. She was on one of her tangents, hating everything about the States, including him. She was threatening to go back to France. It was that time of year, when she was missing spring in Paris. She didn't leave for her three-month summer there till June. He was counting the days, although he hated to admit it. But she was hard to live with at times.

'There isn't much you can do right now till we finish the electrical and the kitchen. I think if you go away for a few weeks, you might be able to move in when you get back. That would be exciting for you,' he said, suggesting the vacation again. He loved helping her with the house. It reminded him of when he had done his own in Potrero Hill. Hers was on a far grander scale, of course, but the same principles prevailed, although every old house had quirks of its own.

'I can't stay away from the office for that long,' Sarah complained.

'Give us two weeks then. If you go away in mid-April, I promise you can move in on May first.' She jumped up and down like a kid when he said it, and that night she thought about it with some seriousness.

She was of two minds about it. She never liked leaving her office. She had nowhere to go. And no one to go with. She hated traveling alone. All of her friends had children and husbands. She called a friend from college in Boston, but she was just getting divorced and couldn't leave her devastated kids. Sarah consoled herself by reminding herself that she couldn't have gone with Phil, either. He had never taken a trip with her in four years, only with his kids. She even asked one of the other female attorneys in the office, who said she couldn't get away at the moment. In desperation, Sarah asked her mother, who said she had just planned a trip to New York with a friend, to go to the theater and museums, so she couldn't go. Sarah thought of giving up the idea, and then decided to go alone. After that, the big decision to make was where. She always got sick in Mexico, and didn't think she should go there solo. She liked Hawaii, but two weeks there was too long. She enjoyed New York, but alone it was no fun. She still hadn't decided, when she was looking at her photograph of Lilli that weekend, and suddenly she knew exactly where she wanted to go. To France, to track her down. She remembered Mimi saying she had gone to see Lilli's French château once, where she had lived with the marquis she left her husband for. Mimi had said it was boarded up, but Sarah thought it would be interesting to see it, and get a sense of where Lilli had lived during her years in France. She had lived there, after all, for fifteen years before she died, a relatively long time.

Sarah went to talk to Mimi about it on Sunday, and found out where it was, apparently in Dordogne, relatively near Bordeaux. It sounded like a nice trip to Sarah. She had always wanted to see that area, and the châteaux of the Loire, if she had time. She loved Paris, and by Monday, Sarah had decided to take a two-week vacation in France. She was going to leave the day after Easter, and she told Jeff she was going to hold him to his promise that she could move into the house on May 1. It was six weeks away, and Jeff said he thought there was a good chance that they'd be ready. Sarah had already decided that she would have the house painted after she moved in. She was going to try and lay the carpet herself with Jeff's help, in the few small rooms where she was going to use it, like dressing rooms and an office, a small guest room, and one bath with a chipped floor. And wherever possible, she was going to do some of the painting herself. If not, it would cost a fortune and impact her budget. Besides, she thought painting some of the rooms would be fun, and learning to lay carpet gave her the illusion that she was saving money. Actually she had done well on the budget so far.

She told her mother and grandmother about the trip to France, Mimi wrote down all the information she had about her mother and the exact location and name of the château. She didn't know much more. Her own trip to find out had been disappointing, but Sarah didn't care. It sounded interesting to her, even more so if she could find someone who had known Lilli, although it was now more than sixty years ago.

For the next month, she caught up with everything she had to do in the office, and started packing her apartment, so she'd be ready to move when she got back. Most of what she owned she was planning to either throw in the garbage or give to Goodwill. All she really had to take with her were her books and clothes. The rest was awful. Looking at it, she wondered why she had hung on to it for so long.

Sarah spent Easter with her mother and Mimi. They had a nice Easter brunch at the Fairmont, and the following day Audrey left for New York. She was excited about it. Mimi was planning to spend a few days in Palm Springs with George, and work on her golf game, and Sarah was off to Paris. She had dinner with Jeff the night before she left.

'Thank you for suggesting the trip,' she said as they sat across the table from each other in an Indian restaurant. He had ordered his curry hot, and Sarah had ordered hers mild, but both were good. 'I'm really excited about it. I'm going to check out the château where my great-grandmother lived.'

'Where is it?' he asked with interest. He knew the story from her, but not the details. He was as intrigued by it as she was. It gave life to the house, and spirit, and soul. Lilli had been an adventuresome and somewhat outrageous young woman for her day. Particularly when one thought that she had been twenty-four years old when she left. She had been born the night of the '06 earthquake, on a ferry going to Oakland to escape the fire in the city. It had been an auspicious beginning to a very interesting and somewhat turbulent life. Her arrival in the world had been provoked by an earthquake and the end of her life punctuated by a war. It also intrigued Sarah to realize that she had been Sarah's age when she died. A brief but fiery life. She had died at thirty-nine, without having seen her two children in fifteen years. Her husband, the marquis, had died the same year, in the Resistance.

'The château is in Dordogne,' she explained to Jeff, as his eyes watered from the curry. He liked to say he loved his women and his curry spicy, though lately more so the curry. Marie-Louise had been getting spicier and sharper-tongued by the hour, but he was hanging in.

'Your ancestors are a lot more interesting than mine,' he commented as they chatted through dinner.

'I'm fascinated by her,' Sarah admitted. 'It's a wonder my grandmother turned out as normal as she did, with a mother who walked out on her, a father who was depressed forever after, all the money they lost in the stock market crash, and a brother who was killed in the war. She's remarkably sane and happy in spite of all that.' Jeff had never met her, but he had heard a lot about her and could see that Sarah adored her. He hoped he would meet her one day. 'She left on a trip to

Palm Springs with her boyfriend yesterday. Her life is a lot racier than mine is.' She laughed at herself. She hadn't dated anyone since Phil, but she was really excited about her trip, and Jeff was happy for her. He thought it was a great idea to follow Lilli's tracks, and would have liked to do it with her himself. 'How's it going with Marie-Louise, by the way?' Just as she used to talk to him about Phil before they broke up, he often talked about Marie-Louise to her. They had become fast friends in their months of working together closely on her house. And as always, she was wearing his antique house pin on her lapel, she almost always did now. It was the symbol of her liberation, and her passion for the house. And she loved it all the more because Jeff had given it to her.

'Things are okay, I guess,' he answered her question. 'Her point of view is a little more Gallic than mine. She says that a life without arguments would be like an egg without salt. I'm about ready for a salt-free diet one of these days. But I think she'd feel unloved if we weren't arguing all the time.' There was no question that he loved her, but living with her was a challenge. She was constantly threatening to walk out anytime he disagreed with her. It was stressful for Jeff. Sometimes he thought she enjoyed it. For her, it was a way of life. Her family was like that. Sometimes it seemed, when he visited them with her, that they woke up every morning and slammed all the doors for the hell of it. It was the same with her aunts, uncles, and cousins. They never spoke in normal voices. They constantly shouted at each other. 'I guess it's just dysfunctional, not French, but I can't say I enjoy it.' He couldn't even imagine living that way for the rest of his life, but he had for fourteen years. Sarah couldn't imagine living that way, either, but as long as he was still doing it, it obviously worked for him.

'I think it's like you and Phil,' he said as they finished dinner. He felt as though he was steaming from the curry he'd eaten, but he loved it. 'After a while, you just get used to it, and you forget there's anything different. It's amazing what we adapt to sometimes. Have you heard from him, by the way?'

'Not in a couple of months. He finally gave up.' She had been true to her word and never spoken to him again. And now she no longer missed him. She missed having someone sometimes, but not him. 'He probably has a new girlfriend, and cheats on her, too. That's who he is, I realize now.' She shrugged a shoulder, and they went back to talking about her trip. She was leaving the next morning. It was a long flight to Paris.

'Don't forget to send me a postcard,' he told her when he dropped her off at her apartment and she thanked him for dinner. He didn't kiss her good night. Now that she was free and he wasn't, she didn't want to play those games with him. She knew she'd get hurt. And he respected her wishes. He cared about her too much to want to hurt her, and he was deeply involved with Marie-Louise, for better or worse. Worse at the moment, but that could change any minute. He never knew who he'd wake up to in the morning, Bambi or Godzilla. Sometimes he wondered if she was bipolar.

'Call me if anything happens at the house that I need to know about, or about any decisions I should make.' He had her itinerary, as did her office, and her grandmother. She was planning to rent a French cell phone at the airport, and promised to call him with the number. And she was taking her computer with her for e-mail, in case her office needed to communicate with her.

'Don't worry, just forget about it. Enjoy your vacation. And I'll help you move in when you get back.' She beamed when he said it. She could hardly wait. But she had a fun trip ahead of her first. 'I'll e-mail you and keep you posted on our progress.' She knew he would. He was good about communicating what was happening at the house. So far there had been no bad surprises, only good ones.

It was as though the project had been meant to be since the beginning. The restoration had been a dream. It was as though both Lilli and Stanley had wanted her to have the house, although perhaps each of them for different reasons. But it already felt like home to her. Moving in would be the icing on the cake. She had already decided to use Lilli's bedroom, and had ordered a brand-new king-size bed, with a pale pink silk headboard. They were going to deliver it as soon as she got back.

'Bon voyage!' he called as she ran up the steps to her apartment, and turned back to wave. She disappeared into the building then, as he drove away, thinking of her. He hoped she'd have a good trip.

CHAPTER 17

The plane landed at Charles de Gaulle airport at eight A.M. Paris time. It took her an hour to get her bags and go through customs. At ten A.M. she was driving down the Champs Élysées in a cab, with a broad smile as she looked around. She had slept well on the plane on the eleven-hour flight. It felt like it took forever, but now finally she was here. She felt like a heroine in a movie, as they drove through the Place de la Concorde with its fountains and across the Pont Alexandre III toward the Invalides, where Napoleon was buried. She was staying at a small hotel on the Left Bank on the Boulevard St. Germain, in the heart of the Latin Quarter. Jeff had given her the name of the hotel, based on a recommendation Marie-Louise had made, and it was perfect.

Sarah left her bags in her room, and walked all over Paris. She stopped for a *café filtre* in a café, and ate dinner alone in a bistro. She went to the Louvre, and rode on a Bateau Mouche the next day, like a proper tourist. She visited Nôtre Dame and Sacré Coeur, admired the Opéra. She had been to Paris before, but somehow this time it was more exciting. She had never felt as liberated, or as free of burdens. She was just happy being there for three days before she left for Dordogne on a train. The concierge at her hotel in Paris had given her the name of somewhere to stay. He said it was simple, clean, and very small, which suited her perfectly. She hadn't come here to show off. And she was amazed at how comfortable she was alone. She felt totally safe, and despite her limited French, people seemed ready and able to help her all along the way.

When she got off the train, she took a cab to her hotel. It was an old Renault that bumped along the roads, and the countryside was beautiful. This was horse country, and she saw a number of stables as they drove out into the country. She also saw several châteaux, most of them in tattered shape. She wondered if Lilli's would be as well, or if it had been restored in the meantime. She was excited to see it. She had carefully written down the name, and showed it to the clerk at the desk of her hotel. He nodded and said something unintelligible to her in French, then showed her on a map and spoke in halting English. He asked if she wanted someone to drive her there, and she said she did. It was late in the afternoon by then, and he promised to have a car and driver for her in the morning.

She ate at the hotel that night. She had foie gras from nearby Périgord, which was delicious. They prepared it with cooked apples on the side, and salad and cheese afterward. Once back in her room, she sank into the feather bed, and slept like a baby until morning. She awoke with the sunlight streaming through the windows. She hadn't bothered to close the heavy shutters. She preferred the sunlight. She had her own bathroom, with an enormous bathtub, and after she took a bath and dressed, she went downstairs to a breakfast of *café au lait* served in bowls, and croissants made that morning. The only thing missing was a companion with whom to share it. There was no one to talk to about how delicious the food was, or how beautiful the countryside, as the driver that the hotel clerk had promised drove her to the Château de Mailliard, where her great-grandmother had lived during her days here.

It was a half-hour drive from the hotel, and they saw a beautiful church before they reached the château. It had once belonged to the château but no longer did, the young driver explained in broken English. And then slowly they drove along a narrow road, and she saw it. It looked enormous. There were turrets, and a courtyard, and a number of outbuildings. It dated back to the sixteenth century, and was very beautiful, although currently under reconstruction. There was heavy scaffolding around the main building, and workmen working industriously, just as they were on Scott Street.

'New howner,' the young driver said, pointing. 'Fix hup!' She nodded. A new owner had apparently just bought it. 'Rich man! Wine! Very good!' They smiled at each other. The new owner had made his fortune in wine.

Sarah got out and looked around, curious about the outbuildings and the property. There were orchards and vineyards, a huge stable, but no sign of horses. It must have been beautiful in Lilli's day, Sarah suspected. Lilli had a knack for winding up in amazing houses, Sarah thought with a smile, and finding men who spoiled her. She wondered as she looked at the château if Lilli had been happy here, if she missed her children, or Alexandre, or her home in San Francisco. This was so different and so far from home for her. And although she had none herself, Sarah couldn't imagine leaving one's children. Her heart went out to Mimi, as the thought crossed her mind.

None of the workers paid any attention to Sarah, and she wandered for nearly an hour, exploring the property. She was curious to look into the château itself, but she didn't dare, so she stood outside and looked up at it. There was a man standing at a window, looking down at her, and she wondered if they were going to ask her to leave. He appeared on the front steps a few minutes later

260

and walked toward her with a quizzical look on his face. He was a tall man with silver hair, wearing a sweater, jeans, and workboots. But he didn't look like the other workmen. There was an air of authority about him, and as he approached, she saw that he was wearing a heavy, expensive gold watch on his wrist.

'*Puis-je vous aider, mademoiselle?*' he asked politely. He had been watching her for a while. She looked harmless, but he wondered if she was a reporter. Tourists rarely turned up here. Because of him, the press sometimes did.

'I'm sorry.' She put her hands out with a shy smile. '*Je ne parle pas français.*' It was all she knew, to tell him she didn't speak French. 'American,' she said, and he nodded.

'May I help you, mademoiselle?' he asked again, this time in English. He was curious about who she was. 'Are you looking for someone?' His English was accented but flawless.

'No.' She shook her head. 'I just wanted to see the château. It's beautiful. My great-grandmother lived here, a long time ago.'

'Was she French?' He looked intrigued. He was a very striking man in his early fifties. He looked rugged, handsome, and smart. He was examining Sarah in intricate detail.

'No. She was American, married to a marquis. The Marquis de Mailliard. Her name was Lilli.' She said it as though offering him credentials, and he smiled at her, as though to offer her safe passage.

'My great-grandmother lived here, too,' he said, still smiling at her. 'And my grandmother, and my mother. They worked here. My grandmother

261

probably worked for yours.'

'She was my great-grandmother actually,' Sarah reminded him, and he nodded. 'I'm sorry to intrude. I just wanted to see where she lived.'

'Not many people come here,' he said, studying Sarah. She looked like a young girl, in her jeans and running shoes with a sweater over her shoulders, and her long hair in a braid. 'The château has been boarded up for sixty years,' he told her. 'I bought it last year. It was in terrible condition. It's been untouched since the war. We're doing an enormous amount of work. I just moved in.'

Sarah nodded and smiled. 'I just bought her house in San Francisco. It's an enormous house, though not as big as this. It's been uninhabited since 1930, except for a few rooms in the attic. Her husband, my great-grandfather, sold it when she left, after the Crash of 1929. I'm restoring it, and I'm moving in when I go home.'

'Your great-grandmother must have liked big houses, mademoiselle, and the men who gave them to her.' She nodded. That was Lilli. 'We have much in common, we are doing the same work, on both her houses, it appears.' Sarah laughed when he said it, and so did he. 'I hope she appreciates it. Would you like to come inside and look around?' He was very hospitable. Sarah hesitated, and then nodded. She was dying to see it, and to tell Mimi about it afterward, and Jeff, and her mother. Now she could say she had.

'I'll only stay a few minutes. I don't want to be a nuisance. My grandmother said she came here years ago, but it was all boarded up, as you said. Why has no one lived here for so long?'

'There were no heirs. The last marquis had no children. Someone bought it after the war, but they died very soon after, and it became a big battle with their family. They fought over it for twenty years, and never lived here. In time, they just left it, the people who had wanted it were gone, the others didn't want to live here. It has been for sale for many years, but no one was foolish enough to buy it until me.' He laughed and greeted the workmen as they walked in.

The inside of the château was vast and somewhat gloomy. There were enormously high ceilings, and a grand staircase leading to the upper floors. There were long hallways where Sarah could imagine ancestral portraits. Now there were rugs rolled up against the walls. There were sconces made for candles, and as they walked farther in, the tall windows let in sunlight. She thought the house in San Francisco was prettier and brighter, but it was also infinitely smaller. There was a cavernous feel to this that Sarah somehow found sad. This was a whole different life. She wondered again if Lilli had been happy here in her life as a marquise. It was such a different life.

The new owner of the château walked her upstairs, and showed her the enormous ancestral bedrooms, and several libraries still filled with books. There was a drawing room with a fireplace that a tall man could stand up in, and her host proved it to her, and then as an afterthought, he held out his hand to her.

'I'm sorry to be so rude. I'm Pierre Pettit.' He shook her hand, and she introduced herself to him. 'Not the Marquis de Mailliard,' he teased. 'You are the great-granddaughter of a marquise, I am the great-grandson of a peasant, and the grandson of a cook. My mother was a maid here as a young girl. I bought the place because my family worked here as long as there were Mailliards here. Originally, they were serfs. I thought it was time to put a Pettit in the château, since there are no Mailliards left. Peasants are of stronger stock, and eventually they rule the world.' He laughed as he said it. 'I am very happy to know you, Sarah Anderson. Would you like a glass of wine?' She hesitated, and he led her into an enormous kitchen that was still a relic of the past. They hadn't renovated it yet. The stove was at least eighty years old, and looked a lot like the one she had just thrown out.

Sarah didn't know it, but Pierre Pettit was one of the most important wine merchants in France. He exported wine all over the world, particularly to the States, but to other countries as well. He took a bottle off a rack, and she was stunned when she saw the name and vintage. He was opening a bottle of Château Margaux 1968.

'That's the year I was born,' she said with a shy smile, accepting a glass of it from him.

'It should breathe for a little while,' he apologized, and then took her to see the rest of the château. They were back in the ancient kitchen half an hour later. It was a once beautiful but now dreary place. He had explained his plans for it to her as they walked around, and asked her questions about her house. She had told him what she was doing, how much she loved it, and she told him Lilli's story, which he found intriguing, too. 'It's amazing that she left her children, don't you think? I don't have any myself, but I can't imagine a woman doing that. Does your grandmother hate her for it?'

'She never talks about her, but I don't think so. She doesn't know much about her, she was six when her mother left.'

'She must have broken her husband's heart,' he said sympathetically.

'I think she did. He died about fifteen years later, but after losing his fortune and his wife, my grandmother says he more or less became a recluse, and eventually died of grief.'

Pierre Pettit shook his head as he sipped his wine. 'Women do things like that,' he said, looking at Sarah. 'They can be heartless creatures. That's why I never married. And it's so much more entertaining to have one's heart broken by many than by just one.' He laughed after he said it, and so did Sarah. He didn't look like he had a broken heart to her, but rather as though he had done the heart breaking, and enjoyed every minute of it. He was a very attractive man, with a lot of charisma, and was obviously very clever in business. He was spending a fortune restoring the château.

'You know, there is someone I think you would like to meet,' he said, looking pensive. 'My grandmother. She was the cook when your great-grandmother lived here. She's ninety-three years old and very frail. She can't walk now, but she remembers everything in minute detail. Her memory is still excellent. Would you like to meet her?'

'Yes, I would.' Sarah's eyes lit up at the prospect.

'She lives about half an hour from here. Shall I take you?' he asked, setting down his glass, and smiling at her.

'Would it be too much trouble? I have a driver, if you give us directions.'

'Don't be silly. I have nothing to do here. I live in Paris. I just came down for a few days to check on their progress.' According to what he had told Sarah, completion was still two years away. He'd been working on it for a year. 'I'll drive you there myself. I enjoy seeing her, and she always scolds me that I don't come often enough. You've given me a good excuse. She doesn't speak English. I will translate for you.'

He strode purposefully across the hallway, and down the main stairs, with Sarah following him, excited to have met him and to have the opportunity to meet a woman who had known Lilli. She hoped his grandmother's memory was as good as he said. She wanted to be able to go home to Mimi with something about her mother. It was like a gift she wanted to bring back, and she was grateful to Pierre Pettit for his help.

He left her in the courtyard and told her he'd be back in a moment. He reappeared five minutes later, driving a black Rolls convertible. It was a very handsome car. Pierre Pettit treated himself very well. His ancestors may have been serfs, but he was obviously a very rich man.

Sarah got in beside him, after explaining to her driver that the gentleman would take her back to the hotel. She tried to pay him, but he said it would be on her bill. And a moment later, she and Pierre sped off. He chatted easily with her on the way, asking her about her work and life in San Francisco. She said she was an attorney, and he asked if she was married. She said she wasn't.

'You're still young,' he said, smiling. 'You will

marry one day.' He said it almost smugly, and she rose to the challenge instantly. She liked him, and he'd been very nice to her. She was enjoying the ride through the countryside in his Rolls. It would have been hard not to. It was a perfect April day, and she was in France, driving around in a Rolls-Royce with a very handsome man who owned a large château. It was all very surreal.

'Why do you think I'll marry? You didn't. Why should I?'

'Ahhh . . . you're one of those, are you? An independent woman. Why do you not wish to marry?' He enjoyed sparring with her, and he obviously liked women. And she suspected they loved him.

'I don't need to be married. I'm happy the way I am,' Sarah said easily.

'No, you're not,' he said smugly. 'An hour ago you were alone in an old Renault with no one to talk to. You are traveling in France alone. Now you're in a Rolls-Royce, talking to me, and laughing, and seeing pretty things. Isn't it better like this?'

'I didn't marry you,' Sarah said pointedly. 'We're much better off like this. Both of us. Don't you think?'

He laughed at her answer. He liked it. And he liked her. She was bright, and quick. 'Perhaps you're right. And children? You don't want children?' She shook her head, looking at him. 'Why not? Most people seem to enjoy their children a lot.'

'I work hard. I don't think I'd be a good mother. I don't have enough time to give them.' It was a comfortable excuse.

267

'Perhaps you work too hard,' he suggested. He sounded like Stanley for a minute. But this man was very different. He was all about pleasure and life and fun, not just work. He had learned secrets to life that Stanley never had.

'Perhaps,' she answered. 'Do you? You must have worked very hard to have all this.' He hadn't inherited it, he had worked for it, and he laughed as he answered.

'Sometimes I work too hard. And sometimes I play too hard. I like doing both, at different times. You have to work hard in order to play hard. I have a wonderful boat I keep in the South. A yacht. Do you like boats?'

'I haven't been on one in a long time.' Not since college, when she had sailed with friends in Martha's Vineyard, but she was sure the boats she'd been on were nothing like his.

They reached his grandmother's house a few minutes later. It was a small, neat cottage with a fence around it, beautifully maintained, with rosebushes in front, and a tiny vineyard behind it. He got out and opened the car door politely for Sarah. It was a remarkable experience being with him. She felt as though she were in a movie. The movie was her life for the moment. And she was starring in it. She was a long way from San Francisco.

He rang the bell and opened the door, and a woman hurried toward them, wiping her hands on her apron. She spoke to Pierre, and pointed to someone in the back garden. She was his grandmother's caretaker. Pierre led Sarah out through the back of the small house. It was filled with lovely antiques, and had bright pretty curtains

268

at the windows. The house was small, but he took care of his grandmother well. She was sitting in a wheelchair in the garden looking out at the vineyards and the countryside beyond. She had lived in this part of the world all her life, and he had bought her the cottage many years before. To her, it was a palace. Her eyes lit up when she saw him.

'Bonjour, Pierre!' she exclaimed with delight, and then smiled at Sarah. She looked pleased to see her, she enjoyed visitors and especially her grandson. He was the joy of her life, and she was very proud of him. It showed.

'Bonjour, Mamie.' He introduced Sarah to her, and explained why she had come. His grandmother responded with a look of interest, many exclamations, and she nodded her head several times at Sarah, as though to welcome her. As she and Pierre chatted animatedly, the caretaker reappeared with cookies and lemonade, which she poured for them, and set the pitcher down on a nearby table, in case they wanted more. The cookies were delicious.

Pierre turned to Sarah then, and pulled up chairs for both of them. 'She said she knew your great-grandmother well, and always liked her. She said she was a lovely woman. My grandmother was seventeen years old, and only a maid in the kitchen when Lilli came here. She said your great-grandmother was very kind to her.' She referred to Lilli throughout the conversation as Madame la Marquise. 'Your great-grandmother helped her to become the cook several years later. She said she never even knew she had children until one day she saw her looking at photographs of them in the garden, and she was crying. But she said that other than that, she was always very happy here. She had a sunny nature, and she adored her husband. He was a few years older than she, and he worshiped her. She says they were very happy. He laughed all the time whenever he was with her. She said it was very hard for everyone when the Germans were here. They took over the stables and part of the château. The outbuildings were full of their men, and sometimes they were very rude and stole food from the kitchen. Your great-grandmother was nice to them, but she didn't like them much. She said Lilli got very sick toward the end of the war. There was no medicine, and she got sicker and sicker, and the marquis nearly went mad, worrying about her. It sounds like tuberculosis or pneumonia, I think,' he added softly. It was a fascinating recital for both of them, particularly Sarah, as she imagined Lilli crying over photographs of Mimi and her brother. Strangely, she realized now, he had died the same year as his mother, in 1945, just before the end of the war. Alexandre, her ex-husband, had died that year too. It was hard to imagine how Lilli could survive for all those years without news or contact with her children, or any of the people she had once loved. She left them all for the marquis, closed the door of her past behind her, and never opened it again.

'My grandmother is saying that finally your great-grandmother died, although she was still very young,' Pierre went on. 'She says she was the most beautiful woman she had ever seen. And the marquis was inconsolable when she died. My grandmother thinks he had been in the Resistance all along, but no one knew for sure. He began disappearing more and more after she died, perhaps on missions with local cells, or in other districts. The Germans killed him one night not far from here. They said he was trying to blow up a train, she doesn't know if that was true or not. He was a good man and wouldn't do anything to kill people, except maybe Germans. She thinks he let himself get shot because he was so grief stricken over his wife's death. They died within a few months of each other and are buried in the cemetery near the château. I can take you there if you wish,' he offered, and she nodded. 'She said it was very sad for everyone when they died. The Germans had kept the servants in the château and worked them very hard. The commandant moved in after the marquis died. And then the Germans left finally. And after the war, all the servants went to other places, the château was boarded up. Eventually someone bought it . . . and you know the rest. What an amazing story,' Pierre said to Sarah, who reached out and took the old woman's hands in her own to thank her. Pierre's grandmother nodded and smiled, she understood the gesture. She was every bit as lucid as Pierre had said she would be. The story she had shared with Sarah was a gift she could take home to Mimi, the story of her own mother's years in France and her last days.

'Thank you . . . *merci* . . .' Sarah repeated, as they continued holding hands. This ancient woman was her only link to her lost great-grandmother, the woman who had vanished, and whose house she now owned. The woman two men had loved so passionately that both died when they lost her. She had belonged to each of them, and had been theirs,

271

and in the end, she had been her own. She was like a beautiful bird that could be loved and admired but not caged. As they sat together, and Sarah mulled over Lilli's story, Pierre's grandmother's brow furrowed for a moment, and she said something more to him. He listened and nodded, and turned to Sarah with a wistful air.

'My grandmother says there was one other thing about Lilli's children. She said that she often saw her writing letters. She wasn't sure, but she thought they might have been to them. The boy who went to the post office said that her letters to America were always returned. He gave them back to Madame la Marquise himself, and she would look very sad. He told my grandmother that she put them in a little box, where she kept them tied up with ribbons. My grandmother said she never saw them until the marquise died. She found the box when she was helping to put away her things, and showed the box of letters to the marquis. He told her to throw them away, so she did. She doesn't know for sure, but she thinks they were letters to her children, all of which were returned. She must have tried to contact them over the years, but someone always sent them back to her unopened. Perhaps the man she had been married to, the children's father. He must have been very angry at her. I would have been, in his place.' It was hard for any of them to understand how she had left a husband and two children, out of passion for someone else. But according to Pierre's grandmother, she had loved the marquis that much. She said she had never seen two people more in love with each other, right up to their deaths. Enough to abandon her children for. Sarah couldn't help wondering if she had regretted it, and hoped she had. Her tears over the photographs and returned letters she saved said something. But in the end, hard as it was to understand, her love for the marquis had been more powerful, and had prevailed, as had his for her. It was one of those passions apparently that defied reason and all else. She had walked away from an entire life to give herself to him, and leave everyone, even her children, behind. She had gone to her grave without ever seeing them again, which seemed a terrible fate to Sarah. And for Mimi, the grandmother she loved so much.

Pierre chatted with his grandmother for a while, and then they left. Sarah thanked her profusely again before she did. It had been an amazing day for her. And as he had offered to, Pierre took her to the cemetery on the way back. The Mailliard Mausoleum was easy to find, and they found them there. Armand, Marquis de Mailliard, and Lilli, Marquise de Mailliard. He had been forty-four years old when he died, and she thirty-nine. They had died within eighty days of each other, not even three months. Sarah felt sad as she left the cemetery, after hearing the story. She wondered how many times Lilli had cried over the children she had left, and why they never had any children of their own. Perhaps that would have consoled her, or perhaps she couldn't bear the thought of having another child, after the two she had given up. Even with as much as Sarah knew now, Lilli would always be a mystery to all of them. What had driven her, who she had been, what she had really felt or not felt or cared about or longed for were all secrets she had taken with her. Clearly, her passion

273

for the marquis had been a powerful force. Sarah knew that Lilli had met him at a consular party in San Francisco just before the crash. How she had decided to run away with him, or when or why, no one really knew and never would. Perhaps she had been unhappy with Alexandre, but he had obviously adored her. But it was, in the end, the marquis who had owned her heart, and only he. Sarah felt as though she had something to go back with, which would satisfy her grandmother and even her mother, although Lilli would forever be an enigma. She had been a woman of enormous passion and mystery till the end. Sarah was planning to tell Mimi about her mother's letters to her when she went back.

'I think I have fallen in love with your great-grandmother,' Pierre teased her as he drove her back to the hotel. 'She must have been a remarkable woman, of enormous passion and magnetism, and quite dangerous in a way. They loved her so passionately, it destroyed them. They couldn't live without her when she was gone,' he said, glancing at Sarah. 'Are you as dangerous as she was?' he teased again.

'No, I'm not.' Sarah smiled at her benefactor. He had made her whole trip worthwhile. She felt as though destiny had brought them together. Meeting Pierre had been an incredible gift.

'Perhaps you are dangerous,' he said, as they drove up to her hotel, and she thanked him for his kindness, and spending the entire day with her, driving her around.

'I would never have found out any of this, if I hadn't met your grandmother. Thank you so much, Pierre.' She was genuinely grateful to him.

274

'I enjoyed it, too. It's quite a story,' he said quietly. 'She never told me all that before. It all happened before I was born.' And then, as she got out of the car, he reached out and touched her hand. 'I'm going back to Paris tomorrow. Would you like to have dinner with me tonight? There's only a local bistro, but it's fairly good. I'd enjoy your company, Sarah. I had a good time with you today.'

'So did I. Are you sure you're not tired of me?' She felt as though she had already abused his hospitality and didn't want to do so again.

'Not yet. If I get tired of you, I'll bring you back.' He laughed at her.

'Then I'd like to very much.'

'Excellent. I'll pick you up at eight.'

She went upstairs and lay on her bed after that. She had a lot to think about. She couldn't get Lilli out of her head. She felt haunted by her, after listening to the story Pierre's grandmother had told, and he said he felt the same way when he came back to pick Sarah up in the Rolls.

The bistro he took her to nearby was simple, and the food was plain but good. He had brought his own bottle of wine. He regaled her with tales of his travels, and adventures on his yacht when he sailed around the world. He was interesting to talk to and fun to be with. She felt as though she were on another planet as she laughed and talked with him. It was a delightful evening for both of them. He was fifteen years older than she, but had a youthful outlook on life, probably because he had never married or had children. He said he was still a child himself.

'And you, my dear,' he scolded her over the last

of their wine, which was yet another exquisite vintage, 'are far too serious, from what I can see. You need to have more fun, and take life more lightly. You work too hard, and now you are killing yourself on your house. When do you play?' She thought about it and then shrugged her shoulders.

'I don't. The house is play for me now. But you're right. I probably don't play enough.' Sarah suspected correctly that no one could accuse Pierre of that.

'Life is short. You should start playing now.'

'That's why I'm here, in France. When I go back, I'm moving into Lilli's house,' she said, looking happy.

'It's not Lilli's house, Sarah. It's yours. Sarah's house. She led her life, she did exactly what she wanted to do, no matter who she hurt or who she left behind. She was a woman who knew her own mind, and always got what she wanted. You can tell that, listening to her story. I'm sure she was very beautiful, but probably very selfish. Men always seem to fall madly in love with selfish women, not the kind ones, or the good ones, or the ones who are good for them. Don't be too good, Sarah . . . you'll get hurt.' She wondered if he had been, or if he did the hurting. But she suspected he had Lilli pegged correctly. She abandoned her children and husband. It was still hard for Sarah to understand. And Mimi probably understood it even less. Lilli had been her mother. 'Who is waiting for you when you go home?' Pierre asked her, and Sarah thought about it.

'My grandmother, my mother, friends.' She thought of Jeff as she said it. 'Does that sound too pathetic?' It was a little embarrassing spelling it

276

out, but he had figured it out himself anyway that afternoon. He could sense that there was no man in her life, and she was at ease about it, which he thought was sad, given her looks and age.

'No, it sounds sweet. Maybe too sweet. I think you need to be harder on your men.'

'I don't have any men.' She laughed at what he said.

'You will. The right one will come.'

'I had the wrong one for four years,' she said quietly. She and Pierre were becoming friends. She liked him, although she could sense that he was something of a playboy. But he had been kind to her. And fatherly, in a way.

'That's too long to keep a bad one. What do you want?' He was taking her under his wing. She was an innocent in his eyes. And he sounded like Santa Claus, asking for her wish list.

'I don't know what I want anymore. Companionship, friendship, laughter, love, someone who sees things as I do, and cares about the same things. Someone who won't hurt me or disappoint me . . . someone who treats me well. I want kindness more than passion. I want someone who loves me and who I love.'

'That's a lot to ask for,' he said seriously. 'I'm not sure you can find all that.'

'When I do, they're married,' she said matter-of-factly.

'What's wrong with that? I do it all the time,' he said, and they both laughed. She was sure he did. He was definitely a bad boy at times. He was too handsome not to be, and rich enough to do whatever he wanted and get away with it. He was very spoiled. 'I'm a man of conscience,' Pierre said

277

out of the blue. 'If I weren't, I would sweep you off your feet and make mad passionate love to you.' He was only half-teasing, and she knew it. 'But if I do that, Sarah, you'll get hurt. You'll be sad when you go back, and I don't want to do that to you. It would ruin the whole purpose of your trip. I want you to go back happy,' he said, looking at her gently. He was being protective of her, which was rare for him.

'So do I. Thank you for being so nice to me.' There were tears in her eyes as she said it. She was thinking of Phil and how rotten he had been to her. Pierre was a kind man. That was probably why the women in his life loved him, married or not.

'Find a good one, Sarah. You deserve it,' he said quietly. 'You may not think you do, but you do. Don't waste your time again with the bad ones. You'll find a good one next time,' he said, speaking to her as a friend. 'I can feel it in my bones.'

'I hope you're right.' It was funny how Stanley had told her not to waste her life working too hard, and now Pierre was telling her to find a good man. They were like teachers who had been put in her path to teach her the lessons she needed to learn.

'Would you like to drive back to Paris with me tomorrow?' he asked as he drove her back to the hotel.

'I was going to go back on the train,' she said hesitantly.

'Don't be silly, with all those awful, smelly people? Don't be ridiculous. It's a long drive, but it's pretty. I'd enjoy having you along.' He said it simply and sounded as though he meant it.

'Then I'll come. You've been much too good to me already.'

'All right, then I'll be disagreeable to you for at least an hour tomorrow. Will that make you feel better?' he teased her again.

He told her he'd pick her up at nine the next morning, and they'd be back in Paris by five in the afternoon. He said he was meeting friends in Paris the following night, but would enjoy taking her to dinner in Paris another night of her stay. It sounded wonderful to her, and they made a date on the trip back to Paris.

They had a wonderful time driving together, and he took her to a delightful restaurant for lunch, where they knew him and he seemed to stop there often on his way to Dordogne. He made the entire experience an adventure and a joy for her, just as he had the previous day. The hours flew by like minutes, and they were back at her hotel in Paris before she knew it. He promised to call her the next day and kissed her on both cheeks when he left. Sarah felt like Cinderella when she walked back into the hotel. The coach had turned into a pumpkin, the footmen to three white mice, and she walked up the stairs to her room, carrying her suitcase, wondering if the past two days were real, and wanting to pinch herself to check. She had found out everything she wanted to about Lilli, seen the château, seen her final resting place, and even made a friend along the way. The trip had been a huge success.

CHAPTER 18

For the rest of Sarah's stay in Paris, she saw
monuments, churches, and museums, ate in
bistros, sat in cafés. She walked down streets,
discovered parks, peered into gardens, and
explored antique shops. She did everything she had
ever wanted to do in Paris, and felt as though she
had lived there for a month by the time she went
back to the States.

Pierre took her out to dinner one night, to the
Tour d'Argent, and dancing at Bain Douche after
that, and she'd never had so much fun in her life.
In his own milieu, Pierre was indeed dazzling, and
definitely a playboy, though not with her. He
kissed her again on both cheeks when he dropped
her off at her hotel at four in the morning. He said
he would have loved to see her again, but he was
going to London to see clients. He had already
contributed more than his fair share to the success
of her trip. She promised to send him photographs
of Lilli's house in San Francisco, and he promised
to send photographs of the château for her to give
to Mimi. She made him promise to call her if he
ever came to San Francisco. And she had no doubt
he would. They had genuinely enjoyed getting to
know each other, and she left Paris knowing she
had a friend there.

She felt as though she were leaving home when
she checked out of the hotel and took a cab to the
airport. She could see now why Marie-Louise
wanted to move back there. She'd have done the
same if she could. It was a magical city, and Sarah's

280

trip had been the best two weeks of her life. It didn't matter at all to her now that she'd gone alone. She didn't feel deprived, she felt richer. And Pierre's words were echoing in her ears, just as Stanley's had, *Find a good one when you go back.* Easier said than done. But in the absence of a 'good one,' she had herself, which was fine for now, and maybe even forever. She wanted to come back to Paris again soon. It had been everything she'd hoped for and more.

She'd only heard from Jeff twice on the trip. Once about a minor electrical problem, and the second time about a replacement refrigerator, when the one they'd ordered didn't come, and wouldn't for several months. His e-mails had been brief. And her office never contacted her at all. It had been a real vacation, and although she was sad to leave, she also felt ready to go back. She wasn't anxious to go back to work. But she couldn't wait to move into her house. Jeff said it was ready, and waiting for her.

She took a flight out of Charles de Gaulle at four o'clock, which got her into San Francisco at six in the evening, local time. It was a beautiful warm April day. It was Friday, and she was moving on Monday, and going back to work on Tuesday. She had the weekend to pack the rest of her things, and even drive some of it over herself. She was thinking of sleeping at her new address that weekend, although the movers were coming Monday, on May 1st, just as Jeff had promised. He had set everything up for her.

She was anxious to see her grandmother to tell her all she'd seen and heard, but Sarah had had an e-mail from her mother, saying that Mimi was still

281

in Palm Springs with George, and she had had a ball in New York with her friends. Her mother had become a wonder of modern communication, and now loved to e-mail. Sarah still thought it was funny. She wondered if her mother had heard from Tom again, or if things had already petered out. Long distance was too tough to really work. Sarah had tried it in college and never liked it. Geographic undesirability had been a turn-off to her ever since.

She took a cab from the airport to her apartment, and as she came through the door, it looked worse than ever. She felt like she no longer even lived there. She couldn't wait to get out. There were boxes everywhere that she'd packed before she left, and the rest of her belongings were in piles all over the floor. Goodwill was scheduled to come on Tuesday to take whatever she didn't move. She wasn't moving much. She was almost embarrassed to give it to Goodwill. She felt as though she had grown up in the last six months, ever since she'd bought the house.

She called her mother that night to say she was back. Her mother sounded rushed, she said she was flying out the door. She was going to Carmel for the weekend. She seemed to be moving around a lot these days, and having fun. Her mother said Mimi was due back on Wednesday. Sarah wanted them all to come to the house for dinner the following weekend. And she had much to tell Mimi, after her visit to Dordogne.

Sarah was surprised not to hear from Jeff that night. He knew when she was coming back, but he was probably busy. She fell asleep early that night, still on Paris time, and woke up at five in the morning, thoroughly jet-lagged. She showered and dressed, made herself a cup of coffee, and headed to the house at six. It was a gorgeous sunny morning.

When she let herself into the house, she felt as though she already lived there. She walked around her domain with pleasure. All the lights worked, the plumbing was fine. The paneling shone. And when she walked in, the new kitchen was gorgeous. It was even more beautiful than she'd hoped for. And she liked the replacement refrigerator even better. She was going to start painting the smaller rooms in the next week, and the professional painters were starting in two weeks to do the big ones. By June the house would be nearly complete. She was going to do the rest of the details slowly, over time, and begin looking for furniture at estate sales and auctions. That would take more time, but her money was holding up nicely, thanks to Jeff's help cutting corners and getting her everything wholesale. She was going to wait to do the elevator for now, because she really didn't need it. He had even given her the gardener he and Marie-Louise used in Potrero Hill. She had gotten everything cleaned up, and had planted neat rows of flowers, and hedges bordering the house.

'Wow!' she said smiling to herself, as she sat down at her new kitchen table. 'Double wow!' She beamed. She loved it.

She had been there for two hours when the doorbell rang. She peeked out a side window, and saw Jeff standing outside holding two cups from Starbucks.

'What are you doing here so early?' he asked, smiling at her. He looked relaxed and happy, as he handed her a Grande double cappuccino with nonfat foam, just the way she liked it.

'I'm in a time zone from another planet.' But from the look on her face, he could see that she had enjoyed it.

'Did you have fun?'

'I loved it . . . and the kitchen looks gorgeous,' she said as he followed her in and looked around. He'd had the cleaning crew in the day before so that when she saw it, it would look perfect. He ran a full-service office, he teased her.

They were sipping their coffee and chatting comfortably when he jokingly asked her if she'd seen Marie-Louise in Paris. Sarah looked confused by the question.

'No. Did she go back? Isn't she early for her summer trip?'

'Not this year. She left me.' He looked Sarah in the eye as he said it.

'She left you?' Sarah repeated, looking startled. 'As in really left you, or as in for a few weeks to hang out in Paris?'

'She moved back. I'm buying out her half of the business. We're selling the house. I can't afford to buy that from her, too. I can use my half of the house money to buy her out of the business. Actually, I'm selling the house for her.' He looked calm as he said it. She could only imagine how he felt. Fourteen years out the window was hard to swallow. But he looked like he was doing okay. In some ways, it was a relief.

'I'm sorry,' Sarah said softly. 'How did that happen?'

'It was long overdue. She was miserable here from the day she got here. I don't think she was happy with me, either. I guess not'—he smiled wryly—'or she'd still be here.' Even if he was taking it well, and knew it was for the best, it was still painful. They had been battling incessantly since Christmas. He was exhausted, and almost relieved now that it was over.

'I don't think it was about you,' Sarah consoled him. 'I think it was about her, and living here, and not wanting to be here.'

'I offered to move back to Europe with her at one point, a few years ago. But that didn't do it for her, either. She's just not a happy person. She's very angry.' She had been angry right up till the last minute, and slammed the door when she left, which was not how he'd wanted to end it. She didn't know how to do it any other way. People left home in different ways, some in gentleness, others in anger.

'What about you? Did you meet the man of your dreams in Paris?' He looked anxious as he asked her.

'I made a friend.' She told him about her visit to the Château de Mailliard, meeting Pierre Pettit and his grandmother, and she told him all she'd seen and heard. She could hear the echo of Pierre's words, *Go back and find a good one.* She didn't say anything about that to Jeff. He had enough on his mind, and was still feeling raw after Marie-Louise left him. It was like when she ended it with Phil. She knew it was for the best, but it still hurt. 'I had a great time,' she said quietly, as she finished her cappuccino. She didn't want to rub it in. He'd obviously had a rough time in her absence.

'I figured you did. You never e-mailed.' He smiled ruefully. It had worried him a little.

'I was savoring every minute, and I thought you were busy.' She told him again how sorry she was about Marie-Louise, and after that they wandered around, checking out the house, while he showed her new additions and details. The place had really come together in two weeks, just as he'd promised. 'I'm going to sleep here tonight,' she said proudly. He smiled at how happy she seemed. She looked better than ever, and he was glad she was home. He had missed her, particularly lately. Marie-Louise had left the week before. But he hadn't wanted to tell Sarah till she got back. He needed time to adjust to it himself. It was still a little weird going home to an empty house. She had taken everything she wanted with her, and told him to keep or sell the rest. She had no great attachment to any of it, not even him, which was painful. Fourteen years was a long time. This was going to be an adjustment. The first couple of nights he almost laughed at himself. He realized that he missed the fighting. It had been the essence of their relationship for fourteen years.

'So what are you going to do today, Sarah?'

'Pack some stuff. Bring some things over. I want to start moving my clothes.' She didn't have that many. She had weeded out a lot of those, too. She was merciless now in her purging, getting rid of all the things she no longer needed or wanted.

'Do you want help?' he asked hopefully.

'Are you being polite, or do you mean it?' She knew he was busy.

'I mean it.' He wasn't as busy as she thought, and he wanted to help her.

'Then I want help. We can drive some stuff over, so I can stay here tonight. I'm not going to sleep at

286

the apartment anymore.' It was over. She hadn't even wanted to sleep there the night before. Her new bed had been delivered on Scott Street. It was gorgeous, and very girly with the pink headboard. It was almost worthy of Lilli.

He went to her apartment with her, helped her carry armloads of clothes and boxes downstairs, and they drove over four loads of her things in both their cars. And then he helped her carry it all up to her bedroom. It was therapeutic for him. She could see that he was distracted. He looked a little shell-shocked.

'Do you think she'll come back again this time?' Sarah asked him about Marie-Louise when they stopped for lunch. She was starving. It was nine hours later in Paris. She noticed that he didn't eat much.

'Not this time,' he said matter-of-factly, as he toyed with the sandwich she'd made him. She had eaten hers in two minutes. 'We both agreed it should be over. It should've been years ago. We were just too stubborn and too cowardly to let go. I'm glad we did this time. I'm putting the house on the market this week.' She knew he loved the house and had worked hard on it, she was sorry for him about that. But they were going to make a healthy profit, which was something at least. He said Marie-Louise wanted every penny she could get. He was paying her a hefty sum for her share of the business.

'Where are you going to live?' Sarah asked with interest.

'I'm going to get an apartment here in Pacific Heights, close to the office. It makes more sense.' They'd never been able to put their office in the

287

house in Potrero Hill because it was too far for clients to come. 'Maybe I should take your old one.'

'Don't. You'd hate it. It's awful.' Still, with his furniture, it would look better than it did with hers.

'I'm seeing a few places tomorrow. Do you want to come?' He seemed lonely and at loose ends, which was normal. Marie-Louise had never spent much time with him, but it was different now, knowing she was gone for good. No matter how difficult it had been, it left a void, and he hadn't yet figured out how to fill it. She was like a phantom limb now that she was gone. It ached at times, but he was managing without her.

'I'd love to see apartments with you. You're not going to buy another house?'

'Not yet. I wanted to let the dust settle first, sell the old one, and see what we get. I'll probably have enough to buy a condo after I pay her for the business. But I'm in no rush.'

'That's smart.' She approved. He was being sensible, practical, and generous with Marie-Louise, which was typical of him.

He helped her move more of her things after that. He hung around, and they ordered Chinese food for dinner. And then he left her. He came back the next day to see apartments with her.

'So how was your first night?' he asked when he picked her up. He was smiling, and he looked better than he had the day before, although he'd been very glad to see her. He had really missed her while she was gone. They had become good friends in recent months.

'It was fantastic. I love my new bed, and the bathroom is incredible. You could put ten people in that tub.' All night she felt like she was home. She had felt that way since the first time she saw the house. And now it was real. Her dream had come true at last.

They found an apartment for him that afternoon. It was small and compact. It wasn't exciting, but it was clean and in good condition, and a block from his office. It even had a small garden. And it was four blocks from her house on Scott Street. The location was perfect. It had a fireplace, which he liked. He commented to Sarah as they left that it was going to be weird living in an apartment, after so many years in his house.

He dropped Sarah off after that. He had to go back to his own place and start packing. He called her later that night.

'How are you doing, Jeff?' she asked kindly.

'I'm okay. It's depressing packing all this stuff. I'm going to sell what I can with the house, but I think I'm going to wind up putting a lot of it in storage.' The apartment he had rented was small, which was all he wanted for now. He had said that, eventually, he would buy another house, but not yet. It was too soon. It was an odd feeling for her now, too. After their off-and-on flirtation for the last five months, and occasional moments of near passion when he kissed her, she didn't know quite where they stood now, and neither did he. They had become friends over the past five months, and now suddenly he was free. They were both moving slowly, and with extreme caution. She didn't want to screw up their friendship for a romance that might not last anyway, or destroy the easy companionship they shared.

She didn't hear from him again until Tuesday at

the office. He said he had an appointment in the neighborhood, and invited her to lunch. She met him at the Big Four at one o'clock. He was wearing a blazer and slacks and looked very handsome. She had his house pin on her lapel.

'I wanted to ask you something,' he inquired cautiously, halfway through lunch. It had been the whole purpose of the invitation. She had suspected nothing.

'How do you feel about dating?' She didn't understand the question.

'Generally, specifically, or as a social custom? At the moment I'm not sure I remember how you do it.' She hadn't been on a date in four months, since she broke up with Phil, or with anyone else for four years before that. 'I'm a little rusty.'

'Me too. I meant specifically, as in us.'

'As in us? Now?'

'Well, okay. If you want to consider this a date. We could call this our first. But I was thinking more like dinner, and movies, kissing, you know all that stuff people do while dating.' She smiled at him across the table. He looked nervous. She reached out and took his hand.

'Actually, I like the kissing part. But dinner and movies would be nice, too.'

'Good,' he said, looking relieved. 'Then do we consider this our first date, or is this just a practice round?'

'Either way. What do you think?'

'Practice, I think. I think we should start with dinner. How about tomorrow?'

'That sounds good,' she said, smiling at him. 'Do you have plans tonight?'

'I didn't want to be pushy, or look too anxious.'

'You're doing fine.'

'I'm glad to hear it. I haven't actually done this in fourteen years. Come to think of it, it's about goddamned time.' He smiled broadly at her across the table, and when they left the restaurant, they were holding hands. He walked her back to her office, and picked her up at eight that night. They went to a little Italian place on Fillmore Street that was in walking distance from her house. It was going to be his neighborhood soon, too, when he moved.

When he walked her back to her place, he stopped outside her front door and kissed her. 'I think that makes this our first official date. Do you agree?'

'Absolutely,' she whispered, and he kissed her again. She unlocked her front door, and he kissed her one last time, and then got in his car and drove home, smiling to himself. He was thinking that Marie-Louise had done him the biggest favor in the world when she went back to Paris.

As Sarah walked slowly up the stairs to her new bedroom, she was thinking of Pierre's words to her again. *Find a good one. You deserve it.* She knew without a doubt she just had.

CHAPTER 19

Sarah gave her first dinner party on Scott Street the weekend after she moved in. She set the table in her kitchen, and invited Mimi and George, her mother, and Jeff. She was going to introduce him as the architect who was helping her with the house, which explained his being there, without telling her family yet that they were dating. It was still very new, and she wasn't ready to share that information with them yet. But it was an easy way for them to meet him. He told her on the phone the day before that he was nervous about it. She told him she thought her mother would be fine, her grandmother was adorable, and George was easy. He was only slightly reassured. This was important to him, he didn't want to blow it.

They had already seen each other three times that week. He came by one night with Indian curry (hot for him, mild for her), while she started painting her dressing room. Her hair was already splattered with pink paint by the time he got there, and he laughingly showed her how to do it, and then wound up helping her. They forgot to eat till after midnight, but the dressing room looked great when Sarah woke up the next morning and rushed to check the color. Powder pink, just as she wanted, in nice, clean, smooth strokes.

He came by the next day, too, and Sarah made dinner. They wound up talking about everything from foreign movies to decorating to politics, and neither of them got any work done, but they had a nice time. And on Friday he took her to dinner and a movie, to 'maintain their dating status,' as he put it. They had a good French meal at a small restaurant on Clement Street, and went to see a good thriller afterward that they both enjoyed. It wasn't a serious film, but they had a nice time with each other, and kissed again for a long time when he brought her home. They were still moving slowly, though seeing a lot of each other. He had spent the day with her on Saturday, painting again, and helped her set the dinner table for her first party. She made leg of lamb with mashed potatoes and a big tossed salad. He had brought a cheesecake and some French pastries. And the table looked pretty when she set a bowl of flowers on it. Everything was in order, and the kitchen looked terrific. She could hardly wait for Mimi and her mother to come. She wanted to tell her everything she had heard about Lilli in France, and the meeting with Pierre's grandmother. It had been kismet that they met.

Mimi and George were the first to arrive. She looked as happy and was as sweet as always, said how pleased she was to meet Jeff and what a good job he'd done helping her granddaughter with the house. They walked straight into the kitchen, because there was nowhere else to sit for the moment, except on Sarah's bed. And as soon as she saw the beautiful new kitchen where the old pantries had been, Mimi clapped her hands.

'Oh my word! How beautiful this is! I've never seen a kitchen so big!' The view into the garden was lovely and peaceful. The arrangement of the counters and appliances was all cleverly done, in sparkling white granite, with bleached cabinets, the big butcher-block island, and the huge round table that felt as though it were in the garden. Mimi loved everything she saw. 'I remember the old kitchen when I was a child. It was always such a dark, gloomy place, but all the people who worked there were always so kind to me. I used to run away from my nanny and hide there, while they gave me all the cookies I could eat.' She laughed at the memory, and didn't seem upset by being in the house. On the contrary, she seemed happy there.

She took Jeff on a tour, with his hand tucked into her arm, and shared a multitude of memories and history with him. They were still upstairs when her mother rang the bell and Sarah let her in. Audrey sounded breathless, and apologized for being late.

'You're not, Mom. Mimi just got here. She's taking my architect on a tour. George was keeping me company in the kitchen.' She took her mother's coat and hung it in the cavernous hall closet that was nearly as big as her bedroom in her old apartment. The de Beaumonts had used it for cloaks and fur coats belonging to their guests when they gave parties in the ballroom. Sarah had said to Jeff that she could have used it as an office, although she had plenty of rooms for that, and was using the study in the master suite for that purpose.

'You invited your architect for dinner tonight?' Audrey looked a little startled, and Sarah told her that her hair was really pretty. She was wearing it differently these days, in a variety of upsweeps that were very flattering, and she was wearing very good-looking new pearl earrings that Sarah complimented her on, too.

'I thought you'd like to meet him,' Sarah said, referring to Jeff, and then lowered her voice conspiratorially. 'I really felt I should invite him. He's done so much for me, he's gotten me so many things wholesale, and he's done a beautiful job on the house.' Her mother nodded in response, and followed Sarah into the kitchen, looking somewhat distracted. Audrey smiled when she saw George, sitting at the table, sipping a glass of white wine, and enjoying the garden view.

'Hello, George,' Audrey said pleasantly. 'How

294

are you?'

'Wonderful. We just got back from Palm Springs. Your mother is turning into quite a little golfer,' he said, looking proud.

'I've been taking a few lessons myself,' Audrey said, as Sarah handed her a glass of wine, and looked at her in surprise.

'When did you start that?'

'A few weeks ago, actually,' Audrey said, smiling at her daughter. Sarah thought she'd never seen her look as well, as Mimi and Jeff walked back into the room.

Audrey and her mother embraced, and Mimi couldn't stop talking about how immaculate the house looked. It still needed a coat of paint, of course, but all the new electric lights and the revitalized chandeliers had already given the place a glow. The paneling shone, the bathrooms were clean and functional. Even without furniture, the house had already begun to look like a home. And Mimi loved what Sarah was doing to her bedroom. Jeff had pointed out every new detail, while Mimi told him tales of her childhood, and pointed out all the little secret cubbyholes and corners of the children's rooms. They had become good friends on their brief tour.

Sarah lit the candles on the table, and they sat down to dinner shortly after that. Mimi said the leg of lamb was perfect, as she and George regaled them all with tales of their activities in Palm Springs. Jeff listened avidly to all of them, he was seated between Sarah and Mimi, and seemed to be enjoying everything they had to say. Audrey asked him about his work, and he explained about his passion for old houses. Everyone thought him very

295

attractive, although Audrey remembered Sarah telling her that he lived with someone, so it was obvious that their relationship was professional and not romantic. Still, they appeared to be very good friends.

'What have you been up to, Mother?' Sarah asked as she put the dishes from the main course into the dishwasher, and Jeff helped her get dessert. He seemed to be very at ease in the kitchen, Mimi commented, and Sarah reminded her that he had designed it.

'A full-service architect,' Mimi teased. 'He even does dishes.'

'I had a wonderful time in New York,' Audrey said in answer to her daughter's question. 'The plays we saw were terrific, the weather was great. It was just perfect. How was France?' she asked with interest.

Over dessert, Sarah told all of them what she had learned from Pierre Pettit and his grandmother, when she visited the Château de Mailliard in Dordogne. She felt a little uncomfortable speaking so openly about Lilli in front of her grandmother, with others present, and she wasn't sure if that would be awkward for her. She told her about the photographs Lilli had cried over and the letters that had been returned and that she had saved. Tears rolled slowly down Mimi's cheeks as she listened, but they didn't appear to be so much tears of anguish as of relief.

'I could never understand why she never even tried to contact us. I feel better knowing that she did. My father must have sent them back.' Mimi sat quietly for a moment, absorbing what Sarah had said. She had listened to every word intently,

296

nodded several times, asked a number of pointed questions, and had tears in her eyes more than once. But she told Sarah afterward that it was a great comfort to her to know what had happened to her mother, that she had loved so deeply, and been loved deeply in return, and to know that her last years had been happy. It was a typically generous statement from her, knowing all she'd lost. She had grown up without a mother, because Lilli ran off with the marquis. It was an odd, empty feeling knowing that her mother had been alive until she herself was twenty-one years old, when she had never seen her again after she was six. It had been a painful time in her life. She said that maybe she and George would visit the Château de Mailliard themselves someday on a trip to France. It was a trip she still wanted to make, to see where her mother was buried, and pay her last respects to the mother she had lost as a young child.

It was a lovely evening for all of them, and they hated to see it end. They were about to leave the table finally, when Audrey cleared her throat and clinked her glass. Sarah thought she was going to say something about wishing her luck in her new house. She smiled at her mother expectantly, as did the others, and Jeff stopped talking to Mimi. They had enjoyed a lively conversation with each other all night, particularly about the house, but on other topics as well. Sarah could see that Mimi had Jeff completely charmed.

'I have something to tell all of you,' Audrey said, looking from her mother to her daughter, and then at George. She then took in Jeff with a brief nod. She hadn't expected Sarah to include him that evening, but she didn't want to wait any longer. They had made the decision in New York. 'I'm getting married,' she said in a single breath as they all stared at her. Sarah's eyes grew wide, and Mimi smiled at her, unlike her granddaughter, she was not surprised.

'You are? To who?' Sarah couldn't believe what she was hearing. She didn't even know her mother was dating, let alone planning to get married.

'It's your fault.' She smiled at Sarah, who still looked mystified. 'You introduced us. I'm going to marry Tom Harrison, and move to St. Louis.' She looked apologetically at both her mother and daughter. 'I hate to leave you both, but he's the most wonderful man I've ever met.' She laughed at herself then with tears in her eyes. 'And if I blow this, I may not get another chance. I hate to leave San Francisco, but he's not ready to retire, and it doesn't sound like he will be soon. Maybe when he does, we can move out here. But for now I'll be living in St. Louis.' She looked at Sarah tenderly, and then at her mother, as they all absorbed what she had said. Jeff stood up and went to give her a hug, to congratulate her. He was the first one to do it.

'Thank you, Jeff,' she said, touched, and then George leaned over and kissed her cheek.

'Well done,' George said. 'When's the wedding?' There was nothing he liked better than dancing and a party, and they all laughed when he said it.

'Soon, I think. Tom doesn't think we should wait. We want to take a trip this summer, and he thought it might as well be our honeymoon. He wants to go to Europe. He proposed in New York, and we thought we'd get married at the end of June. I know it's corny, but I kind of like the idea of being a June bride.' She blushed as she said it, and Sarah smiled. She was thrilled for her. Sarah had had no idea that the match she'd made would turn out to be such a huge success. She had just hoped they would be friends, and occasional dates. This was like hitting the jackpot in Las Vegas.

'Were you with him in New York?' Sarah asked with interest.

'I was,' Audrey said, beaming at all of them. She had never been as happy in her life. Sarah had been right when she introduced them. He was an amazing man.

On the way back from New York, Audrey had stopped in St. Louis to meet Tom's children. They had all been wonderful and welcoming to her, and she had spent some quiet time with Debbie and her nurses. She had read her some of the stories she used to read to Sarah when she was little. Tom had watched them from the doorway of Debbie's room with tears in his eyes. Audrey was more than willing to help him handle the nurses and Debbie's care, as his late wife had done. She wanted to do everything she could to help him. And then she looked around Sarah's dinner table with damp eyes. 'I feel so guilty leaving you both.' She looked at Sarah and her own mother. 'I just don't want to pass this up . . . he makes me so happy.' Sarah got up and put her arms around her then, and Mimi was next in line. All three women were crying tears of joy, while Jeff smiled at George. Jeff was a little embarrassed to be participating, but both men looked touched.

'What a wonderful occasion this has turned out to be!' George announced, as Sarah went to the refrigerator to look for a bottle of champagne she had brought from her apartment. She found it, and Jeff uncorked it for her. They all toasted the bride.

'Best wishes,' Jeff said politely, knowing that you were only supposed to congratulate the groom, and not the bride.

They each toasted Audrey, and Tom in absentia, and then Sarah suddenly realized they had a wedding to plan. 'Where are you going to do it, Mom?'

'Good lord,' she said, setting down her glass, 'I have no idea. Tom and I haven't even talked about it. Out here, of course. His children will come, except for Debbie. We only want family at the wedding, except for a few of my close friends.' In Audrey's case that meant a dozen women she had been hanging out with for the past twenty years. 'Tom's daughter wants to give a party for us in St. Louis. But I don't think we want a big wedding here.' She didn't have a wide circle of friends, and Tom knew no one in San Francisco.

'I have an idea,' Sarah said, smiling at her mother. 'My house will be painted by then.' It was nearly two months away. 'Let's do it here. You could help me stage it, Mom. We could rent some furniture, some trees maybe. We could have drinks in the garden, and do the ceremony in the living room . . . it would be so pretty, and it is a family house. What do you think?'

Audrey looked at her and beamed. 'I'd love that. Tom's not very religious, and I think he'd be more comfortable here than in a church. I'll ask him, but I think it would be terrific. What do you think, Mother?' She turned to Mimi, as her mother smiled lovingly at her.

'I'm thrilled for you, Audrey. I think it would be

wonderful to do it here, if Sarah can do it. It would mean a lot to me,' she said, smiling happily at her daughter. It was wonderful news for all of them to share. Audrey said she would call a caterer, and a few musicians. Her florist could do the flowers. All Sarah had to do was be there. And she and Tom would order the invitations. Sarah couldn't believe it was happening. Her mother was getting married and moving to St. Louis.

'I'm going to miss you, Mom,' Sarah said wistfully, as she walked her mother to the door a short while later. They had a million details to plan now, and Audrey was buzzing with excitement, mostly about the groom, which was as it should be. 'You told me I should rent the house out for weddings once I'm finished,' Sarah said, laughing as she thought of it. 'I never realized the first one I would do here would be yours.'

'Neither did I when I said it.' Audrey put an arm around her daughter and hugged her. 'You can use me as a guinea pig. I hope one of these days the wedding we have here will be yours,' her mother said, and meant it. 'By the way, I like your architect. He's a lovely person. It's too bad he has a girlfriend. How serious is he about her?' Audrey was always matchmaking, but this time Sarah had beaten her to the punch, on both counts. But she wasn't ready to tell her she was dating Jeff. She wanted to keep it to herself for a while, and enjoy it in private while they discovered each other.

'They lived together for fourteen years,' Sarah said honestly in the past tense, but Audrey was too excited about everything else to notice.

'That's too bad . . . and I think you said they own a house and business together. Well, there's always

Tom's son Fred in St. Louis. He's adorable, and just got divorced. He's already got a million women chasing after him. You'll meet him at the wedding.'

'Sounds like I'd have to fight my way through a crowd to find him. Besides, geographic undesirables don't work for me, Mom. I'm a partner in a law firm here.'

'We'll find someone,' Audrey reassured her, although Sarah wasn't worried. She was comfortable by herself now, and she was dating Jeff, even if it was still a secret. She wasn't desperate to find a man. And from all she could see, she had one. A really great one.

'I'll talk to you soon, Mom. I'm so happy for you and Tom,' Sarah said, as she kissed her good night. Mimi and George left a few minutes later. They were adorable together, and made a sweet couple. Sarah teased Mimi, as they left, that theirs would be the next wedding, and Mimi tittered and told her not to be silly, while George guffawed. They were happy as they were, going to parties and dancing, playing golf, and going to Palm Springs. They had all they wanted without marriage. But Tom would be great for Audrey, who was still young enough to want a husband. Mimi said she was happy as she was.

The house was strangely quiet after the others left. Sarah walked back to the kitchen, thinking of how odd it felt to know that her mother would be moving away. She already missed her. They had been getting along so well in recent months that it was really going to be a loss to Sarah, and made her feel a little sad, like a kid being abandoned. She didn't even want to put the feeling into words.

It made her feel silly, but it was real to her.

'Well, that was quite an evening,' Sarah said, as she walked back into the kitchen. Jeff was filling the dishwasher while he waited for her. 'I didn't expect that piece of news,' she said, as she went to help him. 'But I'm happy for her.'

'Are you okay with it?' Jeff looked at her intently. He knew her better than she thought, and he cared a lot. 'Is he a nice guy?' He liked her family, and suddenly felt protective even of Audrey, whom he scarcely knew.

'Tom? He's a fantastic man. I fixed her up with him myself. He was one of the heirs to Stanley Perlman's estate and this house. I had no idea she'd marry him, though. I know they had dinner together when he was out here, and he sent her some e-mails. She hasn't said a word to me about him since. But I think she'll be really happy with him, and once you get past her occasional prickles and sharp tongue, my mother is a really good woman.' She respected her and loved her, even if Audrey had given her a hard time over the years. But those days seemed to be behind them. And now that they were closer than they'd ever been, she was leaving. It made Sarah feel sad. 'I'm going to miss her. I feel like I just got dropped off at camp.' He smiled at her and stopped filling the dishwasher long enough to kiss her on the lips.

'You'll be okay. You can go visit her whenever you want. And I'm sure she'll come back to see you and Mimi a lot. She's going to miss you, too. Speaking of which, I have a confession to make.'

'What's that?' He had a nice way of reassuring her, and she liked it a lot. There was something very steady and comforting about him. He never

303

gave her the feeling that he was about to run away. He was the kind of guy who stuck and stayed, just as he had with Marie-Louise until she left. He had a good track record.

'My confession is that I may be dating you, but I have fallen madly in love with Mimi. I want to run away and marry her, and if I have to, I'm willing to fight off George. She is the sweetest, cutest, funniest, most adorable woman I've ever met, next to you of course. I just want you to know that I'm planning to propose to her in the immediate future. I hope that's okay.' Sarah was laughing at his description, and she was thrilled that he loved her. Mimi was totally irresistible, and he meant every word.

'Isn't she incredible?' Sarah beamed at him. 'She's the coolest grandmother in the world. I've never heard her say a mean word about anyone, she loves everyone she meets, she has fun everywhere she goes. Everyone is crazy about her, and she always has a good time. She has the best attitude of anyone I know.'

'I totally agree,' Jeff said as he started the dishwasher and turned to Sarah. 'So you won't mind if I marry her?'

'Not at all, I'll give the wedding. Gee, that would make you my stepgrandfather, wouldn't it? Do I have to call you Grampa?' He winced as she said it.

'Maybe Grampa Jeff would be a little friendlier. What do you think?' And then he grinned at her. 'I guess that makes me a really dirty old man now for dating you.' He was only six years older than she was. As he said it, he put his arms around her and kissed her. It had touched him to be part of their family dinner, and even share exciting news.

Neither of them had expected it, but it had added a special poignancy to the evening for all of them, even Jeff, and surely Mimi, whose daughter wanted to be married in the house where she herself had been born. They had come full circle.

She offered Jeff another glass of wine then. There was almost no place for them to sit yet. All she had was her kitchen table and chairs, and her bed upstairs. The rest of the time they had been working on the house, and didn't mind sitting on the floors. But on a social evening like this one, the options were limited. And she didn't feel she knew him well enough yet, in a dating context, to invite him to lie on her bed and watch TV upstairs. She didn't even have a chair in her room, although she had ordered a small pink couch, which wasn't due to arrive for months.

He said he'd had enough to drink, and they sat in the kitchen for a long time, talking. He was aware of the social awkwardness her lack of furniture caused. He knew her circumstances well. Finally, she yawned, and he smiled.

'You need to get to bed. I'm going,' he said, as he got up and she walked him slowly to the front door. It had been a lovely evening for them all.

He kissed her just inside the front door, and then looked puzzled for a moment. 'What date is this, by the way?'

'I don't know,' she mumbled as he kissed her again. He was counting something, and she wasn't sure what he was asking. She loved the way he was silly sometimes, it made her feel young.

'Well, if lunch was our first official date . . . Did we ever agree on that? . . .' he said, kissing her some more. 'Then there were three dinners . . . two

305

here, one out . . . that would make four . . . tonight makes five . . . so this is our fifth date, I think . . .'

'What are you talking about?' She laughed at him. 'You're being completely goofy. What difference does it make what date this is?' She was mystified by the point he was trying to make, while they couldn't stop kissing each other. Whatever date it was, it was extremely nice, and she was liking it a lot, also kissing him. She couldn't tear herself away from him long enough to let him leave, and he seemed to be having the same problem.

'I was just trying to figure out,' he said in an ever-huskier voice, born of passion, 'if the fifth date is too soon to ask you if I could spend the night . . . What do you think?'

She giggled. She liked the idea, and had been wondering the same thing. 'I thought you were engaged to Mimi . . . you know, Grampa Jeff.'

'Hmm . . . that's true . . . the engagement isn't official yet . . . and we don't have to tell her . . . that is if . . . unless . . . what do you think? Do you want me to go home, Sarah?' he asked, seriously for a moment. He didn't want to do anything to upset her. He was in no rush, but he was aching to spend the night with her, and had been since they met. 'If you want me to go home, I will.' He wondered if it was too soon for her. It wasn't for him. And apparently not for her, either. She shook her head no in answer to his question. She definitely didn't want him to go home, as she smiled shyly at him.

'I'd love you to stay . . . It's a little awkward here, isn't it? . . . It's not like my bedroom is a few feet away . . .' They had to go up two flights of stairs, including the grand staircase. It was definitely not a subtle little pas de deux into her bed.

'Should I race you?' He laughed as she turned off the lights and put the chain on the front door. It looked to both of them like he was staying. 'I'd carry you up the stairs, but to be honest, I'd be crippled by the time we got to your bedroom. Football injuries from college . . . I might be able to fireman carry you though, if I really had to. That's not as hard on your lower back.' She smiled at him as she took his hand, and holding hands, they walked up the grand staircase, then up yet another flight of stairs to her bedroom on the third floor. Her new bed looked very pink and pretty in the master bedroom, and the light from her two bed lamps cast a soft glow in the room.

'Welcome home,' she said softly as she turned to look at him. He was gazing down at her with eyes of wonder, as he gently released her hair, and it cascaded past her shoulders. Her big blue eyes were filled with honesty and hope.

'I love you, Sarah,' he said softly. 'I loved you the first time I saw you here . . . I never thought I'd be lucky enough for it to come to this . . .'

'Me too,' she whispered as he kissed her, and then gently lifted her onto the bed.

They both took their clothes off, and then snuggled under the covers. She turned off the lamp on her side of the bed, and he turned off the lamp on his, and then they lay holding each other tight as their passion mounted. His hands were beginning to make her body sing as he whispered, 'I'll always remember what happened on our fifth date . . .' He teased her with his words and his lips as she laughed softly.

'Shhhh . . .' she said, and then melted into him in the bed with the pink headboard in the room that had been Lilli's.

CHAPTER 20

Sarah and Jeff's romance blossomed all through May and June. He spent most of his nights with her at the house on Scott Street. He only went home for the night when he had work to do and needed his drafting table. She finally suggested he get one and put it in one of her spare little rooms. She had so many, she had plenty of room for him to set up a makeshift office with her. He liked the idea, and found a good secondhand one. He brought it home one Friday night and dragged it up the stairs. That way he could work while she continued to paint a myriad of small rooms. The painters were doing a great job on the big ones. Each day, the house looked more exquisite.

Jeff turned out to be an excellent cook and made breakfast for them every morning before they left for work. He made pancakes, French toast, fried eggs, omelettes, scrambled, even eggs Benedict on weekends, and she warned him that he'd have to leave if he made her fat. It was a treat to have him pamper her, and she did as much for him whenever she could. They still ordered take-out food most nights because they both worked late, but she cooked dinner for him all three nights on the weekend, except when he took her out to dinner. They had long since lost count of the number of dates, and agreed that there had been many. They had been together for some part of every day since Audrey's announcement of her impending marriage. And he spent just about every night of the week with her. He hadn't officially moved in, but he was there constantly. And one of the master dressing rooms was now his. Everything was working out beautifully for them.

By the first of June, preparations for Audrey and Tom's wedding were in high gear. Audrey had picked out furniture to rent for the main floor, for the dining room and sitting rooms, and the main salon. She had picked topiary trees that would have gardenias in them. She had ordered flowers for the reception rooms, and a garland of white roses and gardenias for the front door. Just as she had promised, she was taking care of every possible detail, and was paying for it herself. The wedding was going to be small, but she wanted it to be perfect. Even though it was the second wedding for each of them, she wanted it to be a day that they would remember for the rest of their lives, especially Tom. She had hired a group of four to play chamber music as people walked in. The wedding itself was going to be in the living room. She had thought of everything. The only thing missing that had her in a total panic was that she hadn't found a dress. Nor had Sarah. She had been too busy in the office to go shopping since Audrey had shared the news. Her mother finally convinced her to take an afternoon off, and they went shopping together, with great results at Neiman Marcus.

Audrey found an off-white satin cocktail dress with crystal beads on the hem, cuffs, and neck. It had long sleeves and looked demure. She found perfect white satin shoes with rhinestone buckles to go with it, and a matching handbag. Tom had just given her a spectacular pair of diamond earrings as a wedding present, and the engagement ring he had given her was a ten-carat cushion cut diamond that knocked Sarah's eyes out when she saw it. Audrey had already decided that she would be carrying a small bouquet of white orchids. She was going to be elegance incarnate.

By five o'clock on their shopping day, Sarah still hadn't found a dress, and was beginning to panic. Her mother insisted she couldn't wear an old black cocktail dress she'd worn to her office Christmas party for the past two years. As the maid of honor, she had to buy something new, and then finally her mother spotted an exceptionally pretty Valentino dress. It was the same brilliant blue as Sarah's eyes. It was satin, strapless, and had a little jacket she could take off after the wedding. Her mother suggested she wear it with high-heeled silver sandals, which looked just right. Her mother was going to have her carry a smaller bouquet of the same white orchids, and she had ordered one for Mimi as well, just so she didn't feel left out. She had boutonnieres for Tom and his sons, and a corsage of gardenias for his daughter. And Audrey had hired a photographer to record it all, in stills and on video. However small the wedding party, she had thought of every detail. And Sarah was relieved to have found a dress she liked. She didn't want to wear something she thought was ugly and would never wear again. The blue dress they'd chosen was the perfect color for her eyes, skin, and hair. It was sexy, as it molded her figure, but at the same time demure, with the jacket, and it had a very low back, which Audrey said looked sensational on her.

'What's with you and Jeff, by the way?' her mother asked casually as they left Neiman's. 'Every time I go by the house to drop something off at night or on weekends, he's there. That can't just be about work. What does his girlfriend think of all that devotion to your restoration project?'

'She doesn't,' Sarah said cryptically, juggling her packages as they headed toward the Union Square garage, where they had left their cars.

'What does that mean?' Audrey didn't want her getting into another situation where she'd get hurt, although she liked Jeff a lot.

'They broke up,' Sarah said coolly. She still liked keeping her business to herself, even though she was closer to her mother these days, especially with the wedding approaching. Knowing her mother was moving away soon, Sarah was spending more time with her, and for the first time in years, enjoying it a lot.

'That's interesting. Did they break up because of you?' Audrey considered that a hopeful sign.

'No. Before us.'

'Before "us"?' Audrey raised an eyebrow. 'Are you and Jeff an "us" these days?' That was news. She had begun to suspect it, but wasn't sure. And Sarah had said nothing. He was just there and always very helpful, courteous, and friendly whenever Audrey dropped by.

'Maybe. We don't talk about it.' That much was true. They just enjoyed each other, without discussing it or putting labels on it. They were both recently out of long-term relationships that hadn't worked, which made them both slightly gun-shy,

311

although they were happy with each other. Happier than she had ever been with Phil, or he with Marie-Louise.

'Why don't you talk about it?' Audrey inquired.

'We don't need to know.'

'Why not?' Audrey persisted. 'Sarah, you're thirty-nine years old. You don't have a lot of years to waste on relationships that go nowhere.' She didn't say it, but they both knew Phil had been a dead end for four years.

'There's nowhere I want to go, Mom. I like where I am. So does he. We're not planning to get married.' She always said that, but Audrey had always believed that if she found the right man, she'd change her mind. And maybe this time she had. Jeff appeared to be nice, competent, intelligent, successful, and solid. What more did she want? Sometimes she worried Audrey. She thought Sarah was much too independent for her own good.

'What do you have against marriage?' Audrey asked her as they found their cars and fumbled for their keys in their handbags.

Sarah hesitated for a moment and then decided to be honest. 'You and Dad. I don't ever want to be where you were with him. I couldn't do it.' She still had nightmares about it.

Audrey looked worried and lowered her voice conspiratorially. 'Does Jeff drink?' Sarah laughed and shook her head.

'No, Mom, he doesn't. Or at least no more than he should. I probably drink more than he does, and I don't drink too much, either. Marriage just looks too complicated to me. All you hear about are people who hate each other, get divorced, pay

312

spousal support, and then hate each other more. Who needs it? I don't. I'm happier like this. As soon as you add marriage to the mix, as far as I can see, you're screwed.' And then she realized what she had said to her mother, on the day they'd bought the dress she was going to wear to her next wedding. 'I'm sorry, Mom. Tom is a wonderful guy. So is Jeff. It's just not for me. And I don't think Jeff is so keen on the idea, either. He lived with his last partner for fourteen years, and they never got married.'

'Maybe she was like you. You young women are strange creatures these days. None of you wants to get married. Just us old folks do.'

'You're not an "old folk," Mom, and you look gorgeous in that dress. Tom is going to faint when he sees you. I don't know, maybe I'm just chicken.' Audrey had tears in her eyes as she listened.

'I'm sorry if your father and I did that to you. Most marriages aren't like that.' With an alcoholic husband who had left her a widow at thirty-nine, the same age Sarah was now.

'No, but too many are. I don't like the odds.'

'Neither did I. But look at me now. I can't wait to do it.' She looked ecstatic, and Sarah was equally so for her.

'Maybe I'll do it when I'm your age, Mom. I'm in no rush in the meantime.'

It made Audrey sad for her, and even more so to think that Sarah might never have children. But she had always said she didn't want any, and even now, with her biological clock ticking, presumably, she was sticking to her guns. No kids. No husband. So far all she had ever desperately wanted was her house. It was her only passion. That and her work,

313

although Audrey suspected she was in love with Jeff and didn't want to admit it. And no matter what she told her mother, Sarah knew she loved him. Which made it all the more terrifying to think about commitment. She wasn't ready. And maybe never would be. For now, it was working for both of them. Jeff wasn't putting any pressure on her. Only Audrey. She wanted everyone to be happy, and in the excitement of her upcoming big moment, she thought everyone should be married, like her and Tom. 'Why don't you work on Mimi and George?' Sarah teased her.

'They don't need to get married at their age,' Audrey said, smiling, although they were sweet together and inseparable now.

'Maybe they don't agree. I think you should throw her the bouquet at the wedding. If you throw it at me, I'm throwing it right back at you.'

'I get the message,' Audrey said with a sigh. Sarah knew what she wanted and what she didn't. She was a very stubborn woman.

They each got into their cars then and drove home, relieved that they had found dresses for the wedding. Jeff was talking to the painters when she got home. They were almost finished. So far the renovation had taken six months, and it looked gorgeous. There were still details to attend to, and there would be for a long time. But the house looked beautiful and was very much in order and, thanks to Jeff, had come in way under budget. She had even finished the bookcase she made and it was now full of law books in her study. There was even room for more. Everything about the house was perfect. She had currently been thinking about starting to order curtains, at least for some of the rooms. She was finishing the house bit by bit. And getting it where she wanted. In the fall, she wanted to start looking for furniture at antique auctions. She and Jeff thought it would be fun to go together. He was very knowledgeable about antiques and was teaching her a lot.

'How was your day?' Jeff smiled at her as she walked in and put down her things. She took off her shoes with a sigh. Her mother shopped hard and took it seriously. She was exhausted.

'Tough day at Neiman's. We found dresses for the wedding.' He knew they'd both been worried about it till then.

'Joe and I are talking about the color for the ballroom. I think you should go with a warm cream. What do you think?' They had already agreed stark white would be too harsh, and in a moment of frivolity, Sarah had thought pale blue, but she liked the cream idea better. She trusted Jeff's eye and instincts. He hadn't steered her wrong so far, and was extremely respectful of her opinions, even though he was the architect. It was, after all, her house, and he was mindful of it.

'I agree.'

'Good. Now go have a bath and a glass of wine or something. I'm taking you out to dinner.' He went upstairs to the ballroom with the painter, to try out samples on the walls, which always made a big difference, depending on how the light hit it.

'Yes, sir,' she said, marching upstairs to her room, carrying her shoes, with her spoils from Neiman's. The stairs in her new house were keeping her in shape. She hadn't started to build the gym in the basement yet. She wanted to do curtains and furniture first.

He was back upstairs in her bedroom half an hour later. She was lying on the bed, watching the news and looking relaxed. He loved just watching her sometimes. He lay down next to her and put an arm around her.

'I told my mother about us today,' Sarah said vaguely, keeping her eyes on the TV.

'What did she say?'

'Nothing much. She likes you. So does Mimi. She just gave me the usual corny crap, about my age, last chance, kids, blah blah blah.'

'Translate that for me,' he asked with interest. 'The blah blah blah part. Fill in the gaps.'

'She thinks I should get married and have kids. I don't. I never did.'

'Why not?'

'I don't believe in marriage. I think it fucks up everything.'

'Oh well, that simplifies things, doesn't it?'

'It does for me. Is that okay with you?' She looked at him then, vaguely worried. They had never explored the subject in detail. Since he had never married Marie-Louise, she had always assumed he felt the same way she did.

'I don't know. I guess so. If it has to be. I wouldn't mind having a kid one day, or even two. And it's probably nicer for the kid if its parents are married, but it's not essential if it's a deal breaker for you.'

'I don't want kids,' she said firmly, looking scared.

'Why not?'

'Too scary. It changes people's lives too much. I never see my old friends. They're all too busy changing diapers and driving carpool. How much

316

fun can that be?'

'Some people seem to like it,' he said cautiously.

She looked at him honestly then. 'Tell the truth, can you really see either of us with a kid? I don't think we're that kind of people. At least I'm not. I like my work. I like what I do. I like lying here on my ass watching TV before you take me out to dinner, and we don't need a babysitter to do it. I love you . . . I'm crazy about my house. Why mess with a good thing? Why push it? What if you wound up with a really awful kid who did drugs and stole cars or something, or like Tom's daughter, blind and brain damaged? I couldn't do it.'

'You paint a pretty grim picture, Sarah.'

'Yeah. You should have seen my mother's life when she was married to my father. He was a vegetable, always drunk, hiding in the bedroom while she made excuses for him. And my childhood was a nightmare. I was always afraid he'd come reeling out when my friends were there, or do something to embarrass me. And then he died, which was worse. My mother cried all the time, and I felt guilty because I used to wish he'd die or leave or something, and then he did, and I figured it was my fault. Forget it. I finally made it out of the trenches into adulthood, and I'm not going back to any part of that. I didn't like being a kid, and I don't want to do that to someone else.'

'Neither of us drinks,' he said practically.

She looked at him, horrified. 'Are you telling me you want kids?' That was a news flash to her, and not a good one.

'Maybe one day,' he said honestly, 'before I'm too ancient.'

317

'And if I don't?' She felt panicked as she asked him, but she wanted to know, before they went any further. It could be a deal breaker for her.

'If you don't, I love you anyway. I won't push it. I'd rather have you than a kid . . . but maybe at some point, I wouldn't mind having both.' She was stunned to hear it. She had assumed he didn't want any, either. This was not good news to her.

'If I had a kid, I wouldn't get married,' she said defiantly, and he laughed at her, and leaned over and kissed her.

'I wouldn't expect anything less of you, my love. Let's not worry about it. Whatever happens, happens.' They were being careful, but listening to him, Sarah reminded herself to be more so. She didn't want any slips, if so, he'd probably want to keep it and she wouldn't. They didn't need the headache or the grief. She thought their life together was perfect just as it was.

'I'm too old to have children anyway,' she said, pushing it further. 'I'll be forty on my next birthday,' she reminded him. 'That's way too old.' But they both knew it wasn't. He didn't comment. It was obviously a subject that upset her, and for now anyway, it was not a pressing problem. For either of them.

They both dropped the subject, went out and had a pleasant dinner. Sarah told him about her mother's idea to rent out the house, or parts of it, for people to give weddings, which Sarah thought was not a bad way to make some extra money to pay for the furniture she wanted. She liked the idea, and Jeff thought it might be fun, although annoying to have strangers in the house who might wander around where they shouldn't. Jeff had

318

another idea, which he thought would be funny, but it would take money to make money, and for the moment she was hanging on to what she had, for her house and all the things she wanted to buy to make it even more beautiful than it already was.

Jeff's idea was that they buy houses together, in bad shape, restore and remodel them together, then sell them at a profit. He loved what she had done to her own house, and said she had a knack for it. She liked the idea, but worried about what it would cost them. It was an idea for the long haul, if there was one. So were marriage and babies. They seemed to be discussing long-term plans tonight. But she liked his idea about redoing houses on spec. She knew she was going to be sad when the house on Scott Street was finally complete. She had loved every minute of doing it, and still did.

He stayed with her that night, and for the weekend. He hardly went to his apartment anymore except to get books and clothes. He had only spent a few days in it since he rented it. And he told her at dinner that he had just had a serious offer for the house on Potrero Hill. Marie-Louise had been sending him e-mails breathing down his neck for the money. After the appraisals, he was keeping the business and she was getting the proceeds from the house. She had told him to accept the offer, so he had. She had bought out his share of the apartment in Paris. She was going to live there, and set up a studio for herself. Their life of fourteen years had unraveled fairly easily, surprisingly so, which only validated Sarah's point to her mother. It was easier not to get married, especially if anything went wrong further down the road. Sarah thought Marie-Louise was lucky. Jeff

319

was a great guy. He had handled everything for her, didn't cheat her out of a penny, was generous to a fault, and gave her everything she wanted. He was a prince in every way. Sarah was impressed by all she saw. The gods had smiled on her this time. So far. For now at least, she didn't want to look past today.

CHAPTER 21

Audrey's wedding came faster than anyone expected. It was hard to believe that the end of June had arrived. One minute they were planning the wedding, and the next, the caterers were bustling around in the kitchen, the videographer was setting up his camera at the right angle, the florist had brought the topiary trees, there were garlands on the stairs and over the front door. A photographer was following every human in the house like a heat-seeking missile, then photographing the decor, the preparations, and the guests as they arrived. The musicians were playing. Tom and his children were standing in the front hall, as Jeff and Sarah chatted with them. Fred had brought his new girlfriend, which made Sarah smile. So much for that, not that she cared, she had Jeff now. And Mimi and George walked in looking like an ad for vibrant old people in a magazine. She was wearing a pale blue silk dress and jacket that harmonized well with Sarah's brighter blue one.

And suddenly, they were waiting for Audrey to come down the stairs. There was no one to walk her down. She came down alone to Handel's *Water Music,* with tears running down her cheeks as she looked at Tom. She took everyone's breath away, she looked so pretty. Mimi looked proud, Sarah squeezed Jeff's arm, and as Tom looked at the woman he was marrying, he cried openly, standing between his two sons. Everyone was moved, as she walked to him and took his arm.

The judge who performed the ceremony spoke wisely about the challenges of marriage, and the blessings it provided when it was right, the wisdom of it between two good people who had chosen well. The food was delicious. The wine was fabulous. The house looked spectacular, the furniture Audrey had rented to stage it looked like it belonged there. Sarah really liked Tom's children, and his sons got on famously with Jeff. It was the perfect day, the perfect time, and before anyone could blink, Audrey was standing at the top of the stairs again in her beautiful white satin dress, and her bouquet of white orchids came hurtling down and hit Mimi in the chest, as Sarah let out her breath, and her mother winked at her. Tom tossed the garter at Jeff. And then the assembled company stood on the sidewalk outside the house, throwing rose petals, as Tom and Audrey drove away in a rented Rolls to the Ritz-Carlton, where they would spend their wedding night, before flying to London the next morning. They were flying from there to Monte Carlo, and then on to Italy for a three-week honeymoon Tom had planned carefully, while following all of Audrey's many instructions. It didn't bother him at all. He loved it.

As Sarah and her new stepfamily walked back

into the house, Mimi was sitting on the rented couch, still holding the bouquet and smiling. 'I'm next!' she said happily as George pretended to faint.

'Not you, George!' Jeff corrected him in his ersatz panic. 'I caught the garter. It's me and Mimi, not you!' Mimi giggled, and they all laughed, as waiters poured them all more champagne. She and George had one last dance, while the young people chatted.

Sarah liked her new relatives, and urged them to come back and stay with her whenever they wanted. Two of them were married, and one had been, and they had all brought their children, who were very well behaved. Audrey now had a whole new family, including six grandchildren, and for a moment Sarah was almost jealous, knowing they would see more of her now than she would. Mimi was going to be the only family she had in San Francisco. Audrey had given up her apartment, and everything she owned had been shipped to St. Louis, to be assimilated into Tom's sprawling house. She had given a few pieces of furniture to Sarah, but kept most of it herself. Sarah knew Audrey's absence was going to be a big change for Mimi and her, but they were happy for her. She had looked like a happy bride when she left, and Tom a proud groom.

It was late when everyone finally left that night. The caterers were still cleaning up. The topiaries were being picked up the next day. There was nothing for Sarah to do, as she walked slowly up the stairs with Jeff.

'It was pretty, wasn't it?' she asked him with a yawn, as he smiled at her. He loved her dress. It made her eyes look even bluer. She leaned against him happily.

'It was beautiful. They were both so cute when they stood there crying during the ceremony. I nearly cried myself.'

'I always cry at weddings. From terror.' Sarah chuckled cynically, and Jeff shook his head with a grin.

'You're hopeless.'

'And you're an incurable romantic, and I love you for it,' she said as they kissed at the top of the stairs, and then went up the next flight to their bedroom. It had been a perfect day. For Audrey and Tom, and all those who loved them. Sarah was happy for her. She had never expected her matchmaking to have this result, but now that it had happened, she was glad it did. She hoped they had a long and happy life together. Her mother called her as they were going to bed, to thank her for letting her use the house, and tell her how much she loved her. She sounded blissfully happy.

Sarah snuggled up close to Jeff that night. She loved cuddling with him in bed, as well as making love, which they did a lot. The relationship was working perfectly for both of them. They had settled into a comfortable routine, and she loved that Jeff was so at ease with her family, especially Mimi, whom he adored. He said he wanted her to adopt him, if she wouldn't marry him. He was willing to do either, or both.

'Good night, sweetheart,' he whispered, as they drifted off to sleep.

'I love you,' Sarah responded, and smiled thinking of the bouquet that had missed her when Mimi caught it.

CHAPTER 22

Sarah and Jeff worked on the house all summer. They started looking at catalogs and going to auctions. He was working on a big restoration/remodel in Pacific Heights, which ate up his time. And Sarah was busy at the office.

In August, they both took a week off and went up to Lake Tahoe. They walked and swam, rode mountain bikes, and water-skied in the icy lake. On Labor Day weekend, at the end of their stay, Jeff reminded her that they had been together for four months. They both agreed they had been the happiest months of their lives. The subject of marriage and children hadn't come up again. It was more of a theoretical question for them. Neither of them had any desire to rock the boat. They had plenty of things to keep them busy.

Audrey called from St. Louis frequently once they got back from Italy. She was busy settling in, and wanted to redecorate Tom's house, so she was occupied and getting to know his children. She missed her daughter and mother, but already knew she wouldn't be back for Thanksgiving. She had promised Tom she would stay in St. Louis with his kids, and Sarah said she would have Thanksgiving dinner with Mimi. Sarah was going to do it at her house this year, and if all continued to go well, Jeff would join them. Sarah told Audrey she didn't want to go to St. Louis, she was anxious to start a tradition of her own, although it would be a smaller group this year without Audrey. And Sarah would have to cook the turkey and make dinner, a first for her.

The fall was exceptionally busy for Sarah at work. She had three big estates to probate, worked on her house on weekends. It was an endless source of delight to her, and would be for years. She and Jeff went to auctions, and even put bids on furniture at Sotheby's and Christie's, in L.A. and New York. She had already acquired several pretty pieces. Jeff had bought a few, too. And in October, he gave up his apartment. He never used it. He moved his things in with her. He had an office and a study now, his dressing room and bathroom, and said he didn't mind living in a pink bedroom. He liked it. But most of all, he liked Sarah. He truly loved her, and she loved him.

He had settled the house and Paris apartment with Marie-Louise. The business was his now. All of her clients shifted their accounts to him. He hadn't heard from her since August, and much to his own surprise, didn't miss her. Even though they had spent fourteen years together, he always knew it was wrong for him. He had just kept investing himself in it. But now that he was with Sarah, he saw the difference. It was as though they were made for each other. He woke up every day, as she did, unable to believe his good fortune. He remembered his own grandfather's old saying that there was a pot for every lid, or a lid for every pot. Whichever it was, he had found it. The only one as amazed by it as he was, was Sarah, who was equally delighted with him.

As Sarah had promised she would, she made Thanksgiving dinner at her house that year. They had a couch and some chairs by then, a coffee table, and a beautiful antique desk in the living room. They actually had somewhere to sit and put down their drinks when Mimi and George came to dinner. Mimi had asked her to invite her two best friends, as she herself usually did, so Sarah had included them, and a friend of Jeff's who was in town from New York and had nowhere to spend Thanksgiving. It was a comfortable, easy group, as the seven of them sat in the living room, while Sarah and Jeff took turns checking on the turkey. Sarah was terrified that it would either be raw, or she'd burn it. It wasn't the same without Audrey. But much to her own surprise, the dinner turned out well. Mimi said the blessing, and this year Jeff carved the turkey. He did a masterful job of it, and George said he was relieved not to have to do it.

He and Mimi had just come back from Palm Springs. Sarah noticed that they were spending more and more time there. They said they liked the weather better, and Mimi enjoyed his friends and the dinner parties they went to. She had just celebrated her eighty-third birthday, but didn't look it. She was as lively and beautiful as ever. George had become a permanent fixture, and was only slightly older than she.

Sarah was serving the mince, apple, and pumpkin pies they had every year at the end of the meal, while Jeff dished out the ice cream and whipped cream, when Mimi looked at them, somewhat nervously, and George nodded encouragement.

'I have something to tell you,' she said timidly as Sarah looked at her. Sarah could sense more than guess at what was coming. But at Mimi's age, what could it be? Her life rolled along without incident, as long as she was in good health. There was a twinkle in her eyes as she looked first at Jeff, then at Sarah. 'George and I are getting married,' she almost whispered. She looked faintly embarrassed, as though there was something slightly silly about it. But they loved each other and wanted to spend their final years together. The only bad news was that they were moving to Palm Springs. George had already sold his house in the city, and Mimi was putting her house on the market. They were going to use George's apartment in San Francisco, whenever they came to town, which Sarah suspected, sadly, wouldn't be often. They had too much fun in Palm Springs, and far less in San Francisco.

'You're marrying *him* and not *me*?' Jeff said, looking outraged. 'I caught the garter, you know, he didn't.' He pretended to look disgusted, and sorely wronged, as the others laughed at him.

'I'm sorry, darling.' Mimi patted his hand lovingly. 'You'll just have to marry Sarah.'

'No, he won't,' Sarah was quick to add.

'Yeah, fat chance of that,' Jeff complained. 'She won't have me.'

'Have you asked her?' Mimi asked with eyes full of hope and wonder. She would have liked that, and she knew Audrey would, too. They had chatted about it several times.

'No,' Jeff answered honestly, sitting down to eat his pie, while Sarah poured champagne. It felt like déjà vu, from when her mother had announced the same thing at the same table in May. Now Mimi was getting married. Sarah reflected that all her female relatives were getting married and moving away. It left only her and Jeff in the city. She was already lonely at the prospect of Mimi leaving, although she was excited for them at their news, and it was obvious they were, too. George just sat there and beamed, while Mimi's eyes danced.

'If I ask Sarah to marry me, she'll probably dump me, or at least throw me out. She's committed to the notion of living in sin as a way of life,' Jeff said, and Mimi laughed. They all knew that Jeff and Sarah were living together, and it didn't bother her at all. She was nearly forty years old, and had a right to do what she wanted.

Sarah ignored his good-natured complaints and asked them when they were getting married. They hadn't set the date yet, but they wanted it to be soon. 'At our age, we can't afford to wait,' Mimi said gaily, as though that were a good thing. 'George probably wants to get married on the golf course, between games. We can't decide whether to do it there or here. We have so many friends down there, it might be too much fuss,' Mimi said pensively, as they all toasted the couple with champagne.

'Why don't you do it here, like Mom did?' Sarah suggested, feeling nostalgic about the whole event. It was so weird that all the elders of the family were getting married. She suddenly felt alone out in left field.

'That's an awful lot of trouble for you,' Mimi said. 'I don't want to give you all that work. You're so busy.'

'I'm not too busy for you,' Sarah insisted. 'I can use the same caterers Mom had for her wedding. They were great. They didn't even leave a mess.'

'Are you sure?' Mimi seemed to hesitate, but George looked enthusiastic. He liked the idea, and reminded her that she had been born in the house.

It made sense to get married there. It was a nice, sentimental thing to do. Jeff's friend from New York was enjoying the exchange of plans and said his own grandmother had remarried the year before and moved to Palm Beach, and was very happy.

'When would you like to do it?' Sarah asked matter-of-factly, as Jeff continued to play the rejected lover, which delighted Mimi. She always referred to him to Sarah as 'that sweet boy.' At forty-five, just recently, he was no boy, although he looked young for his age.

'We were thinking of New Year's Eve,' George interjected. 'It'll give us something to celebrate every year. And I think it would be nice for your grandmother to do it here, in this house. It would mean a lot to her,' he added, and she blushed. She had told him only that morning that she didn't want to burden Sarah, but she had admitted how much she would love it, so everyone was pleased.

'Does Mom know?' Sarah suddenly wondered. Her mother hadn't said a thing. Mimi nodded.

'We called her this morning, and told her when we wished them a happy Thanksgiving. She approved.'

'Traitor,' Jeff muttered darkly. 'I'm a much better catch than he is.' He glanced at George to everyone's amusement. 'Although I have to admit, he's the better dancer. When I danced with Mimi at Audrey's wedding, I stepped all over her feet, and those pretty pale blue shoes. So I guess I can't blame you. But you've broken my heart.'

'I'm sorry, darling.' She leaned over and kissed his cheek. 'Come and stay with us anytime you like in Palm Springs. You can even bring Sarah.'

329

'I should hope so.' Sarah pretended to be miffed, and then they got down to the details of the wedding. She got out a yellow pad and made a list of what they wanted. They wanted to keep it very simple. Only the immediate family. And a simple dinner. They wanted a minister to marry them, and Mimi assured Sarah that hers would come to the house. Mimi wanted to do it at eight o'clock, and have a nine o'clock dinner. Audrey had told her that morning that she and Tom would come. She said they'd probably go down to Pebble Beach after that for the weekend.

'What has my family suddenly become?' Sarah complained loudly. 'Nomads? Doesn't anyone want to be in San Francisco anymore except me?'

'Apparently not,' Jeff answered for them. 'I don't think it's personal. They're just having more fun somewhere else.' He wouldn't have admitted it to her, but as much as he liked Mimi, and even Audrey, he liked the idea of having Sarah to himself.

'Wow,' Sarah said, as she suddenly thought of it, 'we only have six weeks to plan the wedding. I'll call the caterer and everyone else tomorrow.' But there were no invitations to send out, nothing elaborate to organize. What they wanted was very simple. It would just be the immediate family, in the house, on New Year's Eve. It would be even simpler than Audrey's wedding to Tom.

They chatted excitedly about it for the next two hours, and then all the guests went home. Mimi had told them before she and George left that they weren't taking a honeymoon. They were going to do something easy like spend a weekend at the Bel Air hotel in L.A. Mimi had always liked it, and it

330

was an easy drive for them. Jeff had told them that he was disappointed to hear they weren't doing something more exotic, like a trip to Las Vegas. He had hugged both of them when they left.

'Boy, is that a weird feeling,' Sarah admitted to Jeff as they loaded the dishwashers in the kitchen. Jeff had encouraged her to have two, and she was glad she did. It made evenings like this a snap. And it always made things so much easier for her that Jeff helped her. He was a good sport about things like that.

'What? Your grandmother getting married? I think it's really nice for her. It's nice for both of them that they don't have to be alone at that age.'

'She adored my grandfather, and my mother was afraid she'd die when he did, but she's had a whole second life, and sometimes I think she's enjoying it just as much.' It had certainly looked that way tonight. 'I meant that it feels weird that they're all moving away. We've all been here together for all these years. Now Mom's in St. Louis, and Mimi will be in Palm Springs.'

'I'm here,' he said softly.

'I know.' She smiled, and leaned over and kissed him. 'I guess this forces me to have a more grown-up life. I always felt like a kid while they were here. Maybe that's what I meant when I said this feels weird.'

'It must,' Jeff said, as they turned off the lights in the kitchen and went upstairs to what they now called 'their' room, not just hers. It felt that way now.

Sarah called her mother in the morning, and told her she was a sneak for keeping the secret the day before, when Sarah had called to wish her a happy Thanksgiving. Audrey had called another time herself, and said not a word.

'I didn't want to spoil the surprise. She asked me not to. I think it's great, and the weather is better for her down there. It's a better climate. Tom and I will come in for the wedding, at least for one night.'

'Would you like to stay here?' Sarah asked hopefully.

'We'd love it.'

'That'll be fun, to have us all under one roof.'

Sarah got all the details she needed from her mother after that and set it up on Monday. All Mimi had to do was buy her dress. She said she felt too old to get married in white. She called Sarah two days later, sounding victorious. She had found the perfect dress in a color they called champagne. Sarah realized then that she had to get one herself. This time she chose a dark green velvet. And since it was New Year's Eve, she decided to get something long. Audrey said she was going to be wearing navy blue.

For the next five weeks between Thanksgiving and Christmas, Sarah's life was a relay race, with no one to whom she could pass the baton. She didn't want Mimi to have to do any of the work for the wedding, but Sarah didn't have time, either. She told the caterer to do it all. She had them check details with her.

Beyond that, she was frantic at the house, trying to make sure Mimi's wedding would be impeccable, going to holiday parties with Jeff, and trying to get ready for Christmas herself. Jeff was ecstatic. After years of tiptoeing apologetically around Marie-Louise's annual seasonal gloom, as though he had caused the entire event, this year he could celebrate it with abandon. Every day he brought home new decorations, more presents, another tape of carols, and two weeks before Christmas, he came home with a twenty-foot Douglas fir. He had four men from The Guardsmen set it up next to the grand staircase, after which he brought home two carloads of decorations. Sarah laughed when she saw it. The carols he had on the stereo system were so loud she could hardly hear him when he talked to her from the top of the ladder. He had just put the star on the top of the tree.

'I said it's like living in Santa's workshop!' she shouted up at him, and then repeated it three more times. 'Never mind. It looks great!' she complimented him, shouting up to him again, and this time he heard her, and thanked her. He was so pleased with himself, and she loved him for doing it. She had bought him a beautiful antique architect's desk at auction, and it was being delivered to the house on Christmas Eve. He nearly fainted when he saw it.

'Oh my God, Sarah, it's gorgeous!' He loved it. He loved celebrating Christmas with her.

Both her mother and grandmother were away. It was her first Christmas without them. But Jeff made it wonderful for her. She cooked a small turkey on Christmas Eve, and they went to church together at midnight. She realized as she shared dinner with him, and an excellent bottle of wine he'd bought, that the year before, on exactly that date, she had told her mother and grandmother about the house on Scott Street, and now here they were, and she was in it.

She didn't forget either that a year before, she had been alone for the fifth holiday season in a row, and Phil had been in Aspen with his children, while she was once again not included. Her life had changed radically in a year, and she loved it, both Jeff and the house. The only downside was that her family had moved away, and she was not so keen on that. Progress. Sometimes it was good, sometimes not. But at least they had moved away for happy reasons.

Jeff and Sarah shared a lazy day on Christmas Day. He had given her a narrow diamond tennis bracelet, and she kept looking at it and smiling at him. He was very generous with her, and she loved it as much as he did his new desk. She had also given him a bunch of small silly gifts, filled a stocking for him, and even left him a letter from Santa, telling him what a good boy he was, but to please stop dumping his dirty laundry all over the laundry room floor and expecting someone else to pick it up. It was his only flaw. He didn't have many. And he loved everything Sarah had done for him over the holidays. It was night and day from his experience with Marie-Louise. Sarah was the best Christmas gift he'd ever had.

Five days after Christmas, Audrey and Tom arrived from St. Louis. It really felt like Christmas to her then. Her grandmother and George also arrived that night. Both couples were staying at Sarah's house, and she loved it. Jeff helped her cook for all of them. And the three women spent long hours in the kitchen, chatting. Audrey told them all about her life in St. Louis. She loved it. Tom was even better than she'd ever dreamed. She looked genuinely happy. And Mimi looked ecstatic. The original blushing bride. Sarah loved that they were all staying with her. It made her feel like a kid again to have them both around.

They all went out to breakfast the next day, on the morning of New Year's Eve. The caterers were already at work in the kitchen, and even for a small dinner party, the preparations seemed endless. But both Mimi and George seemed remarkably calm. They all had a good time together, laughing and chatting. The three men talked football and stock market shifts. Tom and George talked golf. Jeff flirted with the bride, much to her delight, and Audrey and Sarah talked about the wedding details and went over a checklist. They went for a walk after that, and didn't get back to the house till one o'clock.

After that, Mimi disappeared into a different bedroom, and told George she didn't want to see him till that night. Sarah had arranged for the hairdresser to come to the house, and a manicurist to do nails.

They spent a delightful afternoon enjoying each other. They were all going to stay there that night, too, to see the New Year in after the wedding. The next day the newlyweds were heading to L.A. for the weekend, and Audrey and Tom for Pebble Beach. Jeff and Sarah were going to stay home and relax. Sarah was going to try and paint two more rooms, she was becoming expert at it, and Jeff had to work on a bunch of projects.

The house was filled with bustle as eight o'clock approached. Sarah and Audrey went upstairs to help Mimi dress. When they walked into her room, she was sitting on her bed in her dressing gown, with her hair done, holding the photograph of her

335

mother.

She looked at her daughter and granddaughter, and had tears in her eyes as she set the photograph down.

'Are you all right, Mother?' Audrey asked her gently.

'I'm fine.' Mimi sighed. 'I was just thinking of how happy my parents must have been here at first . . . and that I was born in this house . . . I'm so glad I'm marrying George here. Somehow it feels so right . . . I was thinking that my mother would have liked it.' She looked at Sarah then. 'I'm so glad you bought this house. I never knew how much it would mean to me when you told us about it . . . it sounds silly to say at my age, but after all that sadness growing up, and missing her when I was young, I finally feel as though I've come home, and I found her.'

Sarah took her in her arms then and held her, and whispered softly to the grandmother she loved so much, they all did. 'I love you, Mimi . . . so much . . . thank you for saying that.' It made buying the house seem even more right. In fact, it was perfect.

CHAPTER 23

At the last minute, they had decided to make the wedding black tie. All three women were going to be wearing long gowns, as were Mimi's five or six friends who were attending. The men were wearing tuxedos. The groom looked very debonair with a red bow tie, and ruby studs and cufflinks that had been his grandfather's. Much to everyone's delight, Jeff had volunteered to give the bride away, and she accepted. She was afraid to fall, or trip on her gown, if she came down the grand staircase alone. She felt safer with a strong arm to lean on. They didn't want a mishap at the wedding.

'And since you won't marry me, Mimi, which shows very poor judgment on your part, I decided to be gracious and give you away to George. Although I must say, you should be ashamed of leading me on for the last six months. I'll be right there, in case you change your mind and come to your senses at the last minute.' Mimi loved the games Jeff played with her, and so did he.

He was waiting outside her room when she was ready. She came out in her pale gold and champagne-colored evening gown with gold high-heeled shoes. She was carrying a bouquet of lily of the valley, which she said had been her mother's favorite flower. The groom was wearing a sprig of it on his lapel as he waited for her downstairs. Audrey and Tom noticed with a smile that he was looking nervous.

They chatted quietly with the minister as they waited for her to come down, as a harp and violins began playing. Sarah had lit everything by candlelight and turned the lights down. And then suddenly they saw her coming. She still had a lovely figure, even at her age, and she looked absolutely regal, as she came slowly down the stairs on Jeff's arm. He looked solemn, handsome, and distinguished. She looked up at Jeff and smiled, as he patted her hand, and then her eyes found George, and she smiled. For a moment, Sarah realized that Mimi looked a lot like Lilli, she was just older, but equally pretty. There was the same mischievous sparkle in her eye, the same passion for life. It was as though the photograph Sarah had of her had come to life and grown up. Sarah had a sudden sense of the power of the generations that had followed after her, like ripples on the ocean. Mimi, her mother, herself, and Lilli long before them.

Mimi looked serene as she moved gracefully from Jeff's arm to that of the man who was about to become her husband. They stood in front of the minister, and exchanged their vows in clear, strong, peaceful voices. Then George kissed the bride, and the music started up again, and everyone was laughing and crying and celebrating, as they had done only months before for Audrey.

Jeff kissed the bride, and told her it was now official. He had been jilted at the altar. Mimi kissed him, and then kissed everyone, especially Audrey and Sarah.

They had dinner, as planned, at nine, and the champagne flowed till midnight. The three women who were descended from Lilli all kissed their men at midnight. And then danced briefly to the violins. No one went to bed until after two in the morning. It had been a perfect little gem of a wedding.

Sarah lay in bed next to Jeff afterward and smiled at him. 'I'm beginning to feel like a professional wedding planner.' She laughed. 'It was pretty, wasn't it? You looked so handsome when you came down the stairs with Mimi.'

'She wasn't even shaking. I was more nervous than she was,' he confessed.

'George looked a little anxious, poor thing.' She

turned to Jeff again then. 'Happy New Year, sweetheart.'

'You too, Sarah.'

They fell asleep in each other's arms, and the next morning they got up to cook breakfast. It was a festive morning, and both older couples were packed and ready to leave after breakfast. Mimi was coming down the stairs toward George when she remembered that she had forgotten something. The others were all standing at the foot of the stairs, chatting, when she came back down again, carrying her bouquet of lily of the valley from the night before.

'I forgot to throw my bouquet last night,' she said, smiling down at them. She stopped halfway down the stairs as they watched her. She was wearing a bright red suit, with her mink coat over her arm, and low-heeled shoes. She looked well put together, and far younger than her age, as she took a last whiff of the delicate flowers and gracefully tossed them at her granddaughter. Sarah caught them before they fell to the floor, looked startled, and then, as though they were too hot to handle, she tossed them back to Mimi, almost by reflex, who caught them with one hand, and threw them at Jeff, who caught them with both hands, and stood there grinning, while everyone applauded.

'Nice save,' George complimented him, as Mimi reached the bottom of the stairs and looked straight at Jeff.

'Since Sarah doesn't know what to do with them, Jeff, I hope you do,' she said, and then kissed them all, got into the taxi that was waiting, and left for the airport. The honeymoon had begun. Audrey and Tom left five minutes later, to drive to Pebble Beach, and play golf at Cypress Point for the weekend.

Sarah and Jeff stood in the front hall after they all left, looking at each other. He was still holding the bouquet and set it down gently on a table.

'You give good wedding.' He smiled at her as he put his arms around her.

'Thank you. So do you,' she said, as he kissed her.

CHAPTER 24

It was a quiet weekend after everyone left. Jeff went to his office upstairs to work. Sarah changed her clothes and started her painting project. She brought him a sandwich at his desk around two. They both worked till dinnertime, they ate leftovers from the wedding, and afterward they went to a movie. He had recorded the football game earlier on TV, and watched it when they got home. It was a perfect New Year's Day, and a nice counterpoint to the busy days leading up to the wedding. The house didn't seem as much empty as peaceful.

'What am I supposed to do with Mimi's bouquet?' she asked Jeff the next morning, when she found it in the fridge. He had put it there in case she wanted to save it. The fragrance was heavenly each time either of them opened the refrigerator door. 'Is it bad luck to throw it away?'

'Probably,' he said, as he put the butter away. 'I thought you'd want to keep it. It's a nice souvenir of the wedding,' he said innocently.

'A likely story. You'll probably throw it at me in my sleep.'

'I wouldn't dare. I'd be struck by lightning,' he teased her. 'You could dry it or something, and give it back to her in a year, on their first anniversary.'

'That's a good idea. I'll do that.' She put it in a box carefully, on a shelf in the kitchen. And for the rest of the day, they were both busy.

They went to a party given by old friends of Sarah's on Sunday night, and on Monday the new year began with a bang. It seemed like every client she had wanted to rewrite their will that month. New tax laws had been passed, and everyone was in a panic. She had never been as busy. She had promised her mother they would come to see them in St. Louis, but she didn't see when. She felt as though her workload was never-ending. And Jeff was just as busy. It seemed as though everyone had bought an old house over the holidays, or inherited one, and wanted to hire him to restore it. Business was good for him, but without Marie-Louise there with him now, everything rested on his shoulders, and he was swamped.

After four weeks of working day and night and burning the candle at both ends, Sarah caught a terrible cold at the end of January. She had never been as sick in her life, and after a week of cold and fever that kept her home, it then turned into stomach flu, and she spent the next four days in the bathroom. Jeff felt sorry for her, and kept bringing her soup, orange juice, or tea. It all made her even sicker, and finally she just lay in bed moaning.

'I think I'm dying,' she said to him, as tears

rolled down her cheeks. He felt helpless, and at the end of the second week he told her she had to go to the doctor. She was planning to, and had an appointment the following morning. She called her mother that night, complaining about how awful she felt, as Audrey listened to her long list of symptoms.

'Maybe you're pregnant,' Audrey said matter-of-factly.

'That's not funny. I have a cold, Mom. Not morning sickness.'

'I had colds the whole time I was pregnant with you. It's something about your immune system lowering so you don't reject the baby. And you said you've been throwing up for the past four days.'

'From stomach flu, not a baby.' She was annoyed at her mother's casual and obviously inept diagnosis.

'Why don't you check it out. These days that's very easy.'

'I know what I've got. I have the Asian flu, or consumption or something. Everyone at the office has it.'

'It was just a thought. All right, then go to the doctor.'

'I am. In the morning.' She lay in bed afterward, annoyed at what her mother had said, and silently calculating. Her period was two days late, but that often happened to her when she got sick. She wasn't even worried. Or she hadn't been, until she talked to her mother. Now she was, and she lay in bed thinking about it. That would be truly awful. It was the last thing she wanted. She had a great life, a terrific career, a man she loved, a wonderful house. And she did not want a baby.

She got so nervous about it finally that she got up, dressed, and drove to the nearest drugstore, where she bought a pregnancy test. Jeff wasn't home yet. Feeling stupid for even doing it, she followed the directions, did the test, left it on her sink, went back to bed, and turned on the TV. She'd almost forgotten about it half an hour later, and went back to her bathroom to see what the results were. She knew they were going to be not pregnant. She had been careful all her life, and aside from one or two scares when she was in college, she had never played baby roulette. She wasn't on the Pill. But with rare exceptions, she and Jeff were always careful, except at the right time of month, when she knew she had no worries.

She picked up the test with a smug look, glanced at it, looked again, and then fumbled in the garbage for the instructions. There were two lines on the test, and she suddenly couldn't remember if there were supposed to be one or two if she wasn't pregnant. The diagram stated it clearly so anyone could read it. One line, not pregnant. Two lines, pregnant. She looked again. Two lines. There was a mistake. It was a false positive. The test was defective. There was a second test in the box, so she used it. This time she stood tapping her foot, with a knot in her stomach, staring at herself in the mirror while she waited. She looked awful. This was ridiculous. She wasn't pregnant. She was dying. She glanced at her watch, then looked at the test. Two lines again. She stared at herself in the mirror again and saw herself go sheet white.

'Oh my God . . . oh my GOD! This isn't happening!' she shouted at the mirror. 'I AM *NOT*!' But the test said she was. She threw both of them in the garbage, and then walked around her bathroom with her arms crossed, hugging herself. This was the worst news of her life. 'SHIT!' she shouted out loud, and as she did, Jeff walked into the bathroom, looking worried. He had just come home from the office. Her mother was right.

'Are you okay? Were you talking to someone?' He thought maybe she was on the phone. She looked awful.

'No. No. I'm fine.' She brushed past him, went back to bed, and dug herself under the covers.

'Do you want to go to the hospital? Do you feel that bad?'

'I feel worse,' she said, nearly shouting at him.

'Then let's go. Don't wait till tomorrow, you'll just get sicker. You probably need antibiotics.' He was of the old school that still believed they cured all. He had been urging her to get some all week.

'I don't need antibiotics,' she said, glaring at him.

'Is something wrong? I mean other than that you're sick?' He felt sorry for her. The poor thing had been feeling awful for two weeks. It was depressing. But aside from that, he thought she was acting a little psycho. 'How high is your fever?'

'I'm pregnant.' There was no point hiding it from him. She would have to tell him sooner or later. He just stared at her as though he didn't understand what she'd said. Neither did she.

'What?'

'I'm pregnant.' She started to cry as she said it. Her life was over. This was a nightmare. She still felt sick. In fact, she felt worse. He sat down on the foot of the bed.

'Are you serious?' He didn't know what else to

say. He could see that she did not consider this good news. She looked like she was about to jump off the roof.

'No, I'm kidding. I always kid about suicidal events in my life. Of course I'm serious. How the hell did that happen? We're always so careful. We never slip.'

'Yes, we do,' he said honestly.

'Well, not at the wrong time. I'm not stupid. I know better than that. And so do you.'

He was thinking back, and suddenly looked sheepish. 'I think it might have happened the night of your grandmother's wedding.'

'No, it didn't. We went right to sleep.'

'We woke up in the middle of the night,' he corrected her. 'I think you may have been half asleep . . . I didn't force myself on you,' he said, looking unhappy. 'We just kind of . . . did it . . . and went back to sleep.' She did a rapid calculation, and groaned audibly. That had to be it. If they had wanted to plan it, they couldn't have hit it better. Or in this case, worse.

'Was I out of my mind? How much did I have to drink?'

'You had a few drinks . . . and a lot of champagne, I guess.' He smiled at her lovingly. 'You seemed fine to me, but you were a little out of it in the middle of the night . . . You looked so cute. I couldn't resist.'

'Oh my God,' she said, jumping out of bed again and pacing around the room. 'I can't goddamned believe this. I'm almost forty years old, and I'm pregnant. *Pregnant!*'

'You're not too old, Sarah . . . and maybe this is something to think about . . . maybe it's our last

345

chance. Our only chance. Maybe this isn't such bad news.' It wasn't to him. To her it was dire.

'Are you crazy? What do we need with a baby? We don't want a baby. I don't at least. I never did. I told you that right from the beginning. I never lied to you.'

'No, you didn't,' he said fairly. 'But to be honest, I'd love to have our kids.'

'Then you have it. I won't.' She was storming around, looking like she wanted to kill someone, preferably him. But in her head, she was blaming herself.

'Look, it's your body. You have to do whatever you feel you have to do . . . I'm just telling you how I feel about it. I love you. I'd love to have a baby with you,' he said kindly.

'Why? It would ruin our life. We have a nice life. A perfect life. A baby would just screw it up.' She was in tears.

He looked sad as he watched her. He had been here before. Marie-Louise had had two abortions with him. And for the only time since they'd been together, Sarah was sounding like Marie-Louise. It wasn't a memory he wanted to revisit. He got up and put his briefcase in his office. When he got back, Sarah was back in bed, sulking. She didn't speak to him for several hours. He offered to make her dinner, and she said she was too sick to eat.

Gingerly, he suggested that until they figured out what they were doing, she should. She told him to go to hell.

'I have figured it out. I'm going to kill myself. I don't need to eat.'

He went downstairs, ate by himself, and afterward came back upstairs. When he did, she

346

was asleep, and in her sleep, she looked as sweet as ever. He knew it had been a hell of a shock for her. He wanted her to keep their baby, but he couldn't force her to do it. He knew she had to make that decision herself.

She was sullen and silent at the breakfast table the next day. He offered her breakfast, and she made tea and toast for herself. She hardly said a word. She left for her doctor's appointment, and she never called him. She was already at home when he got back that night, and he could see how upset she was. The doctor had obviously confirmed it. Jeff said nothing, and she went back to bed. She was asleep by nine o'clock, and the next morning, she looked better. She apologized to him at breakfast.

'I'm sorry I've been such a witch. I just need to think this out for myself. I don't know what to do. The doctor said if I ever want a baby, I should probably go ahead with it now at my age. I really don't. But maybe one day I will . . . or I'll regret it if I don't have one. I just never wanted a kid. In fact, I very much *didn't* want a kid. But if I ever did want one, I'd want it with you,' she said, and started to cry. Jeff walked around the breakfast table and took her in his arms.

'Do whatever you need to do. I love you. I'd love to have our baby. But I love you. If you really don't want a kid, I can live with that. It's up to you.' His being so nice about it only made it harder for her. She nodded, blew her nose, and cried when he left for work. She had never been so confused and unhappy in her life.

It went on for two weeks. She ranted. She raged. She tortured herself and browbeat him. Somehow he managed to stay calm. He only lost his temper once, and was sorry he did. It had been the same with Marie-Louise, and in the end, she got rid of it, both times. But Sarah wasn't Marie-Louise. She was just angry and upset and terrified. She didn't feel ready to be a mother, and didn't want to condemn a child to an unhappy life. He offered to marry her, which frightened her even more. All the ghosts of her past had come back to haunt her, mostly her own miserable childhood, and her father. But Jeff wasn't him. He was a good man, and she knew it.

It took her nearly three weeks, and then she made a decision. She never told her mother, or anyone. She figured it out for herself. It was the scariest thing she'd ever done in her life. She told him she wouldn't marry him, for now anyway, but she wanted to have their child. Jeff almost cried when she said it. And they made love for the first time in a month that night. By then, she was two months pregnant, or very nearly. Three weeks later they went to the first sonogram together, and there it was. A little blip with a heartbeat. Everything was normal. It was due on the twenty-first of September. Jeff had never been so excited in his life.

It took Sarah longer to get used to the idea. But the first time she felt it move, she lay in bed and smiled and told him it felt weird. He went to all her sonograms, even the one at five months where they saw it sucking its thumb. He went to the amnio with her, and four weeks later, they told them it was healthy and a boy. By the time she was six months pregnant, she didn't feel ready, but she was glad. She thanked him for putting up with her neuroses and terrors. From then on, she was fine. It was their baby, not just hers. She had told her mother and Mimi, and everyone was excited. He had offered to marry her several times, but that was too much for her right now. She told him one thing at a time. First, the baby, then they'd see. Jeff was almost beside himself with excitement, knowing that he and Sarah were having a son. He told her it was the greatest gift of his life.

They were walking down Union Street one Saturday in August, when Sarah was eight months pregnant, when they ran into Phil. She almost didn't recognize him at first, and then she did, and he saw her. He looked surprised, and was with a girl who looked about twenty-five. She hadn't seen him in over a year and a half.

'Wow, what happened to you?' he said, smiling. All she could remember was the last time she'd seen him, in bed with someone else. She had never seen him again.

'I have no idea,' she said, looking blank. 'I went to this fabulous party about eight months ago, I got drunk out of my mind, and the next thing I knew, I woke up and looked like this. What do you think it is?' The girl with him was laughing. Phil looked embarrassed to see her, as well he should.

'Damned if I know,' he said. She looked beautiful and happy. She could see for a minute that he was sorry. And she was glad. She looked at Jeff with a loving smile, and introduced him to Phil. The famous Phil that he had heard so much about. He looked like a fool with the girl. 'I see you got married,' Phil said, looking at her enormous belly. She could see he hadn't, but neither had she. And for the first time, she realized that she wanted to be Jeff's wife, not just bear his child. All her notions of independence and freedom flew right out the window, as Phil and his bimbo walked down the street. She didn't want to be one of them. She wanted to be with Jeff, and their baby, for the rest of her life. She wanted to be his. For real. Not just because they were living in the same house for now.

'He looks like a jerk,' Jeff said, as he helped her into the car. She could hardly move, and they both laughed.

'He is. Remember?'

'I remember,' he said, as he drove her home. And when they got back, she started dinner.

She was still working, but she was getting tired. She was going to take six months maternity leave after the baby came. She was going to figure out if she wanted to work part-time or full-time after that. He would have loved it if she'd retire from the law firm, and restore houses with him, but that was up to her. It all was. She had to make her own decisions. She always had. In the end, she always made the right ones.

They were finishing dinner when she looked at Jeff with a shy smile. 'I was thinking,' she began, and he waited for the rest. It looked like it was going to be good, but it was better than he thought, or even dreamed. 'I was thinking maybe we should get married sometime.' He stared at her in disbelief, and she laughed.

'What brought that on?'

'I don't know. Maybe it's time. I don't want to be a bimbo all my life,' she said, and he laughed even harder.

'Sweetheart, you sure don't look like a bimbo

350

right now. You look like the mother of my son.'

'I think I want to look like your wife. It's a nice look.' He leaned over and kissed her in response. He had begun to think they would never get married, but the baby was enough. She had to want all of it, and now she did.

'Anytime you want. Before the baby?'

'I don't know. What do you think? Maybe after.' Her mother and Mimi were coming for Thanksgiving, and she wanted them there when they got married. Maybe she even wanted the baby there. She wasn't sure. 'I'll think about it and let you know.'

'That would be nice.'

They cleaned up the kitchen together and went upstairs, and she realized as she lay there that night that Mimi's wedding had been their special gift. It had brought them all this.

CHAPTER 25

As part of her plan, Sarah had decided to work till her due date. She finished work on the last day, they gave her a shower and a lunch, and she couldn't imagine what she would do without going to the office. The whole concept seemed odd to her. She was an attorney. She went to an office every day. Or she used to. Now she was going to stay home for six months, with a baby. She was afraid she would go out of her mind with boredom. She told them she might come back early, and one of the women lawyers told her she might not want to come back at all, which Sarah thought was absurd. Of course she would. Unless she went into business with Jeff, restoring houses commercially. That appealed to her, too, particularly with him. She loved the idea of working with him every day. It was a period of transition and change for her. Everything in her life was shifting and moving, even the baby in her womb. After the shower and the lunch, she packed her briefcase and went home. And then she waited. Nothing happened. Her doctor told her that was normal, particularly with first babies. It was driving her nuts. She was never late, with anything. She wasn't this time, either. The baby was.

'What am I supposed to do?' she complained to Jeff one night. The baby was ten days late by then. It was the first of October. Nine months to the day of Mimi's wedding day. They were having a ball in Palm Springs, and never came to San Francisco anymore. But they had promised to come for Thanksgiving, to see the baby. If it ever came. Maybe it never would. She wished she had kept working. But she was too tired and too big. She needed his help now getting out of bed. She felt like the proverbial beached whale. The baby was huge.

'Enjoy yourself. Have fun. Relax. Go shopping,' he suggested, and she laughed at him.

'Nothing fits anymore except handbags.'

'Then buy some.' She had started seeing her old friends again, the ones who had children. She finally had something in common with them.

Jeff was trying to work from his office at home as much as he could. He wanted to be around if something happened, or she needed him. They had set up the nursery in Mimi's childhood room. It seemed fitting, since the baby had been conceived on her wedding night, and Mimi herself had been born in that room. Her own mother had given birth to her there. Lilli, who had broken so many hearts and died so young. Sarah was forty now. It seemed the right age now for her first child. She had waited a long time for everything to be right. First Jeff, and now this.

They went for a walk around the neighborhood that afternoon. They walked to Fillmore Street and back, and she could hardly make it up the hill, but she did, with Jeff's help. They were talking about what they were going to do, and if they were going to buy a house to resell. She was tempted to do it. She was still thinking about it that night, after dinner, as she sat in the bathtub, with the same contractions that she had had for weeks. They weren't real ones yet, just practice ones. Braxton Hicks. They were getting her ready, if the baby ever came. She sat in the tub, relaxing, while Jeff watched TV. He came in once to check on her, and rubbed her back. It ached all the time now, because the baby was so heavy. The doctor was going to induce her in another week, he said, but not till then. The baby was fine, and so was she.

She went downstairs after her bath, to get something to eat, and then came back upstairs again. She felt as though she needed to move around. She couldn't sit or lie down tonight. It was getting closer, but she wasn't there yet. She was seeing her doctor in the morning, and hoped it might provoke something. She was ready.

'Are you okay?' Jeff had been watching her all night. She was restless, but she was in good spirits and looked fine.

'Yeah, I'm just tired of sitting around,' she said, nibbling a cookie. She had heartburn now all the time, which nothing helped. But she knew it would be gone soon. Jeff felt sorry for her as she struggled back into bed, and then got up three times to go to the bathroom. She said the snack she'd eaten had given her a stomachache.

'Why don't you try and get some sleep?' he said gently.

'I'm not tired,' she said plaintively. 'My back really hurts.'

'No wonder. Come here. I'll rub it.' She lay on her side and turned her back to him. It felt better after he massaged it, and then finally she fell asleep and he watched her, with a loving smile.

These were the sweetest days of his life, waiting for his son to be born, with Sarah lying beside him. He finally fell asleep himself an hour after she did. And in the middle of the night, he woke up out of a dead sleep. He could hear her moaning and panting in the dark next to him. When he reached out for her, her face was covered in sweat, and he quickly turned on the light, suddenly wide awake.

'Sarah? Are you okay?'

'No.' She shook her head back and forth, barely able to speak.

'What happened? What's wrong?' The contractions she was having took her breath away, literally. Finally. She couldn't speak. She had woken up out of a sound sleep, having a baby, and was too stunned to even wake him.

They had both realized by then that the contractions in the bathtub had been real, not 'fake,' and her restlessness, backache, and stomachache had been labor, for a long time. They

354

had missed all the signs. He touched her stomach and looked at his watch. They were two minutes apart. They had been told to go to the hospital at ten. The baby was coming. Now. He didn't know what to do. Suddenly Sarah started screaming. It was a long, primeval howl between sharp screams.

'Sarah, come on, please, sweetheart . . . we have to go to the hospital. Now.'

'I can't . . . can't move . . .' She screamed again with the next contraction, and tried to sit up, but she couldn't do that, either. She was pushing. He grabbed the phone and called 911. They told him to leave the front door open and stay with her. But she wouldn't let him leave her. She had a death grip on his arm, and she was crying.

'Come on . . . Sarah . . . I have to go downstairs and open the door.'

'No!' As she said it, her face turned purple and she looked at him in terror. She was writhing in pain and pushing at the same time, and suddenly in the room there was a long thin wail between her screams, and a bright red face between her legs with silky black hair, as their son slid into the world, looked at both of them, and stopped crying. He just lay looking up at them as they both cried, and hugged each other, as they heard sirens outside.

'Oh my God, are you okay?' She nodded, and he touched the baby's face, and then gently lifted him onto her stomach. The doorbell was ringing. 'I'll be right back.' He raced down two flights of stairs, let the paramedics and fire department in, and ran back to her with them.

After the paramedics checked both of them, they said she was fine and so was the baby. A burly paramedic cut the cord, wrapped the baby in a sheet, and handed him to Sarah as she beamed. Jeff couldn't stop crying. She and the baby were the most beautiful sight he'd ever seen. They put her in an ambulance with the baby, to check them out at the hospital, and Jeff rode with them. The baby was perfect. They sent them home three hours later, and Sarah called Audrey and Mimi. William de Beaumont Parker had been born, in the same house where his great-grandmother had come into the world eighty-three years before, and his great-great-grandparents had lived. His parents were ecstatic. A great blessing had come to them in Lilli's house. Sarah held the baby, with Jeff's arms around her, and all three of them fell asleep. Although she had never expected it to be, it was the best day of Sarah's life.

CHAPTER 26

Thanksgiving was more hectic than usual that year. Mimi and George came, and she invited her usual cronies. Audrey and Tom flew in from St. Louis. Sarah nursed the baby, while Jeff cooked the turkey and Audrey helped him. They ate at the big table in the kitchen, while William slept in a basket after Sarah fed him. Sarah had never looked better, Jeff looked slightly frazzled and sleep deprived, and everyone agreed William was the prettiest baby they'd ever seen. He was a beautiful, healthy boy. His parents had waited a long time to have him, but he had come at the right time. Mimi loved visiting him in her old room. Sarah had painted it blue herself, with Jeff's help, to keep her off the ladder right before William was born.

The meal was the same one they ate every year, following tradition. And Mimi said the pies were perfect.

'He's the best baby, isn't he?' she said proudly. He slept right through dinner, and didn't wake up again until Jeff and Sarah got upstairs, and Audrey had helped clean up the kitchen. William was seven weeks old on that day. He weighed twelve pounds, and had been born at just over nine. George said he looked six months old. And Tom held him expertly, as the master grandfather he was.

Both his grandmother and his great-grandmother held William the next day, and took care of him while Sarah got dressed. Jeff went downstairs to their third guest room to try and get some sleep. He didn't have to be dressed till six. Sarah almost forgot to wake him, and then sent Tom to get him up. They had to wake him twice. Fatherhood was more exhausting than he had expected, but much better. He loved Sarah more than he ever had before.

Sarah was still dressing when Audrey brought the baby in to nurse. It made Sarah half an hour late when she came downstairs, and by then everyone was waiting. Mimi was holding the baby, Jeff was wearing a dark blue suit and was wide awake and looked refreshed. Tom and George were standing side by side, and all heads turned as Sarah came slowly down the stairs in a long white dress. It was a size bigger than she would have liked, but she looked exquisite. The dress was a simple creamy lace with long sleeves and a high neck, and showed off her figure, which was better than ever, even if slightly fuller. She was wearing her hair in a loose bun, with lily of the valley in it, and she held a bouquet of them in her hands. Jeff's eyes filled with tears when he saw her. He had waited so long for this. She had been worth the wait.

They both cried when they exchanged their vows, and their hands shook as they put each other's rings on, and just as they did, William woke up and looked around. The minister christened him at the same time. As Jeff said afterward, it was a full-service wedding. They got it all done at once.

Afterward they ate and danced and drank champagne, and took turns holding the baby. And finally Jeff danced slowly around the ballroom with his wife. It was the first time they had used it. They were going to give a big party there for Christmas this year. They were slowly growing into the house, each other, and their lives. Sarah had become Mrs. Jefferson Parker. She had extended her maternity leave to a year, and they had just bought a small house to remodel, to try it out as a joint project. They would see what happened after that, and how much money they made on it. If it went well, she was going to leave the law firm. She was tired of chasing tax laws and writing wills.

As she danced with Jeff, Sarah thought of Stanley's words way at the beginning, telling her not to waste her life, to live it and dream it and savor it, to look to the horizon, and not make the mistakes he had. He had made it possible for her to do it right. The house had brought Jeff into her life . . . and William . . . and Tom into her mother's . . . So many lives had been touched by Stanley, and this house.

'Thank you for making me so happy,' Jeff whispered, as the ballroom spun around them, with all its splendid gilt and mirrors.

'I love you, Jeff,' she said simply. She could hear their baby cry as someone held him, and his parents danced on their wedding night. The baby that had been born in Lilli's house.

In the end, they had all been touched by Lilli. The woman who had run away so long ago had left a legend and a legacy behind her. A daughter she had barely known, a granddaughter who was a fine woman, a great-granddaughter who had brought Lilli's house back to life with infinite tenderness and love. And a great-great-grandson, whose journey had just begun. The generations had rolled on without her. And as Sarah danced in Jeff's arms, she sensed that the mysterious creature who had been Lilli was at peace at last.